WILL WANTED A KISS.

He wanted to feel her

Just once before she w

Amazon Annie, terror of the river basin, were nothing but another wild story to add to the tally.

"So you've changed your mind about the plane?" There was a slight hesitation in her voice, a slight breathlessness that brought a brief curve to his lips. She wasn't immune to what he was feeling.

"No. I haven't changed my mind." He shifted his weight closer to her, lifting his hand to cup her chin.

She went very still within his light grasp, her eyes widening behind her glasses. Diffuse light streamed through the orchid vines, casting her face in a delicate tracery of shadows, darkening her irises to a jungle-green. In contrast, her hair was a riotous halo of white and gold blond.

"This," she said softly, "is a terrible idea."

"I know," he admitted. But he did it anyway, smoothed his fingers along the curve of her jaw and lowered his mouth toward hers.

"Um ... maybe you better rethink this," she said when he was less than a breath away.

"No," he murmured. "I've done enough thinking." She smelled sweet, like her soft drink, and he wanted to lick the taste off her lips.

"Dr.... uh, Travers. Will, I—"

"Shh, Annie. It's just a kiss." And a bolder lie he'd never told. The kiss was instantly hot, and sweet, and wet, sending a wave of pleasure sluicing down his body to pool in his groin, and as quickly as that, he forgot the plane, the guns, the boat. All of it was lost in the sensual wonder of Annie Parrish's mouth.

Also by Glenna McReynolds

PRINCE OF TIME

DREAM STONE

THE CHALICE AND THE BLADE

RIVER *of* EDEN

GLENNA McREYNOLDS

BANTAM BOOKS
NEW YORK TORONTO LONDON SYDNEY AUCKLAND

RIVER OF EDEN
A Bantam Book / February 2002

ISBN 0-553-58393-X

PUBLISHED SIMULTANEOUSLY IN THE UNITED STATES AND CANADA

Bantam Books are published by Bantam Books, a division of
Random House, Inc. Its trademark, consisting of the words
"Bantam Books" and the portrayal of a rooster, is Registered in
U.S. Patent and Trademark Office and in other countries. Marca
Registrada. Bantam Books, 1540 Broadway, New York, New
York 10036.

PRINTED IN THE UNITED STATES OF AMERICA

OPM 10 9 8 7 6 5 4 3 2 1

TO THE SHAMANS—
STAN, LOREENA, CHAD, JOHN, MICHAEL, ANTHONY ...

Close your eyes and I'll kiss you.

A fiend like thee might bear my soul to hell.

WILLIAM SHAKESPEARE,
TWELFTH NIGHT

CHAPTER 1 ✄

DRENCHED TO THE BONE, DR. ANNIE Parrish stood in the doorway of the ramshackle waterfront cantina called Pancha's and wiped what she could of the rain off her glasses. Putting them back on, she let her eyes adjust to the dim light. Water dripped off her green shirt and baggy khaki shorts, adding to the mud she'd dragged in with her off the street. The tropical afternoon rain poured down behind her, running off the cantina's tin roof and coursing in streams down the dirt slope to the black waters of the Rio Negro where it flowed past the city of Manaus, Brazil. Inside the tavern, a samba beat blared out of a radio, while a toothless young man added percussion with the rapid beat of his open palms against the bar.

A scattering of seedy-looking patrons littered the shadowy interior, their faces obscured by a pall of cigarette smoke, but it was the couple dancing in front of the bar that held Annie's attention.

The woman was mulatto, her skin a creamy café au lait color, her yellow halter top and orange sarong the brightest things in the dingy room. Her partner was chameleonlike in comparison. The most noticeable aspect about him was movement—the flick and sway of his hips to the music, the flash of gold bracelets on his upraised arms, the rippling of his open, midnight-blue shirt against his sun-bronzed skin.

The woman was a sunburst. He was a star-flung night, his dark brown hair streaked blond in places and flying with every toss of his head, then falling back into multihued layers that hung low on his neck. Red seed bracelets stacked four inches high around his right ankle were revealed by the rolled-up legs on his black pants, *shoroshoro* seeds from the forest adding a susurrus of sound with every step he took.

Annie didn't have a clue who the woman was, but the man was William Sanchez Travers, and sure as she was standing there, he didn't look like any Harvard-trained ethnobotanist she'd ever seen, "defrocked" or not. He looked like the kind of man mothers warned their daughters about and the reason fathers kept shotguns. But he was Annie's best chance for getting upriver, and given that one asset, she was inclined to overlook a lot of faults.

With an absent gesture, she shoved her fingers back through her short-cropped blond hair, slicking the wet strands off her face. A quick pat-down of her pockets proved them bulging with the usual junk, too full to organize, so she stuffed what she could deeper, and ignored the rest. Tidied up as best as she could manage, she squared her shoulders. For better or worse, Travers was exactly the type of man she'd been looking for—broke enough to come cheap and shady enough not to ask too many questions. Annie knew plenty of men who fit that description, but she'd worked in the Amazon long enough to add a third caveat: she needed a man who wouldn't slit her throat in the dead of night. When her research sponsor, Dr. Gabriela Oliveira, had recommended Travers, telling Annie he was back in Manaus and headed upriver to Santa Maria, Annie had figured the ex-Harvard botanist, no matter how degenerate, would more than fit the bill. Hell, she'd read every book he'd ever written—twice.

Now she had an offer to make.

As she started forward, the music slid into a lambada rhythm. Without missing a beat, Travers and his partner came together in a hip-swaying Latin swing that bordered on lewd. Then they took it over the border.

Annie's gaze dropped down the length of their bodies and quickly came back up in a warily skeptical onceover. Anything could happen on a dance floor in Brazil—and it looked like anything might.

She only hoped he and the woman stopped somewhere short of actual public copulation. She didn't have the strength for it after spending half the day looking for him in every seedy, portside dive in Manaus he was known to frequent. There weren't many he'd missed, and after observing his favorite haunts firsthand, she wouldn't put anything past him, even if only half of the rest of what she'd heard about him was true.

Three years ago, he'd forsaken academia and his fieldwork and disappeared into the Amazon rain forest. The rumors had been bountiful and gruesome: he'd been eaten by an anaconda; he'd taken one too many hallucinogenic trips on the *Banisteriopsis caapi* liana and was living in a near vegetative state in a cave near the headwaters of the Putumayo; or—and this had been

Annie's favorite—he'd had his head shrunk by the Jivaro.
No bones or body, vegetative or otherwise, and no iden-
tifiable shrunken head had ever been found. A year later,
he'd disproved all the rumors by resurfacing in Manaus
safe, though not necessarily sound. The verdict was still
out on his mental state—way out.

Looking at him now, Annie would guess he'd abandoned botany for his true calling as a *sambista*. The kind
of moves he was making were grounds for arrest in some
countries: arms down, shoulders loose and rolling, his
hips doing a buck-and-shimmy against the woman's.
Rumor said Gabriela had been the one to bail him out
with Howard Pharmaceutical Labs, the company fund-
ing his research. Even so, half a dozen lawsuits were still
waiting for him back in the States, compliments of old man
Howard, who hadn't planned on his high-priced glory
boy disappearing without delivering some new magically
medicinal plant Howard Labs could make millions of
dollars synthesizing.

Well, she thought, that bright hope had sure gone to
hell in a handbasket, with the way smoothed by more
than a few bottles of rotgut *cachaça*, Brazilian sugarcane
alcohol. It was a damn shame, but all Will Travers was
known for now was ferrying people up and down the
Rio Negro and the Rio Solimoes and showing up in the
Manaus bars often enough to qualify as a waterfront
attraction.

At six feet, he had the gringo looks for it, tall and
rangy, with that wild, sun-streaked hair and a face that
had set more than one coed on the path to a botany
degree.

Annie was way past the coed stage of her life, but
from what she could see of him, he hadn't lost his poster-

boy looks, even if the veneer of his Harvard days had worn so damn thin as to be invisible.

He probably didn't know it, but he'd once one-upped her on a plant identification, getting his specimen in mere days ahead of hers. Since then, for all time, whenever anybody enjoyed a certain South American balsam herb in their garden, the label read *Dicliptera traversii*, instead of *Dicliptera parrishii*. It was as close as she'd ever gotten to getting the best of him. Then he'd gone and dropped out of the game—and that was the real damn shame.

As she watched him dance, her mouth curved into a rueful grin. What a waste, she thought, and what a great opportunity for her. With William Travers out of the running, a place in the history books was up for grabs, and she was going to take it. Still, she would have loved to have met him in his prime and given him a run for his money, before he'd gone to seed—and like everyone else in the Amazon and academia, she couldn't help but wonder what in the hell had happened to him. He'd been on top of the world before he'd gone off and gotten himself lost.

The music changed again, and Travers grasped his partner's waist with both hands. The woman went willingly into his embrace, the two of them slithering together in a serpentine mating dance.

"Damn," she muttered. They really were going to do the deed right there on the dance floor, as if she didn't already have enough problems.

Johnny Chang, the two-bit felon she'd been dealing with all week, had warned her to leave Manaus once their business was done, and God knew she'd tried, but the boat she'd been counting on had gone belly-up and left her dry-docked. She couldn't afford any more delays. She had to be out of the city by morning.

She glanced out the door. The rain looked as if it would go on forever.

The radio sputtered to a stop behind her, and the sudden quiet drew her attention back to the bar and a bit of good news: Travers still had his pants on.

Thank God for little favors, she thought and moved forward. She needed to cut her deal while she still had the chance.

"Dr. Travers," she said, pitching her voice to carry above the racket of the rain on the roof.

The man she'd been tracking all over the waterfront turned, weaving slightly with the woman still in his arms, and Annie had to fight back a pang of irritation. Drunk before three o'clock, he was in worse shape than she'd expected, and she hadn't expected much. On the other hand, with him two sheets to the wind, talking herself onto his boat ought to be a piece of cake.

"Dr. Travers," she repeated, approaching him with a smile firmly in place. She'd never been much in the bees-and-honey department, but she knew enough to make nice when she wanted something.

"Will," he said, smiling back, his dark-eyed gaze slightly confused as he studied her face. He had a day's growth of stubble along his jaw, macaw feathers tied into his hair behind his left ear, and possibly the longest, thickest eyelashes she'd ever seen on a grown man. "Just Will." With a glance over his shoulder and a gesture, he ordered a beer. The woman was plastered to him.

Probably holding him up, Annie thought, exasperated with herself for needing him. He and the woman leaned a bit too far, having to take a half-step to stay upright, and

Annie couldn't even keep a forced smile on her face. No doubt about it, he'd started his party hours ago and was headed downhill. His hair was wildly disheveled. His shirt was completely unbuttoned, and with his pants low slung and hanging by a thread and the grace of God on his hips, he looked as if he were coming undone, as if his clothes could finish the slow slide off his body at any second.

She had the most ridiculous urge to straighten him up a bit, pull him together and tell him to get a hold of himself.

Instead, she offered her hand and introduced herself.

"Annie Parrish," she said, noticing the *genipa* dye trailing in a thin line around the base of his throat like a serpentine necklace. A chunk of quartzite strung on a knotted palm-fiber cord, a shaman's crystal, hung around his neck. The biggest jaguar teeth she'd ever seen flanked the stone, two wickedly curved fangs telling her the crystal was meant to be a thing of great power. She wondered where Will Travers had gotten it, and if he had a clue as to what it was.

Glancing up, she met his thick-lashed gaze and lazy grin, and somehow didn't have a doubt.

He knew, and probably thought he was really onto something.

Her opinion of him dipped even lower. He was a scientist, one of Harvard's finest, for crying out loud, or had been. He should know better than to believe in magic crystals and jaguar teeth. At one time, before he'd gone and gotten himself lost, he probably had known better.

Heatstroke, some people said. That's what had happened to him, massive heatstroke leading to temporary derangement, though there were differing opinions on how "temporary" the derangement might be. He'd been back for two years and still looked plenty over the edge to her.

"Annie Parrish," he repeated. "Dr. Annie Parrish?" He took her hand, his expression turning curious—a common enough reaction. Like him, she'd had her moment of notoriety in the past. Unlike him, she hadn't made a lifetime commitment to scandal, not yet anyway.

"Yes. I'm working with the River Basin Coalition, RBC. Dr. Gabriela Oliveira suggested I contact you."

"Ah, Gabriela," he said, still holding on to her hand, his mouth curving into another grin. He turned to whisper something to his dance partner.

The woman smiled and pressed herself against him, whispering back, asking him to come with her, a sultry offer on a hot, tropical afternoon, an offer Annie was afraid he wouldn't refuse—and then there she'd be, left standing in Pancha's, while he and the woman finished their dance behind closed doors.

Or maybe he was thinking of taking her with them. He was holding on to her as if he weren't going to let her go.

Well, he could try, she thought, if he was feeling lucky. She had a reputation, well earned, if a little overblown, of protecting herself. If he'd heard about her at all, he must have heard that.

She tried pulling her hand back, and he tightened his grip, showing surprising strength for someone who was having trouble even staying on his feet, and suddenly Annie wondered just how interesting the afternoon might get. Too interesting, she decided, preparing to retrieve her hand, an effort that proved unnecessary when he loosened his grip and slid his hand up her arm, still touching her, but not holding her, as if he were merely keeping track of her while he murmured a reply to the woman. The dancer pouted through all his softly spoken Portuguese. When he was finished, she brushed her lips across his cheek and whispered, *"Gato,"* before turning to leave. Sexy man, she meant, like a cat.

He was pretty damn big for a cat, Annie thought, but she would admit to a certain suppleness to all that lean muscle—and a damn good bit of pure power. However dissolute his lifestyle, it hadn't taken an obvious physical toll, and possibly just the opposite.

The only photograph she'd seen of him had been on his book jackets, taken long before he'd spent his year lost in the rain forest, and there had been some undeniable changes since then. He was leaner, harder, the lines of his face more stark, his features and his body more carved than molded. From her perspective, eye level with his chest, he seemed to be made up entirely of corded muscle covered with smoothly tanned skin, none of which had shown in the picture of him neatly buttoned and tucked into an oxford shirt with a tie. He obviously hadn't spent all his time drinking in cantinas, and wherever he'd been, he'd covered some ground. She knew the look of long miles and short rations. His body was stripped of any excess. He didn't have an ounce of fat on him.

"So you spoke with Gabriela today?" he asked, his gaze coming back to her after the mulatto woman had finished weaving a drunken path to a bar stool. Watching her, Annie had been forced to revise her opinion about who had been holding up who.

"Yes. She told me you were headed to Santa Maria in the morning."

"You want to go to Santa Maria?" he asked, one eyebrow lifting in question. Sweat-dampened hair clung to the sides of his face, pale blond strands overlaying dark brown, accentuating his cheekbones and overall vagabond appearance.

"Yes."

"But not on the RBC launch with Gabriela?" His beer arrived, and he thanked the bartender. *"Obrigado."*

"The engine broke down," she explained. "The parts are coming up from Santarem. It's going to take at least a week, and I'm in rather a hurry ... very, uh ... busy." She carefully chose a word after a slight pause. "Too busy to wait." She couldn't very well tell him she had to get the hell out of Manaus before her luck ran out. That sort of confession was bound to rouse some questions she had no intention of answering.

His grin broadened again, coming as easy as the rain outside and apparently as often. "Gabriela did mention the possibility of a ... busy ... woman wanting passage." With his beer in hand, he slid his other hand low on her back and gave her a little push toward the cantina's front door, moving her along with more purpose than she would have thought he could muster.

"Yes, I'm ... uh," she said, glancing around, wondering if she'd missed something. "I'm doing research on the—" Her voice trailed off when she noticed two men rising from a table near the bar. One was tall with buzz-cut black hair. The other was younger, shorter, and dumpier with a cigarette hanging from between his lips. Both of them were watching Travers with grim expressions on their faces. The glint of a partially sheathed knife flashed on the shorter one's hip.

O-kay, she thought, remembering a couple of other things she'd heard about the mysterious William Sanchez Travers. One rumor that had picked up some speed was that he'd spent his lost year searching for and finding a city of gold buried in time and lianas in the wilderness of Amazonia. He did have a pair of hefty gold bracelets hanging around his wrist, gleaming dully in the low light of the cantina, and there was nothing like gold to bring out the mercenaries and *bandidos* in backcountry Brazil. Of course, people who had known him before he'd disappeared swore that even if he had found an ancient lost city of gold, the wealth wouldn't have interested him nearly as much as the archaeobotany of the site. But even she could see that he'd changed in some rather dramatic ways from the photograph on his book jacket, maybe more than the people who had known him before realized.

Regardless, he was ushering her out the door, and he had a couple of very *bandido*-looking dudes staring holes in the middle of his back.

"You do know there's a man with a knife watching us. Right?" she asked.

"Think nothing of it," he replied with a shrug.

"Do you know him?" she asked, taking another quick glance and thinking a lot about it. She'd been on more than a few waterfronts along the Rio Negro, and in more than her share of roughneck bars back home in the States, once or twice in less than ideal situations. In her opinion the only situation less ideal than a grim-faced man with a knife was a grim-faced man with a gun. Whether the men were Wyoming cowboys or Brazilian *caboclos,* the outcome was never good.

"The one with the knife in the orange T-shirt is named Juanio. The man trying to hide a shoulder holster under his vest is called Luiz."

"Shoulder holster?" That meant a gun. The day was definitely taking a dive.

"*Garimpeiros,*" he explained, as if that would be reassuring.

"Gold miners," she translated aloud, her curiosity and wariness ratcheting up a few dozen notches. Gold miners were the bane of much of the Amazon and a particularly poisonous thorn in her side.

"Don't worry. They're only here to entertain me."

Annie didn't bother to hide the doubtful arching of her eyebrows. "And are you finding them entertaining?" No one could be that self-assured when he had a man with a knife and another with a gun at his back.

He glanced down at her, and his mouth curved into a mischievous grin. "Very."

"And the woman?" she asked, wondering how, or if, the dancer was involved.

His grin broadened. "Cara? Part of the package. She dances a few dances. Juanio buys me a few drinks, and Luiz makes sure I don't get distracted by any *garotas* who wander in off the street."

Annie slanted him a glance, hardly classifying herself as a *garota,* a lovely girl, who had wandered in off the street. She knew what people saw when they looked at her. "Four-eyed academic" and "muddy-kneed botanist" came to mind, and "pint-sized pit bull" had been mentioned more often than she cared to admit, especially by other field researchers, especially if they were in her field. "Lovely girl" would be a stretch on her best day.

In two more steps, he had her back outside, under the

eaves of the cantina's tin roof, the rain pouring down not six inches from where they were standing.

"I'd say Luiz is doing a damn good job." Drunk or not, and she wasn't at all sure anymore, he'd just given her a first-class bum's rush.

He answered with a negligent shrug and stepped out from under the eaves. The rain sluiced down his body, instantly plastering his clothes to his rangy frame. He tilted his head back and dragged his hands through his hair, letting the water wash over him. For a moment, he looked like a river creature, sleek and wet, all lean muscle and coiled power, half of this world and half of the other, the rain a veil between water and air. Then he stepped back under the eaves, and the moment passed— but not without leaving her oddly disconcerted.

She didn't know what he was, but she was getting the idea that he wasn't just the simple dockside boat tramp she'd set out to find.

"If you want to come as far as Santa Maria, that's fine with me," he said, wiping a hand across his face, and then wringing out the tail of his shirt. "Fare is a hundred and twenty *reais* with meals. I'm tying up at the RBC dock tonight and leaving at dawn."

Before she could say anything, he turned back toward the cantina and within a few steps had melted into the darkened interior with his *garimpeiros* and package-deal mulatto woman. A new song started up on the radio.

"Damn," she swore softly. She'd seen a lot of wild things in the rain forest, but William Sanchez Travers had just shot to the top of her list.

And who in the hell were those gold miners? She knew *what* they were—trouble. *Garimpeiros* were always trouble, especially when you mixed them with liquor and guns. Whatever deal he was working, Will Travers was sitting on a powder keg doing business with them. She just wondered how much business he was doing, and whether or not she ought to be hightailing it in another direction.

But damn, he did have a boat, and she had a place on it at dawn, which was more than she'd walked into Pancha's with, and which still made him her best bet for getting out of Manaus—and above all else, *garimpeiros* or not, she needed to get the hell out of Manaus.

FROM WHERE HE STOOD in the cantina's doorway, Will watched Annie Parrish make her way down the street. He'd given her a minute before coming back to check on her, and he was glad to see she'd left. He had some business on its way to the cantina, the kind of business best transacted without witnesses. Will had sent a message two hours ago to let Fat Eddie Mano know he was in town. Juanio, Luiz, Cara, and a few others had arrived shortly afterward to empty out Pancha's and keep him in place. Fat Eddie was due any minute.

A grin curved his mouth, and he lifted his bottle of beer to take a drink—Annie Parrish, the infamous Annie Parrish. When Gabriela had mentioned a woman, she was the last one he would have expected. He hadn't even known they'd let her back into the country. Gabriela must have really pulled some strings. She'd definitely laid her reputation on the line to be working with Annie Parrish, and the reason old Dr. Oliveira might have for doing that intrigued Will almost as much as Annie herself—almost, but not quite.

Given her reputation, he'd expected her to be bigger,

rougher around the edges, more imposing, but she'd barely reached his chin, and the word "rough" was the last one he'd thought when he'd turned around and seen her standing behind him. "Soft" had come to mind, silky soft and golden skinned despite her scraped-up knee and the calluses he'd felt on her palm, and despite the strength of her grip when they'd shaken hands. She'd looked like a wet kitten, with her cropped blond hair sticking out all over and her gaze scrutinizing him from behind her rain-spotted, wire-rimmed glasses. Amazon Annie, he'd heard her called before the unfortunate Woolly Monkey Incident, as the case came to be known. Afterward, she'd only been called persona non grata.

He'd been way upriver at the time, but he'd heard the stories when he'd returned to Manaus. She'd been kicked out of Brazil by then, but now she was back, her pale hair framing an urchin's face with a freckled nose and cat's eyes—hazel-green—none of which had been mentioned in the stories he'd been told. In them, fact and fiction had melded together to make her sound like one of the original Amazon warrior queens, not the small, intently serious woman who'd been staring up at him from where she'd stood in a puddle of mud with one of her shoes untied. She'd looked a bit scatterbrained, with pencils and a wet notepad sticking out of one of her pockets, soggy papers fanning out of the other, and a muddy magnifying glass hanging from a cord around her neck, but Will had heard enough about her to know she had a botanically brilliant mind. She'd collected plants for some of the most famous herbariums and research institutes in the world. He had noticed a small scar near her right temple and wondered if she'd gotten it in the incident. Apparently, there had been bloodshed all around.

The thought made him distinctly uncomfortable. In another environment, and a lifetime ago, he'd been as liberated as the next man, but upriver in deep jungle no woman was safe on her own. Someone as nubile as Annie Parrish was pure jaguar bait, with every man in the forest being the jaguar—himself included. The laws that governed civilized behavior started unraveling pretty quickly in the heat and humidity of equatorial Amazonas. About the only protection a woman could have was a gun, and everyone had said Dr. Parrish had used a pretty damn big one.

He grinned. It was a little hard to imagine. Wearing baggy cargo shorts with every pocket stuffed like a kid's and a green shirt two sizes too big, she'd looked more like an underfed teenager than an Amazon. But she had known when to stop asking questions and get out of Pancha's, and she hadn't been frightened by Juanio and Luiz. She'd been curious, but not unnerved.

"*Senhor,*" Juanio called from back in the bar. "*Vem aqui, por favor.*"

Will gave a quick glance over his shoulder and saw what he'd been waiting for—a rolling mountain of a man and a package coming through the back door, Fat Eddie and his contraband, Will's ticket to hell. He hadn't wanted Annie Parrish in the cantina when the deal got struck, and it looked as if he'd gotten her out in the nick of time. He certainly hadn't wanted to let go of her until she was out of Pancha's. Juanio and Luiz weren't quite as benign as he'd made out. He'd figured for a few minutes' worth of conversation, keeping her close to him was enough to keep her safe.

He returned his attention to the street and waited until she reached the corner. Only after she was out of sight did he turn and walk back into the bar and realize that he was still smiling. Taking Annie Parrish to Santa Maria on his boat, the *Sucuri*, wasn't going to be a problem. A paying passenger going upriver was always welcome. Wanting to take her farther than just up the river, however, might be a problem, and nothing could have surprised him more.

He didn't remember sopping-wet ragamuffins as being his particular type, but he couldn't deny that Dr. Parrish had held his interest. Fortunately, he'd heard enough about her to be cautious. As he recalled, it had been her lover that she'd shot.

CHAPTER 2 ✵

THREE DAYS, ANNIE TOLD HERSELF. It's only three days to Santa Maria. What could happen in three days?

Not much, she assured herself.

Or apocalypse.

"Get a grip," she muttered, cinching up a set of plant press frames in her hut on the RBC grounds. Three days on the Rio Negro wasn't going to get them anywhere near gold-mining territory. Logic alone told her nothing was going to happen with Travers's *garimpeiros* on the way to Santa Maria.

Unless Juanio and Luiz were going with them.

She stopped in mid-cinch, thinking she couldn't possibly have gotten herself into that much trouble in one short afternoon.

"Nah," she decided, shaking her head and finishing up the frames. Whatever kind of "entertainment" Travers had going with the *garimpeiros,* he and the miners weren't boat-ride friendly.

She set the first press aside and started on the next. Most of the cargo for the trip upriver was already stacked outside her hut, one of the thatched-roof buildings Gabriela euphemistically described as a guest house. Annie just had a couple of things left to finish. When Travers pulled up at the dock, she wanted to be ready to load everything on the boat. She'd wasted enough time in Manaus.

She knew it was a miracle the Brazilians had even let her back into the country after the fiasco that had gotten her unofficially deported, the so-called Woolly Monkey Incident. But by the grace of God and Gabriela Oliveira, the government had been convinced to give her a year to finish her research. If everything went right, at the end of the year she wouldn't be surprised if they gave her the whole damn country. For now, though, she was on shaky ground, knowing they wouldn't hesitate to exile her again if she so much as stuck her nose over any of the big black lines they'd drawn around her visa.

Unbeknown to them, she hadn't returned to Brazil to stay inside anybody's lines. In the week since she'd been back, she'd already broken half a dozen laws. The proof was lying in a pair of long, narrow crates stacked up between the door and her cot—the merchandise she'd purchased from Johnny Chang, the merchandise the slimeball didn't want hanging around Manaus any more than she wanted to hang around herself. One stint in a Brazilian jail had been enough, thank you very much, and if she never saw the inside of another cockroach-ridden cell or Corisco Vargas, the damned megalomaniac army major who had put her there, so much the better.

Truthfully, William Sanchez Travers was the least of her problems. She just wanted to keep it that way.

With the last of the press frames secure, she double-checked her supplies of alcohol, glycerol, and stove fuel and hauled them all outside. She had a milk crate each of rice and beans, and a few tins of canned meat and fruit. Finding fruits and edible vegetables in gardens abandoned by the Indians and in the surrounding secondary forest was part of her research, and she was good enough at it to feed herself and a family of four.

Not that she was going to be spending enough time doing research to feed anybody. She hadn't fought her way back to the Amazon in order to continue her data collection on peach palms and the reforestation of abandoned swiddens, despite what the proposal she'd submitted to RBC said. There was a prize of untold riches waiting for her up the Rio Cauaburi, and if it hadn't been for the army major, the woolly monkey, and the damned *garimpeiro* she'd had to shoot, the prize would already be hers. Now she had another chance, and if she pulled it off, she would be famous with her reputation secure, instead of infamous with her reputation hanging in shreds.

Her gaze strayed past Johnny Chang's crates to the small black fanny pack tucked up under her pillow on the cot. Leaning over, she pulled the pack out and knew she held the future in her hands. Not just her future, but something for the future of all mankind. Johnny Chang's crates were only for any trouble that might get in the way of that future.

The running patter of feet approaching from outside brought her head around, her hands tightening on the pack.

"Annie. Annie," a small voice called. "Grandmama says for you to come."

A smile curved Annie's mouth as she rose to her feet

and crossed to the open door. Lifting her hand high, she hid the pack by stuffing it into the thatched eaves above the jamb, before she leaned outside.

"*Oi, Maria. Tudo bem?*" she said to Gabriela's six-year-old granddaughter, a chubby little beauty with bouncy black pigtails and big, melting brown eyes. As the director of RBC, Dr. Oliveira had a house on the coalition's thirty acres of lushly landscaped gardens and cultivated fields. Another twenty or so researchers were housed in the guest cabanas, some of them just passing through, like herself, others working in RBC's labs. Annie was on her second stint with RBC.

"*Ô, terrível, Annie, terrível.*" Maria scrunched her little face up and gave a disconsolate shake to her head. "Tomas's puppy ate my frog, and now he won't give it back."

Schooling her features into an appropriately grave expression, Annie knelt down.

"Trust me, honey, you don't want the frog back. What you want is a new frog, and I saw lots of them in your grandmother's fountain next to the lab."

Maria's face brightened. "Nice, big fat ones?"

"The fattest," Annie promised.

Maria ran off down the path, shouting over her shoulder, "Don't forget Grandmama!"

Annie was unlikely to forget the formidable matriarch of RBC, the woman who had saved her twice, once from a Brazilian jail, and the second time from the obscurity of a lab assistant's job at the University of Wyoming. Annie had cooled her heels for nearly a year at home on the great western plains of North America, trying to get back to the Amazon. She never would have made it without Gabriela Oliveira's support.

She looked down at herself and grimaced. She hadn't changed clothes since she'd gotten drenched looking for Travers, and a summons from Gabriela required better than shorts that drooped to her knees and a green shirt that had seen better days.

Looking around by the door, she spotted the duffel bag that held her bathroom kit and clean clothes. She reached for it—and froze.

Her outstretched fingers slowly curled back into her palm. A trickle of fear ran down her spine.

Snail snake, she told herself, looking at the small coiled colubrid nestled in the shadows between her duffel and a gallon of alcohol. The snake was nothing more than a harmless *Dipsas indica*—and it still made Annie's skin crawl.

"Damn," she whispered as the snake slithered off and disappeared into the leaf litter. Her best friend, Mad Jack Reid, had assured her she would outgrow her aversion to snakes the same way someday he would outgrow wild women, but neither had happened yet. It was still one of the great ironies of her life that she hated snakes and yet loved the snake-infested jungle of the rain forest—all the lush, overgrown plants and towering canopy trees, and above all the rare jewels tucked in between, the Orchidaceae.

She glanced over at the doorjamb where she'd hidden the small black pack in the palm thatch. Mad Jack would have her butt in a sling if he found out where she'd gone, and what she was doing.

There had been a time before she'd been exiled, a few short days on the Rio Cauaburi, when she'd thought all the world could be hers. The illusion hadn't lasted long.

The Woolly Monkey Incident had changed everything, tumbling her from glory into the depths of doom so fast there had been days she'd wondered if she would survive.

Well, she had survived. Not only survived, but gotten back to Brazil, and this time she would not be denied. Johnny Chang's crates would see to that, friggin' Corisco Vargas or no Corisco Vargas.

With the snake gone, she grabbed the duffel bag and headed off for a quick cleanup at the bathhouse.

"IT'S TIME YOU CAME BACK into the fold, William," Gabriela said from behind her big mahogany desk piled high with papers and various potted plants, most of them straggling toward death's door. At sixty-eight, she had hair that was white as snow and was twisted into a tidy French roll at the back of her head. Her hands shook slightly with palsy, but her mind and her eyes were crystal clear, missing very little of what went on at RBC or anywhere else in the Amazon. "You've been running wild for too long."

Will could hardly disagree with her last statement, and he could hardly agree to the first, which left him in a bit of a bind.

"You could water your plants," he suggested, lifting one limp leaf where it lay comatose on a neatly bound research proposal.

"I'm a botanist, not a gardener," the old woman informed him with a haughty arch to her brow, "and you're avoiding the question."

Will looked up. "I'm taking Annie Parrish to Santa Maria. That's what you wanted, isn't it?"

"Partly. It would be nice if you could set aside a few days of whatever it is you do all day long and make sure she's on terra firma once she gets there."

" 'Nice' isn't the word most people think of when they think of me," he said nonchalantly, picking up a smooth stone from off her desk.

"I know you better than most people," the old scientist said, undaunted.

He rubbed his thumb over the stone. Gabriela *had* known him. There had been a time when a lot of people had known him, but they didn't know him now. Will set the stone down, not bothering to correct her.

"Didn't she work in Santa Maria before? Everything I've heard had her up there until she shot her lover in Yavareté." He named a town far to the west of Santa Maria, a town on the Rio Vaupes where it crossed the border from Colombia into Brazil.

"I found her in Yavareté, yes," Gabriela said carefully, "but she wasn't there by choice."

Will paused, his fingers resting on the edge of a cobalt-blue bowl filled with seed pods. "Found?"

"She'd been taken there for questioning."

"Taken by whom?" He picked up part of a broken seed pod containing four Brazil nuts, *Bertholettia excelsa*.

"Corisco Vargas," the old woman said after a short hesitation.

Will looked up and caught her clear-eyed gaze with his own.

"Where, exactly, did you find her?" he asked. He knew Corisco Vargas. Everybody on the Rio Negro knew the bastard.

"In a jail cell."

"What kind of shape was she in?" It was a loaded question, loaded eight ways from Sunday, and Will doubted very much if he was going to like Gabriela's answer.

He didn't.

The old woman shrugged, her hand making a slight, dismissive gesture.

"You know the way of these things. To save face, the government sent her home and—"

"I heard she was deported," he interrupted, dropping the broken seed vessel back into the bowl.

"Not officially. There were no papers."

"And the lover?"

"There was no lover."

No lover.

"Then who the hell did she shoot?" He was beginning to doubt if anything he'd heard about Annie Parrish was true.

Gabriela made another negligent gesture. "A *garimpeiro* working for Vargas."

It was an interesting quirk of Brazilian politics that allowed Vargas, an army major, to also be one of the country's most notorious, illegal gold-mining entrepreneurs. Vargas had operations in the Serra Pelada and was opening more mines along Brazil's northern border.

Santa Maria was only about a hundred miles from that border.

"If she's planning on messing with Vargas, you shouldn't have approved the research that got her back into the country," he said, moving on and lightly skimming his fingers over a book. They came away dusty.

"She's brilliant," Gabriela said, as if that both explained and excused everything.

He wiped the dust off on his pants and looked over at the old woman, pinning her with his gaze. "She's jaguar bait, and we both know it. Do everybody a favor and send her back to the States, and the next time you ask me to take somebody on my boat, don't leave all the fun parts out."

He turned to leave, planning on getting on the *Sucuri* and getting as far away from RBC and Annie Parrish as possible.

Dr. Gabriela Oliveira had other ideas.

"You owe me, William, and I'm calling in my markers." She paused for effect, then added, "All of them."

It was true. He did owe her, more than enough to cover the hassle of hauling Annie Parrish up the Rio Negro, but he'd taken on another debt that far exceeded any hold Gabriela had on him, a debt wrapped around him as tightly as his own skin. This close to payback, he wasn't interested in dealing with somebody who could easily turn out to be more trouble than she was worth.

He felt the weight of the old shaman's crystal lying against his chest, his protection for now, and had no regrets for the bargain he'd made, or for the "lost" year that had changed the course of his life. For what he'd seen, and heard, and felt, and known three years ago, there had been no choice but to follow Tutanji into the forest. A year later he'd emerged, and for the last two years Tutanji had charged him with plying the rivers of the Amazon. The cord that held him to the medicine man had grown ever longer; his search had ever expanded, until he'd finally found the demon Tutanji sought—Corisco Vargas.

And Vargas was a demon, more so than anyone knew. Annie Parrish couldn't have picked a worse person to tangle with, not in all of Amazonia.

"I could just shoot her now and save us all a lot of trouble." It was the voice of experience speaking. Will knew enough about Vargas to imagine what the Yavareté jail had been like, and the thought was enough to churn his gut.

"And I could just shoot you now and save us even more," another voice said from behind him.

Will didn't know whether to laugh or swear out loud. He did neither, only turned toward the door leading from Gabriela's office to the garden to see Annie Parrish standing there in the last rays of a dying sun.

"When did you come in?" he asked out of curiosity.

"Just before jaguar bait," she said clearly, as if an apology might be in order.

In good conscience, Will couldn't retract a word. Dry and all scrubbed clean, with her hair fluffed out, her clothes too big for her small frame, and her eyes wide behind the glasses perched on her freckled nose, she looked like exactly what he'd called her—a cat snack. Contrarily, she also looked mad enough to chew nails.

"For the record," she went on, "I'm planning on staying as far away from Corisco Vargas as I can get, and the last 'jaguar' that tried to take a bite out of me ended up with a bullet in his leg."

"So I heard." He was glad to hear her stance on Vargas, but the whole Amazon Annie thing was starting to look like a hoax to him—because the woman simply didn't fit the description, any of the descriptions. And she sure as hell didn't look as if she'd survived a Yavareté jail, with or without Vargas involved. An experience like that would have left its mark, and other than the scar near her temple, she had one of the most unmarred faces he'd ever seen, not a perfect face, but an interesting face with pretty skin and delicate, feminine features. She was physically fit and as sleekly muscled as anyone who had walked the Rio Vaupes and lived to tell the tale, but there wasn't a hard edge on her. Not anywhere, he thought, letting his gaze sweep the length of her body before coming back up and getting waylaid by the flinty glint in her hazel eyes.

It was all he could do to fight off another grin. The cat snack came complete with claws. Good, he thought. Given her chosen destination, she needed them, the sharper the better.

"William and I were just finishing up discussing the terms of your passage," Gabriela interjected diplomatically. "If I thought the RBC launch would actually be fixed in a week, I would recommend waiting. It would certainly give me much less to worry about, but I know you don't want to miss the height of the peach palm harvest."

Peach palm harvest? Will couldn't say for sure, but Annie Parrish didn't look as if she were thinking about peach palms, not with her mouth that tight.

"You've got nothing to worry about, Gabriela," she assured the old doctor. Then her gaze slid in his direction, and her attention focused on him in a way he found interesting, if rather obvious. She was checking him out through her little gold-rimmed glasses, sizing him up, and trying to figure out just how much trouble he could possibly turn out to be.

More than she needed, he could have told her—but he didn't.

"Are you still leaving at dawn?" she asked.

He nodded, intrigued. By his own standards, there wasn't a square inch left on him to inspire anyone's confidence. He was damned surprised to find out that Annie Parrish's standards were even lower than his own.

She turned to Gabriela. "Is there anything else?"

"No," the old woman said. "I just wanted you to know William and his boat had arrived."

"Then if you'll excuse me, I'm going to get Carlos and start loading my gear," she said, naming RBC's old caretaker. She hardly glanced at Will on her way out the door. "I'll be on the dock at dawn."

Will nodded, waiting until she was out of earshot before he turned back to Gabriela. There were a whole lot of bad ways for the situation to end, and only one good one.

"Send her home, Gabriela. You can get another researcher to finish whatever work she had going on in Santa Maria, or you could just let it go. She's been gone a year. There couldn't be much left of whatever she started."

"Another researcher wouldn't be Annie."

"Okay," he conceded. "I'll go up there and check it out myself. If there's anything worth salvaging, I'll let you know. Then you can decide whether to send her or not." He was headed in that direction anyway, straight to hell, the Cauaburi, and Vargas, and he could spare a couple of days to look over the Santa Maria station and file a report.

"You're not Annie Parrish, either," the old woman said, and at that, Will did laugh out loud.

"I lost my reputation, Gabriela, not my mind. I doubt if her work is beyond my comprehension. I can still manage an assessment."

"I know enough to only believe half of what I hear

about you," Gabriela countered, "and given my observations and your lack of explanations, I do believe half of what I've heard since your return."

"Obviously the bad half."

She narrowed her gaze at him. "Don't fool yourself, William. It's all bad and some of it worse."

He couldn't argue the point. "Which part makes you think I can't do what Annie Parrish can do?"

"Not can't do, but won't do. You're not interested in benefiting RBC. On the other hand, any work Annie does will come under the auspices of my institute."

"Looking for a legacy, Gabriela?" he asked dryly.

In answer, she raised her hand. It shook like a leaf in the wind, but there was no wind coming in through the garden door. With a heavy sigh, she lowered her hand back to the desk.

"It's time, William. I'm getting older in a thousand ways every day, and the board knows it. They want Ricardo Solano in as the new director."

Will knew Ricardo Solano. The man was good, but worked strictly by the book. Solano sure as hell would have never let Annie Parrish back into RBC.

"A legacy is built on years of work," Will said, relenting from his hard line. "You've done the work. No matter what Annie Parrish finds or doesn't find, it isn't going to change how you're remembered."

A tired smile spread across the old woman's face. "You're too cynical, William, just like me. Annie isn't. She still believes there are wonders in the forest, and it's the believers who find them."

Or fools not quick enough to get out of their way, Will thought, exasperated with her reasoning, even with the shaman's crystal weighing heavily around his neck.

"I still say you should send her home."

"No. She goes to Santa Maria." The old woman was adamant. "You just get her settled. I'll be up as soon as the launch is fixed. I'm sure Father Aldo at the mission can keep her out of trouble in the meantime."

"He didn't manage to keep her out of trouble last time." It was a point too important not to mention.

"Father Aldo wasn't at fault," the old woman said, absently sorting through a sheaf of papers on her desk. "Annie wasn't anywhere near Santa Maria when she came in contact with Vargas."

"Then where the hell was she?"

Gabriela lifted one of the papers. It shook ever so slightly in her hand, but her gaze, when she leveled it at him, was steady. "I wish I knew. Nobody dared to question Vargas, and Annie wasn't talking. She still isn't. If you really want to know, you'll have to ask her yourself."

It was a challenge, the gauntlet thrown, and Will wasn't naïve enough to think Gabriela had done it lightly. To the contrary, he'd just figured out why the director of RBC was being so insistent on having Annie Parrish travel with him.

"You want me to find out what she's up to, and it doesn't have a damn thing to do with peach palms, does it?"

"I don't think so," was the old woman's unacceptable reply.

"I don't have time for this, Gabriela," he said, his anger starting to break toward the surface.

Gabriela was completely unfazed by his unraveling control, meeting his glare without so much as batting an eyelash, her look cool, calm, and presumptuously appraising.

"I don't know what you've been up to the last two years, either, William, but I know it's a damn sight more than drinking your way down the length of the river, no matter what I've heard. I don't know where you were for those twelve months when you were supposed to be doing botanical research for Howard Pharmacueticals, and I don't know what happened to you while you were there, but I do know Elena Maria Barbosa Sanchez's son, and I think I know when he's in over his head."

That she was close to being right didn't make Will any less angry. He wasn't in over his head yet, but he sure saw himself heading in that direction.

"You want to know why I let Annie Parrish come back to Brazil?" she continued. "Because I couldn't keep her out. They beat her in Yavareté, William. I was there to pick up the pieces, and I'm the one who put that girl back on the plane to Wyoming. It wasn't four months later that she was begging me to let her back in. She must have still had the bruises."

Will felt his jaw tighten. He didn't want to hear this, none of it.

"So you tell me what's driving her," Gabriela said. "You're both in the same field. You're both among the very best. You're both a couple of loose cannons hell-bent on something—and this old woman can't help but wonder what." She cocked her head to one side, as if she expected an answer.

An answer she wasn't going to get from him.

"I'm just living my life, Gabriela. What I'm doing has nothing to do with Annie Parrish, and I'd like to keep it that way."

"You're not living your life," she said, all but calling him a liar. "You're biding your time. I've watched you do it for two years, but I've got a bad feeling in my bones that your time is running out. Maybe I'm just an old woman feeling her own end drawing near—or maybe I'm right."

That was the last damn thing Will wanted to hear.

"I've never known you to be quite so philosophical," he said, more than ready to leave.

"Then you weren't paying attention. Take her to Santa Maria, William, make sure she's okay. That's all I'm asking."

It was enough, and as close to a dismissal as Will needed to make a break for it. Without another word, he turned and walked out of her office.

On the front porch, he glanced back toward the garden where Annie had disappeared down an overgrown path. Take a woman up the river, Gabriela had said, but she sure as hell hadn't said, "Take Annie Parrish up the river."

Jesus. Vargas had beat her.

He wished Gabriela hadn't told him—not that he hadn't figured it out for himself. He also knew a beating might have been the least of her ordeal, but he'd be damned if he wanted to think about it.

Jaguar bait he'd called her, and despite the *garimpeiro* she'd shot, at least one predator had gotten his teeth into her. So why the hell hadn't she stayed home? If she wasn't back for vengeance, what was she back for?

"*Merda,*" he swore under his breath. Sometimes, botanists in the tropics went a little crazy, the sheer tonnage of plant material and variety of species cross-wiring their circuits and skewing their perspective. From the looks of things, Annie Parrish was one of those who'd been out in the sun too long.

Damn. It was going to be a long three days to
Santa Maria, but first he had his final meeting with Fat
Eddie. More than contraband needed to exchange hands
if he was going to find his way through the vast expanse
of the Cauaburi drainage. He needed the fat man's map
to the gold fields, those jungle hellholes carved out of the
riverbanks by the *garimpeiros* and ruled by a devil named
Corisco Vargas.

CHAPTER 3 ✘

REINO NOVO, BRAZIL

SHE'D COME BACK, THE *NORTE-americana*. Corisco had known she would. She'd come back to Manaus and would soon be heading straight for him, compliments of Gabriela Oliveira, the River Basin Coalition, and the trap he'd so carefully baited a year ago. Santa Maria wouldn't hold her this time any better than it had the last. She would come up the Rio Negro to the Cauaburi and through the emerald door to the heart of the rain forest, to Reino Novo.

He set the message from his man in Manaus aside and leaned across the top of his desk, reaching for a smooth glass cylinder next to the lamp. Light shone down through the glass, illuminating the delicate, glowing prize inside.

Poor little *cientista*, he thought, pulling the cylinder closer. Annie Parrish had come back, and now the Rio Cauaburi would be her grave. He should have killed her when he'd had the chance, instead of indulging himself in trying to break her.

"Fernando," he called out. *"Vem aqui."*

A hulking giant of a man dressed in an army uniform moved out of the shadows in the corner of the richly paneled office. His face was scarred, his head bald, his gaze deceptively blank. Behind him, something moved inside a huge glass tank.

"Bring the box," Corisco added.

Fernando turned to a shelf on the wall and picked up a small gold box. At the desk he set it down with a deferential murmur.

"Do you remember the woman from Yavareté?" Corisco asked, knowing full well that Fernando had not forgotten her. The great hulk had formed a bit of an attachment to Dr. Parrish, especially on the third day, when Corisco had hung her naked in chains from the jail cell wall and let Fernando look his fill.

The giant nodded, his gaze growing quite discerning.

"She is back in Brazil, in Manaus. Send a message to our man to have her picked up and brought to us here. She'll be impressed by the changes in Reino Novo, don't you think?"

Again, Fernando nodded, and Corisco graced him with a smile before dismissing him with a wave of his hand. For all his intelligence, Fernando was ridiculously easy to please.

Not so himself. The night air was stifling, despite the ceiling fans droning overhead. Rain at dusk had laid a pall of humidity over the Cauaburi, making the fountain in the courtyard outside his office absurdly redundant. He was awash in a water world. Piping in more seemed almost ludicrous.

He picked up the box, appreciating the solid heaviness of the gold. Gabriela Oliveira had played her hand out saving Annie Parrish in Yavareté. The governor of

Amazonas, the man who had issued the order to release the RBC botanist at Gabriela's insistence, had mysteriously died within months of Dr. Parrish's release, and the new governor was deep in Corisco's pocket. There would be no more interference in any of his plans. The government of Brazil could twist and turn and natter all it wanted about tapping the potential of the rain forest, but he was the man who would do it, and in a manner no government official could ever have imagined, let alone brought to fruition.

He turned the gold box over in his hand, admiring the exquisite craftsmanship almost as much as he admired the deadly contents. There were a thousand ways to die in the Amazon, but few as exquisitely painful as the kingmaker beetle. The iridescent carapace of the five-inch-long insect contained enough toxic material to dispatch two governors. Once ingested, the hemorrhagic toxins created an internal bloodbath inside the victim and then disappeared without a trace.

Annie Parrish was lucky. She would have a far more glorious death. She'd been so stubborn, so unyielding, a willful prize to be tamed—and he would have tamed her, if she hadn't been taken from him. She didn't know a woman's place, but he would teach her, and this time she would tell him everything. She'd been so soft to the touch, when he'd had her before, so very, very soft.

He set the box aside and shifted his attention to the cylinder, letting his fingers drift down the smooth curve of glass. He didn't understand scientists and all these damned environmentalists. They didn't seem to have any concept of reality, of his reality. They had no idea of the power waiting to be unleashed in the forest.

He did.

His gaze drifted to the large glass tank in the corner of the room, then came back to the cylinder and the exquisite piece of rain forest jungle floating inside.

Scientists came to the Amazon with their degrees and their books, wanting to understand, but only on their terms. They never took the jungle on its terms. Interpreting through the eyes of the rational gaze, they understood nothing, because the jungles of Amazonia did not fit their rational minds. Left to her own devices, Annie Parrish and those like her would have his world crawling with researchers trying to unlock secrets best left alone. Secrets like the one he was building in Reino Novo, like the one residing in the glass cage, and the one inside the glass cylinder.

The delicate orchid was so very lush, its elongate, midnight-blue petals limned with a cream-colored frill, the whole of it dusted with gold flecks like stars in the night sky. He'd confiscated it from her in Yavareté, one of a pair, and known she'd found a rare prize.

In the dark of night, the flower glowed. Even after twelve months of floating in preservative solution, the petals had not browned or withered, and it still emitted light, a mesmerizing, creamy golden light draped with a hint of green along its edge, like a miniature aurora borealis.

Irresistible, he'd thought, and known then that she would return. That she'd collected the flower near the mines was a foregone conclusion, though she'd refused to tell him where. He'd tried beating the information out of her and gotten nowhere, and before he'd had the chance to escalate to more refined torture, she'd been freed by Gabriela and the doomed governor.

The little fool, to have come back. Her timing couldn't

have been worse. It was so inauspicious as to seem fated, that she would die with all the others, a lovely, exotic centerpiece to the sacrifice that would put Reino Novo on the map and seal his name in infamy. None would dare defy him then. Anyone who wanted to enter the rain forest, whether to rape it or save it, would have to deal with him. He would be king of the last great wilderness left on earth, King of the Great Green Hell, King of the Amazon.

CHAPTER 4 ✄

DARKNESS FELL QUICKLY ALONG THE Rio Negro, and Annie, Carlos, and his son, Paco, finished loading her supplies by the light of the lanterns strung along the path leading down to the river.

Travers's boat rocked on the water at the end of the dock, its white form barely illuminated by a low-wattage bulb hanging from a pole on the docking shed. The riverboat was a thirty-footer with two cabins, a helm forward and a smaller cabin aft with an open walkway in between. A short rail around the upper deck made it a good place to store cargo. Up close, she could see the boat needed paint, but the deck felt solid beneath her feet, and she couldn't help but feel a surge of excitement at being on the river and knowing in the morning she would be heading upstream, back to the Rio Cauaburi, the land of all her dreams.

After storing the last of her cartons, she and the men exchanged good-nights, and Carlos and his son headed back up the riverbank to the hacienda's compound. Annie stayed a moment longer to double-check the lashings holding down her supplies. She also wanted to make sure Johnny Chang's crates were well hidden by the rest of her cargo and the tarps she'd bought to keep the rain off her equipment. Waterfront lowlife or not, she doubted if Travers would appreciate her dragging ill-gotten goods on board his boat. In fact, she was damn sure that was just the sort of thing that would get her kicked off his boat. It was certainly why booking fare on one of the public "birdcage" riverboats had been out of the question.

Even so, in Gabriela's office she'd come damn close to changing her mind about going with him. Damn close. Only the risk of staying in Manaus another day had kept her from telling Will Travers he'd talked himself out of a passenger.

Jaguar bait.

She jerked one of the tie-down ropes, her mouth tightening in irritation. What gall. She'd never heard it put in quite those words, but she knew exactly what he meant—and he was dead wrong. She wasn't anybody's entrée. If anything, he'd be surprised to know just how much alike they were, or had been before he'd lost himself in the rain forest.

Her mouth curved into a brief, knowing smile. Having met him twice now, she'd put a dollar to anyone's dime that Travers had never been lost a day in his life, and certainly not for a whole year.

No, she mused. He'd known exactly where he was and probably knew exactly how to get back. Not that he was telling.

Something more than intelligence was burning in the depths of his dark eyes, and against her better judgment, part of her was damned curious to see how much she could find out about him in three days, beginning with where in the hell he'd been, and moving on to what in the hell had happened to change him from a scientific legend to a waterfront has-been.

Holding on to the last tie-down, she stood on the boat's aft deck and looked down the length of the Rio Negro. Jungle rose up on the near bank, dense and impenetrable, a hothouse of plants and mysteries. The river's black waters reflected a white stream of moonlight all the way to the lights of the city farther to the southeast. She had a year on her visa. By the time she returned to Manaus, there would probably be rumors running all over town about her. Like Travers, she planned on being "lost" for a while herself. Unlike Travers, she planned on coming back a hero, not an outcast. If the Amazon and its creatures had devoured anybody's life, it was Dr. Will Travers's, not hers.

A soft noise coming from the other side of the boat brought her head around. In the next second, she heard a soft thud and the sound of running feet racing up the dock toward shore. Moving quickly to the walkway between the two cabins, she barely caught sight of a man before he veered off the lantern-lit path and disappeared into the palm trees on the riverbank. The palms' fronds gleamed silver in the moonlight, great swaths of curves silhouetted against the sky. Below the trees, all was darkness.

It could have been Paco, she thought, though she doubted it. Paco wouldn't have left the path. It certainly hadn't been Carlos. The old man was incapable of moving faster than a shuffle. That only left the about forty or so people who lived and worked at RBC to choose from for the nighttime runner, any of whom could have had a legitimate reason to board Travers's boat. Given where she'd been standing, they probably hadn't even realized she was on board.

Curious, but not overly disturbed, Annie turned back into the walkway and came to sudden halt, her gaze riveted to the blowgun dart sticking out of the aft cabin's door. The small wad of white kapok fluff on the end shone brightly in the moonlight.

Alarmed, she looked back to the shore to make sure the man was gone, before she moved in closer to the dart and saw the scrap of paper pinned to the door. With a quick tug, she pulled the dart out of the wood and held the paper up to the light.

The message was short and ominously direct: **LEAVE MANAUS.**

CHAPTER 5

SUNLIGHT STREAMED THROUGH THE windows fronting the *Sucuri's* helm, making a hot band across Will's face where he lay in his hammock between the wheel and the door, slowly rousing to the day. The thought of opening his eyes to such a blast of brightness was too painful to contemplate, so he gingerly rolled himself over into a spot of shade. A soft groan escaped him.

The mere fact of the sunlight's existence told him he'd overslept and missed the dawn departure time. He wondered, briefly, if Annie Parrish had found another boat and left without him. Or better yet, if Gabriela had come to her senses in the night and canceled the woman's project.

"A-hem." A purely feminine voice sounded from the doorway.

No such luck.

By pure force of will, he lifted his head a bare fraction of an inch and pried one eyelid open. It was her, all right, looking incredibly fresh and lovely, and incredibly annoyed. With a pained sigh, he sank back into his hammock.

He didn't blame her. He was pretty annoyed himself. It had taken half the night and two bottles of *cachaça*, before Fat Eddie Mano had relinquished the map. Bitching and moaning had been the first two items on the fat one's agenda. The old thief had been robbed, a load of merchandise taken out of one of his warehouses right out from under his nose and undoubtably by one of his own *jagunços*, henchmen, the only people with access to Eddie's various hidey-holes. Eddie hadn't said what had been stolen, but Will had a pretty good idea of the kind of goods Fat Eddie traded in and out of Manaus, and none of it was legal. The man couldn't go to the police, especially since whatever had been stolen from Fat Eddie, Fat Eddie had originally stolen from them—a fact the man had let slip sometime after they'd cracked open the second bottle, then repeatedly forgotten as he'd bemoaned the fate of "honest" businessmen at the mercy of corrupt police officials and perfidious employees. Vengeance had been sworn, with various tortures amply described—hour after hour and shot after shot of brain-numbing *cachaça*.

Will had gotten the point, however unnecessary. He had no intention of stealing the contraband Fat Eddie had given him in Pancha's. For Will, meeting with Corisco Vargas face to face to deliver the goods was far more important than the bag of gemstones Fat Eddie had entrusted in his care. The map was what he'd come to Manaus to get, not a clutch of rough-cut diamonds and emeralds.

He carefully slipped his hand into the front pocket of his pants, felt the folds of paper and told himself the end had justified the means—a reasoning he usually found spurious at best.

His body told him it was still damn spurious thinking. Everything inside his skull had congealed into one, big, giant throb of hangover pain. His mouth felt as if a hundred *pistoleiros* in dusty, old leather boots had tromped through it, and he and Eddie had been drinking the good stuff.

"It's seven-thirty," Miss Bright Eyes said with an edge to her voice. "I've been here since five, and this is the first time you've budged."

Definitely irritated, he thought.

"I thought maybe you'd died."

Close, he could have told her, and still in critical condition.

"Can you get up? Or do I need to go get Carlos?"

He was tempted to tell her yes, go get Carlos. Not because he couldn't get up, but because running back to the hacienda might help her work off some energy. She sounded pretty keyed up and a little on the bitchy side, and with his head pounding, what he needed was a smooth slide into the day, a nice quiet unmooring and a slow drift into the current.

Yeah, he thought. That's what he needed, a nice and easy slide into consciousness—or back into oblivion. There was no reason to hurry, now that he had the map. Hell wasn't going anywhere without him. It would still be up on the Cauaburi, whether it took him a week or two weeks to get there. With the hangover he'd made out of two bottles of rotgut and less sleep last night, his money was on the two weeks.

"Are we going to make it out of here before noon, or not?" she demanded to know. "I am on a schedule. A tight ... very tight schedule."

He snorted in disbelief—and damn near blew his head off. A groan of pure pain lodged in his throat, right behind a foul curse. Tight schedule? There was no such thing in the Amazon. A person had their choice of two speeds on the river, slow crawl and dead stop, with reverse a possible third. Nobody ever went anywhere on a schedule, tight or not. Anybody who tried was destined for the loony bin.

Then he remembered something Gabriela had said.

"Peach palms," he muttered under his breath. Annie Parrish was supposed to research the peach palm harvest around Santa Maria—something he could have done in his sleep.

No, he thought, remembering a little more of the conversation. The peach palm thing was just a cover for something else, but he'd be damned if he could remember what.

"You oughta just go home," he mumbled, too hungover to sort through the mess.

"I beg your pardon?" she said, her voice reaching a new note of stridency.

Merda, he swore to himself, oblivion forgotten. Where was that kitteny, soft-looking woman he'd met yesterday in Pancha's? And who had let this sanctimonious alley cat into his cabin?

"How did you get in here?" he asked, working to raise his voice above a hoarse whisper. With Fat Eddie's gems on board, Will had felt compelled to take a few precautions. Locking the door had been one. The pistol digging into his rib cage was the other.

"I picked the lock," she said without even a trace of apology in her voice.

So much for sanctimony, he thought. She was just plain angry with him and not afraid to show it.

Once again, he could hardly blame her. He could have told her there was a law against breaking and entering, even on a boat, but he was getting the idea she wouldn't give a damn. He was also beginning to think Gabriela was right. Annie Parrish was a woman on a mission— and her mission didn't have a damn thing to do with peach palms. That's what Gabriela had said, or rather, implied. Dr. Oliveira didn't really know what Dr. Parrish was up to any more than he did.

And he was stuck with her on his boat.

"Go get Carlos," he suggested, every word grating across his aching brain. "And coffee." If she wanted to leave before noon, he was going to need Carlos, and coffee wouldn't hurt.

Muttering something about it taking more than coffee to get his sorry hide moving—to which he could only agree—she turned and walked out the door.

Blessed silence descended, and every cell in Will's body begged him to go back to sleep. He ignored them. Putting one hand on his brow to keep his head from exploding, he carefully swung his legs over the side of the hammock and put his feet on the floor. Whether hell was going to wait for him or not, he would be better off out of Manaus.

But twenty minutes later, when Dr. Parrish returned with Carlos, he hadn't gotten so much as an inch closer to leaving. He was still sitting on the side of the hammock, his head in his hands.

"*Como vai, Guillermo?*" the old man asked, shuffling into the cabin and over to the small gas stove sitting on the counter. Carlos was part Indian, about five feet two, and as wizened as an old tobacco leaf.

"*Vou bem,*" he answered, his voice little more than a croak. I'm well.

The old man cackled at his obvious lie, showing blackened teeth, then set about getting some water on to boil.

Stationing herself by the door, Annie watched as Carlos pulled handful after handful of vegetal whatnot out of a cloth bag slung over his shoulder. Most of the debris went into the pot. Some went directly into a tin cup. Considering the shape the specimens were in, she wasn't surprised not to recognize anything, but she trusted Carlos to know what he was doing. Every grad student who had ever worked for RBC knew about Carlos's famous hangover remedies—and William Sanchez Travers was undeniably, colossally hungover.

The man had practically paralyzed himself, she thought with disgust. She'd purposely kept her expectations and qualifications for a boat captain low, but as of five o'clock that morning, he'd bottomed out below any base minimum requirements. She didn't mind that he'd gotten drunk. In fact, after yesterday's confusing conclusions, she took some small comfort in the verification of his cheap and easy character—but his timing sucked. Dawn, he'd said. She did a quick check of her watch, and her lips thinned. They'd be lucky to cast off by ten o'clock.

The last thing Carlos pulled out of his bag was a sheaf of wild *Piperacea* leaves, his *shinki-shinki*. He began shaking it over Travers's head and shoulders, and her expectations slipped even lower. When the old witch doctor started to chant, Annie knew they were sunk.

Noon, she groaned inwardly. If Carlos thought Travers

needed a full-blown healing ritual, they were going to miss half the day.

This was what she got for depending on a down-on-his-luck river rat given to drink and waterfront alliances not so very different from the one making it necessary for her to get the hell out of Manaus.

Yet there she stood, not five feet from shore with the day bearing down on her and a crumpled piece of sweat-stained paper in her pocket telling her she was doomed.

"Could you speed this up a little, Carlos?" she muttered to the old man in a whispered aside.

"Yeah, Carlos," Travers mumbled in Portuguese, slanting her a wry glance from beneath his lashes. "The lady is on a schedule, a tight schedule."

Annie didn't deign to respond. She obviously hadn't spoken softly enough, but she hardly cared. The important thing was to get under way.

"Tight schedule," Travers repeated, a grin flickering across his mouth, and she dared to hope. He could drink himself into a coma after he got her to Santa Maria, and he probably would, but his grin was an undeniable sign of life.

He was coming around.

"I *was* on a schedule," she said doggedly and watched his grin broaden before he turned away and buried his face behind his hands with another soft groan. Long swaths of sun-streaked hair fell over his fingers. For a moment, she feared he'd peaked and was heading back down. Then he let out another soft sound and dragged his hands back through his hair.

Relief flooded through her. He was definitely coming around.

Three days, she told herself, that's as long as she needed him to stay on course. Three days if everything went as planned, which of course it never did on the river. She knew that as well as he, but she was working with a schedule anyway, a tight, year-long schedule with only one goal—to get herself back to the exact spot where she'd been standing when that woolly monkey had fallen out of the sky and landed in her arms.

Carlos had given a slight nod in answer to her question and was shaking his *shinki-shinki* a bit faster. When the old man handed her a cigar out of his pocket, she didn't hesitate to take it. She bit off the end, spit it out the porthole, and bent toward the stove. With a few good puffs, she had the cigar glowing and smoking.

Good God, Will thought, squinting over his linked fingers and watching her blow a smoke ring into the air. Carlos cackled behind him, and Will could imagine that the old man would get a kick out of smoke rings, the drama of them if nothing else.

At Carlos's direction, Annie Parrish applied her healing witchery to him, wreathing him in cloud after diaphanous cloud of tobacco smoke, following a path set by the shaman's sheaf of leaves. The gringa doctor's help seemed to inspire the old man to new heights of singing. Carlos's voice rose higher, the words of the chant filling the small cabin, bound by smoke and the underlying *shhh-shhh-whoosh* of the *Piperacea* leaves.

It was at times like these when Will really began to wonder what had happened to his life. He'd had such a promising future. He could have eventually left the tropics and gone back to a professorship at Harvard. He could have written more books, done a lecture tour, become the director of some famous botanical garden, and in his waning years, dictated his biography to some eager graduate student. God knows, the possibilities had seemed endless.

But here he was, his head splitting in two, hungover in a hammock hanging inside a bucket of a boat, going up the Black River one more time, maybe for the last time. He barely had two hundred *reais* to his name, including Annie Parrish's fare, and didn't need the bare two hundred he had. Sometimes he felt as if he'd disappeared, a feeling Tutanji would only confirm. Dr. William Sanchez Travers had disappeared. Tutanji had called him into the rain forest, and there in the green twilight of a lost glade he'd been devoured by the old shaman's spirit anaconda.

At least that was Tutanji's story. As Will remembered it, there had been way too much blood for the snake to have been a spirit.

Another wreath of smoke settled about his head, and Will realized he was feeling better. Carlos was no Tutanji, and a store-bought cigar was not a forest shaman's roughly rolled sheaf of green tobacco, but the healing ritual was working. He'd expected it to work. He'd been in the forest too long not to take comfort where it was offered, and too long to underestimate the power of a shaman's spells—even a citified, acculturated shaman like Carlos.

When the old man offered him the cup of the steeped brew, he downed it in one foul, bitter-tasting, leaf-laden swallow. Instantly, a trembling seized him, and all Will could do was hold on for the ride.

Jamming the cigar between her teeth, Annie put one hand on his shoulder to help hold him steady and lifted her other arm to check her watch through the clouds of smoke—eight o'clock. Great, she thought. Carlos was moving at record speed. Will Travers was shaking like a wet dog, and if he didn't fall out of his hammock and knock himself out, they should be on the river within the hour.

A flash on the water drew her gaze to the window, and she swore, one crude word filled with all the frustration of the morning. A boat was approaching the dock from downstream, coming around the point that separated RBC from Manaus.

"We've got company," she said, looking around for a pair of binoculars, knowing down to the marrow of her bones that her luck had just run out.

"I'm not in the mood," Travers grumbled, his body slowly settling into a state of calmness beneath her hand, stage two of Carlos's mystery cure.

There wasn't a botanist or biochemist at RBC who hadn't tried to analyze the ingredients in the hangover infusion. All they'd ever come up with was a few innocuous plants that could never elicit such a dramatic, but brief, physical reaction. The secret had to be in the old man's well-guarded admixtures.

"Then maybe you should fire this tub up and get us out of here, before we get boarded by—" She paused and reached for the binoculars she spotted hanging above the wheel. Putting them to her eyes, she let out another curse. "By the police."

"No one boards the *Sucuri*," he told her simply, and at the sound of the words, an ill-omened trickle of fear wound down her spine.

Lowering the binoculars, she turned to face him, her mind coming to a slow halt, the police forgotten.

"*Sucuri*?" she repeated. "That's the name of this boat?"

The wan flash of his grin as he rose to his feet was hardly reassuring, and Annie had to wonder why a woman with a morbid fear of snakes would stay on a boat named after the biggest, most powerfully gargantuan serpent to ever thrash a path through the Amazon—and contrary to what people thought, snakes did thrash, especially giant anacondas, *sucuri,* especially when they had something big in their coils, something about the size of a female Wyoming botanist.

She knew it all for a fact.

She'd seen it a thousand times in her dreams.

CHAPTER 6 ✖

THE SHRILL BLAST OF AN AIRHORN
drew her attention back to the open window and the
boat bearing down on them. Dropping the cigar into the
empty pot, she gripped the sill with her hands and leaned
forward. Even without the binoculars, she could now
see the insignia of the Manaus police painted on the
small speedboat, and she didn't know which was worse,
the launch headed toward her, or the one she was standing on.

Sucuri. Who in the hell would name their boat after
the world's biggest snake? Herpetologists could argue
all day long about which was longer, anacondas or re-
ticulated pythons, but pound for pound, there was more
snake per foot of an anaconda than any other animal in
the suborder Serpentes. Big and muscular, and uncom-
monly aggressive, they defied comparison in the snake
world. Annie had never seen one in the wild, and for that
she could only thank God.

On the other hand, she'd had more than her fair share

of encounters with the Brazilian police, particularly in Yavareté, and she'd be damned if she was ready for another one.

The airhorn blew again, and she whirled to face Travers. She didn't have a choice, it was the *Sucuri* or nothing.

"You know, getting involved with the police could really slow us down," she said as calmly as she could.

"I'm not planning on getting involved," Travers said around a yawn.

Of course he wasn't, she silently snapped, about to tell him he wasn't going to have much choice if he didn't get moving. Then he lifted his arms above his head in a long, languorous stretch, and Annie could only stare, not sure what held her attention more, the sheer nonchalance of his movement in the face of disaster—or the pistol shoved into the waistband of his pants.

One thing she did know for sure: she hadn't thought everything through nearly as well as she should have.

"Son of a bitch," Travers muttered in mid-stretch, his attention arrested by something through the window. In a single stride, he moved to where she was standing, half trapping her between the narrow counter and his large, warm body as he looked over her head to the river beyond—effortlessly breaching the barrier she'd set up around herself after Yavareté, getting closer to her than she'd allowed anyone in nearly a year.

The macaw feathers were still in his hair, she noted from somewhere close to the edge of panic, the quills tied into the dark strands behind his ear with a strip of red cloth. The *genipa* paint had been washed off in the rain, or maybe in a shower. Amazingly, even in the smoke-filled cabin, he smelled faintly of soap.

"Tchau, Carlos. Obrigado," he said gruffly, turning to the old man and moving away from her toward the helm after no more than a few seconds of contact.

It was a few seconds too many. She'd once canoed over two hundred miles of the Javari River in a dugout with three Indian guides and two Carmelite nuns and never once felt overcrowded—but she didn't think Travers's thirty-foot-long riverboat was going to be big enough for the two of them, and not because he took up too much room. Despite his size, lean and broad shouldered, and standing almost a foot taller than she did, she could have held him off, if she'd wanted to hold him off.

That she hadn't lifted a hand to do so was incomprehensible. Her instincts and reactions were honed for self-defense, and had been long before she'd gotten in over her head with Vargas in Yavareté.

So what in the hell was going on? she wondered. He wasn't harmless. She'd figured that much out in Pancha's. And he wasn't to be trusted, the drunken state she'd found him in that morning was proof enough of his unreliability. That only left one possibility, one she refused to entertain.

Forcing herself to take a breath, she turned back to the window. What she saw made all her unsettling thoughts about Will Travers vanish.

Her mouth fell open in astonishment. Never, ever had she seen such a sight. It was Jabba the Hut with a black ponytail and a flowing black mustache piloting a much too small speedboat and sending up a rooster tail of water as he rounded the point.

"Is that who I think it is?" she asked, her eyebrows arching nearly into her hairline.

"Fat Eddie Mano or the cavalry," Travers said, twisting

the ignition with one hand and tapping gauges with the other. "Take your pick."

She'd heard of him, the fattest man in Manaus and the underworld warlord of the stretch of the Amazon running from the jungle city to Santarem, but for all her waterfront dealings, she'd never seen him. According to Johnny Chang, very few people ever did. Fat Eddie held court in a warehouse near the Praça de Matriz, and petitioners of any and all ilks came to him. Most were dealt with by subordinates. A select few were allowed into Fat Eddie's inner sanctum—and a few of those never came back out, making getting in to see Fat Eddie a dubious honor at best.

"Cavalry?" she repeated, watching in amazement as the huge man in the little black boat swerved in front of the police launch. The man with Fat Eddie raised a machine gun into the air and fired off a few rounds.

Merda, she thought, blanching. It was Johnny Chang, his bald head gleaming in the morning sun, his signature queue flying in the wind.

"Yep. The fat man is heading them off at the pass. If you want to bail out, this is the time," he said. "I'll see you get your money back and drop your cargo at Santa Maria."

It was a reprieve, if she dared to take it. Any innocent person would have jumped at the chance.

She didn't budge—a fact he noted with a questioning lift of his eyebrows.

She looked away, toward shore. Carlos was already halfway up the dock, but bailing out really wasn't an option available to her, not with Johnny Chang on board the black speedboat.

"I'm staying," she said, forcing herself to face him.

"Then cast off." Travers nodded toward the door.

Annie didn't need to be told twice. When the last mooring line hit the deck, the *Sucuri* drifted out into the current, no more than a hundred yards ahead of the two speedboats, and Annie didn't see any way in hell for them to stay ahead.

She hadn't counted on Fat Eddie. The fat man sliced his boat in front of the police, nearly crashing into them. More shots were fired, but by the police, and not into the air. A bullet thudded into the *Sucuri,* and Travers swore. Annie's heart leapt into her throat. She'd known there was danger in returning to Brazil, but she hadn't expected to get shot at before she'd even left Manaus.

"Get down," he ordered, gunning the motor for more speed, steering the *Sucuri* as close to the shore as he dared. Tree limbs slapped against the boat and scraped along the hull.

Annie only partially obeyed, keeping her head high enough to scan the riverbank for a channel. A small tributary emptied into the Negro about five miles upstream. During the rainy season when all the rivers flooded their banks, a number of channels were created through the trees and vegetation, all of them running downstream toward RBC. She was sure Travers was doing what she would have done, trying to make it into one of the channels. They could wind around in the resulting maze of trees and water, maintaining cover while making their way up the shoreline.

Another round of gunfire peppered the air, making her flinch. If Johnny had squealed on her to the police, why in the hell was he in that boat with Fat Eddie? she wondered. And if the lot of them were after Travers, she was making one hell of a mistake heading farther up the river with him.

God, just let her get to the Cauaburi, she prayed.

A rumble of thunder rolled across the sky, dragging her gaze heavenward. Beside her, Travers said something under his breath, a soft word that skimmed across her consciousness and made the hairs rise on the nape of her neck without actually registering.

She started to ask him what he'd said, but was stopped by a fresh spray of bullets strafing the deck. *Merda*. She ducked farther behind the helm, looking up again as the light fell all around. Banks of clouds were rolling in from the horizon, blocking out the sun. Lightning streaked in a jagged bolt across the darkening sky, followed by a thunderous cracking sound.

"I'll be damned," she whispered. She'd seen some fast-moving storms in her time, but this one had come out of nowhere. The next crack of thunder reverberated along the length of the river and brought a deluge in its wake. The heavens simply opened up. Sky-high sheets of rain washed over the boat in long, world-drenching, gray waves, coming in through the windows and soaking them both. The decks were instantly awash in water.

Annie turned to check behind them and could just make out Fat Eddie's boat plowing slowly upstream against the current and the rain, stymied by the sudden downpour, but still heading toward them. The police had pulled up at the RBC dock, the dark shapes of officers swarming toward the shore. Two took up posts on the dock and knelt into firing positions. Over the sound of the storm, she heard the cracking reports of a few more shots, but nothing reached the *Sucuri*, and in the next moment, the boat slipped into a channel, gliding between the towering trunks of two half-submerged *lupuna* trees.

Releasing a pent-up breath, she rose to her feet, only to have her illusion of momentary safety undermined by his next words.

"Maybe you better go below and start the pump, *before* we start to sink," he said, as if the possibility were more inevitable than not.

She glanced toward the floor and saw water disappearing through the cracks in the boards between her feet. Her mouth thinned in frustration and a surfeit of nerves She should have known his boat wouldn't be any more reliable than he was himself.

"Where's the hatch?" she asked, telling herself she'd made the right decision. She'd wanted out of Manaus, with all her cargo intact, and for better or worse, that's exactly what she'd gotten.

"Mid-deck. There's a bucket down there, too, in case you need to bail."

Dear God, she thought. It was going to be a long three days.

HOURS OF BACKBREAKING LABOR LATER, the friggin' engine room was relatively dry, the storm had slacked off to a slow, intermittent drizzle, and by her reckoning, they hadn't even made it to Nova Airão. Three days, hell. It was going to take a week to get to Santa Maria.

Travers had moored the boat in a slow-moving backwater thick with trailing vines and overhung with the graceful sweep of palm fronds. Tree frogs and cicadas sang all around, setting up a nighttime chorus as the sun's last rays slipped below the canopy and sunk them into darkness.

Annie lit the two kerosene lanterns she'd found and hung them from the upper deck rail, where they cast broad pools of yellow light over the boat. Travers had a flashlight in the engine room.

"How's it going down there?" she asked, kneeling by the hatch. Contrary to her first opinion, the *Sucuri* leaked like a sieve, and its old pump needed a full-time nursemaid to keep it running.

A grumble was her reply.

The backbreaking labor had actually mostly been his, but listening to him cuss and bang around in the engine room all day had pretty much worn her out. That and peering through the rain, trying to keep to the course he'd kept coming up to set and adjust.

"I've got food ready." A cooked meal, she almost added. Lunch had been a few thoroughly inadequate bites of manioc bread spread with hot pepper sauce— all she'd been able to grab with one hand on the wheel. She'd been starving most of the day, and after they'd moored for the night, she'd had no qualms about helping herself to his kitchen and his supplies. She'd worked her way up too many rivers not to know a helping hand was always welcome.

Travers made another unintelligible reply, his voice no more than a mumbled echo in the cramped confines of the engine room, and Annie rose to her feet, not exactly disappointed. The meal she'd made of beans, rice, and fish wasn't going to get any better by sitting around, but neither was it going to get any worse, and she'd just as soon Travers stayed where he was until she'd eaten and gone to bed.

They hadn't had time for two words since leaving RBC, and if at all possible, she wanted to keep it that way until they reached Santa Maria.

Stretching out a cramp in her back, she cast her gaze across the water and around the surrounding trees, seeing little in the darkness. She could hear the forest, though, everything wet and dripping, filling the night with small cascades of water and a metronome of droplets falling from leaf to leaf to river—and she could smell it. The sheer greenness of the rain forest filled her senses, indulging her with all its rich fecundity. For a woman who'd grown up on the barren, windswept plains of Wyoming, the Amazon basin was a paradise. It was as far away from the two-bit, flyblown ranch she'd called home as a girl could get and then some—and maybe even a little bit farther than that from where she was standing, right smack-dab in the middle of a swampy nowhere.

She'd kept to the course he'd set during her turns at the wheel, but didn't have a clue as to where they were tied up, except she was damn sure it wasn't nearly far enough away from Manaus. They had jigged as much as they'd jagged through the *igapó*, the flooded forest. A couple of times when they'd come out onto the Rio Negro, she'd wondered if they hadn't actually gone in circles—and she couldn't seem to get the picture of Fat Eddie following them through the rain out of her mind. Why hadn't he just stopped like the police? Unlike the *Sucuri*, the black speedboat hadn't had so much as a canopy on it for cover.

A startled croak followed by a few clattering notes

came out of the darkness, a sudden counterpoint to the frogs and cicadas. Annie turned to peer over the bow, her brow furrowed, wondering what kind of bird was making the sound.

"Roraima limpkin," Travers said behind her—and she nearly jumped out of her skin.

Damn. He moved like a cat, or something even more silent and deadly that she didn't even want to think about, not while she was on a boat named *Sucuri*.

"Roraima limpkin. Right. I've heard of them," she said, turning to face him, forcing her pulse to slow down. "Never seen one, though."

They were both soaked, and had been all day, but once again, whereas she was in full control of her clothes, his seemed to be sliding off his body. If it wasn't for his hip bones and shoulders, he'd be naked, his khaki pants and palm-tree shirt in a pile at his feet.

Buttons, she felt like telling him. Buttons were put on shirts and pants for a reason—though she doubted if he gave a damn about buttons. He looked a little tense, as if maybe Carlos's hangover remedy had only lasted so long and then up and left him high and dry.

"Not many people do." He dropped a screwdriver and a wrench into the toolbox on the deck, then picked up a rag and began wiping the grease off his hands. Light from one of the lanterns played across his face, throwing shadows into the hollows of his cheeks and along his jaw. It was a strong jaw, his nose elegantly shaped. His eyebrows had a sharp curve to them, a pair of arched, dark lines contrasting with the pale streaks in his sunbleached hair.

She wrapped her arms around herself, feeling a chill even in the humid heat of the night.

"But you have," she guessed, giving him credit where credit was due, and then angling just a bit, unable to help herself. After all, he was the infamous William Sanchez Travers. "I bet you've seen a lot of things not many other people have seen." Like lost cities of gold and forbidden shaman rites involving chunks of rock crystal. Like a place no one else had ever been that he hadn't told another soul about—just as she'd never told another soul about what she'd seen and where she'd been.

His soft, self-deprecating laughter took her by surprise. "Yeah, I guess so, some things most people wouldn't want to see. How about you? You've been around."

"Plants," she said, deliberately understating the obvious, wholly intrigued by his answer. Everybody in the Amazon liked seeing gold—so maybe that rumor was a bit off the mark, despite its popularity and his bracelets. "That's all I ever see, everywhere I go. Plants. Sometimes there's something interesting sitting on one or eating one."

"Like a woolly monkey," he said, looking up and pinning her with his gaze.

Well, she thought, he'd cut right to the chase, using the last two words she wanted to hear—"woolly monkey." They weren't a question, yet those two words questioned everything about her—including her competence and her integrity. Damn him. She should have eaten alone and left his dinner on the stove.

"I've seen a few monkeys," she conceded without conceding a thing. "Even eaten a few, but tonight it's *prato feito* with a fish I found in your cooler."

His grin, once again, was anything but reassuring.

"I'll bet you've seen more than a few, Dr. Parrish, but there's only one I'm interested in hearing about, and given our departure from Manaus, I figure the quicker you tell me what I want to know, the better off we'll be." He dropped the rag into the toolbox. "Come on. There are dry towels inside."

Which he could stuff in his ears, if he thought she was going to tell him anything. Far from being daunted by his audacity, she was amused. Nobody, but nobody, got the best of Annie Parrish. She'd been playing by boy's rules since she'd been old enough to walk and chew gum at the same time.

"Actually, by my figuring, all I owe you is the hundred and twenty *reais* you've probably already spent, with maybe a refund for keeping your boat afloat," she said, following him into the main cabin.

"We were shot at." He opened a cupboard and pulled out two large towels, handing her one.

"You're the one who knows Fat Eddie Mano and hangs out with *garimpeiros*, not me." She gave her hair and face a quick drying off, then draped the towel around her shoulders, her demeanor as ingenuous as she could make it—which she knew for a fact was pretty damned ingenuous. He hadn't dreamed up his "jaguar bait" insult without some incentive. He'd just misinterpreted the clues.

"Fat Eddie wasn't shooting at us. The police were, and you've got a history of trouble with the police, serious trouble. How long have you been back in Brazil? A week?" He started to shrug out of his shirt.

Annie deliberately turned toward the stove and began filling her plate.

At her silence, he continued, obviously knowing exactly how long she'd been back.

"The Manaus police aren't known for their efficiency.

It probably took them the whole week to figure out you were in town and about two seconds to decide to finish whatever unfinished business you left behind when they kicked you out of the country. That's what I want to know about—what you were up to that got you kicked out, and why in the hell you came back, and don't try to pawn me off with the peach palm business. Not even Gabriela is buying that."

"Go to hell," she said pleasantly, spooning a chunk of fish on top of her rice.

"Funny you should mention that," he muttered, rummaging around in the cupboards behind her. Something clanked, and he cursed, and unbelievably, the sound tweaked her conscience.

It had been a long day, with little to eat and plenty of hard, physical labor, especially for him. It was a miracle that he'd held up as long as he had, especially since he'd been dead drunk asleep when she'd come aboard at dawn.

"Look," she said, relenting a little as she spooned around for another piece of fish. "We don't know each other well enough to argue about anything, and there's no reason we can't keep things that way. All we really have to do is get to Santa Maria. I'm happy to help out where I can, no refund. You keep the money. Let's just work together to get up the river."

I'll be a son of a bitch, Will thought, squinting over his shoulder at her with a sense of utter disbelief. The woman had the balls of a bull and all the friggin' philosophy of a Girl Scout.

Let bygones be bygones?

He didn't think so, not when he would be pulling slugs out of his bulkhead, not after the painfully lousy day he'd suffered through. Carlos's cure had lasted almost until noon, when it had worn off with a vengeance. He'd been paying hell ever since, wanting nothing more than to just tie up and wait the damn storm out—an option unavailable to him because of his passenger and the trouble he was sure she'd dragged into his wake. The police had no gripe with him.

She was a real piece of work, all right, and it was completely against his better judgment that he let his gaze drop down the length of her body—for about the hundredth time that day. Fluffed up by the towel, her hair was doing that stick-out-all-over thing again, but he had to admit that on her it looked good. Or rather, she looked good whether her hair was sticking out or not. Her face was delicate in profile, her nose slightly upturned with a dusting of freckles, her glasses reflecting the amber glow of the lanterns. Her shirt was still two sizes too big, and her shorts were all bags and sags, but the legs inside the shorts from mid-thigh down were perfect—which had been his problem all day.

Perfect legs, the kind a man wanted to eat his way up—a thought he'd had more than once since the first time he'd come up from the hatch and found himself at eye level with the backs of her knees, a thought that unnerved him more than the bullets lodged in the *Sucuri*'s hull. A lot more. He didn't have time for her, or her trouble, or her knees, yet there she was, on his boat, and for the next three days, in his life.

Take a woman up the river, Gabriela had said, and then made it impossible for him to refuse. Or so he'd told himself last night.

It had been a mistake. One he was paying for. In the cruel light of a head-splitting hangover and a truly rotten day, he had to ask himself who he'd been kidding. Sure he took passengers all the time, nearly every trip, but he usually had enough sense to steer clear of the ones who were more trouble than they were worth—and Annie Parrish was nothing but trouble.

He should have put her off the *Sucuri* at the dock. Carlos's cure must have temporarily clouded his judgment— either Carlos's cure or Dr. Parrish's legs. He honestly wasn't sure which. He did know this trip up the river wasn't like any of the others he'd taken in the last two years, and that alone should have been enough reason for him to have told her no in Pancha's, or told Gabriela no, or to have abandoned her when she'd gone off to get Carlos that morning.

Gabriela was right. He was nearing the end. The end of what, he wasn't sure. But since putting Corisco Vargas's face on Tutanji's demon he'd felt a lot of endings looming near. Perhaps Vargas's life, perhaps his own. Certainly his bargain with Tutanji and all the mysteries that had held the two of them together since the night the great *sucuri,* the giant anaconda, had awakened him from his dreams.

Even for an *Eunectes murinus,* the animal had been big, twelve meters, over thirty-six serpentine feet of pure constricting brawn.

A faint ripple of unease coursed its way down his spine, following a path Will could have traced in his sleep. He had not forgotten. He had not forgotten anything, not the pain, the power, or the fear. The teeth marks on the front and back of his left shoulder were over a hand-span apart. Tutanji had stood by and watched as he'd been bitten, and then made it even further impossible for him to ever forget. The monstrous snake would be with him for the rest of his life, the marks on his shoulder proof of the pain and fear, the marks down his back proof of the power he'd glimpsed, the power that had bound him to the jaguar shaman.

A sudden wave of weariness had him dragging his hands back through his hair. This was no time for him to be looking at a woman's legs.

He pulled a dry T-shirt out of the cupboard and slipped it over his head, and was just about to lay things out for the good doctor a little more clearly, let her know her options were a little slimmer than she thought, when a sound came to him from off the water, a low vibration he almost felt before he heard it. In seconds, the sound clarified itself into the recognizable rhythm of an outboard motor chugging along at quarter speed.

She heard it too and whirled around, her gaze snapping to his, and for the first time all day, he thought he detected fear in her eyes.

Her words confirmed it.

So did the sound of her voice.

"Fat Eddie was still following us when we slipped into that first channel into the *igapó*," she said.

He'd figured as much, but hadn't really thought the man could keep on their trail through a whole day of rain. He should have known better. This whole trip was turning into one disaster after another. Meeting up with Fat Eddie in a backwater swamp half a mile off the main river and a hundred miles from anywhere else was way down at the bottom of his list of safe things to do on a Saturday night, but he was guessing the odds were pretty good that the increasingly loud *chug-chug-chug* coming across the water was the sound of the fat man in pursuit.

Like any good crook who'd gone on to claim the title of "Boss," he was dangerously tenacious.

"Don't worry. Nobody boards the *Sucuri*, not even Fat Eddie Mano."

That was the second time he'd told her as much, Annie thought, and she hoped to hell he was right. She watched him pull out the pistol he'd kept shoved in his pants, his face a mask of quiet concentration as he checked the load, his hands skilled in handling the weapon.

Her own hand was clenched into a fist at her side. The absolute worst ending to the day she could possibly imagine was about to happen—Fat Eddie Mano and Johnny Chang pulling up alongside in their little black speedboat while she and Travers sat like a couple of dead ducks in the middle of a nowhere swamp all by themselves. Calvary, her ass. She was tempted to tell Travers that she had two Israeli Galils, a nickel-plated Kalashnikov, a couple hundred rounds of ammunition, an old Remington rifle with twenty-eight boxes of cartridges, half a dozen 9-millimeter Brazilian Taurus handguns with a stockpile of bullets, twelve grenades, and twenty sticks of dynamite in two crates on his upper deck—but something told her that might not exactly be the kind of news he wanted to hear right now.

CHAPTER 7 ⚡

"GUILLERMO!" A VOICE CALLED OUT of the darkness. William!

It was Fat Eddie, all right, Will thought, shoving the pistol back into his pants and covering it with his T-shirt. He'd know that voice anywhere, gravelly, with every word sounding half swallowed, as if it were too much effort for mere syllables to fight past all the rolls of fat to freedom.

He stepped halfway out the door, motioning for Annie to stay put.

"*Senhor Eduardo,*" he answered, hailing the small spotlight he saw winding toward the *Sucuri* through the trees. It was one of those quirky local facts about a place that while a sizable portion of the one million residents of Manaus knew or had heard about Fat Eddie Mano, the big man himself answered only to Mr. Edward.

"You stay in here," he told his passenger, reaching up and dousing the cabin's lantern. Shadows fell inside the room. "It's probably best if the fat man doesn't know

Amazon Annie is back on the Rio Negro and heading to Santa Maria."

Amazon Annie? Annie wrinkled her nose. Next to "woolly monkey," those were her two least favorite words. The alliterative nickname made her sound like some two-bit matinee heroine out of the forties.

"I hate that name," she said.

"Yeah, well, can't say as I blame you, so let's keep it to ourselves."

A beam of light streamed through the cabin's window, just missing her, and continued on, sweeping over the *Sucuri*'s deck. She glanced out the window and saw a huge, shadowy shape behind the wheel adjust the light until it fell directly on Will where he stood in the doorway.

He lifted his hand in front of his face to shield his eyes.

"Remember, stay in here and keep out of sight," he said under his breath, then walked out onto the deck.

"Guillermo, meu amigo!" the fat man said.

"Oi, Senhor Eduardo," Travers replied, his voice a warm and lazy drawl Annie barely recognized, his words slightly slurred. If she hadn't known better, she would have sworn he'd spent the last few hours tossing back shots and chasing them with beer, just a guy out on the river who wasn't going to let a few bullets at dawn ruin his whole day.

"Tudo bem?" the fat man asked, and Annie felt the speedboat bump up against the *Sucuri*.

"Vou bem. Vou bem," Travers replied, and the two men fell into an easy chat about the weather, and the rain, and the river. Annie couldn't see Travers from her position by the window, but she could see Fat Eddie, at least his back, the fat straining at the seams of a striped

brown and orange shirt, his black ponytail making a chunky question mark at the base of his neck. He was amazingly huge, seemingly too huge to move, certainly too huge to climb out of the speedboat and board the *Sucuri*—not without sinking them both.

She waited to see if Johnny would appear from beside the gargantuan man and add a greeting. When he didn't, she figured he was standing stoically near the helm, hidden by the fat man's bulk. Every time she and Johnny had met, he'd had a thug standing near, silent and threatening. It was probably to her advantage if Johnny wasn't "amigos" with Travers. She didn't think this was the time or place to be admitting she knew Johnny Chang, either.

Of course, there was the possibility that Fat Eddie and Johnny didn't even know she was on the *Sucuri*. No one could have seen her from where she'd been inside the cabin. She hadn't been at the porthole that long.

"The police this morning. It was close for you, no?" Fat Eddie asked when the conversation drifted into a lull.

"Yes, close. *Obrigado*, your interference was much appreciated," Travers said.

"*De nada, Guillermo, de nada*. I am pleased to see you safe, but what of the woman? The little blond cat?" Fat Eddie rasped in his strange, word-garbling voice. "Where is she?"

Annie's heart sank into her stomach. So much for not being seen.

"Elena Maria Barbosa?" Travers asked with drunken artlessness, rattling off some unknown woman's name without a moment's hesitation. "I left her in Santo Antonio, gave her back her money. She was trouble, *senhor*. This morning, well, I was still too drunk to notice, but today on the river, ahh"—he made a sound of disgust—"today I could tell she was trouble."

Annie swore silently and glanced toward the door. If Travers was wrong, and they did get boarded, his lie wouldn't hold up for any longer than it took for Johnny to walk into the cabin. There was no place to hide in the small room—but she could slip over the side of the boat, into the water. Ten feet from the *Sucuri* no one would be able to see her. When Fat Eddie left, assuming he would, she could climb back on board, assuming Travers wouldn't leave without her.

Those were some pretty big assumptions—and what else was out there hunting tonight? she wondered. A twelve-foot caiman? Or a hungry school of piranhas?

Or something even worse?

"I'm so sorry to tell you this, my friend," Fat Eddie said, sounding truly contrite, "but this woman, she lied to you. Her name is not Elena Barbosa. It is Annie Parrish—*Doutora* Parrish—and she has some cargo that belongs to me."

Another silently virulent curse left Annie's lips. Johnny had sold her out.

"Cargo?" Travers's voice rose indignantly. "Yes, the woman has cargo. Too much cargo for what she paid. She loaded it last night, while I was with you, my friend, drinking *cachaça*, but I put it off, all of it, four hours ago on the dock in Santo Antonio. It was a mess ... *bagunça*. Too many boxes, too many crates for my boat."

"Crates, eh?"

"A dozen," Travers confirmed. "Far too many for the *Sucuri,* when I already had a full load of freight going from Manaus to São Gabriel."

Fat Eddie looked toward the upper deck, where Travers must have gestured.

"I am only missing two," the fat man said, then grew silent, as if he were thinking. After a moment, he lifted his hands to his sides in a gesture of reluctant acceptance. "She has stolen from me, Guillermo, two crates of guns, I fear, and I must have them back."

Annie closed her eyes and called herself every kind of fool. Johnny had sold her guns he'd stolen from Fat Eddie Mano.

In actuality, she decided, her chances of being eaten by a caiman were pretty slim, ditto for the piranhas, especially when compared to the chances of something bad happening to her at the hands of Fat Eddie.

"Guns?" Travers suddenly didn't sound nearly so drunk. "She stole guns? From you?"

"Sadly, yes, my friend." Fat Eddie shrugged again. "Did you see any guns when you left her in Santo Antonio?"

"None, but I wasn't looking for guns, *senhor*. In the rain, after last night and this morning, I just wanted to be rid of her."

"I must have them back," Fat Eddie sighed, "or a banker in São Paulo is going to be very unhappy."

Annie was unhappy, pretty damned unhappy, and growing more so by the minute. She narrowed her gaze as she peered out the window, trying to see around Fat Eddie's bulk. Where was Johnny, the slimy bastard?

"Yes, yes, this is all very sad," Travers agreed, utterly convincing in his drunken empathy. "But Elena—this Doctor Parrish—is in Santo Antonio tonight."

"Then I must return to Santo Antonio." Fat Eddie heaved another big sigh. "And you, Guillermo, what will you do?"

"Sleep," Travers answered simply, "and in the morning I will continue up the river. I guarantee you, *senhor*, that the cargo you entrusted to me last night will be delivered as promised."

"Good. This is good news. I know I can always count on you, Guillermo. Some people say you're crazy, but me"—he tapped a finger on his forehead—"I say crazy is good."

Travers's response was too soft for Annie to hear, but it made the fat man laugh.

"Yes, this is true." He chuckled a bit more, then eased himself with a deep breath. "Before I go, I would like to see the stones once more. Could you get the bag for me, Guillermo?"

"*Sim*, of course, *senhor*."

Stones? Annie could only think of one kind of stones Fat Eddie might be interested in, gemstones—and after an amicable night of drinking themselves under the table, William Sanchez Travers was transporting a bagful of them for the jungle city's biggest crook.

Damn. She was in more trouble than she'd thought. Maybe she should get one of those guns she'd gone to so much trouble to buy.

For someone pretending to be drunk, though, Travers moved awfully damn fast. He was at the door before she'd gotten halfway across the cabin—and when he advanced inside, she retreated. In three steps, the wheel was at her back.

"Guns?" he said under his breath, leaning in so close she could see the dark glint of anger in his eyes. "Stolen guns?"

"I paid for them," she whispered, standing perfectly still, her heart racing, noting that once more he'd gotten incredibly close to her—and she still hadn't put him to the floor.

"You and the São Paulo banker," he growled, reaching over her with one hand to open the cupboard door above her head.

"What did the fat man give you? Brazilian diamonds? Emeralds from Colombia?" she shot back, a little more breathlessly than she liked.

He stopped his rummaging around, his gaze narrowing down at her as he lifted a small bag out of the cupboard.

"Both," he said, hefting the bag in his hand.

"So we're each carrying a little contraband, compliments of Fat Eddie Mano," she quietly accused him.

One of his eyebrows arched in a skeptical curve. "I've got a little contraband, Dr. Parrish. You've got two crates of guns Fat Eddie stole from the Manaus police."

Annie blanched. No wonder the day had gone to hell so quickly. Her name was going to start showing up all over, in all the wrong places, official places.

She had to disappear, the sooner the better. Thank God the northwest Brazilian frontier was big enough to do it in. All she had to do was get out of the swamp without getting shot, get to her canoe in Santa Maria, and ditch Will Travers. On her own, nobody would find her.

"Next time I'll ask for provenance," she said with false bravado, giving a small shrug and starting to slip away.

She didn't get far. He stopped her with his hand on her waist, holding her where she stood.

"Don't move," he said, his voice lowering to a dead-serious timbre. "Don't move one inch, unless I tell you to, and maybe—just maybe—I can get us out of here in one piece."

"I can take care of myself," she said, forcing a calmness into her voice she was far from feeling with Fat Eddie less than twenty feet away and Will Travers looming over her.

He held her gaze for a long moment. Amber light from the lanterns gilded the planes of his face, throwing the lean, artful lines and curves of his features into sharp relief.

Annie hardly dared to breathe.

His gaze shifted, drifting downward to her mouth, his lashes lowering, and something about him changed, something subtle but undeniable. Suddenly Annie was even more aware of the nearness of his body, of its sheer physicality, the sound of his breath, his scent—rainwater and a faint trace of engine grease, and the underlying scent of his skin, warm and so very male. He wasn't any closer than he had been, but he felt closer, much closer.

"Yeah," he said softly, lifting his eyes back to hers. "I'll just bet you can, but it's my boat, and tonight I'm the one taking care of everything. Get used to it, and don't make another move for the door."

He released her and left, stepping back out onto the deck.

Annie let out a shaky breath. She had to give him points for nerve, but she hadn't survived all her years in the jungles of South America by depending on anyone for anything, and she wasn't about to start now, especially with someone on such friendly terms with an underworld warlord.

Keeping close to the cabin's walls, she slipped back to

the window, where she could see what was going on. Fat Eddie's boat had drifted back toward the bow a bit, and she could see more of him besides his back, more of his face—little dark eyes sunk between heavy lids and fat cheeks, a small, nearly delicate nose looking thoroughly out of place amid his other, overly rounded features, the sweat gleaming on his skin. His black hair had been slicked back with pomade into his ponytail, leaving nary a strand out of place. He didn't look particularly ruthless—until he opened his mouth.

Annie gasped despite herself. He had the dentition of a piranha, his teeth filed to sharp, triangular points, giving his fleshy countenance a demon's grisliness.

"Ah, yes," the man chuckled with pleasure, leaning over the side of his speedboat to where Travers was kneeling on the edge of the *Sucuri*'s deck.

Just looking at him made her skin crawl. Men in the Amazon had some pretty peculiar ideas in their heads, ideas about animals and sex. It was all tied up with the social order of machismo, the rabidity of South American testosterone, and the wildness of the local fauna. Annie didn't want to dwell too long on what Fat Eddie's piranha teeth might say about his sexual proclivities. She just knew she was getting a gun out of one of her crates, and she was going to strap it on and not take it off.

"They are beautiful, are they not, Guillermo?"

Diamonds and emeralds—Travers was shaking them out into his hand, showing the fat man without exhibiting any of the aversion churning through Annie's veins.

The stones were rough cut, unfaceted, yet they still caught the light, looking like bright pebbles in the palm of his hand. He had a small fortune's worth in the bag, and Annie wondered who he was delivering them to in the northwest. After Manaus, there was little but rain forest and *caboclo* settlements all the way to the border in any direction.

And mining camps, she silently added, hundreds of illegal mining camps, run by hundreds of *donos,* mine bosses, who could easily be dealing in gemstones as well as gold.

What in the hell, Annie wondered, had Gabriela been thinking to suggest she book passage with Will Travers? The old doctor had to know what he was—which was everything the rumors had made him out to be and then some. He was intelligent, all right. Annie hadn't been wrong about that, but like him, she'd misinterpreted the clues. The intelligence she'd seen so clearly in his eyes had a decidedly criminal bent. Hustling jewels for Fat Eddie Mano was not the idle pastime of a disenchanted scholar. It was a fully colluded crime ... not so very different from buying an illegal stash of guns and ordnance from a piece of waterfront riffraff like Johnny Chang.

Okay, she admitted to herself. She wasn't any better than he was, and a fat lot of good that was doing either one of them. Hell, all she really wanted was to get to Santa Maria and from there to the Cauaburi.

Her hand went to the small, black fanny pack she'd belted around her waist at dawn, before she'd ever boarded Travers's damn boat. All she really wanted was a chance to understand what she'd found. She was on the brink of the most exciting discovery of her career, of anyone's career—and she refused to be waylaid by a thick-bellied, gun-toting, piranha-toothed freak like Fat Eddie.

"Get rid of him," she muttered under her breath, urging Travers to finish up with the gemstones and send their most unwelcome visitor on his way.

Travers couldn't have heard her, but he did rise to his feet, and was in the act of pouring the stones back into the bag when something near the waterline caught his eye. His body went still, and he said something soft—words she couldn't hear, but that caused Fat Eddie to smile again, showing his double row of razorlike teeth.

With a hearty laugh, the fat man reached over the side of his boat, grabbing a black rope and hauling an oddly shaped creature up into the air.

Annie stared at it for a moment, trying to figure out what it was, and then, with an awful wave of shock rolling through her, she knew.

Her knees buckled, and slowly, ever so slowly, she slid down the wall, her hand clasped over her mouth, her mind reeling.

Will felt his stomach roll over. He'd been around. He'd seen a lot of things, and he knew a man's head when he saw one, even if it had been dragged through the Rio Negro for a few hours.

Kneeling on the *Sucuri*'s deck, he'd noticed the dark skein trailing off Fat Eddie's boat into the water. Black, thick, and twisted, it had gleamed in the light, looking too fine to be a rope. Following the dark skein down had revealed the reason for its fineness and the grisly trophy at its end. The river warlord had tied a man's head to his boat by its long, braided queue.

"Your thief from the warehouse," he said flatly, when the fat man pulled up his prize. It wasn't a question. The only question Will had was how Fat Eddie had managed to behead the guy without getting himself covered in blood.

"One of them." The fat man chuckled. "His name

was Johnny Chang. Now all I need is the woman, the blond cat. They'll make a good pair. No, Guillermo?"

Will shrugged, ignoring the alarm Eddie's comment generated. He'd seen the man in the speedboat that morning. He'd been stocky, well muscled, and armed with a machine gun. Fat Eddie hadn't gotten the best of Johnny Chang without one hell of a struggle, and Fat Eddie wasn't one for struggling—ever. He paid people to do that for him, and any dread the sight of Chang's flaccid, waterlogged head hadn't dredged up was more than compensated for by the dire realization that the fat man wasn't alone. Somewhere out in the swampy channels, someone was watching them—watching for Annie Parrish, the blond cat.

Will finished putting the stones in the bag, careful to keep his attention focused on the task.

"I have a friend from Ecuador, a Jivaro friend, who will shrink the heads for me," Fat Eddie continued, letting Johnny's head drop back into the water. "When I hang both of them in the Praça de Matriz, no one will think to steal from *Senhor* Eduardo again, hey?"

"No, *senhor*," Will agreed, shoving the bag in his pants pocket, wondering what kind of guns Dr. Parrish had in her crates and how quickly he could get to them. Whatever she'd bought, it had to be bigger and better than the pistol he had tucked in his waistband. "But only a fool would have stolen from you in the first place. From Yavareté to Belém, everyone knows better than to steal from *Senhor* Eduardo."

"Everybody who isn't already dead—or about to be!" The fat man laughed. "So I am back to Santo Antonio to collect my guns and the little cat's head. *Tchau*, Guillermo."

"Até a próxima, senhor." Until we meet again—and Will was going to do everything in his power to make sure they never did.

With a short wave, Fat Eddie pushed the boat's throttle up a notch and spun the wheel to head off into the flooded forest, on a course back to the main flow of the Rio Negro.

Will watched the speedboat's spotlight wind through the trees and lianas until it disappeared. Then he walked across the deck and blew out both lanterns, plunging the *Sucuri* into the rich, velvet darkness of an Amazonian night. Santo Antonio was two hours behind them, which gave him and the little cat a four-hour lead.

He hoped to hell it would be enough.

CHAPTER 8 ✈

STEPPING INSIDE THE *SUCURI'S* CABIN, Will felt an instant surge of panic. She was gone.

Damn her. He'd told her to stay put. He swung around to check the deck outside, and a flash of blond hair caught his eye. She was huddled on the floor in a pool of moonlight, her knees drawn up, her glasses pushed up on top of her head with her face in her hands.

He let out a soft curse in relief. She looked damn small in her oversized shirt and ratty tennis shoes, but without a doubt she was the biggest friggin' disaster to come into his life since Tutanji's anaconda.

Fat Eddie's guns, for God's sake. What was she working on? A death wish?

He let out another curse, not so softly, and her head came up. Their gazes locked in the dim light, hers startled and tinged with wariness, his probably far fiercer than he meant it to be—but damn, she'd cost him.

He'd lied to Fat Eddie Mano to save her, and he could smell his bridges burning the length of the Rio Negro.

"What am I going to do with you?" he asked, a rhetorical question if he'd ever heard one.

"I have to get to Santa Maria."

That was the last thing he'd expected her to say. She was scared. She couldn't hide it, not with her eyes that wide and her mouth that soft.

Soft, soft mouth. Sweet legs. God save him. This was a damn poor time for lust to start figuring into his life.

"No good. You heard him. He wants your head, and if you were watching out the window, you know that is *not* a figure of speech."

"I was watching."

Of course she'd been watching, and he'd found her huddled on the floor. It took more than a disembodied head to unnerve Will, but she couldn't have seen many, and probably none belonging to someone she knew.

"I think we can outrun Fat Eddie to São Gabriel," he said, wondering where his sense of responsibility for her was coming from, and wondering just how damned misplaced it might be. She'd been around. She was a big girl. She knew the rules. No one who didn't know the rules and play the game damn well could have hustled Fat Eddie's guns out from under him. "From there you can catch a plane to Bogotá, or São Paulo, or Rio. Take your pick. Within twenty-four hours after that, you could be back in the States."

It was the best he had to offer, the absolute best. She had to know it, but she wasn't jumping at his great plan, only staring up at him, her face pale, and her chin—so help him God—set at a determined angle.

"Fat Eddie owns this river," he explained further. "You've got nothing to look forward to but dying young if you stay." He couldn't say it any plainer.

"You don't know what I'm looking forward to," she said quietly, adjusting her glasses back down over her eyes and rising to her feet.

A wave of frustration rolled through him, tightening his jaw. She was a big girl all right, and what she had—that damnable unflinching grit—was an admirable quality. It was also the sort of thing that got people killed.

"Yesterday," he said, "in Pancha's, when I agreed to take you to Santa Maria, you were a slightly notorious botanist with Gabriela Oliveira's stamp of approval, a busy woman in need of passage. That started to change last night when Gabriela told me about Yavareté."

He saw her stiffen and hold herself a little taller.

"Yavareté has nothing to do with you."

"Maybe not," he agreed easily enough, "but when Fat Eddie gets to Santo Antonio, he's going to know I lied about you, and then he's going to want three heads to hang in the Praça de Matriz."

As an accusation, it beat hers hands down—and she knew it. Her gaze shifted away from him with a long sweep of lashes, an action so purely feminine it nearly halted his breath—and he suddenly had a gut-awful feeling that he knew exactly where his sense of responsibility for her was coming from.

His problem wasn't lust. Not just any woman would do. He wanted *her*—man to woman, me Tarzan, you Jane. It didn't make sense, but it didn't have to make sense. She was just there, a usually sopping-wet little grab bag of a renegade botanist with misbehaving hair, perfect legs, and a backbone of pure steel, and he wanted her—jaguar bait.

He wanted to groan. God, his life was already hanging

by a thread. He did not need the trouble she stirred up, literally, by the boatload. What he needed was to get rid of her, and the farther away he could send her, the better.

Amazon Annie, he thought with a stifled curse. With the evidence standing in front of him, it was hard to believe she was the one he'd heard all the stories about. Amazon Annie had bushwacked her way across the watershed of the Vaupes River in eastern Colombia and confirmed half a dozen viable populations of *Griffinia concinna,* the long-endangered elegant blue amaryllis, a species devastated by the felling of rain-forest habitat from Panama to Brazil. Thanks to her, the botanical garden in St. Louis was cultivating a scientifically viable population of its own. Her published dissertation on the family Bromeliaceae was backed up by years of fieldwork and countless hard-won miles trekking through the tropical forests of South America, and like all the naturalists who had gone before her, every mile had yielded a story of hardship and close calls. Some of her stories had become legend on the Amazon, until the last legend, the Woolly Monky Incident, had ruined her.

Rallying, she lifted her chin and met his gaze square on. "I owe you for that," she admitted. "But it's going to be a hard debt to repay."

Will appreciated her concession, but in truth, it was an impossible debt to repay.

"I heard you shot your lover." If she wanted a chance to even the score, he'd just given her one, and by the subtle tightening of her mouth, he knew she understood exactly what he wanted.

"He wasn't my lover."

When she didn't offer anything more than what

Gabriela had already told him, Will arched his brow, encouraging her to go on.

"He was a *garimpeiro*, a gold miner," she responded defensively. "I didn't know they were in the area where I was doing my fieldwork, and they sure as hell didn't expect to find me within a few miles of their camp. It was ... uh, a clash of culture thing."

"Clash of culture?" The look he gave her was purely skeptical. Researchers of her caliber didn't make their reputations by clashing with indigenous cultures. "And the monkey?"

"A couple of the miners saw fresh meat in the canopy and shot it. I was on the forest floor and ended up with an armful of terrified, bloody woolly monkey. By the time I'd finished it off, the *garimpeiros* had shown up and were accusing me of trying to steal their game. Things got a little ugly after that."

Will could imagine.

"So you pulled your gun and shot one of them?"

"No ... not quite," she equivocated. "Back then, I didn't carry a gun, but one of the miners had one, and there was a bit of a scuffle."

It was remarkable, he thought, how little information she managed to cram into an answer. He tried to imagine her standing out in the rain forest, covered in monkey blood and "finishing off" the wounded animal with her knife, he supposed, though God knew she could have just wrung its neck with her bare hands. Nothing seemed beyond her. Even so, his imagination hit a brick wall when he came to the part about her coming out one gun ahead in a scuffle with a couple of *garimpeiros*.

"And from there to Yavareté?" he asked, accepting

her condensed version of events for now, taking what she offered without giving her any grief. If she followed his advice and left for Bogotá, she never had to tell him another damn thing for the rest of her life—a depressing thought. If she didn't leave, he was going to stop being nice.

She mused over his question for a good long while, before she deigned to answer.

"Well," she started slowly. "The gun aside, I ended up in their camp, an illegal mining operation with the biggest mother lode I've seen anywhere in the Amazon. The mine boss wasn't too happy to see me, but he didn't want the responsibility of killing a *norte-americana* scientist outright. So he called in a Cessna and sent me to Yavareté, where his boss could decide what to do with me."

"Corisco Vargas."

"Right." She nodded, a subtle look of relief passing over her face, as if she'd managed to satisfy his questions without incriminating herself in any more crimes.

Well, he was far from being satisfied with her whitewash.

"And Vargas didn't want to kill you, either." He made it a statement, since the truth was obvious.

"No," she said, again without any elaboration. "Three days later, Gabriela came and the next thing I knew, I was deported."

She made it all sound so straightforward, so simple. A little tussle in the jungle with a dying monkey and a few *garimpeiros*, then three days in Yavareté with Corisco Vargas.

Will wanted to shake her—shake some sense into her. He wanted to drag Johnny Chang's head back out of the water and scare the shit out of her. How in the hell, he wanted to ask her, have you kept yourself alive this long?

And that was not a friggin' rhetorical question. Nobody could skate on that much luck.

Will glanced out the windows fronting the helm. They had to leave, find a new mooring miles from where Fat Eddie had found them.

He angled his gaze back to her. *Take a woman up the river for me, William, a botanist working out of Santa Maria* ... Gabriela had lied to him. Annie Parrish wasn't just a botanist. At her heart she was something else, something more, and that something more was dangerous. Will had hauled any number of scientific researchers up and down the Rio Negro for RBC, some women, some men. Most had lasted the full term of their grants, a few of them hadn't.

They had all been fine people, academics with a sense of adventure. He'd never met a one besides himself who could have managed an illegal arms deal on the Manaus waterfront, until he'd met Dr. Parrish, and he sure as hell hadn't been attracted to any of them—until Annie Parrish.

His gaze skimmed over her. She was still wet, her shirt clinging to the small curves of her breasts, an intriguingly erotic detail of the type he hadn't noticed in too long to remember.

He sighed, then rubbed his hand across the back of his neck and gave her a sideways look.

You're both among the very best, and you're both hell-bent on something up the Rio Negro ... Gabriela hadn't lied about that. He and Dr. Parrish were both hell-bent on something. Tutanji had set his course, but Annie Parrish was all on her own, and by his estimation was sinking fast. He didn't know how many pieces Fat Eddie was going to leave her in if she refused to leave the country, but he knew for damn sure he didn't want to find out.

"Cast off," he said, turning back to the wheel. "We've got a long night ahead of us."

CHAPTER 9 ⨽

ANNIE WOKE WITH A START, ON THE verge of a scream. She couldn't breathe. Her lungs felt crushed, her rib cage cracking, her legs tangled up with a moving, surging force she couldn't break. She gasped in a breath, opening her eyes wide, ready to fight—but there was nothing, no giant snake squeezing her, no anaconda wrapping her tighter and tighter, using her own exhalations to crush the breath from her body and snap her bones. There was nothing, only the nightmare of being wrapped in coils.

She took another breath and pushed her hair back off her face. It was morning, the boat gently rocking beneath her, the sound of waves lapping up against the hull. A pale light shone through the port window of the *Sucuri*'s small aft cabin. She twisted in her hammock to look out the other window. Leaves, green and dripping, were pressed up against the glass.

She let out a soft curse and dragged her hand back through her hair again. The storm had returned and lasted most of the night, the rain beating at them as they'd slowly chugged up the river. More than once, water had come pouring over the decks, breaching the bow as they had bucked the waves. Just after midnight, Travers had changed course, leaving the main river and once again heading into the *igapó*. By the time he'd found a suitable mooring, the rain had diminished into a pattering of drops on the roof. Annie had fallen asleep to the soft sound, exhausted from the day's trials.

Travers had slept in the forward cabin, rehanging his hammock by the helm. The boat was very quiet, and she wondered if he was awake. She didn't hear anyone moving around, only the scratch of tree limbs scraping against the starboard side and the creak of the hull in the water. Off the boat, the forest was alive with morning. Howler monkeys croaked and roared in the distance, their calls sounding like a herd of prehistoric beasts. Closer to the boat, she heard the squawks and cries of birds rousing from their roosts—comfortingly familiar sounds. With a cup of coffee, strong, black, and Brazilian sweet, she figured she could face the day.

"Damned dream," she muttered, sinking back into her hammock and rubbing the bridge of her nose. She'd not had it in Manaus, nor during her year stuck in Wyoming, nor in Ecuador or Peru. It was strictly a Black River nightmare, coming to her the first time years ago up on the Vaupes, one of the Rio Negro's biggest tributaries—and her first night back on the river, it had returned in full force.

She swore again, tying not to let the fact of the dream's geographical boundaries freak her out any more than usual, just because she was on a boat with the unbelievable name *Sucuri*. It wasn't the first time she'd come back to the river and suffered the snake nightmare. It probably wouldn't be the last.

Rousing herself, she slipped out of the hammock. Her glasses were close at hand on a small shelf, so was the gun she'd taken out of one of her crates while Travers had tied up the boat, a 9-millimeter semiautomatic Taurus. She buckled the holster around her waist and put an extra clip in her fanny pack.

Outside the cabin, the world was cool and serene, blanketed in a heavy layer of mist rising off the water. Trees loomed in the white drifts of vapor. Somewhere, something splashed in the river. It was Annie's favorite time of day, before the sun burned a blazing path along the equator and turned the forest into a sauna.

Stepping over to the port side, she noticed the *Sucuri*'s canoe was missing. Travers wasn't asleep, she realized. He was gone. The information settled in without too much alarm. Even if he'd wanted to abandon her—which he probably did after the Fat Eddie fiasco—she was nearly one hundred percent sure he wouldn't abandon his boat.

Nearly.

She glanced over her shoulder at the jungle of trees and lianas rising from the flooded forest and the long greenish and white aerial roots of the aroids going down. If she had to, she could find her way out and back to the main flow of the Rio Negro.

Her gaze slid over the trees and epiphytes sheltering the boat. Every species was familiar to an eye trained to find the unfamiliar. The river was not at full height, and with the morning mist draping around every branch and limb, much of the canopy was still out of sight. But there were orchids up there somewhere, and the rainy season was a good time of year to find many in flower.

Annie, though, had honed her interest down to just one species of orchid, *Epidendrum luminosa* or *Epidendrum parrishi*. Her hand absently went to the fanny pack belted around her waist. She hadn't decided yet what to name the exquisite anomaly she'd discovered on the Cauaburi. Certainly the latter classification would assure her renown throughout the remaining history of the world, another comforting thought on a cool Amazonian morning when she found herself alone, as usual, and somewhat lost, which was not exactly unusual. The rain forest was a big place, and she'd wandered too far from home on more than one occasion.

A bright spot of red on the water caught her eye, a ceiba flower, and she bent down to scoop it up as it floated by. With her fingers just breaking the surface, a dark, sinuous form streaked away from beneath the boat and disappeared into the watery shadows below the trees.

She jerked back, the flower forgotten, her pulse racing.
Sucuri, the image flashed through her mind.

Peering into the dark water, she strained to see what was undoubtably already gone. After a minute of fruitless searching, she told herself the animal had probably been a caiman, or one of a hundred large species of fish that inhabited the rivers of the Amazon, but least likely an anaconda. Contrary to her nightmare, giant snakes were not lurking in every pool.

Curious, though, she leaned over the side of the deck and let her gaze run over the hull, looking for the damn letters she might have seen yesterday morning, if the paint had been in better shape. As it was, she could just make out a blue *CUR* above the waterline. The *SU* at the beginning of the word was hopelessly chipped. The *I* at the end was no more than a faint bluish-gray shadow blending into the weathered plank it was painted on, but it was there, **SUCURI**.

"*Merda,*" she swore under her breath. She rose to her feet and wiped a hand across her damp brow. Johnny was dead, murdered by Fat Eddie Mano, his head severed and waiting to be shrunk by a Jivaro tribesman, his body dumped in the river for fish food.

"*Sucuri,* hell," she muttered, turning toward the cabin. She needed a cup of coffee.

Inside, a fresh stalk of bananas hung from a hook in the ceiling. Papayas and guavas were piled in a basket on the counter. She set a pot of coffee to start on the kerosene stove and opened a cupboard, looking for sugar. On her fourth door, she came to a sudden halt, her search forgotten.

Books. Dozens of them.

Lifting her hand, she ran her fingers across the spines, encountering a veritable cornucopia of classic Amazonia, books on botany, plant structure and classification, books written by the great nineteenth- and twentieth-century botanists who had explored the Amazon and the Andes, discovering thousands of new plants for western science. She owned them all and had been deeply influenced by most of them, especially the works of Spruce and Schultes, and the adventures of Humboldt and Waterton. Their true-life stories in the tropics had become the stuff of dreams for a girl living on the dry, western plains of North America.

And Travers had them all, including his own, hardly the library of a man who'd completely abandoned botany for criminal vice. She could only conclude that on some level, he was still in the game.

A small smile curled her mouth. The Dr. William Sanchez Travers whose name was on the books would have been damned impressed by what she'd found up on the Cauaburi.

The last book in the row didn't have a title on the spine, and when she pulled it down, she saw only one word on its cover: **TRAVERS**.

An excited thrill went through her. His logbook.

A thousand rumors had gone around about him, one for every day since he'd disappeared—and she was holding the answers to them all. Heady stuff for someone who needed a little leverage after Fat Eddie had all but pronounced her dead.

With only the faintest twinge of guilt, she opened to the first page—and frowned. Her brow furrowed, and she pushed her glasses a little higher on her nose.

"I'll be damned," she muttered, flipping through the pages one by one. The dates were there, starting well before his disappearance, along with line after line of daily entries—every one of them written in a language she didn't even recognize, let alone understand.

But the details—her gaze skimmed another dozen pages, all of them covered with a distinctively illegible script and spare, concise drawings, both botanical and geographical.

Forget the rumors, she thought. He hadn't been lost for a moment, let alone a whole year. He knew exactly where he'd been every minute of every day, but without a latitude and longitude or a translation, he was the only one who knew.

So what had he been doing? she wondered, paging forward through more of the log.

And what was he hiding?

A splash outside brought her head up and her hand to her gun. Her heart pounded in her chest. If it was Fat Eddie and his goons, this could prove to be a pretty short trip for somebody.

Leaning forward, she peeked through the window and saw Travers pulling up in his canoe. He was naked from the waist up, propelling the boat through the water and leaving a swirling trail of mist in his wake.

She unconsciously relaxed her grip on the pistol, her sense of danger forgotten as she watched him—lithe and powerful, the muscles in his chest and arms bunching with each paddle stroke. With his hair damp and his skin sheened silver with morning dew, he was the river creature again, a picture of primitive grace and near preternatural beauty.

Her mouth thinned into a tight line. It was the last thing she wanted to admit, the absolute last—that he was beautiful.

With an annoyed admonition at herself to stop staring, she started to turn her attention elsewhere, but got sidetracked by two white scars marking his chest above his heart, just under the curve of his shoulder, an interesting detail she tucked away. Anything could have happened to him. She had a few scars herself and wouldn't have given his a second thought, until he glided by her down the side of the boat, and she saw his back. Startled, she could only stare, her breath caught in her throat.

He'd been tattooed, thoroughly, disconcertingly, the images running in a line down his spine from the base of his neck to below the waistband of his shorts, their crude precision far beyond what could be achieved with *genipa* or *rocou* body paint. She'd seen the design before, two snakes intertwined, one dark, one light. It was common up on the Vaupes River in Desana territory.

He'd been changed by it—the truth came to her with chilling clarity. Whoever had marked him, had changed him. Without knowing when, where, or why he'd been tattooed, she knew she was looking at the moment when he'd ceased being Dr. William Sanchez Travers, world-renowned botanist with the Harvard pedigree, and become what he was today . . . a mystery.

Snakes. God. Her nemeses. No artisan had put the paint beneath his skin. The serpents were crudely drawn, yet there was power in the simple, bold lines crossing and recrossing each other down his back.

Eaten by an anaconda, so the rumor went, and so it might have been, she thought, her gaze drifting down the long, intertwined curves, his former life devoured by what had happened to him.

Travers shrugged into a shirt he'd picked up out of the canoe and turned toward the cabin. For a moment, he stood still, looking off into the mist-bound forest, and her gaze went to the chunk of rock crystal and the jaguar teeth hanging from the cord around his neck—a shaman's crystal.

Another uneasy sensation coursed a path up her spine. This was him, she realized, not the reprobate of the rumors. He was no waterfront tramp, no drunk, no matter how drunk he'd gotten with Fat Eddie. He was something altogether different, and this was his place—the wild river and the rain forest.

In Pancha's she'd wondered if he knew how to use the crystal. It was considered a powerful talisman, both a protection from one's enemies in the Otherworld, and a way of seeing beyond the boundaries of this world. In

Pancha's she'd wondered just how far over the edge he'd gone.

Far enough and then some, she decided ... and then some more. She glanced down at the book in her hands. She doubted if Gabriela had underestimated him, but she knew Fat Eddie had, and so had she. Before his disappearance, he'd been a lauded naturalist, a scientific adventurer who had built a reputation for going beyond the proscribed boundaries of conventional wisdom, geographically and academically.

She would put a dollar to anyone's dime that he hadn't changed in that respect, that he was still going beyond the proscribed boundaries, maybe even into the shaman's realm—or so he might believe. She lifted her gaze from the writhing snakes drawn in his log. She wasn't sure what she believed about him, but there he stood, the most brilliantly infamous Harvard ethnobotanist to ever come out of the Ivy League, with row upon red row of *shoroshoro* beads wrapped around his ankle, barefoot and more than half naked on the deck of an Amazon riverboat with feathers tied in his hair.

And that tattoo, the shamanic abstraction of a man's cerebral fissure if she'd ever seen one, and she'd seen plenty up on the Vaupes.

His existence didn't revolve around something as simple as taking passengers up and down the river or being the fat man's pawn, quite the contrary. The edge he'd gone over was the border onto an abyss—and there the hell she was, trapped with him on a boat named *Sucuri*.

CHAPTER 10 ✄

RELEASING A DEEP BREATH, WILL glanced over his shoulder toward the cabin where he'd left her sleeping. She'd ruined him. One little blond-haired, too-smart-for-her-own-good woman with two crates of illegal guns had gotten on his boat and ruined him. It seemed almost impossible.

He'd spent two years working the river, getting to know every *caboclo* settlement and tributary on both shores, and doing a lot of chasing of his own tail, and the same trip that had finally nabbed him Corisco Vargas had also saddled him with Annie Parrish—the one-woman riot squad.

Good God. His life was on the line, and she was gnawing at the rope.

The signal he'd been waiting for sounded through the trees, a pounding rhythm of *manguare* drumbeats that would be picked up and repeated the length of the river north, and those who understood the message would be warned to beware and to watch for the *Sucuri*.

"Watch her sink like a stone or go up in flames," he muttered, heading toward the main cabin. Fat Eddie was out for blood, more than blood, if he could get it.

While Will would be the last person to certify his waterfront *amigos* as reliable, they all knew chaos when they saw it, and when he'd finally raised Diego Martinelli in Santo Antonio on the radio just before dawn, the old sot had confirmed that chaos had arrived with hellfire and a torch.

Stepping inside the cabin door, he was surprised to see his own personal bête noire awake and stirring. She looked slightly rumpled, but no worse the wear for their long night.

Good, he thought, she's going to need her strength—just as he was going to need his to keep from shaking her, or doing something really stupid, like making a pass. Anything between them had nowhere to go. He wasn't crazy enough to let it go anywhere. But rumpled, like everything else, looked good on Annie Parrish. Damn good. In that respect, she was the most amazing creature. Wet, muddy, scraped up, and wild haired—she managed to look good through it all, fresh faced and soft skinned, her small body lithely curved, her eyes bright and curiously aware behind her gold-rimmed glasses.

And the little white T-shirt she'd put on that morning looked especially good.

It fit.

It more than fit, and all he could think was that she'd picked a damn poor time to run out of baggy shirts. God help him if it rained and she got wet.

"Good morning," she said, her expression oddly subdued, wary even.

Justifiably wary, in his opinion.

"Not exactly," he said, not even attempting to lie. It was a hell of a morning, no matter how he looked at it. He had to get rid of her, the quicker the better, and he'd be damned if he knew how to do it.

She accepted his curmudgeonly greeting with an equanimous nod and a question. "The *manguares*. What are they saying?"

"It's a warning to stay off the main river. Fat Eddie torched Santo Antonio about ten o'clock last night," he said, reaching past her and pouring himself a cup of coffee. "They're still fighting the flames."

He sipped the hot brew, strong and black, and had to admit she made good coffee. The *prato feito* she'd made for dinner had been good, too, even if he had eaten it hours later.

"Fat Eddie set the town on fire?" A note of guilt crept into her voice. Also justifiable in his opinion.

"Actually, just the dock, but then somebody's fishing shack caught on fire, and it was all downhill after that." He took another sip, looking at her over the rim of his cup. She'd done a good job of making herself at home in his galley, such as it was, but he didn't recall culinary skills as being at the top of his list of desirable traits in a woman. As he recalled, he'd usually just stopped at desire, his and the woman's, and called it good.

"Was anybody hurt?"

"Not when I talked to my friend on the radio this morning, but I thought it best to send out a warning. There's a rubber-tappers settlement not too far from here, and an Indian village a few miles beyond that."

She glanced away at his answer, doing that slow sweep of the eyelashes thing that he swore to God he'd never noticed on another human being. But he noticed it on her. He noticed how long her eyelashes were, their color a golden brown to match her eyebrows. He noticed the softness of her cheeks ... her mouth.

His gaze drifted farther, down the front of her T-shirt, over her shorts and down the length of her legs, before settling on her bare feet. He'd like to call it good with her—but the last time he'd checked, and appearances aside, he didn't have a death wish.

He sighed and lifted his gaze back to her face. He was glad to see she was wearing a gun. He was afraid she was going to need it. He didn't know what was in her little black pack, but when he'd left her shortly after dawn, she'd had it buckled around her waist, and she'd worn it all the previous day. It was the only thing she owned that he hadn't gone through with a fine-tooth comb—and what an amazingly deadly cache of treasures she had hauled on board his boat. If he'd been a policeman, he would have arrested her himself.

But she'd looked damned sweet asleep—damned sweet and perfectly, metaphorically edible—her body limply relaxed in her hammock, her lips partly open. He'd wanted to kiss her, press his mouth to hers and slip his tongue inside, taste her. He'd wanted to feel her come awake in his arms, rise against him and return his kiss. Instead, he'd checked to make sure her pistol was loaded and closed the door behind him.

"São Gabriel is out, but I think we can make it to the Salesians at Barcelos tonight," he told her. "If we can get Gabriela to call in a plane, Bogotá is still your best bet for an international flight, but Venezuela is closer, and anywhere out of Brazil will be enough to throw Fat Eddie off your trail." It wasn't that he didn't have a plan. He just didn't have a way of forcing her to buy into it—other than force itself. He hoped it wouldn't come to that, but he certainly wasn't above it. Not by a long shot.

"And your trail?" she asked, surprising him by meeting his gaze directly, a flash upward of hazel eyes shot through with green and gold.

She was a cat. Fat Eddie had gotten that much right.

"I can handle Fat Eddie."

"So can I." She leaned back against the counter and crossed her arms over her chest. She was still wary, still looking guilty as hell, but there wasn't any hesitation in her statement. She could handle Fat Eddie.

He didn't doubt that she would try. She'd made her claim to fame long before the Woolly Monkey Incident. What he couldn't figure out was why she would still want to "handle" the fat man. *Merda,* she'd seen Johnny Chang's head.

"There's a point where ambition crosses the line into foolishness." And she was skirting the edge.

"If I get there, I'll send you a postcard," she said coolly, too coolly to suit him.

"It's not just Fat Eddie Mano," he said, though he knew damn well that she knew the facts as well as he did. "He's got a hundred *jagunços* working for him and access to hundreds more."

"You're not working for him. Wherever you're taking his gemstones, it's no favor to him," she said, surprising him again.

Okay, he thought, she's shrewd, just one more reason to get rid of her.

"Let's say it's mutually beneficial," he conceded, and so help him God, she smirked, twisted her lips up into a wry little curve that all but called him a liar.

He let out a short laugh in disbelief and set his coffee aside.

"Can you explain to me just exactly what it does take to scare you?" He really wanted to know. Hell, he was scared for her. He'd been scared for her since Eddie had dragged that damned head out of the water.

"Fat Eddie scares me," she admitted—much to his relief. He didn't like to think she was crazy. "Just not enough to turn me around and send me packing."

Of course not.

"Nobody needs the kind of firepower you have up on my deck to research peach palms. Israeli Galil rifles? With two hundred rounds of ammo? Hell, you're better armed than half the Brazilian army. Why?" He arched his brow, demanding an explanation, which—from the look on her face—he wasn't going to get.

"You opened my crates?"

"Opened, inventoried, and catalogued, and I have to tell you that, including the piece you're wearing on your hip, you've got one hell of an arsenal working for you. I mean, what *are* you planning on doing with two dozen grenades?"

Her gaze narrowing, she pursed her lips and told him exactly nothing.

"And the dynamite, for God's sake?"

Still nothing.

"Who is Jackson Reid?" he asked, changing tactics, and because he was damned curious about the man whose name had shown up three different times in her supplies— once on a duffel bag address tag, once in indelible marker on a flashlight, and once on a very expensive camera.

"A friend," she said after a considerable pause, giving

him plenty of reason to doubt her answer, but he'd be damned if he would sink so low as to grill her about the men in her life.

"Well, how about telling me where you got this." He took two steps across the cabin and reached behind the wheel, pulling out a blowgun dart. He'd found it in one of her packs with a piece of crumpled paper shoved in next to it. " 'Leave Manaus,' " he quoted the message. "That's a little too anonymous for Fat Eddie, so I'm guessing Johnny Chang sent this to you?"

"Is there anything I own that you haven't been through?" she asked peevishly.

"Other than the pockets on the shorts you're wearing and your little black pack, nothing."

The startled look she gave him quickly transformed into one of galled sensibilities, as if he were the real piece of work on the *Sucuri*.

He wanted to kiss it off her face.

"The dart was stuck in your boat, Dr. Travers," she said, commandeering the high ground, such as it was. "Certainly, I considered showing it to you, and if you'd been sober yesterday morning I might have remembered to drag it out."

"Considered?"

"In case it was meant for you."

"No." He shook his head, not buying her theory. "Nobody would threaten me with something like this. It's too simple, a cheap jungle trick meant to scare a—" He stopped suddenly, recognizing his error.

"A woman?" she finished, her eyebrows rising above the rims of her glasses.

"A *turista*," he filled in, a concession she seemed to

accept, though she was the only woman he would have conceded the point to, her and Gabriela.

"Okay. Let's cut to the chase. I can pay you a lot more than I already have to get me to Santa Maria. A lot more," she said, proving that she at least understood that he was holding most of the cards.

But the offer was ridiculous.

With a flick of his wrist, he impaled the dart into the wooden cowling above the helm's windows. "You're working on a grant. You don't even have gas money, unless Gabriela doles it out. So what are you going to pay me with?"

"Guns."

He added resourcefulness to her list, but shook his head.

"If I can get rid of you, I don't need any guns. I can patch things up with Fat Eddie, tell him I was *mulher louco*, crazy for a woman, so I lied to keep you with me for the night." He reached for his coffee. "He'll understand that." At least Will thought it was worth a shot.

She glanced out the window, and he noticed a trace of color tinging her cheeks. Intrigued, he looked at her more closely, thinking she couldn't possibly be blushing—not Amazon Annie.

"And what are you going to tell him happened to me when he notices I'm not around anymore?"

His mouth curved into a quick grin. "This is Brazil, Dr. Parrish, where the most common postcoital response in a woman is to throw something and walk out."

"We're in the middle of nowhere," she objected, tossing a glance in his direction and making an absent gesture toward the forest all around. The color across her face deepened to a rosy hue.

Will paused with his cup halfway to his mouth, going from being mildly intrigued to utterly fascinated, wondering if it was the thought of being in a postcoital situation with him that disconcerted her, or just the thought of sex in general—because she was blushing, definitely blushing.

He took a slow, considering sip of his coffee. He should have asked Gabriela more questions about her, more about Yavareté. The old doctor had always been straight with him. She would have told him anything, if he'd asked.

"Being in the middle of nowhere is no deterrent to a determined woman," he said, "and you, in particular, have proven to be a very determined woman."

"Money, then," she offered, tightening her arms across her chest, a body signal he didn't have any trouble interpreting in and of itself, but when combined with the blush burning up her cheeks, the message got a little more complex. "I will have money, more than grant money, a lot more. You can set your own price, and I'll pay you when I get it."

He gave his head another slow shake. "You're working way too hard here, Doctor. You only have two things I'm interested in, and money isn't one of them."

She went very still across from him in the cabin, and he knew beyond doubt that he had her full and undivided attention.

"The first thing is information," he told her, not waiting for her to ask. "And the second ..." He shrugged, letting his voice trail off. He had no intention of telling her the second. Her imagination was doing fine at filling in the blank all on its own. Her eyes widened slightly, before shying away from his. Her blush deepened even more, and he pretty much instantaneously figured out at least one thing that disconcerted the hell out of her—him and the thought of sex in the same breath.

I'll be damned, he thought. She was tough, all right, but he'd bet his boat and everything in it, including Fat Eddie's emeralds, that whatever Corisco Vargas had done to her, it hadn't included rape. Her reaction to him was too unabashedly coy, not frightened. She hated reacting to him at all. He could tell. But she couldn't control it. She couldn't meet his eyes and think about sex at the same time.

His grin broadened. If she wasn't careful, she was going to charm the pants right off him, and then there would be hell to pay.

"I'm talking a lot of money," she said, her gaze firmly focused somewhere in the vicinity of her feet.

"And I'm still thinking Barcelos, by nightfall if we're lucky. By this time tomorrow you could be on your way to Miami."

"So you get the guns either way," she said, flashing him a mutinous look. It was a flat-out accusation she didn't sound any too happy about.

"Yeah," he admitted, forcing himself to get back to business. He could fantasize all he wanted, but Annie Parrish was off limits. "I get the guns either way." And a hell of a lot of use he had for a bunch of guns. Of course, giving them back to Fat Eddie would go a long way toward mending the bridges he'd burned last night.

"I'm not getting on a plane in Barcelos," she insisted, not surprising him in the least. But as far as he was concerned, it was a done deal. He was going to save her and help himself, whether she liked it or not.

"Well, go ahead and cast off. The idea might look a lot better to you once we get there." And if it didn't, Will figured that was just too damn bad. One way or the other, he was getting her the hell out of Brazil.

CHAPTER 11 ✠

BARCELOS CAME INTO VIEW SHORTLY before nightfall, its riverfront marketplace bustling with people buying up the day's last bargains. Merchants up and down the docks were hawking their wares. Fishermen had their catches laid out on pallets, undercutting each other with cries of *"Barato! Barato!"*

Travers found a mooring on the north end of the waterfront, tying up on the low-rent end of the docks between a small barge piled high with cargo and a riverboat that made the *Sucuri* look new. Three mongrel dogs patrolled the barge, a brindle bitch and two half-grown pups, all of them emaciated and looking junkyard mean. An old man lay sleeping in a hammock strung between the crates, his arm wrapped around a shotgun. The public launches and the *gaiolas* were docked to the south, near the fruit and vegetable stands.

There wasn't a plane in sight.

Annie was relieved, but it was a backhanded victory at best. The day had gone from bad to worse. Travers had finally raised RBC on the radio about mid-morning, but it had been Dr. Ricardo Solano who had taken the call; Gabriela was ill. How ill, Dr. Solano hadn't felt at liberty to say, but Annie had a bad feeling. Gabriela was a tough old bird, but not even tough old birds lasted forever.

All Solano had promised was to do what he could, which might not include sending a plane to pick up Dr. Parrish. He hadn't thought the situation warranted such an expensive, unfunded measure, but neither had Travers mentioned Fat Eddie, the shrunken heads, or the guns.

She owed him for that now, along with everything else. If Solano knew what she'd done, he'd be the first to notify the police and have her arrested. Travers had called her situation a medical emergency, and she had to admit that having Solano dismiss her supposed health crisis with a noncommittal "I'll do what I can" had been disconcerting. Gabriela was her connection to RBC, her lifeline, if she needed one, and without the old doctor, Annie realized she was on her own—or at least she would be, if she could get away from Will Travers.

"Let's get something to eat," he said, walking out on deck, buttoning his shirt—a first, she was sure. "If the plane still isn't here by the time we finish and pick up a few supplies, we'll head farther up the river."

"Why not spend the night in Barcelos?" she asked, feigning a casual tone.

He grinned, obviously seeing right through her. "Because there are a hundred men here you could talk into taking you to Santa Maria, all of whom would be more than happy to do it for guns or grenades, and most of whom think dynamite is a fishing lure."

He was right, but she'd figured it was a long shot. She

wouldn't have any reservations about approaching one of the fishermen or *caboclos* and taking her chances on another boat. She'd been on a hundred boats in the Amazon basin, from private, first-class launches filled with scientific equipment, to dugout canoes, and she'd never gotten into trouble until the Cauaburi. On the other hand, she'd already paid Travers, and he had her cargo. When the plane didn't come—and she was sure it wouldn't—he would have little choice but to continue on to Santa Maria.

She changed into a pair of pants and took the extra precaution of tying a long-sleeved shirt around her waist to conceal her Taurus 9-millimeter. Wearing a gun was one thing. Advertising it was another.

As she came back out on deck, Travers was paying a group of children to watch the *Sucuri*. Ragged and cheerful, they eagerly caught the coins he pitched in the air and could be counted on to hang around for the promise of more on his return.

With their band of diminutive guards on duty, and a few more in tow, they wove a path through the waterfront marketplace, heading in the general direction of a cantina sporting a sign proclaiming **Carne e Cerveja**.

"Why the kids, if no one ever boards the *Sucuri*?" she asked.

"Keeps them out of trouble for an hour." He stopped and bought a dozen pieces of *cana*, sugarcane, on sticks. The children jumped and laughed around him, scrambling for their share of the sugarcane, while one of them ran the extras back to the boat.

"Um ... thanks," she said, when he handed her a piece.

"My mom used to buy these for me all the time when I was a kid."

"Your mom?" Now that took a stretch of Annie's imagination, thinking of the six-foot gringo with snakes tattooed down his back as a little kid at his mother's side, sucking on sugarcane.

"Elena Maria Barbosa Sanchez Travers," he said. "She's Venezuelan. I was born in Caracas. How about you? Where were you born?"

"Wyoming," Annie said slowly, casting him a disbelieving look. "You gave Fat Eddie your mother's name?"

"She's in the States, has been for twenty-five years. I don't think there's much chance of her running into Fat Eddie Mano. What about your folks?"

"Probably not going to run into Fat Eddie, either," she granted wryly, wary of where he might be going with this sudden rash of personal questions.

He chuckled from deep in his throat, looking at her from over the top of the sugarcane in his mouth—and Annie had to admit that he made sugar look good. She also had to admit that having the chance to get rid of her had improved his mood.

Greatly improved.

It was almost insulting.

"I meant where do they live," he said.

"My dad is in Wyoming." An easy enough answer to come up with.

"Great place, Wyoming. And your mom?"

"Tahoe or Vegas. Or sometimes Jackson Hole. She's hard to keep track of." She took a taste of the sugarcane and hoped that was the end of the "mother" conversation.

"Like her daughter?"

Annie nearly sighed. He was plowing some pretty old ground.

"Look," she said, wiping the juice off her chin with

the heel of her palm. "You can draw all the conclusions and similarities you want, and you won't get a fight from me. I'll be the first to admit I'm permanently scarred from my mother's abandonment, and there isn't a doubt in my mind that's how I ended up down here in the middle of nowhere with a washed-up botanist like you, waiting for a plane that isn't going to come, when all I really want is to get back on the river and get to Santa Maria."

"Washed-up?" He laughed again, obviously unfazed by her opinion. But then, he was William Sanchez Travers, and she knew for a fact that he'd been called worse— much worse.

"What else would you call a Harvard man smuggling gems for the likes of Fat Eddie Mano?"

He grinned down at her, his unrepentant smile broadening. "Hungry," he said. "Come on."

At the cantina, he chose a table outside in the small courtyard fronting the bar, where they had a full view of the river and the docks. Vines and greenery draped over the top of the patio wall, bougainvillea and fuschias entwined with lacy fronds of *dryopteris*. A pair of scarlet macaws were for sale in a cage across the alley, their raucous cries cutting through the diminishing hum of activity on the waterfront.

"We're wasting time here. There's no plane," she said, helping herself to the manioc flatbread the waiter had brought.

"Not yet," he agreed.

A thin string of lights came on around the patio, sparking to multicolored life and giving the dingy little place a festive air.

"There's not going to be. Rick Solano would just as soon I died as to ever darken RBC's door again, and that's a direct quote heard through the grapevine." She dipped her bread in pepper sauce and sprinkled it with salt. "He was the only vote against my proposal, and he was a loud one."

"What does Solano have against you?"

"Professional jealousy." She took a bite and felt her eyes start to water and her tongue start to burn. It was heaven.

Travers paused with a piece of bread in hand. "He can't afford to be that irresponible, not as the director of RBC."

"Tell him that."

"I did. This morning," he said and gestured at her soft drink. "Do you want another *guaraná*?"

"Sure." She nodded.

"*Moço, mais um cervejinha e um guaraná,*" he called to their waiter, then turned back to her. He took a drink of beer before continuing. "Gabriela said you're not here to study peach palms. She thinks you're up to something else."

She didn't so much as blink an eye. "That's interesting."

"Yeah. Real interesting," he agreed. "She also said if there were any wonders to be found in the forest, you would be the one to find them, not me."

Unbidden, Annie's mouth curved into a grin, and she reached for another piece of bread. "Then she hasn't seen your tattoo, because you sure as hell found something out there. Or, from the looks of it, something found—" she stopped suddenly, her gaze snapping up and slamming into a pair of darkly amused brown eyes.

"No," he said slowly. "Gabriela has never seen my tattoo. When did you?"

"This morning, when you pulled up in the canoe."

And the last thing she'd wanted to do was admit it. She was appalled by what had been done to him—and because of her damned nightmare, more than a little unnerved by the tattoo itself.

She had found a wonder in the forest, an orchid unlike any other, and it was going to make her name. Whatever Travers had found had taken his and left him marked for life, and even as curious as she was about him, it had set him on a course she was damned sure she didn't want to follow. He was a fascinating man, for all he'd once been and for whatever he'd become, but his tattoo had erased any doubts she might have had that he was treading waters far deeper than she wanted to brave. She wanted her orchid. That was all. Just her orchid.

"So what did you think?"

She thought about telling him the truth, that she knew he was wearing a shaman's crystal and would place bets that he knew how to use it in ways she hadn't even heard about and probably wouldn't believe. That she knew the snakes wound so sinuously down his back represented shamanistic knowledge far beyond the temporal world, and it frightened her to think about what the damn things meant or who had put them there. But then she reminded herself all she really wanted from him was passage to Santa Maria, and the quicker she left him, and the less she knew about him when she left, the better off she'd be.

"I think you could have gotten better work in the States," she said. "Tattooing is all the rage there now."

His gaze shifted away from hers. "All the rage." He let out a short laugh. "Yeah, I'm sure I could have gotten better work in the States." He lifted his beer to his mouth and drained the last of the bottle.

With impeccable timing, the waiter returned with drinks and their food. Annie took the respite and waited until they were both mostly finished before she broached their impasse again. She could get off the *Sucuri;* the Salesians would give her a night's lodging at the mission, she was sure. But she was also sure that Travers would not give up her guns. Not when returning them to Fat Eddie would go a long way toward getting him back in the fat man's good graces.

He was going to be disappointed. She'd spent her life savings on those crates, and she wasn't at all sure she could get her orchids and get back in one piece without them. There was too much gold on the Cauaburi for the area to be secure, too big a chance of running into Vargas. A year ago, the mining had just been starting. It would be utter chaos now, and she wasn't walking into chaos without protection. There would be no repeat of Yavareté. None. On that one fact, she was undeterrable.

"There isn't going to be a plane," she said, repeating her earlier prediction. "So we have to decide what's going to happen here."

He looked up from his plate, and the light fell across his face, delineating the dark wings of his brows and the expressive curve of his mouth, and Annie had to admit he was dangerous in more ways than one. Despite a reputation that even at its worst was undeniable, and that damned tattoo that told her he was definitely more trouble than she needed, maybe even more than she could handle—and that was saying quite a lot for a woman with her plans—he fascinated her on levels she had no business thinking about.

"Solano wants the directorship of RBC," he said, sitting back in his chair. "He can't afford to have you show up dead right now. Dead scientists are an anathema to pharmaceutical companies and their research money. He'll send the plane."

"And if he doesn't?"

"Then we've got a problem."

"Which needs to be addressed," she said, agreeing with him and adding the bonus of a smile that was meant to tell him they could work together on this. It was her bargaining smile, a smile to ease any uncertainties he might have about the outcome of their discussion.

Will grinned back. He couldn't help it. She was going into Girl Scout mode again.

"Okay. It's time to level with you," she continued, still smiling, so candid he could see right through to her ulterior motives.

His grin broadened. "That would be refreshing."

"Yes, well, in the interests of RBC—and I have to hold their interest even above my own, even with Fat Eddie involved—I can't tell you what project I'm working on, and I can't walk away. It's simply not an option."

"The project you need all the guns for, not the one where Father Aldo is sitting next door watching you count peach palm fruit."

"Yes, I guess that's one way to put it," she finally said, after a long pause.

"I see." She was in trouble up to her pretty little neck.

"Yeah, well, I think it's important here to point out that we're only a day's travel from Santa Maria, and I have already paid you."

"True."

Obviously surprised by the ease of his concessions, she relaxed her smile into a genuine expression of pleasure—

and Will's heart slid to a slow stop, his easy mood disappearing.

He hadn't seen her smile before, not like this. He hadn't thought her particularly beautiful, only haphazardly cute in a way that attracted him—but when she smiled, he saw beauty, that little cat beauty of hazel eyes and ditzy hair, of fine cheekbones and a turned-up nose, the kind any man would want, and suddenly he felt a surge of possessiveness that could only make his life difficult. He didn't need or want his emotions tied up in what he had to do to Corisco Vargas. He didn't want to be thinking about what Vargas had done to her.

Merda, he swore to himself.

"Well, given that we agree on the basics, I don't see any reason why we can't—"

"Wait a minute," he interrupted, shoving his plate out of the way and leaning onto the table. "I want to backtrack a bit."

"Okay." Her smile wavered, and an uncertain light came into her eyes.

"If you're going to try to talk me into taking you to Santa Maria, when I'll be the last person to see you alive if Fat Eddie gets a hold of you, I want a little more information."

"I can't give you any information. Like I said, RBC's interests preclude—"

"Personal information," he interrupted.

The look she was giving him turned wary as hell again, but she was the one who had offered to level with him, and he doubted she would back down just because the going got a little tough, not while she still had a chance to win.

"What kind of personal information?"

"Simple stuff, like what's your backup plan if things start going bad? How are you going to keep yourself from getting killed out there once you're on the river alone?"

"The same way I always have," she said bluntly. "I've been taking care of myself for a long time."

"True," he admitted. "But I bet you never had anyone like Fat Eddie on your case."

"Try Corisco Vargas." She angled a look at him from over the tops of her glasses.

"Oh, right. I forgot," he lied smoothly.

"Believe me, Vargas makes Fat Eddie look like a choirboy, piranha teeth and all." She brought her soda to her mouth for a drink.

"Pretty nasty character?"

She nodded, setting the bottle on the table. "You've been on the river a long time, too. You must have heard the stories."

"Like the one about him sacrificing virgins on a bloody altar made of beaten gold hidden somewhere in the jungle?"

Her gaze slid away, and she let out a short burst of nervous laughter. "Yeah, right, that one. Thank God I wasn't a virgin when he got a hold of me."

Of course she hadn't been—and there Will was again, wanting to shake her, and then shake her again, because Vargas had gotten a hold of her, beaten her and God knew what else, and she'd come back. She was crazy. Certifiable. It took every ounce of strength he had not to jump over the table and grab her.

"Yeah, right," he said, sitting back in his chair and

forcing himself to calmly take another drink of beer. "I guess you're a little better protected this time."

She gave him another suspicious look, but nodded, and his mood darkened to a dangerous shade of black. A handgun was a viable form of self-defense for a woman. If she was the nervous type, a woman might also get herself a rifle, maybe a semiautomatic. But only a woman hell-bent on going out and taking on the devil himself would buy two high-tech Israeli Galils and a Kalishnakov with two hundred rounds (two hundred rounds!) of ammuntion and then back it up with grenades and twenty friggin' sticks of dynamite.

"So," he started in again, unable to help himself. "How did he know?"

"Know what?" She gave him a quizzical glance.

"That you weren't a virgin."

She was fast, but he was faster. He had a hold of her before her butt even came off the chair.

"Bugger off," she growled.

"Anytime, Annie." He was so furious, he could hardly see straight. "But not until you're out of here."

"This is none of your business."

"I'm making it my business." He tightened his grip on her wrists. "You're not here doing research, no matter what your damn proposal said. You're here to get back what you lost in Yavareté, and you want the man who took it from you. Corisco Vargas."

"You've got a wicked imagination, Will Travers, but you are *way* off the mark on this." She was spitting mad, strung tighter than a bow. For as small as she was, she was strong, and though he wasn't worried, he definitely felt like he had a tiger by the tail.

"I know Vargas beat you. Gabriela told me."

"Well, that's all he did, you jerk, and believe me, it looked worse than it was."

Jerk? In all his life, no one had ever called him a jerk. But then, in all his life, he'd never manhandled a woman the way he was manhandling Annie Parrish.

Yet he didn't let her go.

He didn't dare.

He thought back to those *garimpeiros* she'd tussled with over the damned woolly monkey, and the results of that escapade gave him pause. He could take her, but maybe not without hurting her, not if she was going to fight him—and wasn't that the damnedest thing. God, he had seventy pounds on her, if he had an ounce.

A silver flash out on the river behind her caught his gaze, a fractured beam of light dropping out of the sky. In seconds, the murky silhouette behind the light resolved itself into wings and a fuselage.

"Are you going to kick my butt, if I let you go?" he asked, returning his attention to her.

"Maybe," she said through gritted teeth.

"I don't want to hurt you."

"I can't say the same."

Definitely angry.

Quickly, before he could change his mind, he released her and stepped back.

She didn't so much as budge. Not a muscle. Just held him with a steely-eyed glare, until she heard the same thing he'd just seen—a Cessna 106 floatplane taxiing down the Rio Negro toward the Barcelos dock.

CHAPTER 12 ⚑

SHE WHIRLED AROUND, HER EXPRESSION one of utter disbelief. For himself, he was disgustingly ambivalent. Yes, it was best all around if he got rid of her immediately, especially best for her. But damn, she'd cross-wired then hot-wired a whole slew of his nonlogical, rather loudly clamoring male impulses and natural instincts—all of which were telling him to keep her.

Keep her for what? his intellect demanded to know—and he'd be damned if he had a reasonable answer for that.

"I could shoot you," she snapped, turning back around, her frustration palpable. "Just shoot you and steal your damn boat."

She was still wearing her gun, but Will wasn't too worried. She was crazy in some ways, but not in that way.

The plane was about two hundred yards off and closing in.

"Okay," she said suddenly. "Okay. Let's deal. I'll give you all the information you want."

He was tempted. Whatever she was working on had to be amazing.

"All right," he said, trying to sound noncommittal enough to keep her from calling him a liar when he put her on the plane anyway. "Tell me what you've got."

She let out a deep breath, still hyped up, but visibly relieved, and he felt a twinge of guilt for getting her hopes up. If he knew what she was after, he could help her out, but she wasn't staying in Brazil, not as long as Fat Eddie breathed.

"Okay," she repeated, as if steadying herself for a confession. Then she confessed, all in one breath, all with appropriate reverence. "*Aganisia cyanea.*"

"That's good," he admitted slowly. "That's real good, but not worth risking your life for."

Her expression told him she disagreed. "It's only been collected half a dozen times"—she leaned in closer over the table—"and I found hundreds of them, *hundreds,* all blooming the first week of March up on the Rio Marauiá."

"Hundreds?" He was impressed, damned impressed. No one had ever found more than a single blue orchid anywhere. "Where on the Marauiá?"

"Toward the headwaters."

"And how in the hell did you get up there?" Over a hundred miles off the main river, the headwaters of the Marauiá were born in the lost world straddling the Brazil-Venezuela border, a wild land mostly uninhabited, except for the Yanomani to the east, and farther west, between the Marauiá and the Cauaburi, by the nomadic

Dakú when he'd first encountered them, or rather when they'd chosen to encounter him. He sure as hell hadn't been looking for a tribe known more by rumor than account, and he most certainly had not been looking for a man like Tutanji.

Tutanji, though, had been looking for a man like him—a man exactly like him.

"The last time I did research here, RBC had a river launch that docked in Santa Maria about every two months." She glanced over her shoulder, talking fast. "Sometimes Gabriela would put it at my disposal for a week or so."

"I didn't know anyone was mining up on the Marauiá. The whole damn river is infested with caimans. Most miners won't go near the place. Too many crazy stories about monster *jacarés*, real man-eaters."

"I didn't know anyone was up there at the time, either." Her gaze flicked again to the incoming plane. "Come on. Do we have a deal, or not?"

"*Aganisia cyanea* at the headwaters of the Marauiá," he mused aloud, then shook his head. "No. I'm not going to let you die for blue orchids, not even a hundred of them."

"I don't have to die for them," she insisted. "I just have to go and get them."

"Give me the exact location, and I'll do what I can. I'll send all the specimens I collect to Gabriela with your name on them."

The blank look she gave him would have been comical, if she hadn't been so serious.

"You?" she said. "You'll go get them?"

"Yeah. I'll fight my way through all the *Crocodilia*

and send any blue orchids I find to RBC through your peach palm project." He repeated his offer. "No one needs to know."

"*I'll* know," she begged to differ. "They're *my* orchids, and I'm going to be the one collecting them."

"Not after I put you on that plane."

It was the truth, and as it settled in, she got a look in her eyes he didn't quite trust, a look that seemed to question his ability to put her anywhere.

"Yes I can," he assured her, reaching in his pocket and pulling out a few bills to throw on the table.

Glancing back at the plane, she ran her hand through her hair, making it all stand on end. And somewhere within the space of that movement, she made a decision he was sure he didn't like.

"Then that's it," she said. Without sitting down, she finished off her soft drink, then set the bottle on the table and took off walking across the patio with a very purposeful stride.

Will worked his way around the table, getting slowed down by a batch of potted plants he hadn't noticed on the way in.

"Damn." He speeded up his steps, catching her just at the edge of the courtyard, by the wall.

He took her by the arm; she turned—and suddenly the night was different than it had been before. She didn't seem to notice, but he felt it with his very next breath. The darkness was richer, deeper, enveloping them in a curve of night-shadowed adobe and trailing vines lush with bougainvillea and vanilla orchids. She shifted her stance, the subtlest of movements, but he knew it was the moment she became aware of the change, aware of the scent of flowers infusing the air, aware of him.

"No," he said. "That's not quite it." Her skin was soft beneath his fingers, her eyes growing warier by the second—with good reason.

He wanted a kiss.

He wanted to feel her mouth beneath his—just once. Just once before she was gone and his two days with Amazon Annie, terror of the river basin, were nothing but another wild story to add to the tally.

"So you changed your mind about the plane?" There was a slight hesitation in her voice, a slight breathlessness that brought a brief curve to his lips. She wasn't immune to what he was feeling.

"No. I haven't changed my mind." He shifted his weight closer to her, lifting his hand to cup her chin.

She went very still within his light grasp, her eyes widening behind her glasses. Soft, diffuse light streamed through the orchid vines, casting her face in a delicate tracery of shadows, darkening her irises to a jungle-green. In contrast, her hair was a riotous halo of white and gold blond.

"This," she said softly, "is a terrible idea."

"I know," he admitted.

But he did it anyway, smoothed his fingers along the curve of her jaw and lowered his mouth toward hers.

"Um ... maybe you better rethink this," she said when he was less than a breath away.

"No," he murmured. "I've done enough thinking." She smelled sweet, like her soft drink, and he wanted to lick the taste off her lips.

"Dr. ... uh, Travers. Will, I—"

"Shh, Annie. It's just a kiss."

And a bolder lie he'd never told. He touched her mouth with his, softly, so softly, capturing the small gasp of her response and tunneling his fingers up into the silky disarray of her hair.

Her hand came up between them, pressing against his chest, and he stopped with his mouth on hers—but it wasn't enough. It wasn't nearly enough.

Just a kiss, he'd said, but he hadn't even gotten that yet.

Slowly, he slid his other hand down the length of her arm and twined his fingers through hers. Then he moved both of their hands to the base of her spine and pressed her forward, into his hips. His response was jointingly physical, one of those flashes of heaven and hell. It was heaven to have the pressure of her body up against his, and hell knowing he wasn't going to get much more—but this moment, this moment was about a kiss, and he wasn't going to be denied.

He rocked against her, bringing her tight against him, and she groaned, a barely spoken word sounding a lot like "disaster," before her mouth parted and her fingers curled into the fabric of his shirt. It was all the encouragement he needed. Opening his mouth over hers, he claimed her as his own.

The kiss was instantly hot, and sweet, and wet, sending a wave of pleasure sluicing down his body to pool in his groin, and as quickly as that, he forgot the plane, the guns, the boat. All of it was lost in the taste and the surprisingly sensual wonder of Annie Parrish's mouth. She fit against him so perfectly, her small breasts pressed against his chest, the wondrous curves of her buttocks, her *bunda*, filling his palm. Her mouth was delicately formed, her lips soft, her tongue shy, until coaxed by his into a tantalizing exploration that left him wanting a lot more than he could get with her backed up against the wall in a public cantina.

But he took what he could, sliding his hand under her T-shirt, marveling at the sleek strength of her back. She wasn't very big, but she was solid. She didn't feel fragile in his arms. She felt like the woman who had walked the Vaupes—and far more startlingly, she felt like his.

It didn't make sense. He didn't have a place for any woman in his life, let alone a wild card like Annie Parrish. She was trouble, nothing but trouble, an actual danger to life and limb, but the longer he kissed her, the more fascinated he became. The tomboy of the Amazon was intrinsically, delightfully, mysteriously female, and everything male inside him wanted her, all of her, for as long as he could keep her—which, given his current life expectancy, he estimated would be all of two weeks. Which, he admitted, could be why he was even thinking in such terms. Two weeks of "till death do us part" really wasn't that big of a stretch, but it wasn't going to happen, so he kissed her. He kissed her until he was hot everywhere, and she was making little sounds in the back of her throat that told him she'd passed the same barrier of common sense he had and was only seconds away from doing something totally crazy and totally wonderful, like sliding her hand down the front of his pants.

God, just the thought made him hard. He wanted her to hold him. He was ready to be teased into an oblivion of sexual languor. He was ready to rent a room with a bed and say to hell with the plane.

"*Senhor* Travers?"

Will was aware of the voice, but it took hearing his name two more times before the reality registered enough for him to lift his head. Yet even when he did, he stayed focused on her. Her eyes were closed, her glasses skewed, her head back, revealing the satiny column of her throat. Her lips were still parted, wet, and he could think of a thousand truly magical things he'd like her to do with her mouth.

"*Senhor* Travers?" The voice intruded again.

Her eyes came open slowly, a deep, gray-rimmed green, fringed in thick, golden lashes.

"I'm going to hold this against you for a long, long time," she whispered.

"Yeah. I'm not going to forget you, either," he promised, removing his hand from beneath her shirt, though he lingered for a few seconds at her waist, molding his palm to the warm curve, as if with the light gesture he could hold on to her.

"The plane is here, *Senhor* Travers. Tied up by the boat. With the moon full and the river to follow, the pilot, he wants to leave again."

"Yeah. Right, but we may be talking a change in itinerary." He turned to the man behind him and instantly froze. "Juanio." It was one of Fat Eddie's henchmen from Pancha's. Short and round, with a mop of black hair, the young man had a nervous twitch in one eye, a cigarette stuck behind his ear, and a Colt revolver in his hand.

Another man came out of the shadows, the one called Luiz, and Will's alarm heightened. Leaner and meaner, taller and more muscular, with buzz-cut hair, a cold, black-eyed gaze, and a big bush knife on his hip, he was by far the more dangerous of the two. Both of them were armed. Both of them were pointing their guns at him and Annie.

He swore silently to himself. He'd known kissing her would be dangerous. He just hadn't realized how dangerous.

"*Uma pistola, garota?*" Luiz gestured with his gun at the protrusion on Annie's hip, and Juanio stepped forward to disarm her. To Will's relief and her credit, she didn't offer any resistance, just raised her arms and let him take her gun. Drawing against two-to-one odds when the other team was already cocked and loaded was bound to bring things to a quick end, especially when Fat Eddie would just as soon have her dead as alive.

"We don't want any trouble from you, *Senhor* Travers," Juanio said. "No trouble from you, no trouble from us. *Compreende?*"

"*Compreendo,*" he said. I understand. Though he didn't really know how they were going to keep from having trouble, if they tried to take Annie. He had to get her back on the boat. "How did you find us?"

"*El rádio.*" Juanio grinned, revealing a curve of stained, yellow teeth. "We been waiting upriver for you, two days now, *senhor,* two steaming, stinking days in the plane, but when you call for help, Juanio and Luiz bring help, though the woman, she don't look too sick to me. But we help you; you help us. No?"

Waiting upriver? Now why in the hell had they been doing that? he wondered. "Help you how?"

Juanio's grin broadened, and he brought his free hand up, rubbing the tips of his fingers together. "*Esmeraldas. Diamantes.*"

Will's gaze shot to the other man, who snarled at Juanio.

"Silence! *Idiota.*"

"You want *Senhor* Eduardo's gems?" Will asked

disbelievingly, wondering just how many rats were fleeing Fat Eddie's ship and why. First, Johnny Chang had stolen the fat man's guns, and now the second-string *jacunços* were trying to make off with his gemstones. Johnny had had a plane ticket on him. Luiz and Juanio had a whole damn plane—but they didn't want Annie, and they hadn't mentioned her guns.

Things were looking up—way up, if all the two *bandidos* wanted was the gems.

"We know you have them, *senhor*," Luiz warned. "We were there in Pancha's when the fat one gave them to you."

"Yes. I have them. They're on the *Sucuri*."

A look passed between the two men, as well it might. Fat Eddie Mano hadn't chosen Will as his courier simply because of his less-than-sterling reputation. The *Sucuri* had a reputation that easily equaled his, a reputation forged in the very murky waters of the upper Amazon Basin. People didn't board the boat uninvited for a reason. A reason Juanio and Luiz were obviously well aware of, or they would have simply scared off the kids and tried to take what they wanted.

Luiz jerked his head toward the docks in an unspoken command, and Will reached for Annie's hand. The look she cast him was very steady, coolly controlled, easing a good deal of his worries. If he was going to be shanghaied on the Barcelos waterfront, he could do far worse than to have Annie Parrish by his side—and he probably couldn't do better.

At the *Sucuri*, Luiz gave a curt command. "Get rid of your *filhotes*, your puppies." He'd concealed his gun by holding it under his greasy leather vest, but once near the boat, he'd gotten close enough to jab Will in the back with it. Juanio had simply draped the tail of his shirt over his hand. In the dark, it was enough to keep other people from noticing.

"*Embora!*" Will said, approaching the group of rag-tag children. "*Agora mesmo!*"

Used to quick shifts of fortune, the children didn't hesitate to run off.

A light was on in the dry-rot hulk floating next to the *Sucuri,* but the barge still had only the dogs and sleeping old man on board. The Cessna had been moored at the end of the dock, next to the hulk. A party was getting going farther up the waterfront, and the sounds of music and laughter drifted across the haphazard jumble of canoes, skiffs, barges, *batalones,* and riverboats at ever-increasing decibel levels.

"Fat Eddie isn't going to like this," Will said.

"Well, we don't like stinking Fat Eddie," Juanio proclaimed with a sneer.

"Corisco Vargas isn't going to like it, either." Will voiced a deeper warning with a noticeable effect.

Juanio crossed himself and looked to his partner, a nervous shift of his gaze Luiz refused to acknowledge.

"Fat Eddie doesn't own this river anymore," the bigger man said.

"And Vargas?" Out of the corner of his eye, Will saw Juanio cross himself again.

"I spit on Corisco Vargas," Luiz declared, then spit on the dock instead and stamped on the wet spot with his boot, rubbing the smear into the wood.

Will glanced up and saw a weak smile cross Juanio's face as the younger man watched the macho display and took heart in Luiz's bravery against a wad of spit.

Will gave them a week on the outside, before their

bodies were hanging, gutted and skinned, from some tree in the rain forest, monkey meat for whatever passed by.

"You won't be safe anywhere in Brazil, if you steal those stones," he said.

"But we'll be safe in Miami!" Juanio offered with a shaky laugh, as if affirming it out loud would help make it so.

Luiz thought differently and wapped Juanio up the side of the head, shutting him up. " 'Ta louco? Take the woman and get the jewels."

Juanio winced and grabbed his right ear, protecting it from another blow. "You go," he grouched, slanting his partner a mutinous look. "I'll watch the *senhor*."

"Go," Luiz growled. "Or I'll shoot off your balls."

Will just wanted Annie on the *Sucuri*, and he didn't much care who else was on the boat with her.

Juanio cared, though. He cared a lot.

"Make her go alone," he insisted. "If she doesn't bring us the stones, we'll kill him."

"And then he's dead, and she takes off in the boat, and we have no jewels?" Luiz laid it all out in rising tones of disgust. "Move!" he ordered. "And don't come back without the gems."

Juanio held firm, his mouth tightening in a stubborn line. "You never said I would have to get on the devil boat."

"The boat's devil is here," Luiz assured him, giving Will a poke with his gun. "Without him, the boat is just a boat, a simple boat, you fool."

"That's not what they said in Manaus. In Manaus, they said the *sucuri* is real, that it lies in wait on the boat to devour the *senhor*'s enemies."

"And isn't Manaus full of fools? A bunch of fools

who work for Fat Eddie and don't know shit about what's going to—" Luiz stopped suddenly and changed tactics. "Juanio. Didn't we work our way out of the mines because we were smarter than the others?"

"Yes," Juanio reluctantly agreed.

"And haven't we both seen the true devil?" Luiz's voice lowered to a rough whisper. "You don't want to see him again, do you?"

Juanio vehemently shook his head no, turning pale in the moonlight, his right hand racing once more through the stations of the cross.

"Think Miami, Juanio. We'll be safe in Miami. Nothing bad ever happens in *os Estados Unidos*. But we need the emeralds to get there, Juanio. We need the diamonds to pay to get in. They don't want our stinking *reais* in *os Estados Unidos*. We're going to have to pay the border guards in *diamantes*. The *diamantes* on that boat." He pointed to the *Sucuri*.

Juanio struggled with indecision for a moment or two longer, but in the end, Luiz's threats and promises proved harder to ignore than the superstition and rumors about the *Sucuri*. Muttering under his breath, Juanio took hold of Annie's arm and shoved her forward, toward the boat.

She didn't hesitate, only glanced back at Will once, before stepping onto the deck, and he would have given every emerald and diamond Fat Eddie owned to know what she was thinking.

Annie was thinking she'd been crazy to let Travers kiss her. Her senses were still reeling from those long, glorious minutes when she'd been consumed by the taste and feel and the utter seductiveness of William Sanchez Travers's mouth. Truly, she would never forgive him for the experience.

She was also thinking she was in more trouble than she'd thought, if Travers was invoking Corisco Vargas's name to scare off Luiz and Juanio, and she was thinking about how dangerous stupid people could be, stupid people like Juanio. So she didn't waste any time once she was on board.

Despite his capitulation, the man was far too nervous to be paying close enough attention to her. He was a bundle of sweating nerves just waiting for a giant snake with a heart full of hunger to lunge into view, jaws gaping. For herself, she absolutely refused to entertain any such idea, because if she did, she'd be sweating as much as Juanio—and if for a moment, when she first stepped on board, she did feel a strange, fleeting sense of malevolence, she ignored it, walking boldly to the main cabin's door, where she was going to cold-cock little old Juanio and get her gun back.

Confidently, she reminded herself that she'd been on and off Travers's boat dozens of times in the last two days, and the only snakes she'd seen had been tattooed down his back—until she opened the cabin door and her eyes lit on a coiled shadow of bulky, gargantuan, serpentine proportions looming up out of the darkness.

Terror shot through her with all the speed and crackle of a lightning bolt, electrifying every cell in her body, and without a thought in her head that wasn't absolutely petrified with fear, she opened her mouth and let loose a bloodcurdling scream.

Behind her, Juanio crashed onto the deck in a deadaway faint.

CHAPTER 13

IN THE FIRST SPLIT SECOND OF THE attention-riveting sound of Annie Parrish coming completely unglued, Will raised his arm and smashed his elbow back into Luiz's face—from the feel of it, breaking the man's nose. It was quickly downhill after that for the would-be jewel thief. Will grabbed his gun, knocked him out cold where he was bent double over himself, his bleeding face in his hands, and was running for the boat before Luiz even hit the dock.

Juanio was a limp pile of blubber and bones Will had to fight his way past, before he could get to her, to Annie.

She was still standing—no fainting dead away for Amazon Annie—and she'd stopped screaming, but she was as white as a sheet, her hand clutching the cabin's door.

He swore under his breath and took another step into the cabin.

"Annie." He called her name softly, warning her of his presence. She hadn't felt fragile earlier, but she looked fragile now, like the merest breath of wind would crumble her into dust.

Without moving so much as an inch, she said rather breathlessly, "I've been doing some thinking, and I've decided you're right. It's best if I go."

"Great," he lied, alarmed by how she looked, so pale, her hand white-knuckled on the knob. "But we're going to have to find another plane, someplace else. This one here tonight is no good."

"No," she argued, making a small, fluttering gesture with her free hand. "Everything will be fine. Just fine. I'll arrange things, transport and all, just grab my stuff and be on my way. You can have the guns."

"We can talk about it later," he said calmly, "but we have to leave now. Together."

"We?" Her expression changed to one of blank incredulity as she slanted her eyes in his direction. "Together? Oh, no. No, I'm done."

That didn't sound good.

"Annie," he began, but she hushed him with a wave of her hand, her gaze wandering away from him again.

"You see"—the furrow in her brow deepened—"I—I can't begin to imagine what you've been up to. Or actually, I can ... almost. It's the tattoo. It's not a simple thing, Will, not like I said. Nobody in the States could have given you an image of a rainbow boa and the ancestral anaconda twined together in man's cerebral fissure. I mean, you might get some Celtic imagery, or Christian, or Native North American, but no South American stuff, not at that level. That's pure *payé*, shamanistic, and all I can think is that some medicine man got a hold of you, a real heavy hitter, and he's casting spells like a Master of

Animals and sending you helpers from the Otherworld. Or at least that's as close as I can figure, and to get that far I have to concede every one of my most dearly held scientific principles." Her eyes met his, and though she was frightened, her gaze was crystal clear. "You're trouble, Will, so much trouble, you make Fat Eddie's vendetta against me look like a date to the prom."

For someone who'd only been back on the boat for two minutes and spent half of that screaming bloody murder, she'd done some pretty fast figuring. Even terrified, her mind had been working like a steel trap, and he wondered why Tutanji couldn't have sent him somebody like Annie Parrish as a helper, instead of all these damn snakes all the time—because he was sure that's exactly what had turned her pale with fright. Twice before, someone had tried to board the *Sucuri* without his permission, and both times, the men had seen a huge snake, an anaconda in the main cabin. The stories of those sightings had spread fast, and far, and wide. Hell, his boat hadn't even had a name until the first time it had happened.

"I've got a few things going on," he admitted. "But nothing I can't handle."

For such a small movement, the raising of her eyebrows packed one hell of a punch, casting every ounce of his integrity and judgment into doubt. "The smart thing for me to do is to get as far away from you as I can, and—"

"Right," he agreed, interrupting her, not wanting her to say more. "But not in Barcelos, Annie. Not tonight."

"You're dangerous," she said.

"Yes," he admitted. "But so are you, and we seem to get along okay."

"I'm afraid of snakes," she told him unnecessarily.

"Terrified" would have been his choice of words, based on the look in her eyes when he'd walked into the cabin. He just hoped she wasn't afraid of him, but that could have been asking a lot at this point.

"Lots of people are."

"I have dreams," she confessed. "Snake dreams. Nightmares. I wake up sweating, Will. Sweating and strangling."

So did he when he dreamed about snakes, but he always dreamed about the same snake, just the one—over and over.

"We can talk about dreams, if you want," he promised. "Later, after we're out of here."

A groan from Juanio backed up the rightness of that decision.

"You can't stay, Annie. Not here."

She looked at him for a long moment, before glancing away and rubbing her hand over her face.

"*Meu Deus,*" she murmured. My God.

IT WAS AN hour before Will guided the *Sucuri* close in to one of the river islands and found a mooring, an hour that Annie had spent trying to sort things out and calm down. Juanio was still on board and out cold, and she was beginning to wonder if someone could literally scare themselves into a coma. Luiz was behind them, but Will had grounded him with the simple expediency of jimmying the plane door open, cutting the ignition wires, and handing out the Cessna toolkit to every kid who had come running when he'd whistled. Like a chattering, giggling school of piranhas, they'd swarmed over the plane with flying arms and nimble fingers, stripping it down to its bones. The first wing had been disappearing down the dock even as the *Sucuri* had drifted into the current off the Barcelos waterfront. A pair of urchins clutching Cessna seat cushions to their chests had been following the wing. Luiz would be lucky to have a pontoon strut left by the time he woke up.

The emeralds and diamonds were another story altogether. Will wasn't just hauling them someplace for Fat Eddie. He was taking them to Corisco Vargas, according to what he'd told Luiz and Juanio, which meant she and Will were more than heading in the same direction. They were headed for the same damned place, and the man she was trying to avoid was the one he was intending to find.

When she'd stumbled onto Corisco's Cauaburi operation a year ago, she'd been so far out in the boondocks, there wasn't a place she'd stepped that had been on any map. But Will must have a map, and even though at this point in time, he thought the only treasure to be found at the end of it were the gems he was taking there, the man wasn't an average type of guy. No matter how far he'd fallen off the botanical research bandwagon, he would always look at the forest as a botanist, a brilliant, highly skilled botanist with an eye for plants, which meant he'd become just one more big problem she had to contain. He could have all the *Aganisia cyanea* he could find, but she doubted if he would find very much. No one had ever found more than a single flower on the Marauiá or anywhere else. Her concern was *Epidendrum luminosa,* and it was all hers, every last luminous petal and sepal, every glowing calyx and corolla.

Perched on the galley countertop, her head already in her hands, she let out an exasperated sigh. She was beginning to feel decidedly star-crossed.

And the damned snake. She'd recognized the *sucuri* looming up out of the dark, known the serpent for what it was, and would never forget it, whether it had been real or her imagination.

It sure as hell had looked real, but either way left her on shaky ground and with the uncomfortable conviction that Will Travers was a man privy to more freaky supernatural hoodoo than a person could beat with a stick, the kind of stuff she'd made a career out of avoiding.

Beneath her, she felt the low throb of the engine slowing to a halt, and she looked up to see Will throttling down.

"I'll tie up," he said, latching the wheel. "There's some tobacco in that last drawer over there. Blow a little smoke on Juanio. See if you can get him to come around."

Tobacco was a cure-all in the Amazon. *Nicotiana tabacum* was smoked, chewed, made into a syrup, and ingested, all with amazing results. More often than not, it was a shaman's first line of defense, and that Travers's first thought was to blow a little smoke on Juanio only proved her point about his experience.

"Blow a little smoke," she muttered, rummaging through the drawer. It was full of all kinds of leaves and stems, flowers and buds, some bagged, some not, some labeled, most not. He had at least two dozen small jars holding plant material, a lime gourd, and about a pound of *Erythroxylum novogranatense* leaves, coca. She finally came up with a cotton bag of tobacco, some whole leaves, some cut, and a packet of papers. Taking the civilized route, she used the papers, rolling a cigarette and licking it closed.

By the time Travers returned, she was sitting on the

floor next to Juanio, blowing smoke rings around the chubby guy.

"You want some coffee?" he asked, offering the other Brazilian cure-all.

"*Por favor.*"

In a few minutes, he sat down next to her and handed her a steaming hot, sugary sweet *cafezinho.*

"Thanks."

He took the cigarette from her hand, and she watched as he took a long draw and blew the smoke out, wreathing the Brazilian bandit. "Come on, Juanio, *acorda.* Wake up."

Annie took a sip of coffee, inhaling the fragrant smoke and thinking how cozy it all would be, if it wasn't ninety-eight degrees with ninety-nine percent humidity, and he wasn't the single most disturbing man she'd ever met.

Half the problem, she decided, was the way he looked, a little too wild, a little too far over the edge, a little too beautiful to be the derelict she'd thought he was in Pancha's. Of course, the bigger half was about Vargas and the gems, and the snake thing, and that he hadn't denied a word of what she'd said about a shaman getting hold of him.

"Juanio," he said softly, coaxingly. "Come back so we can talk, amigo."

The half about him kissing her hardly bore thinking about. She'd been kissed, if not by a lot of people, at least enough to know Will Travers did it with skilled concentration and an intensity that could completely undermine a woman's moral fabric. She'd definitely been left a little frayed around the edges by the experience.

Frayed and curious. If that's what his kiss did to her, she wondered, letting her gaze drift to his mouth—what would the rest of it be like?

She remembered how he'd danced in Pancha's, and she remembered how it had felt to have his lips moving over hers, his mouth open, the taste of him, the gentle aggression that had kept asking for more, and delivering more every time she gave in. It had felt like sex, at least the sex of her fantasies, the sex no one ever seemed to have in real life.

"How are you feeling?" he asked, and her head jerked up, a blush streaking across her cheeks.

"Um ... fine." She could hardly tell him the truth, that he'd short-circuited her common sense, and she'd be damned if she didn't wonder if he could do it again.

"You've got a little color back," he said.

Right, she thought, feeling the warmth in her cheeks.

"So what's this with Vargas and the gems?" she asked. She didn't want to think about his mouth, or his kiss. For that matter, she didn't want to think about Vargas, either, but she'd better.

"A little business."

"What kind of business?"

He shrugged and took another long drag off the cigarette.

"I meant what I said back at the cantina, about Vargas being worse than Fat Eddie."

He blew the smoke out. "What makes you think so?"

"Fat Eddie likes being a honcho in Manaus. He likes pushing people around with his money. Even the head-shrinking thing is to make a big macho statement about what a tough character he is, about how people better not mess with him. But Vargas ..." Her voice trailed off.

Talking about Vargas was dangerous. She didn't want to stir up too much of what she'd put behind her.

"Vargas is what?" he asked, watching her more carefully than she liked.

"Unpredictable. You can't count on him going for the money. His idea of power is far more refined than Fat Eddie's. He likes mind games, and he's very good at them."

"Are you afraid of him?"

"I'd be a fool not to be, and so would you."

"Are you afraid of me?"

She should have seen that one coming, but she hadn't.

"No," she said after a moment's hesitation, giving him that much even if it was half a lie. "I'm not afraid of you. I figure we have at least one more day together on this damn boat, probably more, unless my luck takes a big swing to the good, and I would like to forge some kind of working relationship. You are Dr. William Sanchez Travers. Or were. I've read all your books, and we haven't shared so much as a single insight on Amazonian botany. All we seem to do is—"

"Run for our lives," he filled in for her, then took another drag off the cigarette and blew it over Juanio. "I've read your work, too. You were last published in the *Journal of Ethnobotany* two years ago."

Annie couldn't help herself, she was ridiculously pleased. "The article on beekeeping by the Barasana?"

He nodded, squinting at her through the smoke. "I had an entomologist on board just last week. She'd read it, too."

She? "Who?"

"Dr. Erica Grunstead, brought her down from São Gabriel. Do you know her?"

Did Annie know the lovely and brilliant Dr. Erica Grunstead?

"Um, yes. We've met a couple of times at RBC." A couple of times when Erica had proven over and over again that it was possible to be a Class A scientist, a Grade A field researcher, and a perfect lady at the same time. Annie had been frankly amazed at the woman's sophistication.

"She's a nice person."

"Very nice," Annie had to agree. The woman had treated her with all the kindness of a sister.

"Smart, too."

"Harvard, wasn't she?" Annie asked, though she knew perfectly well that Dr. Erica Grunstead indeed came from the same prestigious Harvard line of Amazonian research scientists as Dr. William Sanchez Travers.

"Three years behind me. I knew her in Cambridge."

"Oh." Annie was completely disgusted with what that little news item did to her.

"She hasn't changed much. Still real pretty. Knows how to use a comb. Doesn't know how to detonate a grenade."

He was baiting her. Annie knew it, and still rose to her own defense. "It's the humidity that makes my hair fluff out like this."

"Right." He laughed. The bastard laughed, and her cheeks burned. "Annie, we're going to have a hell of a lot more than one more day together on this damn boat. Barcelos was supposed to be the solution. It wasn't the problem."

"Barcelos was your problem," she pointed out. "I'm not the one being chased up the river by a couple of *garimpeiro* jewel thieves."

"No. You're the one with the piranha-toothed, machete-wielding psychotic on your trail."

Damn him. She was too tired to fence with words. "You should really let me win once in a while just to keep the game interesting."

"You can have the galley award," he conceded graciously. "Erica didn't cook, and you've done a real nice job with the meals."

She shot him a look that would have killed a lesser man, and ran into a grin that was pure, unadulterated mischief. It curved the corners of his mouth, lit the depths of his eyes, and did the most awful thing to her heart.

"Are you going to make a career out of teasing me?" she groused, trying to counteract the damned sense of longing his grin inspired.

"But it's true," he said, all innocence. "She couldn't boil water, or gut a fish, and not once, the whole week she was on my boat, did she make me want to back her up against a wall and kiss her until our eyes crossed."

Innocence should have been difficult to hold on to after a statement like that, but he managed without so much as breaking a sweat. Annie couldn't say the same for herself. The picture he'd put in her mind made her feel flushed all over. She wanted to tell him that he must be mistaken, because for the most part, men did not find her particularly attractive, especially after they got to know her.

But he wasn't most men, and he had no reason to be intimidated by her intelligence, or her degrees, or her wealth of experience tracking over a large section of the world's last unknown rain forest, a deed that set her outside the realm of most men's egos. And he certainly didn't have any reason to be intimidated by her reputation. His easily exceeded hers on all counts, the good, the bad, and the ugly, and would continue to so right up until she brought back the *Epidendrum luminosa*. Then all bets were off.

"I don't know why not. She's damned pretty." She shrugged, holding on to her nonchalance by a thread.

"And you are something else," he said, his smile fading. "Did you know your nose was crooked?"

"Yes," she said ascerbically.

"And when you smile, which you don't do very often, one of your eyes scrinches up more than the other?"

"Don't you have a life?"

"God, I used to, Annie." A sigh left him, and he took another long drag off the cigarette. "Up until about two days ago, I had a life I was working real hard to keep, but you have thrown a giant wrench into my plans. I've got to get rid of you, and I don't have a damned place to put you."

"Put me where I paid you to put me, or help me get my canoe and put me up on the Marauiá." She could make it to the Cauaburi on her own from there.

"Actually," he said, turning his attention to Juanio and giving him a shake. "I'm thinking about leaving you here."

"Here?" She didn't understand. They weren't anywhere. Then it dawned on her. "The hell you will."

"Nice island in the middle of the river. You've got enough firepower to blow half the state of Roraima to hell and back, if half the state of Roraima decides to come up the river—and I can return in a couple of weeks to pick you up and take you to the Serra da Neblina on the Venezuelan border. We'll go straight up the Marauiá and find your *Aganisia cyanea.*"

"I won't let you do it, Will," she warned him. "I won't." Being stranded on an island in the middle of the Rio Negro during her prime orchid-hunting weeks was out of the question, unacceptable, but she didn't believe for a second that he hadn't already made up his mind. Like her, he was running out of options.

"And how are you going to stop me, An—"

The last thought he had was that, damn, she could really move fast.

CHAPTER 14 ✐

IT WAS THE DEAD OF NIGHT WHEN Will awoke, the only sounds the flowing of the river and the hum of cicadas on the shore. He lay on the floor where she'd left him. No lantern was lit inside the cabin or anywhere on the boat. They were moving slowly through the water with Annie at the helm, piloting by the light of the moon, the engine throttled down, the sky above them a ribbon of darkness studded with stars.

Mutiny, he thought. That's what they called what she'd done. Mutiny. She'd put a pillow under his head, though, and that was sweet. He didn't hurt anywhere, and it took him a minute to remember exactly what she had done to him. She hadn't kicked him, or hit him. She'd grabbed him. Grabbed him on the side of his neck and checked him out like a library book.

He turned his head one way and then the other, making sure he still functioned and having a look around. There was no pain, no permanent damage—and no Juanio.

Now what in the hell had she done with the *garimpeiro*? Will wondered. Probably the same thing he'd been planning on doing. They seemed to think a lot alike. He just hoped she'd asked all the right questions before she'd gotten rid of him.

He carefully stretched his legs and arms, and again found no damage. Actually, he felt pretty good, pretty rested. It had been a hell of a last few days, with not much sleep to go around. His inadvertent nap might have been just the thing he needed.

Stretching himself out again, he folded his hands under his head and settled in to watch her. She was hell on a man. She was hell on him. Where he was going, she couldn't go. Where she wanted to go, he couldn't let her. And where he needed her to go was a place he couldn't get to from where he was.

Damn. The island had been his best idea, maybe his last idea.

"I think we're in love," he said, loud enough to make sure she heard him. "What do you think?"

She glanced over her shoulder. "I think we're in trouble. How do you feel?"

"Refreshed." He told her the truth and was heartened to see her relief. She hadn't wanted to hurt him. "So what do you call what you did to me?"

"Vulcan death grip," she said without batting an eyelash.

"Will you teach me?"

"Nope." She turned back to the helm and made an adjustment with the wheel. He felt the *Sucuri* respond.

"Is that what happened to the Woolly Monkey *garimpeiros*?"

"Mostly."

An ambiguous answer if he'd ever heard one, or maybe a warning that she had plenty of other tricks up her sleeve.

"With a Vulcan death grip on our side, we should be unbeatable."

"I doubt it," she said, tilting her head to look up through the window at the sky. A small tree limb slapped against the bulkhead, plastering the window with leaves, before snapping off.

She didn't budge, but Will leapt to his feet. "Whoa, Annie. You're way too close to shore."

He reached for the wheel, but she'd already killed the engine.

"Shh," she said. "Listen."

He cocked his head and soon enough heard what she wanted him to hear.

"Plane," he said.

"Look." She pointed out the window, at a small beam of light rising out of the trees on a bend in the river. "This is its third pass in the last hour."

The light quickly grew bigger, and Will realized it was a spotlight shining down on the river, sweeping along the shore, looking for something.

He didn't have a doubt that something was the *Sucuri*.

"What did you do with Juanio?"

"Well, I thought about dumping him overboard, but I didn't do it until we were just above Losas, so I'm not sure that counts. All he had to do was float down and hit the dock. I watched somebody pull him in."

Losas was a fishing camp north of Barcelos. Two or three boats were usually in residence, and others were always coming and going. It was exactly where Will had planned on dropping off the Brazilian.

"Did you question him first?"

"Wrung him out all the way down to his skivvies, took every salient fact he had in his head, and almost got enough information to fill a thimble."

"So you didn't learn anything." He couldn't keep the disappointment out of his voice. Luiz had been the one they should have dragged on board. Juanio had just been taking up space.

"Well, he did have one thing to say, just one, and he said it over and over and over, babbled it, actually. To be honest, whatever brain cells he had before he got on your boat were scared out of him the minute I opened that cabin door, and now he's running on empty. Or so I thought. He obviously had enough gumption left to tell somebody about us, somebody with a radio. I don't know what in the hell else they'd be looking for out here at three o'clock in the morning."

Will didn't, either.

"It's got to be Vargas," he said. "Fat Eddie only had one plane, and that was the one we left in pieces in Barcelos."

"That was Fat Eddie's plane?"

He nodded. "Luiz was his pilot."

"Does Fat Eddie know his organization is falling apart around him?" she asked, craning her head back to keep the plane in sight.

"He's got to be figuring it out by now. The power is shifting all along the river, and if Vargas has his way, it will all be coming to him. Guys like Fat Eddie are going to end up running numbers games on the streets."

"No way," she said. "Fat Eddie Mano has owned Manaus for twenty years. He isn't going to give it up without a fight."

"This from a woman who just stole a whole load of his guns."

She let out an unladylike snort. "He's got plenty more where those came from, and let's keep the record straight I paid good money for what I got."

"But to the wrong person."

She shrugged. "Illegal arms sales are a bitch to keep aboveboard."

A classic bit of waterfront philosophy, Will thought, refraining from an incredulous snort of his own, and just the sort of thing that kept her in trouble. "So what was this thing Juanio kept saying?"

She turned to face him, her eyes locking onto his, and he immediately realized she was far more tense than he'd thought, given her easy banter.

"He kept saying *noite do diabo, noite do diabo,* night of the devil. Or sometimes he'd get it a little twisted around, and it would come out *diabo noturno,* night devil, but those few words and that one burning concept pretty much encompassed his whole vocabulary and every brainwave he generated. *Noite do diabo.*"

Will swore softly under his breath. Maybe he didn't have as much time as he'd thought. Maybe Vargas was moving his plans forward faster than expected.

They waited a minute in silence as the plane passed them by and continued on down the river, its light sweeping the shoreline. When it was out of sight, he leaned around her and started the engine.

"So what's this *noite do diabo?*" she asked, stepping aside and letting him have the wheel.

"It's a superstition that's taken hold in the goldfields along the border. The *garimpeiros* have gotten it in their heads that there's going to be a Night of the Devil, a night when the devil comes down the river and destroys everything in his path, stealing souls and tearing up the rain forest. West of São Gabriel, people seem to think the demon will take the shape of a jaguar. East of São Gabriel, they say it's going to be an anaconda."

"An anaconda? Like the one I saw in here."

"No," he said. "No, not like that one. They're talking cosmic proportions, like the ancestral anaconda, the one that brought the Indians here in the beginning and gave them this place and all the gold. In some ways, the miners see it as a purging of their sins. They poison the rivers with mercury, bring malaria and disease, steal women, enslave the Indians and *caboclos* with debt servitude, and this will be the forest's retribution. You know the situation."

It was the other rape of the rain forest, the creation of hundreds of illegal mines in the Amazon Basin.

"Yes, but a Night of the Devil? That seems a bit big for a bunch of *garimpeiros* to come up with on their own."

"Well, it has another side. Anyone who survives will be rich beyond their wildest dreams, cleansed of all their sins."

"By the devil?" She sounded highly skeptical, with good reason. It was a stretch for anyone with an ounce of catechism under their belt.

"God and the devil share a lot of space down here." He turned the wheel, taking them back out into the current.

"So who's the devil? Vargas?"

"I think so."

"But Juanio thinks it's you."

One of his eyebrows arched. "Did he say that?"

She nodded. "On the dock at Barcelos. He said this was the devil's boat, and Luiz said without you the boat was just a boat."

"Ah, that's right," he remembered. "But then he went

on to talk about the true devil. I may get credit for being a minor demon, but I don't think I have the necessary reputation to get tagged as the true devil."

Annie tended to agree, even after what she'd seen in the cabin.

"I'm in trouble here, though, aren't I?"

"I think we established that fact the morning we left RBC."

"I'm not talking about Fat Eddie. I mean with you, with the tattoo, with the snake rising up out of this place when Juanio and I boarded without you."

He eased the *Sucuri* a little farther from shore, piloting around a downed tree.

"That wasn't for you, Annie. I can't say that I exactly understand what happened, but I know the warning was for Juanio. I won't hurt you, and I've been doing my best to make sure nobody else does, either, but the spot you're in seems to get tighter every time I turn around."

"What about your spot?"

"My spot hasn't changed that much. I half suspected somebody might try to get Eddie's cache, but they never would have found me in Barcelos or anywhere else if . . ."

"It hadn't been for me," she finished for him, when his voice trailed off.

He shrugged. "I don't need anybody's help to find trouble."

She seemed to accept his exoneration, her gaze drifting back to the river. She looked exhausted, and the fact made him feel guilty as hell. He remembered how soft she'd been to hold in the cantina, how she'd held on to him, her mouth hot and sweet, and she'd known about his tattoo then. Of course, she hadn't yet seen the *sucuri*.

Damn snake.

Moonlight and tiredness gave her a starker look, turning the warm blond of her hair to cool silver, drawing a tightness at the corners of her mouth, smudging the skin beneath her eyes.

"Why don't you get some sleep. I'll wake you when we get to the mission."

"Can't. Too scared," she said bluntly.

"Of me?" He should never have stopped kissing her, Juanio and Luiz be damned. Should never have let her board the *Sucuri* with Juanio, except she'd been safer on the boat than with Luiz—or so he'd thought before he'd known about her Vulcan death grip. She could have handled the *garimpeiro*, just like she'd handled the others.

"No. Of dreaming about the snake I saw when I opened the door, a green anaconda, upward to thirty feet or more and five hundred pounds, a real mother of a *Eunectes murinus*, huge, almost took up the whole damn cabin—definitely female, so it's not you."

There was a compliment in there somewhere, if he worked at it hard enough.

"It was pretty dark in here," he said. "Even an expert herpetologist would have needed a better look than you could have gotten to sex a snake, any kind of a snake."

She let out a weary laugh and dragged her hand back through her hair, shaking her head. "No. I recognized her. She's the snake from my dreams. She's been with me on the black-water rivers since I first stepped foot in the Vaupes three years ago. What I can't figure out is what she was doing on your boat while I was awake." She laughed again, tremulously. "God, I'm not sure I even want to know why she was on your boat."

Every now and then, something happened that made Will think he'd been in the Amazon for too long, way too long. It was an enormously big place, the river a thousand-headed hydra draining an area of almost three million square miles, and it was forest, endless forest, living and breathing, eating the equatorial light and turning it green—deep, lush, full of spirits and demons, who were often one and the same. Sorcery abounded, a place where invisible darts were secreted in the wrists of shamans who could send them flying through the dark to pierce an enemy's skin. A place where people were descended from jaguars, the proof in their blue tattoos and the palm spine whiskers arcing gracefully from above their upper lips. A place of sympathetic magic where there were no gods, only beings, some seen, some unseen, and man was not separate, but moved within the same stream of breath as every creature, every plant, every living thing in this world and the other. It was a fluid place, geographically and within the mind's consciousness.

He'd been lost in it, been found, and once been close to death, wrapped in the coils and held by the daggerlike teeth of a snake that was also the *sucuri* on his boat. He should have died. Instead, he'd killed the snake, Tutanji's anaconda, an act of survival he had yet to escape, and he had to wonder what in the hell the old shaman's spirit-serpent was doing in Annie Parrish's dreams. That's what made him think he'd been in the Amazon too long.

Three years ago, she'd entered the land of the black-water rivers and had her first anaconda dream. Three years ago, he'd killed a giant anaconda while journeying up another black-water river in the northwestern frontier of Brazil. Hell. He had been in the Amazon too long.

"Here," he said, removing the crystal on its cord from around his neck. "Wear this, and I promise you, you won't dream, at least not about snakes."

She looked over at him, surprised, and for a moment, he thought she would refuse. Then she took the necklace, and he helped her slip it over her head, the backs of his fingers grazing the silky strands of her hair, the jaguar teeth clinking softly against the clear chunk of quartz.

"Thanks," she said when it settled on her chest. "I . . . uh, know you aren't in a position to cast doubts on my sanity." How very generous of her, he thought, thoroughly put in his place. "But I know what I saw. I'm just not sure why I saw it, or if it was real or not. I have a friend who did his research down here, and Gerhardt always said that sometimes the metaphor isn't a metaphor at all in the Amazon."

"Anthropologist, right?"

"Yeah," she admitted with a look as if to say who else but a soft-science anthropologist would have come up with such a idea. "Gerhardt would say a giant snake looming up out of the dark and then disappearing might be exactly that and not a fear-induced hallucination imposed on a susceptible mind, and maybe he's right. Maybe science simply hasn't caught up to this place yet."

"Maybe," he agreed, because of course, science hadn't caught up to him in the last three years, either.

"That doesn't mean what I saw doesn't scare me."

"It just doesn't scare you off." He was beginning to figure her out.

"No," she said softly, fingering her shaman's crystal, her gaze slipping ever so artlessly to his mouth.

His reaction was swift and mysteriously profound, something deep inside him shifting, an emotion he couldn't name beyond surprise. He hadn't expected her to want a kiss, his kiss.

Without a word, he closed the distance between them

and pressed his mouth to her brow. He knew the comfort of a kiss, the reassurance to be found in a simple act of contact. Her hand came up to his waist, and he moved his mouth to her cheek, skirting the golden fan of her lashes with his lips, inhaling the lovely scent of her skin. Sliding his nose down the length of hers, he felt her soften even more deeply into his arms, and he wanted to say, Stay with me, Annie Parrish, open your mouth for me, make love with me.

But she wasn't just softening in his arms, she was falling asleep on her feet.

"Hold on," he said, releasing her long enough to unhook his hammock from the wall and string it across the cabin. "Sleep here tonight. Then if anything happens, I won't have to go looking for you."

It was a polite excuse to keep her close, and to keep her from having to ask. He was sure she didn't want to be alone in the aft cabin any more than he wanted her to be back there by herself.

Once she settled in, she drifted off to sleep almost immediately, an overly tousled, strung-out botanist curled up in a pool of moonlight with her arms wrapped around his pillow and her little black fanny pack snug around her waist.

It really was the only thing she owned that he hadn't gone through, and it wasn't where she kept her passport. He'd found all her papers in her green backpack.

He hesitated, but for no more than a few seconds, before he gave in to his common sense and reached for her pack. He couldn't afford for her to have secrets, any secrets. With a few deft moves, he unsnapped the pack and slipped it from around her waist. She didn't so much as sigh in her sleep.

Carrying it back to the helm, he adjusted the boat's course, before unzipping the top. Inside was another zippered bag, this one also black. He took it out and immediately realized there was a specimen jar inside. *Aganisia cyanea*, he figured, the blue orchid she was so intent on collecting again up on the Marauiá. Considering that she'd been gone a year, he didn't expect the flower to be in very good shape.

Neither did he expect it to glow—but the moment he unzipped the bag, light leaked out and bathed his hand.

Carefully, he lifted the jar out, and a sense of wonder slowly infused his senses. My God, he thought, turning the container over in his hand. No wonder she'd come back. No wonder she was so damned determined to stay.

The orchid inside the jar was not *Aganisia cyanea*. He didn't know what it was other than exquisite, a biological anomaly. Bioluminescence in and of itself was not so unusual, but the quality of light coming off the orchid was remarkable. It wasn't static, but vacillating in waves, creamily golden waves tinged with green. The petals were midnight-blue with a cream-colored frill, the sepals pure midnight-blue, elongate and twisting, the whole perianth dusted with gold flecks. He'd never seen anything like it.

No one ever had—except for Annie Parrish. She'd offered him money, told him he could set his own price to take her to Santa Maria, and she'd been right. She had a fortune's worth of orchid in her pack, if she could find more.

He glanced over at her, knowing now what had driven her to return, no matter what had happened in Yavareté.

She'd lied to him, though, and a wry smile curved his

mouth at the realization. Facing off with him in the
Barcelos cantina, thinking the plane was coming to take
her away and having nothing else to lose, she'd still lied
to him about what she was after.

He couldn't say he blamed her. At any other time in
his life, a botanical specimen of such stunning genetic
rarity would have demanded his full attention and
commitment—and caution. It was an unprecedented find.

She was good. He had to give her that, and she was
bloody single-minded, but orchid or no orchid, by the
time she finally got frightened enough to be scared off, he
was afraid Fat Eddie would already have her under his
knife with Corisco standing in line.

Anybody else would have bailed out in Manaus, or
after they'd seen Johnny Chang's head, or after seeing the
snake in the cabin.

Okay, he thought, remembering. She had tried to bail
out after the snake, and he hadn't let her, but hell,
Barcelos had not been the place to leave her. Still, nobody
else had walked the Vaupes or earned the damned nickname of Amazon Annie, and nobody else had a damned
Vulcan death grip.

Hell, he was scared, but he had to go up the Cauaburi.
He had to stop Vargas or the last three years and his deal
with Tutanji all meant nothing. He could not fail, not for
his own sake, not for anybody's—which still didn't tell
him what in the hell he was going to do with Annie
Parrish or what he was going to do about her amazing
orchid.

He turned his gaze back to the jar in his hand and
again felt a sense of wonder flow through him. The light
was magical, curiously mesmerizing, the pulsing brightness like a beacon.

Glancing up, he checked the boat's position, before allowing his attention to return to the orchid. The light moved in drifting waves along the edge of the petals, cresting on gold and falling off into troughs of deeper green, and the longer he watched, the more intrigued he became.

Hours and miles of river later, he carefully put the specimen jar back into her fanny pack, then stood for a long time staring out into the night, watching the river ebb and flow beneath a shimmering cast of moonlight, looking upward into the sky and tracking the course of the Milky Way across the depths of deep space, millions and billions of bright points of light layered into infinity.

Plants had always fascinated him, how they turned sunlight into food, the sheer, unbelievable variety of them, and their colors, from the most amazing shades of blues, reds, and yellows to everything in between and their thousands of shades of green. He'd spent his life studying plants, appreciating them and being in awe of their delicate complexity, from the giant *Sequoia sempervirens* of the Pacific Northwest to a single blade of grass in any backyard lawn. He'd collected plants, held them, dissected them, classified and contemplated them for hours on end, and he'd talked about them ad nauseum in lecture halls and during fieldwork. But never, not once in all his years of research, had he ever felt even the remotest possibility of a plant talking back—not until tonight.

CHAPTER 15 ✍

FERNANDO HAULED THE CHUBBY GAR-
impeiro into the courtyard by the scruff of his neck and
let him drop like a stone at Corisco's feet.

"The message from Losas," the hulking man said.
"And one from Manaus." He held out an envelope.

"Interesting," Corisco drawled, looking the man
over while taking another sip of his morning coffee. He
held out his other hand for the envelope, and Fernando
carefully laid it in his palm. A servant girl dressed in
yellow set a plate of fresh rolls on the table and gave a
slight curtsy before retreating back into the house. Four
soldiers guarded the perimeter of the patio—four ramrod-
straight, well-armed men standing beneath the lush palms
shading the breakfast table from the tropical sun. The
fountain bubbled and babbled in the background, helping
to disguise, if not drown out, the noise of the generators and
hydraulic pumps used in the mining pit down at the river's
edge.

Setting his coffee aside, Corisco tore open the envelope

and retrieved the paper from inside. He snapped it open, read it, and his mood instantly soured.

He'd heard the plane return from its nighttime sortie on the river. Two flights a day came in to the muddy hellhole of the camp, bringing in supplies, contraband, and a growing horde of deserters from the Brazilian army who came to Reino Novo for wages paid in gold—and messages, like the one from Losas lying at his feet, and the one inside the envelope from his man in Manaus saying Annie Parrish had disappeared.

He crumpled the piece of paper. He would put out a bounty on her, a huge bounty. Every *garimpeiro*, *caboclo*, rubber tapper, and Indian in the northwest frontier would be out looking for her—and they would bring her to him for gold.

"Fernando, do you still have the photographs you took in Yavareté?"

The man hesitated, an unusual occurrence worthy of a withering glance.

"Well? Do you?" he snapped.

"Yes, Major."

"Make up a wanted poster for the woman. Offer ten thousand *reais*. I want every settlement south to Manaus covered by nightfall."

"Yes, Major." The man turned to go.

"And Fernando?"

The giant stopped and glanced back. "Major?"

"Make sure it's her face you use on the poster."

The faintest hint of color washed into the man's face—anger, not embarrassment, Corisco knew—before Fernando nodded and left.

His morning thoroughly ruined, Corisco went back to drinking his coffee. She'd come back to Brazil almost exactly at the time of his sacrifice, and by all the devils he could bring to bear, that's exactly what she was going to be.

Within the last year, the mining operation had boomed, with the pits around Reino Novo producing two kilos a day. The camp boasted three cantinas, two whorehouses, and at least one dead body a week for which he took no responsibility. Gold miners were a volatile group and quite capable of killing each other without any help from him. The deaths he did claim at least had a purpose, as the gold he took from the mines had a purpose.

The *garimpeiro* groaned. Corisco used his foot to push the man over onto his back, and his interest was instantly piqued. He never forgot a face, and he knew this one.

"Juanio," he said. "It's good to see you again."

The man opened his eyes, and the color drained from his face.

"M-Major V-Vargas," he stuttered, then crossed himself, his lips moving frantically in a silent prayer.

"Juanio, Juanio," he implored, shaking his head. "Tell me you are not praying to God. God has no place here in the mines ... ah, but you're not a miner anymore, are you? No, the last I heard, you and Luiz were working as *jagunços* for *Senhor* Eduardo in Manaus. He is a friend of mine, did you know?"

A dead friend, if the fat man's cache of gemstones did not arrive as promised. Fat Eddie Mano was an abomination, a gross distortion of a human being who truly offended Corisco's refined sensibilities, but he did have his uses—or rather he had. Soon there would be only one power on the river, and all the petty bosses like Fat Eddie would find themselves cut out of the trade routes in illegal goods.

Juanio shook his head, his ill-cut mop of coal-black hair flying.

"As a matter of fact, he's on his way here to check on a shipment he's sent, a shipment on the boat that dropped you off at Losas."

If possible, the man paled even further.

"I find it very interesting, Juanio, that you were on this boat with my diamonds and emeralds. *Senhor* Eduardo is also very interested, and very interested in what happened to his plane." Apoplectic, actually. Corisco only feared the fat man might explode before he himself had a chance to make an example out of him.

"It—it was Luiz, Major Vargas." The man struggled to his knees, still trembling, and gave a pitiful imitation of a salute. "Luiz stole the plane. He made me get on the devil boat. I begged him not to make me. It was awful, just as the stories say. The snake, she was . . . was . . ."

"Was?" he prompted.

"Hungry."

Corisco nodded. He'd heard the stories about Will Travers and his boat and the vision snake that guarded it—a drunken gringo's conceit, if he'd ever heard one. At one time, the botanist had been an interesting potential adversary, but a year lost in the rain forest had robbed him of his senses. Corisco knew Fat Eddie derived a sort of perverse pleasure out of using the once famous derelict as a courier, but in this instance, the fat man had erred—possibly fatally, if the gems didn't arrive at Reino Novo.

"What were you supposed to do on the devil boat?" he asked. "Not steal my gems, I hope."

There was nothing deceptive about Juanio's blank gaze. The man was completely overwhelmed by the complexity of the answer required to save himself. The truth, which Corisco already knew, was easier to come by, but spelled certain doom, whereas a lie took more imagination than he could muster.

Corisco let him struggle for a solid minute, before he relented.

"And where is Luiz, my old *piloto,* do you think?" he asked.

"Barcelos," Juanio was quick to answer.

A game answer, but woefully incorrect.

Corisco snapped his fingers and heard a cart start rolling into the courtyard behind him. From the look on Juanio's face, he knew exactly when the little man recognized his compatriot. Luiz had been bound and gagged and caged and now awaited what was surely going to be a regrettable fate.

"It was the woman," Juanio said, thinking faster than Corisco would have thought possible. "I went on the boat to be with Travers's woman. Luiz, he wanted the *esmeraldas,* the *diamantes,* but me, I only wanted to be with the woman, the little blond *garota.* She was skinny, *Senhor* Major, so skinny and mean, but I thought I would try her."

"Woman?" The pilot who had picked up Juanio in Losas hadn't heard anyone mention a woman. "What woman?"

"The one with all the questions and the big gun she kept poking in my face, the little, skinny, mean one with her hair all short and wild on her head. She shoved me off the boat above Losas, and I had to swim for the dock. It is a miracle I am alive today, *Senhor* Major, a miracle."

Corisco couldn't have agreed more or cared less, but Juanio had given him pause.

"Do you know the name of this woman you would have tried?"

"She didn't have a name," Juanio said with conviction. "She was just a *puta* from Barcelos."

Ah, yes, Corisco wanted to say. Barcelos is full of blond-haired, gun-toting whores with the *bolas* to push a man overboard. Juanio was an idiot and would not be missed. As for the woman, he wouldn't describe Annie Parrish as either skinny or mean, but he had an aesthete's appreciation for slender curves and what intelligence did for a woman's mien. Little blond *garota* with a big gun and lots of questions was dead-on, though, and Annie Parrish didn't lack for courage—which left him with the intriguing thought that possibly, through some odd coincidence of timing and perhaps an old professional association, she might be on Will Travers's boat with Fat Eddie's cache of emeralds and diamonds, instead of on the RBC launch he'd been told she was taking to Santa Maria.

How his man in Manaus had missed that piece of information made him wonder about the reliability of his own network of spies and informants, and once more brought home the truth that good help was damn hard to find in the middle of nowhere.

He sat back in his chair and snapped his fingers for more coffee. The *Sucuri,* as Travers's boat was known, had been impossible to find in the dark, though Corisco's pilot had made half a dozen passes on the river above Losas. His suggestion to Fat Eddie, when he'd tracked him down by radio in Santo Antonio, was that he get back on the river himself and find the gems, before someone else tried to steal them. The fat man had responded with all the fawning enthusiasm of a bought whore, but he would do it. He didn't dare not.

It was interesting that Fat Eddie hadn't mentioned a woman being on the boat, Corisco thought. Either he hadn't known, which wasn't good. Or he'd known and deliberately withheld the information, which was far worse—which made Corisco wonder, not for the first time, what Fat Eddie had been doing in Santo Antonio. The fat man himself had been vaguely jovial about his little river romp. Too jovial and too vague for someone who seldom left his lair in the Praça de Matriz.

Santa Maria, Corisco decided. She would stop at the mission, regardless of where else she was going, and if Fat Eddie was quick, he might be able to catch her and the gems there tonight.

A rare smile curved a corner of his mouth. Annie Parrish and the gems in one fell swoop. The fates, indeed, were on his side.

Sadly, the same could not be said for Juanio.

"Fernando," Corisco called out, and the huge man appeared. "Take them both to *El Mestre* and put them in the cages with the others. How many *cordeiros* will that give us?"

"Ninety-one." Fernando was always succinct. "A fair mix of Indians and *caboclos*."

Ninety-one sacrificial lambs to be offered up to the devil himself, more than enough to get the Brazilian media's attention. He only needed nine more to make an even hundred. Annie Parrish would definitely be one.

Skinny little *garota*. Juanio couldn't have been more wrong. She was like a bird-of-paradise with her white-blond hair and her green-gold eyes, her soft, pink skin and her surprisingly lush mouth.

He hadn't kissed her. He'd wanted her begging for mercy, before he kissed her, and the woman had not begged, for mercy or anything else. This time, he would bend the rules.

If she did come with Will Travers on his boat, Corisco would take the drunken ex-scientist as one of his *cordeiros*. Having two *norte-americanos* die in his jungle glade might garner him international attention. Others had killed thousands in the Amazon, the rubber barons being the worst, but no one had ever killed a hundred in a single night, and no one had offered their blood to the devil, a quasi-religious touch guaranteed to strike an extra chord of terror in those Corisco would bring to heel. He already had half of the northwestern frontier dreading his *noite do diabo*, his Night of the Devil, and he had his devil—his gaze flicked up to the house, to where the glass cage lay within the confines of his office.

Everything was falling into place, and so would Annie Parrish. The altar he'd built for the sacrifice, *El Mestre*, was nearly complete, needing only Fat Eddie's emeralds and diamonds to finish the eyes—*Los Olhos de Satanás*, the Eyes of Satan. When those eyes gazed upon the good *doutora*, he would be triumphant.

CHAPTER 16 ⚓

She knew. Even before she came fully awake, Annie knew her fanny pack was missing. The hand that automatically went to her waist only confirmed the truth: Will Travers had taken her orchid.

But he hadn't taken it very far. Halfway out of the hammock, she spied her pack hanging from a hook above the stove. She reached up and slipped it off. A quick check inside proved he'd taken nothing, except her exclusive knowledge that the flower even existed.

Or nearly exclusive knowledge, she amended, turning the specimen jar over in her hand. She'd showed it to Mad Jack in Belize, and Corisco Vargas knew about the *Epidendrum luminosa*. The bastard had stolen one from her in Yavareté.

With a soft curse, she set the orchid aside and made quick work out of her morning ablutions. Her green pack was lying next to the galley's small sink, with everything she needed inside except a comb. She did the best she could with her fingers and poured herself a cup of coffee, before picking up the orchid jar again. She couldn't help but wonder what Will had thought when he'd first seen her prize. Mad Jack had been impressed, damned impressed. He'd also told her it wasn't worth dying for, and if he got so much as an inkling as to where she'd gone after leaving his place, he would have her butt in a sling so fast it would make her head swim.

She turned the jar to better catch the light. When she'd been released from Yavareté, Gabriela had helped her gather up all her botanical specimens, but the orchids hadn't been among them. More than her physical condition, the loss had come close to sinking her into despair. Then, just before she'd boarded the plane, Vargas had pressed a wrapped package into her hand. Why he'd given it to her, she still didn't know, but she'd known exactly what it was, and hadn't let it out of her sight since.

If she could find more blooming orchids, she would let the one he'd taken go. She'd promised herself as much in Wyoming, that she wasn't coming back to Brazil with a vendetta in mind.

But if she couldn't find another one—and the odds were against her—she might have to reconsider her plan to avoid Vargas at any cost.

The muscles in her back twitched, an involuntary and unnecessary reminder of Yavareté, and her mouth tightened. In Wyoming, everything had seemed so clear. In Wyoming, all she'd wanted was more orchids: whole flowers, cuttings, dried specimens, roots, stems, leaves, seeds, everything. On the Rio Negro, nothing was clear, least of all what she wanted.

She thought back to the previous night, her hand going to the large chunk of rock crystal hanging around her neck. The jaguar fangs on either side curved against her fingers.

He'd kissed her. Twice. And everything Corisco Vargas had beaten out of her was coming back. She'd sworn off men, so help her God, but Will Travers kissed like an angel, his mouth so hot, and sweet, and tender. He made her feel like a woman, and that was the one thing she couldn't afford. Because, quite simply, it wasn't safe to be a woman in the Amazon. She'd known it long before Vargas had spent three days proving it to her.

Swearing softly to herself, she slipped her hand to the back of her neck and turned her head to stretch out a kink. She ached from all the tension she was holding in her body. Nothing was going the way she'd planned, not a single damn thing.

"It's incredible," Will said behind her.

Once again, she hadn't heard him approach. She lowered her hand before turning to find him standing in the cabin's doorway, the afternoon light streaming in behind him. She'd slept most of the day away.

"I know." She didn't feel guilty for having lied to him. She was beyond guilt—but not suspicion, not after he'd seen her orchid. Wearing low-slung black shorts, a half-buttoned white shirt, and a pair of old flip-flops, he was obviously dressed to go somewhere, and they were in the middle of nowhere.

"Did you dream?"

"No," she said, surprised to realize she hadn't. She would have expected at least Johnny Chang's severed head to have haunted her sleep. "Thanks. I guess your crystal works." It was a small concession to make after everything they'd been through—two close calls, two escapes, and those two kisses, one sweetly hot, the other surprisingly tender.

She hadn't had much tenderness in her life, and she would not have suspected that Will Travers would turn out to be a source. It was disconcerting, to have breached that small barrier with him.

"Actually, I think the jaguar teeth are what holds nightmares at bay." His face was in shadow, unreadable, but the tone of his voice was oddly flat.

"And why's that?"

"Because the night I cut them out of the big cat's skull was the night I quit having mine," he said, moving out of the doorway, toward the stove and the pot of coffee.

"You killed a jaguar?" Her eyebrows went up. "This jaguar?" Her hand went to the necklace, her fingers curling around the huge teeth. It was hard to believe an educated scientist would come down to the Amazon and kill an endangered species to cut it up for talismans. They would be drummed out of every respectable—She stopped right there. The words "Will Travers" and "respectable" hadn't been mentioned in the same breath for three years.

He turned to face her, a steaming cup of coffee in hand.

"Ran him down, cut out his heart, and drank his blood." He took a sip of coffee—and Annie could only stare.

He was serious. He'd done it. He'd drunk jaguar blood, hot and fresh, right out of the cat's body.

"Are you trying to scare me?"

"Yes." He was unequivocal.

"Why?"

"We're about an hour and a half out of Santa Maria,

partway up the Marauiá. There's a plane at the mission. It might be somebody who can get you out of here."

"And you think if you can prove to me that you're practically crazy, I'll be happy to turn tail and run?" No wonder he was all dressed up.

"Yes." He took another sip of coffee, his gaze un-flinching.

She returned the favor, looking him over and trying like hell to find some resemblance to the man on the book jackets.

There was damn little. The photograph had been meant to convey his authority and his scholarship, and he'd pretty much lost both of those. His most noticeable aspects now were physical—the lean dynamics of his body, the clarity of his dark-eyed gaze, which was too often set off by the sardonic arch of one of his eyebrows. He'd lost his expensive, razor-cut hairstyle years ago. Long and silkily disheveled, his hair was purely pagan now, the top layer bleached even more by the sun, the layer beneath richly dark and feathered down the length of his neck.

And he had those tattoos on his back. They sure as hell hadn't been there in his Harvard days.

Maybe he was right. Maybe she'd be the crazy one, if she went on.

God help her. To have come all this way for nothing.

She rubbed the back of her neck again, turning her attention out the window.

"You saw the orchid. You know what I'm after—or have you decided to try for it yourself?"

"Sure, I want it," he admitted, "but I'm not going to take it away from you, Annie. I just figure you've got a better chance of finding it if you're alive."

"It could be one of Vargas's planes," she said, believing him for now.

"Could be," he conceded. "He's got a network of spies running the length of the Rio Negro. I thought I'd go in, check it out. If it's missionaries or a cargo run, I'll get you a seat on it."

"Going where?"

"Bogotá or bust. You've got to be out of the country, not just off the river."

The rain started again, a soft wash of it dappling the surface of the water and streaking the windows around the helm. On the shore, two caimans slipped into the water, *jacarés*. The largest was near ten feet, big by normal standards, but still far smaller than one of the reported monster caimans of the Marauiá.

"Missionaries and cargo flights don't normally leave Santa Maria for Bogotá, and I don't have enough money to convince anybody to do otherwise." She looked back over her shoulder at him.

"We'll let this one be on Fat Eddie," he said, pulling the bag of gems out of his pants pocket and hefting it in his hand.

"You're going to a lot of trouble to get rid of me." And she wasn't going to ask why. She had a feeling the answer wasn't quite as simple as it had been before Barcelos.

What he said next proved her right.

With his dark eyes narrowed at her, he asked the million-dollar question. "Where in Wyoming are you from?"

She let her gaze slide away. William Sanchez Travers and Amazon Annie were not a match. It was impossible, and she'd be damned if she would let herself think otherwise.

"Laramie. But if you get out of here alive, don't come looking for me. I don't think I could survive the wait, if I thought you were coming."

"You don't have much faith in me, do you?"

"No jaguar gave you the scars on your chest." A jaguar who had gotten its teeth into him that deep would have taken off his shoulder.

"No, it wasn't the jaguar," he said. When he didn't offer more, she just waited.

His gaze didn't waver from hers, not for a second—and suddenly she knew. A cold, disbelieving dread washed down the length of her body.

"*Sucuri.*" She barely breathed the word.

"I was camped up on the Cauaburi the night it happened," he said, "and nothing has been the same since."

The snake had been huge, as big as the snake in her dreams, as big as the one in his cabin.

"Are all the rumors true?"

"Mostly." He nodded. "Except for the one about having my head shrunk, but Fat Eddie is going to do his best to change that."

"The *caapi*?"

"Drank my share and then some," he admitted. "Wouldn't recommend it to anyone. It's not a recreational high, but you'll learn things you can't learn any other way."

"Things about plants?" She couldn't quite keep the interest out of her voice. The orchid had proven to her that there was more to learn in botany than she'd once ever dreamed possible.

"Yes." His voice remained perfectly neutral. "And things about fear and snakes and death, and your own terrifying insignificance that will forever change the way you look at the world. I was killed once by a jaguar in the Otherworld, a golden cat with black spots, and after I died, my spirit rose up as the *sucuri* and killed him."

There it was, the hoodoo, voodoo shamanistic sorcery she'd spent her career avoiding. Not that any shamans had offered to share the Otherworld with her, or given her a chance to have her skull crushed or her neck snapped in a vision dream starring *Panthera onca*. Woman weren't allowed to drink the *yagé* made from the *Banisteriopsis caapi* vine, the vine of the soul, the sky rope that connected heaven and earth and revealed the secrets of the forest.

"Must have been one hell of a fight." She gave him that much.

"Very real, very desperate, very terrifying," he said, and she believed him. *Banisteriopsis caapi* was a powerful hallucinogen. That much was undeniable scientific fact.

"But in this world, you killed the jaguar." That was the true reality, the world she lived in.

"And cut out his incisors to make a charm. That doesn't make me much of a scientist anymore, does it." It was a statement of fact, not repentance, and he finished it off by taking another sip of his coffee.

"What about the *sucuri* on the Cauaburi, the anaconda? Did you kill it, too?"

"Cut it open with my bush knife, but don't ask me how. I nearly drowned in the blood. I did pass out, and when I came to, it was to the smell of roasting meat, the sound of an old man chanting, and pain. Pain everywhere, inside and out."

"The old man saved you?"

He let out a short laugh and dragged his hand back through his hair, his first sign of emotion while telling his whole amazing story. "No." He shook his head and laughed again, a dry, disparaging sound. "Tutanji didn't save me. He sicced that snake on me, and after it cracked two of my ribs and nearly asphyxiated me, he spent the rest of the night putting a tattoo on my back."

"Why?"

"To make me into what he needed, a weapon to use against his enemies."

Annie's dread deepened. "Have you killed for him?"

"Not yet. But it's starting to look like an inevitability."

"Vargas." She said it without thinking.

He nodded. "Your timing is awful, Annie. You've shown up at the end. If you were just a botanist doing research on peach palms at Santa Maria, I could take you there, and you would be well out of it. Very few people in the rest of Brazil are ever going to know what happens up on the Cauaburi, and by the time *Carnaval* hits Rio, it will all be over, one way or the other."

"But I'm not just a botanist," she said.

"No. You're not. You're trouble, the most amazing amount of trouble I've ever seen."

This from a man who'd been bitten by a giant anaconda? And lived to tell the tale? Annie was pretty sure she'd just been insulted.

"I think you've got bigger problems than me."

"Probably, but right now it doesn't feel like it."

She looked back out the window. Bogotá.

If she left, the dream was over. Vargas would win. But the price of staying could very well be her life.

Her fingers tightened around the small jar in her hand. She could feel the heat coming off the orchid. It was ever so slight, but it was there, a faint bit of warming from the miraculous light emanating from the petals. It was to have been her chance for glory and world renown: Annie Parrish, Queen of the Tropics, discoverer of the *Epidendrum luminosa.*

It was to have been her redemption. Why else would she have spent most of her adult life alone in the wilderness of South America, if not to finally come home with a prize?

Home. The word went through her mind shadowed by an old ache. She had no home. She hadn't had one since her mother had walked out on her when she'd been five years old, walked out and never looked back.

She dropped her face into her hand and swore softly. Now was not the time to be hashing over old emotional baggage, not when she was literally up the creek without a paddle.

She lifted her gaze to the jar in her hand. As always, the flower inside filled her with wonder. It wasn't just light coming off the orchid. It was waves of light, creamily golden light tinged with a border of green, and within its vacillating luminescence was a message. She knew it as much by scientific observation as by intuition. She just hadn't been able to crack the code. She'd spent her year of exile studying all forms of bioluminescence, and the orchid was different. It didn't fit the norms. The only thing she'd ever seen that even came close to it wasn't biologically luminescent at all.

It was the aurora borealis, those far northern lights that draped the sky above the frozen lands at the top of the world. And here was its sister, locked in the steaming jungle of the equatorial tropics, the orchid's long, midnight-blue sepals twisting in a delicate Art Nouveau spiral, the cream-colored frill spilling off the edges of lushly dark petals flecked with gold.

"You can come back in a year," he said next to her. "I have relatives in Venezuela. Fly into Caracas, and I'll bring you in over the mountains and down to the Marauiá."

"No," she said on a sigh, rubbing a hand across her forehead. "I lied about that, too. I found the orchid on the Cauaburi, near the place Vargas calls Reino Novo, not on the Marauiá." She put the orchid jar back in her fanny pack and zipped it up.

He was silent for a long moment. She could just imagine what he was thinking, but all he said when he finally spoke was, "All the more reason for you to leave now. There's nothing but danger waiting in Reino Novo. When you come back, the Brazilian government doesn't have to know where you are or what you're doing. If you find what you're looking for, I've still got legal status as a researcher for RBC. We can collect and ship anything you want and be in compliance with the law as long as Gabriela and the Brazilians get their share."

It was a long shot, a very long shot, that his plan would work, and she could get back into the country undetected, find the orchid, and get back out with everything she needed, while he funneled specimens through RBC. But maybe it was a better plan than going up against Vargas and his Night of the Devil, and all these damn snakes that seemed to be everywhere, and Fat Eddie Mano with his piranha teeth and shrunken-head plan.

"And what do you get out of all this?" she asked, slanting him a long look.

He laughed, a low chuckle. "If I'm still alive this time next year to bring you in over the border, I'll call it good. Don't worry, if I was going to ask you for something, it wouldn't be your orchid."

Typically, he made it damn hard to hold his gaze, and she looked away.

"Okay," she reluctantly conceded. "If you can buy me a place on that plane, I'll go. You can have the guns to give back to Fat Eddie, maybe get him off your back."

The minute the words were out of her mouth, a knot formed in the pit of her stomach, as if she'd just made a huge mistake.

"Wait," she said quickly. "Wait just a minute. Don't ... don't give Fat Eddie both Galils. Keep one for yourself. Tell him I sold it in Barcelos or something." That's what she needed to say—protect yourself.

"You want me to keep one of the Israeli rifles?" The look he gave her was slightly confused.

"Yes." She was adamant now. "They're the best money can buy. Accurate, reliable. If you want, we can get one down, and I'll show you how it works. You'll want to keep at least fifty rounds of ammo, and maybe a couple of grenades, and—"

Will let a grin slowly spread across his face as he settled back against the counter and let her ramble on, extolling the virtues of her arsenal and how he could use it to save his ass. She was amazing.

"Everybody worth their salt in Colombia is using the Galil now. You won't have any trouble getting more ammunition. The dynamite is fairly lightweight for the amount of punch you get, and it's easy to fit a stick or two in a pack. You might—"

"Annie," he finally interrupted her, setting his coffee aside and pushing off the counter. "That's about the sweetest thing anybody has ever said to me."

"Sweet?" Now she was the one who looked confused. "We're talking ordnance."

"You don't have to worry. I can take care of myself."

"Bullshit, Will," she was quick to protest, her brow furrowing and her hands going to her hips. "I put you down with a move you've never even heard of. I don't care how long you were out there in the jungle chasing down jaguars and anacondas with your bush knife; these are men you're going up against now. Bad men. Very bad men, and you . . . you're a *botanist,* a plant guy with a snake tattoo and a magic necklace, and they are all going to have guns and—"

"Annie, Annie." He moved in closer, his hand coming up to capture her chin. She went perfectly still, though her expression remained mutinous. "I've been running contraband for Fat Eddie for over a year now. Believe me, I know these guys a hell of a lot better than I ever wanted to know them."

"But you haven't met Vargas, have you?" Her voice was soft, intent, and edged with a type of fear she hadn't shown even with the snake.

"No. That's what this trip is all about. Fat Eddie finally trusting me enough to deliver straight to Vargas." She was a mess, her hair flying every which direction from a night in his hammock, her clothes so rumpled she looked like a walking laundry bag, but her skin was soft and flushed from sleep, and her eyes were flashing with sparks of green and gold, and he wanted to kiss her more than anything else in the world.

"Do you know what the gems are for?" she demanded.

"I think so, yes."

"I think I do, too, and I think you should tell this Tutanji that you've changed your mind about working for him."

He could have told her he'd tried doing that about a thousand times those first few weeks with the Dakú. It hadn't worked then, and it sure as hell wasn't going to work now. He was in too deep.

"I don't exactly work for him, Annie," he said, releasing her chin with a reluctant shrug. "I belong to him. I'm his apprentice."

She looked perfectly nonplussed. "A shaman's apprentice? Like the sorcerer's apprentice in the Disney movie?"

"No." He shook his head. "More like *Faust*."

Her face fell. "The guy who sold his soul to the devil for knowledge," she said flatly, pretty much summing up the bargain he'd made with the Dakú medicine man.

"Yeah. That guy."

She stared at him for a moment, then made a strangled sound and buried her face in her hands. At first he thought she was stifling sobs, but when he listened, he heard differently. She was swearing a blue streak in two languages, cussing him out and calling him every name in the book.

He didn't blame her. From her perspective, the price he was paying must look kind of high.

"So what do you think the gems are for?" he asked during the first lull in her *sotto voce* diatribe.

She looked up and her glasses were skewed, the lenses so spotted with fingerprints, he doubted if she could see much past her nose. Without asking, he slipped them off her face and started polishing them, blowing on the lenses and rubbing the glass with his shirttail.

"All I think is that you are crazy, really crazy. You've convinced me. Congratulations."

"Come on, Annie," he chided her. "Give."

After a moment in which she practically seethed with silent exasperation, hopefully getting it out of her system, she told him what he wanted to know.

"Vargas is building something in the jungle west of Reino Novo."

"Something?"

"I don't know what. I just caught a glimpse of it before the monkey fell on me, but it made me think those virgin-altar stories might not be all hearsay. There was gold on it, whatever it was, lots of gold. I could see it glinting in the sunlight, and I figure anybody who's willing to squander that much gold on some edifice in the middle of nowhere might also want diamonds and emeralds on it, but I'll be damned if I can figure out what in the hell *you're* doing going in there after him." Her voice started rising on the last few words and kept going up. "I'll be damned if I can figure out what this shaman Tutanji could know that's worth your life, and I'll be *damned* if—"

"No." He stopped her with the simple expediency of capturing her face in both his hands, letting her glasses dangle from between his fingers. "No, Annie," he said, adamant himself now. "You won't be damned. That's the whole point of the plane."

"If it's not Vargas's," she grouched, still trying to make her point. "*And* if you can buy the pilot off. *And* if—"

"Sempre tem jeito," he insisted, interrupting her tirade. There's always a way. It was the national mantra of Brazil.

" *'Ta louco,"* she told him. You're crazy.

"Maybe, but I'm going to get you on that plane, and you're going home to Wyoming, and when I'm finished with Vargas—"

"What if Vargas finishes with you first?" she demanded to know.

It was a legitimate question with a lot of unpleasant answers—none of which he wanted to dwell on.

"Then I'm going to wish I'd had time to make love with you." And that was the truth, a truth she apparently wasn't ready to handle.

Color washed into her cheeks—and there he was, holding a blushing Amazon Annie and wanting nothing more than to kiss her senseless.

"Time has nothing to do with it," she said. "I don't ... I just don't."

Given how she'd kissed him, that was one of her more interesting statements.

"You will." He didn't have a doubt. "With me." If he lived past Reino Novo.

"You're awfully sure of yourself," she reproached him, an accusation ameliorated by her downcast gaze and her all too obvious doubts.

"No. I'm sure of you," he said, sliding his thumb across her mouth, loving its silky delicacy, the petal softness of her lips.

"Will," she said, her gaze finally rising, her voice softly vexed. "This solves nothing. You ... I ... we can't ..."

"We can," he whispered, then lowered his mouth to hers. Her response was instant, and instantly gratifying, proving him right. Her lips parted on a soft groan, her hands coming up to his waist and bunching up his shirt before slipping underneath and sliding across his skin. It was heaven, having her hands on him, having her mouth hot and sweet beneath his. There was no resistance in her, only a wondrous giving way.

He opened his mouth wider, capturing her deeper and pressing himself against her. She was so unexpectedly, so damnably alluring, and he wanted to kiss her endlessly.

Annie arched up on tiptoe, irresistibly drawn by the lazy, pleasure-inducing forays of his tongue into her mouth. He tasted so good, his kiss as boldly lewd as his dancing in Pancha's. Again and again, he filled her, slowly, deliberately, making an aching heat rise in her belly, the same heat she felt hardening his body. He was aroused, his kiss meant to entice and please and arouse her, and the knowledge acted like a drug on her common sense. Smoothing her hand all the way up his chest, she tunneled it into his hair, feeling the long, silky strands slide through her fingers, feeling the soft edges of feathers drift across her skin. He was seduction incarnate, the taste and feel of him, all sleek muscle and leashed power where her other hand lay low on his abdomen, and despite what she'd said, she wanted to be closer, so much closer—and that was the danger.

Damn, she told herself when his hand brushed the underside of her breast and she felt everything inside her melt and slowly curl into a pool of desire centered between her legs. *Damn. Damn. Damn.*

One more minute and there wouldn't be any accounting for what might happen.

Will was lost, in over his head—way over, his senses reeling. She was ready to come apart for him. He felt it in the soft giving way of her body, in the way she was touching him, and he was tempted, so tempted to take her. The only thing that kept him from pushing her shirt up and her pants down was the plane in Santa Maria. It wouldn't do him a damn bit of good to make love to her and then not be able to save her. In fact, he couldn't think of anything that would make him feel worse.

"Annie," he murmured, sliding his mouth off hers and kissing her cheek, forcing himself to slow everything down. "Annie, I have to leave, or we're going to be here all night long, and you're going to miss that plane."

"The plane," she whispered, her eyes still closed, her breath coming in soft gasps that made him even harder than he'd already been.

He kissed her mouth again. "The plane. I'll be back around sunset."

"No." Her eyes drifted open and slowly refocused. "No, I've ... uh ... reconsidered. I think I better stay." She retreated an inch, just enough to break contact, her fingers sliding out of his hair, her breasts no longer pressed up against his chest.

Somehow, as much as he would have liked to tell himself otherwise, Will didn't think it was his kiss that had changed her mind. It should have been. The kiss was changing his mind about a lot of things. But a sneaking suspicion told him she had something else in mind.

"Is it the orchid?" he asked straight-out, knowing her too well to fool himself or sop his ego. "Or Vargas?"

She at least had the courtesy to look embarrassed. "I like you, Will, maybe too much. But I haven't made it a habit to organize my life around a man, or to take orders from one."

She liked him.

Will actually felt his jaw clench, and he had to work damn hard not to take her words as a challenge. She liked him. After that kiss, she had the audacity to say she *liked* him?

"Well, Annie," he said, carefully controlling his voice to keep from sounding as if he were biting off bullets. "I like you, too. Way too damn much. But you're still getting on that plane, if I can get you a seat on it, and with over a hundred rough-cut diamonds and emeralds in my pocket, I can pretty much buy everything in Santa Maria, including whoever is piloting that plane. So get your bags packed. I'll be back in four hours."

His point made, he turned on his heel and walked out of the cabin. Amazon Annie be damned. She could do whatever the hell she wanted in Wyoming, but tonight, on the Rio Negro, she was his to do with as he pleased, and he pleased to put her on that damned plane and get her off his damned river.

CHAPTER 17 ✍

ANNIE WAITED UNTIL HE'D PUSHED off in his canoe, before she dared admit anything, even to herself. She'd had a moment of insanity, that was all, just a moment when he'd had her running scared, but his kiss had kicked in her natural instincts—not just her little-used, rusty ones, but her good, old, reliable natural ones, which were to win, to win that damned orchid and drag it out of the deep, dark forest into the light of day and make its mysteries hers.

Months ago in Laramie, she'd known the dangers she would face, and nothing had changed. Not even the addition of Fat Eddie was enough to skew her odds of survival. They had always been slim, but she'd been living on slim odds since the day she'd first stepped foot in the Rio Vaupes, and living on the edge of those odds is what had brought her everything she'd ever dreamed of in botany—an enviable reputation as one of the best, one of the very best, naturalists in South America, and a discovery to cement her place in history.

It was the kissing that messed her up, and where all that kissing was bound to lead. Sex was a sure trip to trouble. Three days spent chained to a jail cell wall in Yavareté, the last one stark naked, had more than proved that to her.

Vargas was a whacko son of a bitch, and though he hadn't raped her, he'd given her plenty to think about. Plenty she kept forgetting every time Will Travers kissed her. She didn't remember ever being kissed the way he kissed her, ever reacting to a man the way she reacted to him. She was beginning to think the reason she'd been so successful in ignoring men for so long had more to do with her never having met the right one than it did with her lofty goals. Plants now, men later, had always been her motto, and except for a couple of diversions—the first the result of teenage hormones and curiosity with a wrangler on the next ranch over, and the second with a professor she should have been smarter than to believe— she'd pretty much kept to her plan, especially these last few years, when her work had begun to consume her.

Guns—that's what she needed, not a man, and guns were what she'd brought with her up the river.

Fortified with a reality she could handle, she picked up her coffee and headed outside. It would be dark before he returned. She would have to set out a lantern for him to find his way back.

Or not, she thought, taking a sip of coffee. She looked downriver, toward Santa Maria. The water was full of caimans, more than she was used to seeing this close to Santa Maria, their knobby hides just breaking the surface. Maybe the stories about the monster *jacarés* were true. She'd never been to the headwaters of the Marauiá, but the caimans down near the mouth of the river tonight actually did look bigger than the ones she'd seen elsewhere in the Amazon.

A splash behind her had her whipping around, just in time to see what looked like a tree trunk submerge beneath the river. An uneasy feeling coursed a path down her spine.

"Great," she muttered. Now was not a good time for her to suddenly get spooky about the animal life of the Amazon. Hell, she hadn't trekked across half of northeastern Colombia without seeing a few caimans. She had real problems tonight, like what was she going to do about Will Travers. He could probably find his way in the dark, but if she and her orchid were still on the *Sucuri* when he returned, there was bound to be an argument about the plane at the mission.

So maybe she shouldn't be on the boat when he returned.

It was a thought.

A good thought.

Santa Maria was just down around the bend, and her canoe and her supplies were waiting for her there. All she had to do was go get them, come back for her guns, and be on her way without him catching her. He would never find her once she was on the river by herself.

But he would still find Vargas, and he'd be alone when he did.

Hell.

She couldn't do it. She couldn't leave him. She didn't care how long he'd been hauling contraband for Fat Eddie, he didn't know Vargas the way she did, and even without figuring in his kisses, she liked him too damn much to leave him to face a maniacal despot alone.

"*Merda,*" she swore again, under her breath. Nothing

was working out the way she had planned, absolutely nothing. Would she be crazy to throw in with him? Or was it crazy to think she could go into Reino Novo alone to find her orchids and get back out without being part of what he was up against?

It all boiled down to Vargas, and his Night of the Devil, and whatever it was she'd seen in the jungle near Reino Novo. Maybe it was a sacrificial altar for virgins. That was the story whispered around the waterfront in Manaus. She wouldn't put anything past old Corisco, certainly not a little blood sacrifice, or even a great big blood sacrifice. The major showed a marked predilection for the substance and some godawful, unsavory methods of indulging his interest.

Unbidden, an image came to mind, and she lifted a hand to her brow, rubbing her temple, her lips pursed in consternation. Now that was a memory she'd tried damned hard to suppress, she thought, and she could have happily gone a whole lot longer without dragging it up.

Maybe a cigarette was in order. Will had all the makings—and a cigarette, and her coffee, and a little time spent on the top deck with her crates would be just the thing to settle her down.

Minutes later, she had a hand-rolled cigarette dangling from between her lips and a crowbar in her hands, prying open the lid on one of her crates. It was time to break out the firepower, probably past time. She wanted a fully loaded Galil close at hand from here on out, and she was going to snap a couple of grenades to her belt next to her 9-millimeter Taurus. There was no sense in being underprepared at this stage in the game.

The lid gave way, and she set the crowbar aside for a moment to take a long drag off the cigarette, managing the feat without actually inhaling too much of the smoke. It was the essence of it she was interested in, the taste of it rolling across her tongue, the comfort of having it wreathe her face. Exhaling, she put the glowing stub on the base of the lantern and bent over the open crate—and instantly, quite suddenly, knew she wasn't alone. Her first thought was that the *sucuri* had returned and was lurking in the cabin beneath her, but when she looked up, what she saw was a man, a wizened old man with weathered brown skin and feathers stuck through his nose and tied into the long, lanky black hair trailing down across his bare shoulders and chest nearly to his waist, a wizened old man who had boarded the boat and climbed up on the top deck to stand in front of her without making a single sound.

Or maybe he'd floated down from the sky. Nothing could have surprised her more than his sudden, soundless appearance, no matter how he'd arrived. He was dressed in a scrap of a loincloth and had rows of red *shoroshoro* beads wrapped tightly around the leanly muscled biceps of both his arms. His sternly silent face was deeply lined with age, but his eyes were bright, black as night, and shining with an inner fire.

He didn't look particularly threatening, but when he spoke—a sharp, guttural command—she heard movement behind her. She whirled around, lunging to her feet, but was captured before she could grab her gun, one Indian hauling her up against his chest, while another snaked a rope around her legs.

SHE LIKED HIM.

Even as Santa Maria came into sight, Will was still seething. For the first time in years, his focus had been jerked out from under him, and Annie Parrish had been the one to do it. Gabriela had been wrong. He wasn't nearing the end of anything, because when he was finished with Vargas, he was heading north to Laramie, Wyoming, and a little blond-haired, wild woman who *liked* him—liked him so much she'd nearly sucked his tongue down her throat, liked him so much she'd had her hand halfway down his pants. Another inch, and he would have been on top of her.

He was still suffering, his loins still aching, and all he could do was let out a soft groan and try not to laugh. It was ridiculous, the way she got to him. Good God, he'd probably be dead inside of a week, and all he could think about was *her*.

He hoped to hell she didn't *like* Jackson Reid the way she *liked* him.

Merda. He didn't want to think about it.

Keeping close to shore, he took a good look around the dock. The one boat tied up was Father Aldo's ancient *batalone*, a huge dugout with built-up sides for carrying cargo. The canoe Annie was expecting was nowhere in sight, but it wouldn't have been unusual for the priest to have loaned it out until she arrived. On the Amazon, everything got used.

He'd stopped at Santa Maria hundreds of times in the last two years, and as far as he could tell, no more than usual was going on, which meant absolutely nothing was going on. The pilot would be at Father Aldo's, and after tying up the canoe, Will headed in that direction.

The mission was little more than a runway bordered

by half a dozen buildings. One was Father Aldo's, the others the mission school, which doubled as the church, a storehouse, and the rest homes, one of them maintained by RBC for their researchers. A stack of crates and boxes next to the last house in the row looked as if they could be Annie's supplies. More supplies were stacked up next to Father Aldo's house, the cargo probably delivered by the plane at the end of the runway. The place was quiet, with a few lanterns on inside the houses, the forest all around humming with the sound of cicadas. If Fat Eddie had figured out Annie was on her way to Santa Maria, he hadn't gotten here yet.

"*Guillermo!*" a voice called out, followed by the sound of several guns being cocked in the dark.

Will froze where he stood, mentally retracting his last thought and calling himself the world's biggest fool.

"Where's the woman, Guillermo? The little cat? And my guns?"

It was Fat Eddie all right, and how in the hell had he been stupid enough to walk into the fat man's trap? There were no other boats tied up at the dock, but he should have realized that Fat Eddie could have half a dozen moored just out of sight.

And he obviously did.

The plane wasn't Eddie Mano's, though, and it wasn't Vargas's. Will could see the markings of a service that flew out of São Gabriel. It would have been perfect for getting Annie into Colombia. São Gabriel was only two hours from the border by plane.

"I still have her, *senhor*," he called out, trying to locate everyone in the dark. Fat Eddie had to be behind the cargo crates next to Father Aldo's. Nothing else was big enough to hide him. On the other side of the street, the end of a rifle barrel could just be seen poking out from behind the mission school. "I'm keeping her for myself."

" *'Ta louco, Guillermo.* You are very, very crazy, yes. This woman has brought you nothing but trouble, and will only bring you more."

An understatement, if Will had ever heard one, but Fat Eddie would never hear it from him.

"You were right about the guns, *senhor*. She did have them on my boat. You can have them back. All I want is the woman." Will heard a boat engine starting a little ways down the river, to the east; then he heard another and another, and another, until there was no distinguishing one motor from the rest.

Merda.

Laughter rang out from behind the crates, good old belly laughter, but Will didn't like the sound of it.

"Of course you can have her, my friend. Most of her. I only want the one part." More laughter filled the air as Eddie's men joined in on the macabre joke, and Will had to fight to keep his panic at bay. Panic wasn't going to save her—or him.

Out of the corner of his eye, he caught sight of a single boat chugging down from the west.

"Drop your gun on the ground, my friend, and we can talk."

It wasn't a request, and Will obeyed, slipping his pistol out of his waistband and slowly lowering it to the ground. The instant metal met dirt, Fat Eddie and his men walked out from where they'd been hiding.

"Guillermo, Guillermo," Fat Eddie sighed, walking forward with the rolling, side-to-side gait of the dangerously obese. He was still wearing his orange and brown striped shirt and a billowy pair of black pants. After two steps, he began to pant, the effort of ambulating three hundred and twenty pounds proving to be a huge strain. "This is all so very bad for you."

It didn't look too good for Fat Eddie, either. Will watched him come closer and closer, and wondered what the chances were of the man having fatal cardiac arrest in the next ten feet.

Eddie stopped and snapped his fingers, and Will's hopes faded. The man knew his limits. Two of his *jagunços* brought out a big wooden chair on poles for lifting, and the fat man descended with a wheezing groan.

"Where is she, my friend? Still on your boat, I think?" Will shrugged.

Fat Eddie made a quick gesture with his hand, and two of his men came forward to frisk Will down.

So much for the gems, he thought, when they got to his front pockets. One of the men pulled out the bag, and with a ragged-toothed grin, took it over to Fat Eddie.

"Ah, this is good." The fat man smiled, looking inside and then hefting the bag in his hand. "You are not so far from the Rio Cauaburi, Guillermo, and because I like you, I will think you were still taking these to Corisco Vargas. You will still die, but at least not as a thief."

The distinction, which seemed to make a difference to Fat Eddie, was lost on Will.

"But the guns and the woman, these I still want. These I still need. Where is the *Sucuri*, my friend?"

Will only had one answer to that question, and he knew it wasn't the one Fat Eddie wanted to hear.

"I want the woman. All of her." And the importance of that distinction was not lost on him at all.

"Is she worth your life?"

"Yes." As a commodity, his life had been sold any

number of times over the last few years. Once more for Annie seemed like the bargain of the century, especially given the way these things had been going for him, because in the end, he was Tutanji's. No matter what Fat Eddie Mano, or Corisco Vargas, or anybody else came up with to do to him, the bargain he'd made with Tutanji was the one that bound him.

And it beckoned, that bargain did. He'd been struggling for so long to fulfill his part, he sometimes lost sight of what awaited him, if he ran his quarry to ground and vanquished the shaman's demon. A glimpse of the beginning of life, Tutanji had promised, a journey to an Amazonian Eden, to the garden where the Dakú had first been born into a lost world, a place untouched by time.

Knowing Tutanji, the least Will expected to find was a living fossil, a plant previously known only from the fossil record of plants that had died millions of years ago, and if that's all he found, it would still be the discovery of the century. Or would have been. Annie's orchid could very well eclipse any discovery of his.

A wry smile curved his mouth, and he saw Fat Eddie's brows knit together. The fat man had no idea what was out there in the rain forest, and whatever Vargas was hoping to gain with his Night of the Devil, it wasn't the true treasure. Annie had found a true treasure. Tutanji had promised another to him. Or maybe they were both one and the same. The thought had crossed his mind more than once since seeing her orchid. Either way, he wasn't going to be denied, not after three long years of sacrificing everything he'd ever thought he believed in.

No, he thought. Fat Eddie Mano wasn't going to be the end of him, not when he was this close.

"Yes, *senhor*," he repeated. "She is worth my life, but what good is she to me, if I am dead?"

Back on familiar ground, the fat man relaxed his furrowed brow, and his grin returned. "Dead men don't need women. This is true, my friend."

Behind him, Will heard the boats arriving and tying up. Men began jumping onto the dock. He glanced over his shoulder to get an idea of how many reinforcements Eddie had called in, and swore under his breath. His odds, already bad, had just become impossible. There were dozens of boats on the river, all shapes and sizes, all of them with at least seven men on them.

"*Marcos. Olá*," Fat Eddie called out. "*Que é que você sabe?*" What do you know?

A tall, powerfully built man brushed by Will where he stood on the edge of the dock. Marcos was better groomed than most of Eddie's henchmen, with a fairly clean, blue T-shirt tucked into a pair of recognizably khaki slacks, and a cowboy hat set at a rakish angle over his neatly trimmed black hair.

He bent to whisper in Fat Eddie's ear, handing him a piece of paper.

"You left her on the Rio Marauiá, Guillermo." Fat Eddie's smile broadened. "Marcos saw your canoe coming into the Negro. I'm sure you would have told me this yourself."

Will wouldn't have put money on it. He'd been planning a nice, simple lie about leaving her in Barcelos. With that option gone, he was going to have to rely on Annie.

Fat Eddie looked down at the paper Marcos had handed him, and his smile grew even wider. "*Incrível*," he exclaimed and looked up at Will. "It seems you are right, Guillermo. She is worth much more in one piece. Ten thousand *reais* more."

With that, he burst into another round of rolling laughter, setting his whole body shaking like a boatload of Jell-O.

Sweet Christ, Will thought, staring at the paper Fat Eddie was waving around. Even in the fading light, he could see the worst—Annie's face on a wanted poster with a bounty of ten thousand *reais* printed in big bold numbers at the bottom, and the words "Wanted Alive" printed at the top.

Right then and there, she became the single most amazing woman he'd ever met anywhere on the planet. She was like a friggin' magnet for disaster, and how in the hell he'd ever thought he could simply give her a lift up the river without his whole life coming unglued was beyond him, totally beyond him.

He swore, a single succinct word that didn't begin to encompass his frustration. She'd said she'd decided to stay, and he doubted she'd waited too long after he'd left to break out something a damn sight more deadly than her 9-millimeter handgun.

He only hoped she wouldn't hesitate to use it.

CHAPTER 18 ✄

FULL DARK HAD FALLEN BY THE TIME Fat Eddie's henchmen had gotten him levered into his little black speedboat and headed west up the Rio Negro to the Marauiá. Motoring up the mouth of the tributary in Marcos's *gaiola* riverboat, Will spotted his landmark, a *lupuna* tree towering above the rest of the canopy, its crown silhouetted by a waning half-moon. The *Sucuri* was tied up in the *igapó* on the other side of the tree.

There was no way for Fat Eddie and his half a dozen boatloads of goons not to see the *Sucuri* once they passed the bend. Annie was smart, though, he kept telling himself. She wouldn't take any chances. She'd seen Johnny Chang's head. She knew the price she was going to pay, if Fat Eddie got a hold of her. She just didn't know there had been another price put on her head. Will only wondered how good she was with her Galils and how long she would hesitate before she used them, and whether or not she could manage to protect herself without killing him by accident—and it would be an accident, if she shot him. She more than liked him. He knew it down to his bones.

Standing on the deck, he watched the night-black wall of the jungle slip by. The river was quiet, the sound of rushing water a low undercurrent as their boats turned into the bend and passed beneath the *lupuna* tree.

"How much farther, Guillermo?" Fat Eddie asked from where he was shoehorned into the speedboat running alongside the *gaiola*.

"A few more miles, *senhor*," It wouldn't be much of a lie in about another minute, but it might buy her a few extra seconds, when she would see them, but they'd all still be looking up the river for her.

"Marcos?" Fat Eddie called out.

"*Sim, senhor?*" the man answered.

"Put Guillermo in front. The woman has guns, many guns."

Marcos didn't hesitate, grabbing Will by the arm and shoving him toward the bow of the boat.

Okay, Annie, he thought, stationing himself at the prow, a gun at his back. Be careful.

As they came fully around the bend, he was relieved to see she hadn't put out a lantern. Then he was concerned. She should have lit a lantern by now—unless she was lying in ambush.

Honest to God, he wouldn't put it past her. She hadn't survived all these years without a sixth sense for danger.

But as the boats continued up the river, Will realized there was more than just a lantern missing. The whole damn *Sucuri* was gone.

He swore under his breath, leaning forward on the rail and scanning the western shore, looking for the pale silhouette of a boat floating on the water—and not finding it.

Son of a bitch. She'd stolen the *Sucuri*, and ten to one said she was heading straight for Vargas. It hadn't taken her long to make her decision, either. Hell, she must have practically followed him down the Marauiá to the Negro and just missed Marcos. God knows where she was now. The Cauaburi was only fifty miles west of the Marauiá, the two rivers on a parallel course as they wound down from the Venezuelan highlands to the Rio Negro. She'd be at the mouth of the Cauaburi by morning, and he knew from Fat Eddie that Vargas was patrolling the whole river. If she lasted until dark tomorrow, it would be a miracle.

A great commotion from the other boats brought his head around.

"*Jacaré! Jacaré!*" the men shouted. "*Um monstro!*"

Will couldn't see the *jacaré*, the caiman, they were pointing at, but every man jack of them was shouldering a rifle or pulling a pistol and holding their lanterns high. Some of the men were laughing, but it was laughter with an edge of fear.

Fat Eddie motored toward the fray as the boats began circling around in the middle of the river, a broad grin splitting his face as he pointed into the water.

"One thousand *reais* to the boat that brings me the beast's hide!" he shouted.

"*Um jacaré monstruoso!*" Another boatload of men caught sight of the reptile.

"*Jacaré! Jacaré!*"

More men took up the shouting, the activity on the boats growing more frenzied. A few men fired off shots.

Others were dragging out ropes and pieces of net. Marcos's boat moved closer, with Will torn between watching for the giant beast and trying to find some sign of Annie or the *Sucuri* where he'd left them at the shoreline.

Damn it all! What in the hell was she thinking to head for Reino Novo alone? It didn't make sense.

"Ooohhh!" A wave of fearful awe rose in a crescendo, and Will whirled around—just in time to see a huge, leathery snout rising out of the water, rows of fearsome, conical teeth bared and glinting in the light of a dozen lanterns, the animal's knobby, scaly hide cutting through the inky black surface of the water in a long, unbelievably long, unbroken line.

Sweet Jesus! His breath caught in his throat on an instant of pure primal fear. The thing had to be twenty feet or more, an unheard-of length for an Amazonian caiman.

"Two thousand *reais*!" Fat Eddie shouted louder, maneuvering his boat nearer the action. The flotilla of boats and men drifted and motored closer to the shore, ineffectually trying to cage the caiman thrashing in the water. Nets had been thrown into the river, and shots were still being fired off. Someone had gotten a hold of the gargantuan reptile with a boat hook.

God, what a beast, the hide easily worth double the two thousand *reais* Fat Eddie was offering, but it wasn't going down without a fight. Water was flying everywhere, waves splashing into the boats, the caiman's tail cracking against the surface of the river.

With everybody overly excited, circling around each other, and shooting off their guns, Will figured it was only a matter of minutes before somebody got killed. He hoped to hell it wouldn't be him.

Letting out a strangled bellow, the animal sank back below the water, taking the nets and boat hook with him, and in a heartbeat, all the laughing and shouting stopped. Tension filled the air as men watched over the sides of their boats, playing out rope where they still had a hold on the caiman, everybody waiting, some in anticipation, some—from the looks on their faces—in abject dread.

Will's gaze was pulled back toward the shore. It didn't make sense for Annie to have left him, but there wasn't a person in the Amazon who could have taken that boat away from her. No one boarded the *Sucuri*. No one.

Except for Tutanji.

The thought came out of nowhere to take hold of him, and with his own sense of abject dread, he felt his heart sink into the vicinity of his stomach.

The old shaman could have come this far south.

He thought back to Annie's nightmares and what she'd said about the *sucuri* on his boat, and his sick feeling got even worse. He didn't understand Tutanji any more than he had to, but during the year he'd spent with the Dakú, he'd understood the shaman enough to survive. Annie didn't stand a chance. Will didn't care how smart she was, or how strong she was, no woman was a match for a *payé* witch doctor with Tutanji's skills. The old man had nearly killed him half a dozen times with his concoctions and his trials, always pushing Will to his limits, to the end of his rope, and then cutting him free to fall where he may. Will's future had been read and molded as much by his failures as his successes. They were all the same to Tutanji, whose only goal was to destroy the demon who had invaded Dakú land, his method of destruction to create his own white devil to fight the white devil who dared to bring his sorcery to the lost world at the headwaters of the Cauaburi and the Rio Marauiá.

Something bumped against Marcos's *gailoa,* and everybody drew back with a gasp, expecting the giant caiman to rise up and snap the boat in two—but it wasn't the overgrown reptile. Will looked down with everybody else and saw a board knocking against the hull.

The board was old and needed paint, but the faded letters written across its sun-bleached face were clear to him in the yellow light of someone's lantern: SUCURI.

His boat hadn't been stolen. It had been destroyed.

So where the hell was Annie?

The sick feeling in his stomach turned into a cold hard knot.

"What is it?" someone asked. "The monster?"

"No, no, no. It's wood," another answered. "Just a piece of wood."

"Where's the monster?"

"There!"

"No, there!"

"Shut up, you fools!" Marcos hissed. "It's wood. It's all just wood. Stay sharp! Two thousand *reais* to the boat that captures the beast. Stay sharp!"

Looking back up to shore, closer now, Will could see the debris strewn across the forest floor and piled up between the trees like tidewrack. Dozens of other boards were drifting out into the river, some of them from her weapons crates, the pieces churned up by the wakes of the boats.

The *Sucuri* had been blown apart—or torn apart.

Behind him, the cries of *"Jacaré!"* started up again, with everyone rushing to the far rail, but Will couldn't quite convince himself that a giant caiman had risen up out of the Marauiá and eaten his boat. He didn't care how damn big the animal was. It hadn't been Annie's dynamite going off and taking all her ammunition with it, either. They would have heard an explosion of that size— which brought him full circle back to Tutanji and the cold, hard knot in his stomach.

The shaman had given him the boat, an ancient wreck beached deep in the jungle and overgrown with vines, left high and dry by the receding waters of the annual flooding of the rivers. It had never been much more than a floating hulk, but it had been home for the last two years, until tonight, when he was sure it had been Tutanji who had destroyed it.

So be it, Will thought, his gaze scanning the rubble. They were nearing the end, he and the shaman. The *Sucuri* was just the first of many things about to change, but the old man had gone too far when he'd taken Annie. Tutanji wouldn't kill her, not outright, but that's as much as Will dared to concede.

Jaguar bait—that's what he'd called her, and Tutanji could be the worst kind of jaguar. He just prayed she wasn't somewhere on the shoreline as broken up as the *Sucuri*, and the only way he was going to know that was by getting off Marcos's boat.

And swimming to the riverbank.

With a monster caiman thrashing in the water, maddened by pain behind him.

Shit.

Grim faced, he swung his leg over the side rail, hoping the *jacaré monstruoso* knew who in the hell he was, *pa-suk panki* to the great shaman Tutanji, Master of the

Otherworld, and friggin' king of the hoodoo metaphysics of this world.

Shit.

He swung his other leg over, and as soon as he cleared the rail, jackknifed into the river—before anyone could notice that he was escaping, though he doubted if anyone would think it was much of an escape. "Suicide" was the word most likely to come to mind.

The water engulfed him, still warm from the day's sun, the current around the bend strong and pushing him into shore. He dove deep and with every stroke prayed he wouldn't find her hurt, and that the giant caiman wasn't in the mood for man.

THE OLD MAN had disappeared. One minute he'd been with them, leading the way through the forest, and the next he'd been gone. Either way, the pace hadn't slackened, and Annie was bruised from the knees down from all the tree roots she'd run into and tripped over. She'd done her share of rain-forest bushwacking and then some, but she hadn't made a habit of doing it in the dark.

The Indians who'd kidnapped her weren't having any problems. Their naked bodies gleamed in the moonlight, their faces painted black, their torsos red.

The sound of splashing ahead and a sudden sogginess of the earth underfoot warned her they were coming to another stream. They'd already forded three, the last one chest high. She was soaked and more worried than she cared to admit.

She'd never been kidnapped before. It seemed so unlikely, the farthest thing down on her "things I need to worry about tonight" list, but she didn't know what else to call her situation.

He'd destroyed Will's boat, the old man with the enigmatic expression and *shoroshoro* beads. Blown it to bits—and she'd be damned if she knew how. He'd stayed on the boat alone for a while, then come back to shore and started blowing and singing and stomping. After a few minutes, the *Sucuri* had crumbled, more imploding than exploding, and taken her guns to the bottom of the friggin' river. It hadn't been much of a boat to begin with, but she would have thought it could hold up to the "I'll huff and I'll puff, till I blow your house down" threat.

She heard the stream up ahead and braced herself. Anacondas were water snakes. They liked grubbing around in forest streams, and they weren't averse to doing it at night, when it was dark, and she couldn't see them.

Damn, she thought, trying hard to distract herself. She'd had some good stuff on that boat, stuff she was going to need, besides the guns, and now it was all floating down the Rio Marauiá. The old man had ruined her.

So who in the hell was he?

She had a few ideas, but none she thought she could handle while she was slogging through a windless swamp and getting eaten alive by mosquitoes while not having a clue as to where she was going to end up.

The Indian in front of her stepped into the stream and sank up to his knees. By his second step, he was in up to his waist and wading deeper. Annie started swearing under her breath. She was going to end up swimming this one, which meant she wouldn't have her footing if something big, and long, and extremely muscular decided to wrap itself around her and pull her under.

She swore again, muttering a stream of invectives as she went deeper and deeper into the water. When the water reached her chin, and she had to lift off the streambed, her panic and anger melded into one perfectly awful emotion, and it was in that state that the name she'd half forgotten and been trying to avoid came back to her, emblazoning itself on her consciousness in fiery letters— *Tutanji.*

"YOU ARE CRAZY!" Fat Eddie bellowed. "Crazy, Guillermo! One crazy son of a bitch!"

Lying on the shore behind a tree, gulping in a breath, Will had to agree. Those minutes in the Marauiá, swimming in the current and hearing the giant caiman thrashing and lunging about in the water behind him, had been some of the longest in his life. He would swear to feeling the beast snap at his toes.

He looked down, checking his feet for missing parts.

"Hell," he sighed in relief, letting his head fall back to the ground. All he'd lost was a flip-flop.

"Where are my guns, Guillermo? My fucking Israeli guns?" Fat Eddie shouted from his boat.

At the bottom of the river, Will thought, ignoring him.

"Annie?" he called out, wiping the water off his face.

"You crazy son of a bitch! You won't get away with this!"

Will had to agree to that depressing statement, too. He was beginning to doubt if he was going to get away with anything on this trip.

"Annie?" he tried again from his prone position, listening intently, but still getting no reply.

A shot rang out from one of the boats and ricocheted, pinging off a tree trunk, and he rolled onto his stomach and scrambled farther up the shore, keeping low to the ground.

"Crazy son of a bitch! Next time I see you, my friend, you are a dead man!"

Yeah, yeah. Take a ticket and get in line, he thought, pushing himself to a sitting position behind a broad tree trunk. He sat quietly, catching his breath and letting his eyes adjust to the darkness.

"Annie?" he called out again, looking around. Boards were tumbled around everywhere, all topsy-turvy. His galley sink was overturned in a pile of rotting leaves. The *Sucuri's* wheel had caught on a low-lying branch, but Will didn't see any guns and he didn't see Annie. He didn't know whether to be relieved or not. Then he saw the arrow stuck into the ground, a palm-wood shaft with black-and-white striped feather fletching, and at the bottom of the shaft, his bush knife stuck into the ground beside it. A quiver and bow were next to the knife, the whole of the edifice draped in a boar's-tooth necklace.

It was an invitation, painfully clear. Tutanji had her, and if Will wanted her back, he was going to have to come and get her.

More shots zinged into the rain forest, some cracking into trees, others burying themselves somewhere in the jungle. Then the cry of *"Jacaré!"* went up again out on the river, and Will knew, for the moment, he was forgotten.

He didn't waste the chance.

Slipping the necklace over his head, he scanned the soft ground of the riverbank, until he found what he needed— footprints heading away from the river, into the forest. With only a half-moon to light the way, he picked up the weapons and took off down the path.

CHAPTER 19 ×

REINO NOVO

FAT EDDIE MANO WAS SWEATING. Corisco could see the dampness staining not only the man's shirt, but his pants legs, could see a regular stream of sweat running down the man's brow and wished he'd held the audience someplace other than in his richly appointed and extremely difficult-to-maintain office. Rot and mildew were constant enemies, and both of them were born of humidity, the water thickening every square centimeter of air in the tropics. Profuse sweating only added to the problem. Now he not only had to deal with the humidity and the rain and the occasional flooding that did its damnedest to inundate his sanctuary above the riverbank, now he had Fat Eddie adding his own personal water supply to the one place in the whole damned Amazon Corisco tried to keep livable. His damned office.

Nobody else dared to sweat in his office, or even in his presence.

He didn't sweat.

Ever.

A pencil snapped in two in his hand, and with a small sound of disgust, he threw the pieces onto his desk.

"And the woman, *Senhor* Mano? What happened to the woman?"

Fat Eddie and his ragged little entourage had arrived at Reino Novo just as the sun was setting, the promised emeralds and diamonds in hand, retrieved from William Sanchez Travers the evening before in Santa Maria, apparently mere hours before the man had been eaten by a giant caiman near the mouth of the Rio Marauiá.

It was a mildly interesting story, the type of larger-than-life escapade that could only come out of a landscape as immense and incredible as the Amazon, but it was child's play compared to the reality Corisco would soon impose on the area.

"Ah, the woman," Fat Eddie said, looking thoughtful, a feat he pulled off with remarkable skill for someone with filed teeth. "Which woman in particular are you interested in, Major Vargas? I have many in Manaus."

Corisco's mouth twisted in disgust. "I am not interested in any of those *putas* you sell out of the Praça de Matriz. I want the doctor, the woman on Travers's boat."

Fat Eddie lifted his arms in a bulky shrug. "The boat was destroyed. I said this, no? And the woman—if there was a woman—maybe she was destroyed, as well."

"But you didn't find a body."

"No bodies. No," Fat Eddie said.

"Her name is Annie Parrish. Doutora Parrish," he told the fat man, carefully watching him for a reaction. The bastard was lying to him. Corisco knew it. Annie Parrish had been on that boat on the Marauiá last night, and if she wasn't dead, she was somewhere in the forest, but for some reason, Eddie didn't want him to know she'd been on Travers's boat, and that meant the fat man was hiding something.

He wouldn't be for long, though. Fat Eddie's twenty or so men were no match for Corisco's elite squad of soldiers. Torturing Fat Eddie might prove to be a disgustingly fascinating experience.

"Ah, the Woolly Monkey woman," Fat Eddie said. "I heard she was back in Manaus, but she has nothing to do with me or my business."

More lies, Corisco thought. Every *jagunço* from Reino Novo to Manaus knew about the price on Annie Parrish's head by now.

"She is with the River Basin people, a meddler, a *cientista*. It was you who had her deported, wasn't it?" the fat man continued.

Corisco wasn't surprised by the question. Everyone knew the Woolly Monkey story, even if they knew it wrong. What they didn't know was where Annie Parrish had really been, what she'd been doing, or what had happened to her in Yavareté.

All he cared about now, though, was what had happened to her on the Marauiá. She'd come back to Brazil, and if she wasn't already dead, he wanted her, by God. He wanted her for his sacrifice.

"Yes, I had her deported," he told Fat Eddie, "but I'm afraid she still has something to do with my business. Something I would like finished."

"So maybe she's worth her weight in gold?" Fat Eddie asked with a chuckle, his eyes lighting up with avarice. "If someone could bring her to you?"

Corisco snapped his fingers, and Fernando stepped forward. Corisco handed him one of the wanted posters off his desk and gestured for him to give it to Fat Eddie.

"Yes, *Senhor* Mano. She is worth a great deal," he said as the fat man looked the poster over and did a fair job of feigning surprise. Yes, she was worth a great damn deal, and the closer she came to slipping through his fingers, the more he wanted her. It was time to send his own men after her. If she'd been near the mouth of the Marauiá last night and her boat had blown up, she couldn't have gotten far. He had men leaving Reino Novo today to capture the rest of the needed *cordeiros*. He would split them up, and they could search for Annie Parrish, as well. He would put the men under Fernando's command. The giant would sniff her out.

"Then for you, Major, I will find this woman and bring her here. If she is still in Manaus, I can have her picked up in a matter of hours. If she is already on the river, it will take longer, I fear. The Rio Negro, she is a very big place." He smiled, showing off his sharp teeth.

But not big enough for the two of us, Corisco thought, not in the least bit intimidated by Fat Eddie's gruesome grin. The Night of the Devil was coming, and after the dark sacrifice, Eddie Mano would either be dead or destroyed. Corisco hardly cared which, but he could see where it might be to his advantage to forgo torturing Fat Eddie today in hopes of a greater benefit tomorrow. Annie Parrish was far more important to him than the fat man from Manaus. If Eddie Mano could bring her in, so much the better, and if not, he and his henchmen would become sacrificial lambs for *El Mestre*.

A startled gasp from one of the *jagunços* had Fat Eddie turning around. The man was staring at the huge glass tank.

"I see my pet has come out of hiding," Corisco said, gesturing for Fernando to turn on the lights in the shadowed tank.

The scarred giant moved forward to a bank of switches on the wall and flipped them on one by one. Slowly, by muted degrees, the full dimensions of the tank came into view, the lights coming on in the back first. Full of vegetation and carefully chosen tree trunks with branches for climbing, it looked like the rain forest just outside the door, complete with a small stream running through the middle of it, continuously cycled by a pump from the river.

It was a rare event when the tank's inhabitant could actually be seen. Corisco was pleased by the snake's timing.

"Thirty-six feet, *Senhor* Eduardo," he said. "The largest anaconda ever held in captivity. Six hundred pounds. I usually feed him deer. I insist that you come back in a week, as my guest at a function I'm hosting, very elaborate, very festive. You can watch him hunt. It's a fascinating sight, I assure you, nearly as fascinating as watching him swallow his kill."

Fat Eddie didn't doubt it for a minute. No more than he doubted that Major Corisco Vargas was dangerous, powerfully dangerous, with his own private army culled from the elite Brazilian forces he commanded, and his gold.

Gold was power, and Vargas was loaded with it. Shipping less than half of what he pulled out of the mines, it was said, and using the other half—it was also said—for darkly demonic purposes.

Fat Eddie had to fight to restrain his laughter. The fucking Amazon was full of friggin' demons, and he had met them all. Vargas, a city boy from São Paulo, didn't know the first damn thing about the *jurijuri* and the *brujos*, the *boraro,* and the *wawekratins*. Whatever the hell he thought he was up to, Fat Eddie's money was on the demons. He just wanted to be around to pick up all the gold when Vargas fell on his prissy, sadistic, epauletted ass.

Idiota.

It was impossible for Fat Eddie to have any respect whatsoever for a man who couldn't think of anything better to do with virgins than to cut them open on an altar—but he wanted the altar. Solid gold, according to rumor, and hidden somewhere around Reino Novo.

He wondered if the altar was what awaited the little cat, when he found her—and he would find her. He'd already set those wheels in motion, ordering a hundred of his *jagunços* up the river to meet him on the Cauaburi.

The major would pay more than ten thousand *reais* to have the woman. He could see it in the man's eyes. Vargas wanted the little *doutora* very badly, indeed.

No body meant she hadn't been on Travers's boat when it had fallen apart, and it had fallen apart. There weren't any burn marks to indicate an explosion. The *sucuri* had left, that was all, and when the snake had left, the boat had fallen apart and mostly fallen into the river, including the *Sucuri*'s cargo.

A smile flickered across his lips. He'd gotten his guns back, by God, and only lost one man doing it. Whatever protection Travers had enjoyed these last couple of years hadn't quite left him, or that giant caiman would have had him for dinner instead of one of Fat Eddie's boat captains.

Travers had gone after the woman, Fat Eddie knew, and he'd been in a hurry to do it.

Taking the woman away from him might not be so easy. Guillermo had lied and stolen his way into an early grave for Annie Parrish, and he'd jumped into the Rio

Marauiá with a twenty-foot caiman in order to go after her.

Eddie was beginning to think his old friend was in love, but love wouldn't be enough to save either one of them. It never was. When Eddie got back to his boat, he would radio the band of men he'd left on the Marauiá. They'd had a day to track the pair through the jungle and must be closing in. The woman he would bring to Reino Novo.

And Guillermo?

Fat Eddie had told Vargas he was dead, more for Guillermo's sake than his own. He liked the man too much to kill him. Guillermo was no fool, not like the major. Guillermo knew the *jurijuri* and the *brujos*. There were times when Eddie wondered if Guillermo was a *brujo* himself. There was a look he got in his eyes sometimes that reminded Eddie of his father, a *brujo* from Ecuador. Like Eddie's father, Guillermo had blood on his hands. Not the weak blood of women, like Vargas, but blood rich with power.

No, Guillermo was not to be underestimated.

A movement in the tank caught his eye, drawing his attention, and Fat Eddie had to admit that Vargas had gotten himself a fine snake, big and brutish looking, its coloring dark and splotchy, its head blockishly large without any of the delicacy or fineness of the other rain-forest serpents.

His glance strayed back to Vargas, sizing him up. The snake was big, and the major was a skinny son of a bitch. A good fit, he thought, his face splitting into a big grin.

Yes, he would be back in a week.

CHAPTER 20 ✖

WILL PASSED HIS HAND OVER A CIRCLE of burned wood in a rain-forest clearing, feeling the warmth left by the fire. Tutanji and his group were no more than two hours ahead of him, and Fat Eddie's men were still somewhere behind him—and somewhere behind Fat Eddie's men was another group. He'd heard them when he'd circled back to see how many *jagunços* Eddie had put on his tail. There were fifteen men from Fat Eddie's boats, and the group following the fifteen had sounded much larger than that. Either way, the drainage between the Marauiá and the Cauaburi was getting damned crowded. He looked up at the circle of sky outlined by the canopy trees. It would be dark before he caught up with the Dakú.

A soft scrabbling in the forest brought his head around, his gaze quickly scanning the perimeter of the clearing. When a paca, a spotted rodent, trotted out of the deepening shadows of the trees and made a beeline for the overgrown gardens, Will looked back to the fire ring.

He'd been in the camp before ... *before he'd killed he jaguar and set himself free*. He'd lived in the clearing vith the Dakú during the first few months after his en-ounter with the anaconda. He'd done his healing here >eneath the peach palms, before they'd all headed farther 1orth.

He sifted his fingers through the cooling ash before lowly rising to his feet.

Tutanji was heading north again and had been for the ast four days with his band of men and Annie. Will had ost the trail the first night at a stream crossing, but ound it again at dawn. Fat Eddie's men hadn't been far >ehind him then, but had been losing ground ever since. The larger group would be moving even more slowly. He 1adn't heard Eddie's men for the last night and a day, but 1e didn't doubt that they were still there, any more than 1e doubted the others were still behind the *jagunços,* racking them with the same diligence he was using to rack the Dakú.

Marcos was good. Damn good.

Tutanji was better, but he'd lost his advantage when 1e'd reached the clearing and taken on women and chil-lren.

Will looked around the area again, noting signs of lomestication: manioc gratings on the ground, a half-inished basket woven from palm fronds. The Dakú's vomen and children had waited here while the men had gone south to get Annie. She must be exhausted by now. [t had been a long time since he'd run night and day chrough the forest. He doubted if Annie had ever had to push so hard.

It had been even longer since the first time he'd jour-1eyed into the low mountain ranges at the base of the

Serra da Neblina, into the lost world where Tutanji's ana
conda had found him. The shaman could be taking he
there, to the misty headwaters of the rivers.

It was a land under siege, like all the Amazon, an
Will knew Tutanji would go to any lengths to save i
from the white man's incursions, even share its secret
with him if that would save it from gold miners' gree
and rampant scientific exploration, both of which tor
away at the Dakú's way of life, upsetting balances an
creating discord. The mere act of observing, however ob
jective the gaze, changed what was observed. Tutanji knew
this and had kept his people hidden, a people know
only by myth and rumor, until gold had been discovere
on the Cauaburi and the demon Corisco Vargas ha
brought in his hordes of *garimpeiros,* his diesel-powere
engines, his hoses and planes and began tearing up th
earth and poisoning the rivers with mercury. No woma
was safe from the *garimpeiros,* no settlement safe from
attack. Many of Tutanji's people had already been lost
much of their once rich hunting grounds decimated b
the hundreds of miners needing food, the fish-poor black
water rivers giving less every year. Soon there would be
nothing but starvation and hardship and disease left i
the land between the rivers.

The wind picked up, rustling through the palms, an
with one final look around, he turned back to the trail
The Indians were moving too fast for anybody to be get
ting any jaguar-bait ideas about her—which was going to
save Tutanji a whole lot of trouble when he finally caugh
up to the old man.

A tired Annie he could handle. A hurt or raped Anni
would make him cruel.

ANNIE RAN IN HER DREAMS, *chased through the forest by a thousand demons, purple agoutis with sharp, tearing teeth; bloodred caimans of enormous size, hungry and searching; orange frogs with poisonous skin leaping at her from every direction; scorpions glowing blue underfoot, their tails raised to strike.*

Run. Run. Run.

She jerked awake in her hammock, her heart racing, ready to flee.

But the night was not full of demons, only a warm wind and the chirping of tree frogs. All around, the Indians were sleeping under *miritisabas*, temporary palm-thatched roofs, mothers with babies at their breasts, children snuggled together, men with their wives. Fires burned at regular intervals around the camp. Men guarded the perimeter, some with bows and spears in their hands, others carrying her guns with rounds of ammunition slung across their chests.

Two men sat by the closest fire, talking in low voices. One was Tutanji, the paint on his legs and arms glowing red in the light of the flames.

The other was William Sanchez Travers, his blond-streaked hair unmistakable.

He'd come.

Relief washed through her in a slow-moving wave, easing the tension from her body.

He'd come.

He'd found her.

Her hand went to the necklace she wore, his necklace. The chunk of quartz was jagged without being sharp.

The teeth were smooth, weighted around her neck. There had been no snakes in her dreams, no giant anacondas, and no jaguars, only the lesser demons.

Will had found her, and now everything would be all right.

Her eyelids, so heavy, drifted back down over her eyes. A sigh left her mouth.

Everything would be all right ... *everything would be all right*.

Will glanced over to where Annie slept, checking for himself one more time that she was okay. Being the only towhead for a good five hundred miles, and the only person wearing clothes, she was easy to spot among all the hammocks full of naked Indians. She was also still wearing her fanny pack.

For himself, he'd long since stripped out of his own clothing, tearing his shirt into a makeshift sling and stuffing his shorts inside. He'd come to the Dakú as one of their own, with a loincloth strung around his waist and toucan feathers tied into his hair. The transition—as always—had been disturbingly easy, like walking into warm water, making him wonder if he only fooled himself on the river, pretending to be a civilized man, when at heart he'd been claimed forever by the rain forest.

It had been six months since the last time he'd been with the Indians, too long, perhaps, and he didn't want Tutanji to make any mistake about who and what he still was, the man who had run the shaman's jaguar to ground and cut the cat's fangs out of his skull, the man who had killed the shaman's anaconda. There was blood on his hands, powerful *pasuk* blood, and Tutanji forgot it at his peril, especially where Annie was concerned.

"The Dakú do not sell their women," he said, his

voice utterly emotionless, his gaze fixed on the paper Tutanji had given him.

She looked like hell in the photograph. Even in the poorly made black-and-white copy, he could tell she'd been hit. Her cheek was bruised. What he thought was blood matted her hair, and even though the picture had been cut off just below her shoulders, she didn't seem to be wearing a shirt—details he'd missed in Santa Maria.

"She is not Dakú," Tutanji said, the words coming out softened on the edges, the result of many missing teeth.

"She is mine, and I am Dakú." He brought his gaze up to meet the old man's. "You have seen the truth of my blood. It is the same as yours." Through a *yagé* vision, they had watched their histories twine together, backward to an ancient Dakú ancestor. Neither of them had doubted what they'd seen at the time. Will wasn't going to let the old man doubt it now. When Tutanji had gone looking in the forest for a white devil apprentice, it was not a stranger he'd been looking for—and the shaman knew it.

"You've had many women on your boat and claimed none of them in all these years."

"I have claimed this one." And a fine mess he'd made of it, losing her on the river to an old friend who wanted to sell her to Corisco Vargas for ten thousand *reais*. Where in the hell, he wondered, had Tutanji gotten hold of a wanted poster while the ink was practically still wet? Vargas had worked fast. There had been no wanted posters in Barcelos.

"No, little brother," the old man disagreed. "No one has claimed this woman. She is still wild."

"Wild or not, she is mine," he said, knowing by Dakú

standards Annie was wild. Hell, even by his own standards she was pushing the envelope—not such a bad thing considering that they'd ended up in a camp with a bunch of Indians who had been pushed to the edge of desperation by forces neither their shamans nor their warriors could control.

That, of course, was where he was supposed to have come in, and a damn lousy job he'd done of it so far. He'd been fooled by the pace of life on the river, fooled into believing time ran on forever and he could take as much as he wanted.

His glance strayed back to the wanted poster in his hand.

He'd been wrong. He should have taken care of Vargas a year ago, before the bastard had gotten his hands on a blond-haired Wyoming botanist who'd been minding her own business making the plant find of the century.

But a year ago, he hadn't known it was Vargas that he wanted. The mine bosses on the Cauaburi had been reporting to a man named Fernando, and the connection between Vargas and Fernando had taken a long time to make—too damn long.

Without Fat Eddie, he might still be looking.

"*Merda,*" he whispered under his breath.

She hadn't had the scar on her right temple before Yavareté. The fresh wound showed up in the photograph as a black line on her pale, frightened face.

He forced himself to take a deep breath, looking for a calm that wouldn't be his until Corisco Vargas was dead.

No shirt.

Blood on her face.

Yes. He would kill Vargas.

"The Dakú have never wanted white man's money or trade goods before," he said, glancing back up at the old man. "Why now?"

"Kiri and Wawakin, Shatari and Mete, they are all gone, along with many others. We will buy them back with the money we get for the white woman." Tutanji spoke in the punctuated rhythms of the Dakú language. "Look around you and see all the missing faces. We hear their cries at night in our dreams, but we cannot find them."

Will had already noticed how many people were missing from the tribe, and wondered if they'd stayed at another camp. If they'd truly all been stolen, things had gotten far worse in the last six months than he'd imagined.

"Buy them back from whom?"

"The *pishtacos*," Tutanji said, using a Quechua word for white men who came into the rain forest and killed Indians to extract their fat. They were a horror to the Dakú, whether they existed or not, and Will wasn't putting any money on it. Not even Corisco Vargas would kill Indians for their slim resources of body fat. There simply wasn't enough to make it worth anybody's while. Anybody who wanted human fat would be better off in Manaus, lying in wait on the Praça de Matriz.

"*Pishtacos*? Or *garimpeiros*?" he asked.

"Are they not one and the same?" Tutanji said. "They raid. They steal. They kill. Then they run to their motored boats and fly up the rivers with our people in chains."

"Where do they go?"

"To the mines. A Tukano man saw many Indians and *caboclos* at the Cauaburi mines. A hundred, he said,

Tukano, Desana, Dakú, Yanomani. The mine bosses work them until they are broken, the women in their whorehouses and the men in the pits, then they put them in cages, cages built around a small gold mountain."

The altar at Reino Novo. Nothing Tutanji could have said could have alarmed him more. A hundred caged Indians and *caboclos*, Corisco Vargas, and the Night of the Devil were a combination for disaster of nightmarish possibilities.

Sweet Jesus, what was the man thinking of doing?

"The dark moon is coming, little brother," the shaman went on. "The woman may be our only hope. Ten thousand *reais* will buy many people and keep them from being slaves."

"No." He pinned the shaman with his gaze, fearing far worse than slavery for the captives and Annie. "Vargas wants the woman for herself. The money he's offering means nothing to him. He won't trade or sell Indians for her."

Tutanji stabbed at the fire with the stick, his face set in grim lines. "No, brother. In this you are wrong. All white men want money. They tear the world apart and burn down the forest for money. This is true." He stabbed the fire again, raising a shower of sparks, his voice rough with the forceful expulsion of his words. "I speak the truth."

It was true, but it wasn't the only truth.

"And all men want power," Will said. "There is power in sacrifice, in a man killing his enemies. The woman is the enemy of Corisco Vargas, the demon who takes our ancestors' gold, the demon who has stolen the Dakú and Yanomani, the Tukano and Desana. He will not give up the Indians or her for money, not when he already makes himself rich on Dakú gold."

He held the old man's gaze as his words sank in, watching the subtle play of emotions on the weathered and lined face. The shaman had magic, powerful magic in the Otherworld, but Vargas was in this world. It was why the shaman had taken Will that long-ago night.

With a grunt, Tutanji looked away.

"Can you take me to where they keep their boats?" he asked.

"Yes. It is a long day from here. Two with the women and children."

"Then send them north with the warriors." They didn't have time for women and children. "We will go alone."

"And the white-haired woman?" the old man asked.

"She's mine," he said succinctly. "She goes where I go."

The old man accepted his ultimatum with a sage nod. "The *sucuri* left your boat. It was best that I brought her with us, even if we don't get the money. She wasn't safe alone."

Hell, she wasn't safe anywhere, Will thought, and certainly not where she was now, practically in Vargas's lap with Fat Eddie's men and God knew who else on their trail. He'd tried to get her out of it, but he was beginning to believe that in some inescapable way, Annie was as much a part of what was happening as he was—an unpalatable truth confirmed by Tutanji's next words.

"I recognized her, you know, when I saw her on your boat."

"Recognized her?"

"From before, when she was here and killed the monkey. She is wild, this woman you have taken, with a spirit anaconda of her own. She needs much working on." Tutanji stabbed the fire again, and more sparks rose into the night.

Unlike most tribes, the Dakú were truly nomadic. If Annie had spent any time at all on the Cauaburi when she'd collected her orchid, it was likely that they had known about her.

But Will was more interested in what else the old man had said.

"She has a spirit anaconda?"

"Yes. She is *wawekratin,* a sorceress, I think. It could have been her snake on your boat all this time."

Nonplussed, Will could only stare. "I thought it was your snake on the *Sucuri* all this time."

The old man looked up from the fire, surprised. "You killed my snake, little brother. Don't you remember?"

Of course he did, but sorcery and the metaphysical Otherworld always left him a little short of firm footing. The snake he'd killed had been real—powerful, bloody, and real. And the snake on his boat had been more of a vision, albeit one he'd never seen for himself. The way he understood things, their different corporeal states didn't necessarily make them mutually exclusive.

Obviously, he'd been wrong, which left him to wonder why Annie's snake had been on his boat these last two years, protecting him, and why it had left just when the two of them needed protecting the most—questions he was unlikely to get answered anytime soon.

"Why didn't you wait for me at the boat?" He was curious to know. "You must have known I would return."

"I did wait for you." If anything, the shaman seemed a bit affronted by the question. "Didn't you see me there in the water, making all the noise and distracting your enemies?"

The caiman.

"That was you?"

"Yes. Yes." A toothless grin spread across the old man's face. "That was me. A giant caiman."

"Did you make the storm in Manaus? The rain that moved faster than the wind?"

"Yes, yes. That was me."

Somehow, Will didn't doubt it for a minute.

"You should take your woman to the river," the shaman advised. "Wash her in the warm water and put your seed inside her to calm her down. Do this every day and feed her only fish and fruit. Then she won't be so wild."

And according to Dakú wisdom, that would be that. Will couldn't fault the old man's reasoning. The Dakú considered all women inherently wild and kept tame only by regular doses of their husband's semen.

But he didn't think Annie would concede him or his semen that much influence.

No, he thought, that was a long shot at best, a damn long shot.

The Dakú also stole women when they could, and Will didn't doubt for a minute that Annie had been as much stolen as saved, no matter who she was, how much bounty was on her, or where she'd been found.

"I have run her hard to wear her out," Tutanji went on. "She shouldn't give you too much trouble, if you want to take her now."

Will glanced back to where Annie was sleeping, and

had to agree with Tutanji. She didn't look as if she could put up much of a fight, but that wasn't exactly the way he'd planned on making love to her, when she was too tired to give a damn.

Hell, he was too tired to give a damn. He'd only had an hour's rest here and there for the last four days. The hammock looked almost as good to him as the woman inside it.

Almost.

It had been a long time since he'd shared a hammock or a bed with a woman.

"Go," Tutanji said, rising to his feet. "Go, and in the morning, take her down to the river. She will be more content."

So would he, but that didn't mean it was going to happen. In the short week he'd known her, contentment hadn't been anywhere on the priority list.

Will watched the old man leave, then looked around the hastily prepared camp. Only the fires proclaimed it a place of men. The shelters and the hammocks were nearly invisible against the backdrop of shadows and tangled vegetation, no more than cradles of leaves and lianas turned with a deft hand out of the forest itself.

Climbing into Annie's hammock, Will considered the shaman's advice. It hadn't been lightly given. Dakú men took the taming of women very seriously, as did Dakú women. More than sex, it was the order of things, a claiming of responsibility, a way of taking care.

Slipping his arm around her, he rested her head on his shoulder and relaxed, letting her settle against him, and nearly was content.

The tree frogs had grown silent, allowing the other night sounds to be heard: the distant flowing of the river, the descending notes of a nightjar's song. He could smell the leaves on the trees, the rich greenness glossed by the fire's smoke. Rain was coming before dawn, building in the clouds coursing across the moon. Six months ago, he'd drunk Tutanji's *yagé* and seen the serpent vision again. The moon tonight was a portent from that vision, a silver scythe cradling Venus through streams of mist, heralding the coming darkness of the new moon.

He wanted to take Annie and run.

He wanted to keep her safe.

He wanted to kiss her—and when she sighed and settled in even closer to him, he did just that, sliding his fingers through her hair, brushing it back off her forehead, and lowering his mouth to press against her skin. She was warm, and soft, and so very sweet to hold, her body sleepily pliant. He'd found her before anything too awful had happened, and for tonight, that was enough.

Or would have been, if she hadn't rearranged herself, sliding her leg up between his.

Interesting, he thought. Damned interesting and bound to get even more so, if she didn't move her leg someplace other than where she had it.

She did, but only to make things worse—or better, depending on how much he thought he could take. With her now lying half across him, her thigh pressing up against his groin, he was ready to say to hell with contentment. Then she sealed his fate, running her hand up his chest and bringing it slowly back down, her fingers absently tracing the ridges of his muscles.

It was heaven, pure and simple, her soft breasts cushioned against his rib cage, her hand warm on his skin, and her thigh creating just enough pressure to make arousal hum throughout his entire body.

He kissed her forehead again, then the bridge of her nose, and in an act of unconscious acquiescence, she tilted her face toward his. The offer was irresistible. Knowing she wasn't quite cognizant of what she was doing, he gently touched his mouth to hers, and when her tongue instinctively came out to taste him, he discovered he wasn't nearly as tired as he'd thought.

Perfect.

He opened his mouth wider, hoping for more of her, and she did not disappoint, licking at his lips and teeth in a delicate exploration, making him wet, and playing inside his mouth with a lazy indulgence that told him she was still at least half asleep.

As a kiss it was artless seduction, his body awakening to hers in quickly escalating degrees, the muscles she lingered over tightening at her touch. Her unconscious desire fascinated him. He wasn't even sure she knew it was him whose mouth she was mating, but her body knew. He recognized every move she made, every response from when they'd kissed before, right down to the way her hand slid down his chest and over his abdomen toward his groin, leaving a trail of heat in its wake—but this time she didn't stop. She went the extra inch and then some.

He stifled a groan, his body slowly arcing into her hand. In the back of his mind, he remembered they weren't that far away from the next palm-thatched lean-to, but he wasn't going to stop her. Everything she was doing, he wanted more of.

Yes. His hips rose again to meet her, a primal reaction as her fingers wrapped around him, the soft warmth of her palm sheathing him.

God, it was too good.

He captured her mouth with his own, filled his hand with her breast, indulging himself in her softness, the taste and feel of her a powerful catalyst to his arousal. He'd been hard since her first kiss, and now he was hard and aching, too hot to be teased, and not yet hot enough. He wanted every stroke of her hand doing to him exactly what it was doing, and through the haze of his thoughts, he knew he wanted to be inside her when he came.

But, God, she was all over him, languorously, with drowsy, seductive imprecision, the catch of her breath in his ear, damp licks of her tongue along the side of his neck, her teeth grazing his chin—and her hand. She was going to devour him and take him right over the edge without ever waking up—and he would have let her do it, if he hadn't wanted more.

He flipped the button on her shorts and slid the zipper down, and with a wonderfully unselfconscious grace, she moved to help, lazily sliding one leg out to free herself. It was a haphazard business at best, but she was wet, and ready, and more than willing when he pushed up between her legs and slid inside, her breath coming in short, panting gasps against his shoulder that went into overdrive when he slipped his fingers into her soft folds and gently, so gently, rubbed the soft, sweet place on her body designed for her pleasure—and for his. He wanted his tongue on her there, promised himself that next time he would lick her until she melted into his mouth. Just the thought of it added intensity to what he was feeling, made him thicker, harder. He thrust once, moving his mouth to hers to kiss her deep, and her body tensed. Holding her to him with his other hand, he thrust again, losing himself in her soft, wet heat, and she started coming undone. He thrust again and caught her cry with his mouth over hers, her contractions rippling down the length of his shaft, her climax tautening her like a bow. Again, and every muscle in his lower body tightened and pulsed with the need for release. Again, and he jerked against her, shattering into ecstacy, pouring himself inside her.

Minutes later, he slipped free of her body, and still felt as if he'd been hit by a freight train. Annie had fallen asleep on top of him and was softly snoring in his ear, completely oblivious to the fact that they'd just set some sort of world record for a quickie in a hammock with one partner asleep.

That had been sex, pure, unadulterated sex. Animal need had met animal need and refinements had gone out the window. Tutanji had been right, though. She was about as calmed down as he'd ever seen her. For that matter, so was he, more relaxed than he'd been in years.

With a little bit of effort, he got her shorts back on her and zipped and buttoned without precisely waking her up. She'd mumbled a little bit, and complained, and made him feel like some sort of pervert for having unadulterated sex with someone who hadn't been precisely awake—but then he remembered where her hands had been before he'd even thought about her shorts, and absolved himself of all guilt.

Amazon Annie.

Good God, he thought, a tired grin spreading across his face. They were a long way from a first-class hotel suite with hot towels, clean sheets, and room service, but she was reminding him of all the luxuries he'd been so long without, and of a luxury he'd never had.

Her, with her tough-girl reputation, her Israeli rifles, and the softest mouth he'd ever kissed. He hoped like hell she didn't hate him in the morning when she realized what had happened, because he was afraid he'd just fallen in love in a hammock.

CHAPTER 21 ✠

CORISCO WALKED ALONG A JUNGLE path bordered by a hundred flaming torches, one for each *cordeiro* to be sacrificed on the *noite do diabo*. He was carrying a well-wrapped package close to his chest. Soot wafted up into the trees in smoky ringlets, blending into a night lit by a bare sliver of moon. In two nights, there would be no moon at all, only a dark circle in the sky, an opening to the netherworld and the hell he would bring into the glade.

Excitement thrummed through his veins. His long years of labor would soon be rewarded. Major Vargas would no longer exist. In his place would be King Corisco, sovereign of four thousand miles of river and three million square miles of mountains, and forest, and plains. Fear would rule where politics forever failed.

No government truly understood power. Bureaucracy tied their hands and their minds. He'd been in the army long enough to see firsthand what kind of mess bureaucracy created. Half-measures were the hallmark of government.

But not in Reino Novo. In Reino Novo, he ruled, and because he ruled, he was creating what other men had only imagined—a true El Dorado, its central plaza already in place, the keystone of all that would come, and all of it in gold.

The path flared at the end, opening onto the golden plaza, the torches continuing around its outer edge, their light caressing the sinuously curved statue rising out of the middle of the square—*El Mestre* in the shape of a truly giant anaconda, ten feet wide and towering twenty feet above the forest floor, its mouth open and gaping, its fangs—like the rest of it—glinting gold in the flickering light.

The emeralds and diamonds Fat Eddie had brought had been added to the statue's eyes, completing *Los Olhos de Satanás,* making them shine with demonic life. The coils of the snake made up the base of the building. A spiral of stairs incised into the snake's scales led to a door in the serpent's throat.

All around the plaza, he heard the sounds of fear, wailing women and the mutterings of old men. Indians and *caboclos* alike became afraid when he lit the torches at night. In a very real way, the torches illuminated their fate, to be consumed by *El Mestre,* their blood to flow over the plaza. He knew they whispered of it. How could they not? He'd made no secret of his plans.

The cages ringed the plaza, a circle of iron bars set into concrete pilings. As a concession to the weather, he'd had thatch roofs laid on top of the top bars to keep out the rain. In the short time since he'd constructed his prison, the rain forest had added its own touches, sending up shoots and vines to twine around the rusting bars and leaf out, making the whole thing nearly picturesque.

He took the stairs up the snake tower to the first level and the small room he'd had built into the golden anaconda's throat. The upper level was the snake's mouth, built like a platform and flanked on either side by seven-foot-high fangs. He'd killed a small paca earlier in the day, using the slightest amount of ground beetle carapace, and the bowl of blood would be well congealed by now. He would build a fire under it, get it boiling and steaming, add a few select ingredients, some powders and pastes he made himself from jungle plants, and one highly poisonous and highly hallucinogenic frog skin. It was a risk to drink the blood potion. It was always a risk, but he was in need of visions, of a night given over to strange pleasure and carefully skirted terror. *Uyump* the frogs were called, vision beasts—and the visions they gave were beastly, indeed. Less than an inch long, the tiny frogs exploded a man's mind into an infinite number of pieces. Only the truly strong came back whole.

He had ... barely. After the first time, he'd had to struggle to regain his sanity, and yet he'd been drawn back to the shaman's shack up on the Rio Papurí again and again, until one night he'd seen his shining path to greatness open up and spread out like a path of stars.

He opened the door to his sanctuary and was greeted by a heartening sight. Beetles, everywhere, scuttling over tables and walls. Thousands of five-inch-long kingmaker beetles, their iridescent carapaces adding a surreally colored and ever-shifting surface to everything inside the room.

Hungry beetles, he thought, moving to the nearest

table and ripping open the package. A pile of raw and bloody monkey parts spilled out, and the beetles descended in a horde to feed on the fresh kill.

A thoroughly satisfied smile curved the corners of his lips. Even without his gold, he was a rich man, a very rich man—and he was unstoppable.

CHAPTER 22 ⚔

ANNIE WAS AWAKENED AT DAWN BY A
soft touch on her shoulder, the woman Ajaju coming to
take her to the river as she had every morning. She
looked around as she swung her legs over the side of the
hammock. The camp was breaking up, everyone packing
and shouldering whatever they would carry for the day.

At the river, the same sense of urgency prevailed.
Children were part of the women's morning time, and
mothers quickly washed their broods in the pool of clear
water below the waterfall rushing over a rocky ledge in
the river.

The morning was lovely and cool, with mist pooling
along the forest floor and rising off the water. Birds were
awake and taking to the air from their nighttime roosts.

With the children washed up, the women hurried
back to the camp. Being the only one with clothes to put
on left Annie alone at the riverbank, a surprising occurrence it took her a moment to realize. She hadn't been
alone since the Indians had caught her. The possibilities

weren't lost on her, but as she slipped on her shorts and looked around the forest, the realities weren't lost on her, either. Striking off on her own might not be in her best interest. The Indians hadn't harmed her, and Will—

Will.

She stopped with her shirt only half on.

Will had come into the camp.

How could she not have remembered? She'd been so relieved to see him. So incredibly relieved.

Maybe too relieved.

She finished slipping on her shirt, and clipped her fanny pack back around her waist, her gaze going to the trail the women had followed back to the camp. A warm blush coursed up her cheeks. She'd had a dream in the night, an incredibly erotic dream in which William Sanchez Travers had played the starring role, his body lithe, and lean, and hard—and for a few, brief, wondrous minutes, a part of hers.

Inexplicably, a warm blush coursed over her cheeks. The dream had felt real, damned real.

Maybe too damned real.

A birdcall to her right brought her gaze back to the waterfall just as a flock of egrets burst out of the trees on the shore. As one the birds took flight, flashes of white against the blue sky, dipping over the misty falls to the water, and then rising again against a backdrop of lush, green forest. At the top of the canopy, they turned, changing direction, and came flying down the river.

And there he was, standing on a slab of rock jutting into the water at the top of the falls, nearly invisible within the rising mist of early morn and the long shadows of the rain-forest trees. Her heart slowed in her chest. He had feathers tied into his hair, green parrot and blue macaw, and long, black toucan. His face had been painted with *genipa* stripes on both cheeks. Another line of paint went down the whole side of his body, all the way to his foot. He was armed with a spear and his machete, its long blade hanging down the length of his thigh tied by a strip of twisted cloth, a line of white against his body. A bamboo quiver and a bow were slung diagonally across his chest.

He was naked except for a loincloth, and the sight of him started a tumult of longing inside her.

It had been no dream. Looking at him, she knew. They had made love, and it had been wonderful—the taste of his mouth, being cradled in the strength of his arms, that first slow thrust of his body into hers.

The memory washed through her, turning longing into an ache of desire she wouldn't have believed herself capable of feeling, not after Yavareté.

From where he stood on a rock in the river, he turned and caught her gaze with his own. A warm blush coursed up her cheeks. They had made love. It seemed impossible to her that she'd let him get that close, even more impossible that she might have been the one to initiate their closeness—but she remembered the way he'd felt beneath her hands, the tautness of his muscles, the silken softness of his skin, all of him hers to explore—and explore him she had.

Her blush deepened. The more she looked at him, the more she remembered.

He started down the rocks at the side of the falls, and she let herself look her fill, her gaze trailing over a landscape of lean muscles and brown skin to his face. He was beautiful, physically elegant, an animal in his prime, and looking at him, she was afraid what she was feeling was more than lust, a truly disturbing turn of events. She hadn't been in love with the wrangler in Wyoming. She'd been in the midst of a teenage crush, but when the pro rodeo circuit had called him back, she'd also been relieved at how easily she'd gotten out of the relationship. She and the professor had shared a passion that was more intellectual than physical, at least on her side. It had been his mind that had attracted her, and her heartbreak had been pretty damned minimal when he'd dumped her for the next coed in line.

Coming up off the trail, Will stopped in front of her, his body sheened with morning mist.

"Good morning," he said. *"Tudo bem?"*

"Vou bem." With him standing close, she was fine.

She had an intellectual passion for his mind, too, and had for years, ever since she'd first read his *Medicines of the Milk River and the Healing Forest,* long before they'd started putting his photograph on his book jackets. But it wasn't the thought of having intellectual discourse with him that was making her heart race. It was the way he smelled—very warm and masculine, very different from her, like *genipa* and earth with traces of smoke from the morning fires. It was his hands and the tendons that ran down his forearms and met like the confluence of a river at his wrist. All she had to do was look at the taut plane of his abdomen and the arrow of dark hair that started at his navel and disappeared beneath his loincloth, and her mouth went dry.

There were probably dozens of scientifically biological reasons for what she was feeling. She'd read some of the published material on the genetic forces at work in mate selection, the literal chemistry of sexual attraction—and at the moment couldn't have cared less.

"Come with me," he said. "I want to show you some thing."

Annie followed him up the path beside the waterfall to the calmer water upriver, intensely aware of his naked ness as she walked along behind him. He was a six-foot tall gringo, a white man burned brown by the equatorial sun, his hair bleached to near whiteness in a wild disar ray of streaks, his muscles long, and lean, and powerful. The loincloth barely covered him in front and wasn't even meant to cover him in back. Every step he took was a study in grace, long flanks of smoothly flexing muscle moving under his skin. She remembered how it had felt to have him hot and hard inside her, the pulsing beauty of his release—and she wanted to feel it all again.

He glanced back over his shoulder, offering her his hand. When their eyes met, she blushed, and he smiled, slow and easy, like a promise—and Annie suddenly under stood that whatever he wanted to show her was only part of the reason they were walking away from the camp.

Anticipation washed through her in a lush wave, heightening her senses, making them hum with aware ness. Her hand was small in his, his palm rough against hers, his fingers longer and bluntly squared. The strength of his whole arm was in his light grasp, and she felt that as a promise, too. His strength was hers. It was some thing she'd never had on her side, a man's strength, something she'd never truly understood.

She understood it now, her gaze drifting over Will's broad shoulders. She understood it even better when she followed the trail of his tattoo. Black snake, white snake, twined in a serpentine spiral down the length of his back. The old shaman had marked him for life, using palm spines and black dye. She saw the scene in her mind's eye:

the dark of a rain-forest night, Will lying on the forest floor, the snake's blood and his own running down his body, and Tutanji chanting hour after dark hour until dawn, his old hands guided by a *caapi* vision through wreaths of smoke.

Knowledge, he'd told her, had been the shaman's promise. For three years of his life and the destruction of Corisco Vargas, he would be given shamanistic knowledge. He was a smart man, brilliant, and for the sacrifices he'd made, Tutanji must have made a damned convincing case.

"What exactly is the old man going to give you, if you overcome Vargas?" More than curiosity prompted the question. She wanted to know everything about him, especially what had changed him.

"A map," he said, stopping and looking back at her. "A map to an ancient, sacred place somewhere north of where we are now."

"The lost city of gold everybody mentions whenever your name comes up?" The rumors about him were near legend in themselves, and the lost city of gold was the most persistent.

"No. Not gold, Annie. A place of plants, ancient plants, something from the fossil record that hasn't been seen alive and growing for millions of years. Maybe a lot of ancient plants." He started walking again, her hand still in his. "To be honest, the night I saw your orchid, I thought it might be part of Tutanji's promise."

She shook her head. "There aren't any orchids in the fossil record. You know that as well as I do."

"Yes, but your orchid is no regular flower. Something unusual is happening with its bioluminescence. Something I would love to research in a lab."

So would she, so help her God. So would she. "We're going to need fresh material to get anything. I did a lot of tests on the flower while I was in Wyoming and didn't find anything that hadn't been found in other biologically luminescent specimens. Yet it is different. I can see that it's different, and sometimes ... sometimes—" Her voice trailed off.

"Sometimes what?"

She let out a short laugh. "Sometimes I think it's trying to tell me something. That the light waves are some sort of Morse Code."

To her surprise, he agreed. "Yeah, I thought the same thing after spending a couple of hours looking at it."

A slow smile curved her mouth. "It is amazing, isn't it."

"Yes," he agreed again, his mouth curving into another smile.

"Like your tattoo?" She had to know what it meant, or even if it meant more than what Gerhardt had once told her about the design up on the Rio Vaupes.

A look of resignation came over his face, and his smile turned decidedly humorless. "The tattoo ... what's amazing about my tattoo is that I didn't die getting it or from some horrific infection afterward. The rest is all Tutanji's game. Basically, it represents the cerebral fissure of a man's brain, like you said that night in Barcelos, but the way Tutanji did it, the drawing also represents the creation of man's cerebral fissure by the cosmic anaconda, in essence, the awakening of man's consciousness, the beginning of human existence, the whole Garden of Eden story from an Amazonian Indian point of view, which ties in with the sacred place from the beginning of time."

"Is it the map itself?"

"No," he said. "It's more of a charm. I won't get the map until after Reino Novo."

If there was an "after" after Reino Novo. Annie didn't want to think about it, but the grimness of the possibilities was impossible to ignore.

Growing quiet, they walked on through trees drenched by mist, wading through shallow streams and ducking under overhanging vines. It was what she'd always done—walked through the rain forest, looking for plants, following little-used paths that only the most discerning eye would even have noticed. For all her fear of snakes, she'd actually seldom seen one in the wild. She'd been in certain regions of the tropics where iguanas dripped from the trees, and in the Brazilian Patanal where caimans crowded every beach, but her days in the lowland rain forests had been relatively free of snakes, and lately, so had her nights. She hadn't dreamed about the anaconda since putting on Will's necklace. Whatever power he'd brought to himself by killing the big cat, the jaguar teeth worked.

And there went another of her most dearly held scientific principles—straight out the window. She was wearing a charm she believed in, a charm whose power had been taken from a jaguar by Will's strength and cunning.

It was the strength that would protect him in Reino Novo. It was the strength that would protect her.

Farther down the trail, they crossed another shallow stream, the muddy water lapping at their ankles, and scared up a flotilla of Morpho butterflies. Blue wings like unreefed sails caught the light drifting down through the shadows of the trees.

Annie held her breath watching them flutter above the

water with a delicacy reserved for forest sprites and spirit beings. She'd seen Morpho butterflies before, but never so many. The imperceptibly tiny scales on their large wings shone with saturated iridescence, more blue than the sky.

The forest was full of riches. It always had been, and as they walked, she fell into the once familiar rhythm of her days, before the woolly monkey had changed her life, days spent walking through the jungle forests of the equator, always searching for plants.

At a deep pool of water below another waterfall, Will gestured to a trail leading beneath a rocky ledge. Annie followed him along its edge, getting soaked by the cool water pouring down from the river above. They had to swim the last few feet to the far shore.

Coming up by his side, she slicked her hair back off her face and took a deep breath. The sound of the water rushing and tumbling over the falls set them apart from the rest of the forest, encasing them in a world of their own made up of the blue sky above and a rich carpet of ferns below. Annie kicked off her shoes and sank her toes into the soft greenery, all the while looking around at the magical glade.

Tsunki, Will thought, mesmerized by the sight of her wet with her clothes clinging to her body. *Tsunki,* a river spirit known to lure men with the promise of sexual favors. According to Tutanji, it happened all the time. A man would come down to the river to bathe or fish, and there would be an erotic incarnation of all his human desires, a spirit woman in flesh-and-blood form who would bind the man to her with an enchanted seduction. Tutanji had experienced two such sexual encounters in his youth, he'd once told Will, the second of which had conferred shamanistic powers upon him.

His gaze swept over her again and he felt the first slow flames of desire lick into life. Annie Parrish, *tsunki* of the Amazon. He was definitely enchanted, and more than half seduced.

Last night aside, it had been a long time since he'd been with a woman, and there were a few things he'd almost forgotten, especially that a woman had to be won, every time, and that no matter how many times a woman had walked the Rio Vaupes, a man's power, sexual and physical, could overwhelm her in an instant.

Annie knew that better than most.

She glanced over her shoulder at him, and with a gesture, he directed her gaze to the shore, to the broken limb of a tree near the water, and watched in satisfaction as her eyes widened. It was his gift to her.

"I found them this morning, right where you'd said they would be."

"My God," she murmured, stepping nearer the log and reaching up to touch the flowers blooming in such rare profusion.

"Look up," he told her, following close behind. "Into the trees." And when she did, he saw her wonder turn into amazement.

There were hundreds of blue orchids in full bloom, enough to make it seem as if there were two skies, the one above the canopy, and another in the understory.

It was a living miracle, and Will knew she understood that as well as he did.

"*Aganisia cyanea*," she crooned, caressing another delicate blue petal.

"I lost count earlier, but from what I can tell, there's a few hundred flowers blooming here, a world record. If you can verify, Dr. Parrish, we can at least submit the find for posterity."

She laughed at that, her eyes brightening. "And can you imagine them wondering how Dr. William Sanchez Travers and Dr. Anne Parrish just happened to end up in the same middle of nowhere at the same time to verify each other's count of an unprecedented number of blooming *Aganisia cyanea* somewhere in northwestern Brazil."

He smiled along with her. "They would never believe the truth."

She laughed again, a sound that rippled along his senses with near physical pleasure. He liked making her laugh. He liked seeing the weight of seriousness lifted from her shoulders, even if only for a short while.

He liked her—more than liked her. Tutanji could have all the other *tsunkis*, Annie was the embodiment of his sexual desire, silken skinned and gently curved—and sweet. It had been so sweet to sink into her liquid heat and lose himself in the sensual wonder between her legs, to spiral out of control with her, with his mouth on hers and her body pulling him deeper and deeper under her spell, until he'd come, his body buried in hers to the hilt and her sweet gasps of pleasure burning her into his soul.

The memory washed through him, making him hard beneath the scrap of cloth he wore. She knew why they'd come away from the camp. He'd seen the knowledge in her blush.

She'd returned her attention to the closest flower and was touching it gently, her fingers moving over the petals, exploring the secrets of its inflorescence exactly the way he wanted to explore her. He wanted to kiss her, make love to her, devour her with lust and passion and love. He wanted her to be his.

His gaze strayed to the necklace around her throat. The cat had been tawny and green-eyed like her, sleek and beautiful, but without the creamy curves of her shoulders and breasts, without her soft mouth.

He moved closer to her, close enough to kiss, and reached out and took one of the jaguar fangs in his fingers. Her gaze locked onto his, and the slow, burning heat in his veins became a fire.

"Tutanji says you are wild and need to be tamed," he told her. He'd brought her here to make love to her, because he might not ever get another chance, and he wanted it badly enough to steal time. They should be on the trail, but he had to have her again.

"Tamed?"

"Yes." His fingers slowly moved up the necklace, caressing the skin of her collarbone beneath. She knew what he wanted, and she wasn't backing away. "He said you need to have my seed inside you to make you content, and that if you are reluctant, I should suck on you with my mouth until you are ready to accept me. He says even the wildest woman will take a man, if she is first worked on in this manner."

Another blush washed over her face and down her throat, reminding him of how easily she'd been aroused in the hammock, of how she'd responded to his touch.

"We made love last night, Annie." His voice grew husky as he smoothed his fingers up the side of her throat, tracing the line of her jaw with his thumb.

Golden lashes swept down over her eyes, resting in half-circles on her cheeks. "I know. I remembered this morning."

"I wondered if you would. You were mostly asleep."

"Not nearly as asleep as I might have seemed," she whispered, slowly lifting her gaze to meet his again. Her eyes were green streaked through with gold, her hair gold streaked through with silver—the little cat—her mouth softly pink and beckoning.

Watching her, holding her gaze, his heart beat heavier in his chest. He could smell her, the warm animal scent of her skin, so alive, the scent of her growing arousal. He remembered how she had tasted in the night, her tongue teasing his, her lips parting on a gasped breath—and everything inside him wanted her.

He'd watched her bathe in the pool with the other women, seen her naked in the river, cloaked only in the rising mists of morning, and he wanted to see her naked again. He wanted to feel her against him, the length of her body pressed against him, her skin hot from his touch.

"Annie," he murmured, lowering his mouth and brushing his lips across hers. "I want to tame you with my mouth, to suck on you here, *querida*,"—he slid his hand down the front of her shorts and cupped her with his palm—"until you are wild with wanting me inside you again."

Her response was immediate, the tension of desire tautening her body, her mouth opening beneath his. She moved against his hand, her pelvis rocking against him as her tongue slid across his lips, and Will groaned, wondering who was seducing whom.

He opened his mouth wider, hungry for her kiss, one hand holding her to him while the other undid the buttons on her shirt, before moving lower and releasing the snap and opening the zipper on her shorts. He worried that he was rushing her, but the time they had was short and he wanted to spend it all on top of her, losing himself inside her. She made a soft sound as he eased his hand into her shorts, his fingers slipping beneath her panties and sliding into her soft curls, and then sliding deeper into an even softer place.

She was slick, already wet, and they'd barely begun. Aroused and aching down to the core of his being, every muscle in his body, every breath became focused on one thing—to make her his, completely.

Dragging his mouth from hers, he reached up and picked one of the blue orchids, then pulled her down beside him on the forest floor, sinking with her onto the green earth.

He would have her the way he wanted, all of her.

Annie felt as if she'd slipped back into a dream. Within the shadows of the forest, he was seducing her, his body hot and hard along the length of hers, his thigh capturing her between him and the ground, holding her in place while his mouth teased and made promises she knew he could keep. With his hand, he pushed her shirt open and followed the path with his tongue, licking a trail of fire to her breast. When he took her in his mouth, she melted and knew this was the beginning of heaven on earth, with the forest all around and Will above her, his body turning her wanton with need—and the orchid. He trailed it over her other breast in a delicately soft path.

"Will." She gasped his name, and he switched his mouth to her other nipple, nuzzling her, soothing the ache he'd started.

The silken fall of his hair draped over her skin in a lazy, sweeping motion that followed the movement of his head. She buried her hands in it, running her fingers through the multicolored strands and along his scalp, holding her to him. Using the flower, he continued the path of petals down her belly and farther down between her thighs.

She sighed and moved restlessly, parting her legs, and Will let go of the flower to touch her with his fingers. Lifting his head, he held her gaze with his own, his eyes darkly slumberous as he spoke to her in soft Portuguese, telling her how beautiful her body was, how soft and wet she was and how her readiness made him hard for her, how he wanted to taste her. Then he kissed her, deep and wet, and began following the flower's path with his mouth, laving a trail of heated desire across her breasts and down to her navel, until he was there, his hands pulling her shorts down over her hips and off her legs, his tongue hot and sweet on her most secret place.

He took her slowly, lingering in his pleasure, licking her like a cat, a big cat, a jaguar who teased with his tongue, who knew when to push her harder and when to gentle her with long, soft strokes. Above them, hyacinth macaws broke free of the trees with raucous cries. In the distant canopy, howler monkeys could be heard making their guttural calls, but within their bower, all was the rhythm of love, hot skin slickened by desire, breathing heightened to a rapid cadence, and Will, taming her with the patience of the ages, until she didn't think she could bear any more.

"Will, please ..." She groaned his name, and he moved up her body, taking her mouth deep as he pressed into her below, inch by inch, claiming her, his senses primed by her response.

When she gasped, pleasure skittered down the base of his spine, adding urgency to his thrusting. She was his to love, the soft, female place between her legs his to quicken and please. Lust powered the act, pure and bewitching. His hips met hers on every stroke, pushing her higher, their bodies united by a fever pitch of friction and tension and his bone-deep need to take everything she had to give.

He pushed inside her again, pleasured as he'd never been before, tantalized by the sliding of her foot down the back of his leg, the thrust of her pelvis forward to seat him more deeply between her thighs. She was so wet and hot, and when her climax came, he was with her, consuming her and being consumed, his cry echoing in her mouth, his seed spilling into her.

Annie hung suspended with him in the long, pulsing moments of physical release, her senses drenched with the pleasure emanating from where their bodies joined, with him so deep inside her. The heat and wonder of him filled her completely, and when she fell back to earth, she knew irrevocably that she'd fallen in love.

CHAPTER 23

RIO CAUABURI

FAT EDDIE WAS FURIOUS. "TEN THOUsand *reais*!" he screamed into the shortwave radio on his boat. "She is worth more than your life, Marcos!"

"*Sim, senhor,*" the man answered from somewhere deep in the jungle between the Marauiá and the Cauaburi Rivers, where he was failing miserably to track down Annie Parrish and Guillermo Travers.

But Fat Eddie didn't want agreement, he wanted the damned little cat. He wanted the gold Corisco Vargas would pay for her. He'd sent Johnny Chang's head to Leticia, and was expecting a perfectly gruesome shrunken head, a *tsantsa,* from his Shuar Jivaro friend. He wanted Annie Parrish's to complete the pair.

That Marcos had been unable to catch Travers, Fat Eddie could understand, but the woman should have been captured days ago. She was a woman. How fast could she run in the forest?

Fast enough and then some, according to Marcos. But Fat Eddie wasn't interested in excuses. He didn't pay people to give him excuses.

Merda. There was nothing upstream in the direction they were heading except for Reino Novo, and having Annie Parrish walk right into Vargas's hands was a disaster so profitless, Fat Eddie couldn't bear to imagine it. If she was going to end up dead on the jungle altar Vargas so ridiculously revered as *El Mestre,* why couldn't she do it after Fat Eddie had squeezed his money's worth out of her?

Ignoring the sputtering radio and a sputtering Marcos, he yelled out over the water to the dozens of other boats now with him on the river. "Turn around! Turn around! We go north again, back up the Cauaburi!"

Why in the name of God Travers and the woman were going to the gold mines was a mystery—with plenty of profit in it somewhere, he was sure. People didn't risk their lives without the promise of some kind of profit. If he had to, he'd catch the little cat on her way up the riverbank itself in order to be the one to turn her in, and he would squeeze her skinny little arms all the way to Vargas's office to get her to tell him what she was after.

Women were the most vengeful creatures God had ever put on Earth, but something told Fat Eddie that a smart woman like Doutora Parrish would figure some profit into her vengeance. Murder alone wasn't enough to get her to walk into the jaguar's jaws.

She was after something.

"*Senhor! Senhor!*" Marcos's voice came crackling through the radio. "We've found them, *senhor*! We're closing in now!"

It was about fucking time, Eddie thought.

"*Chocante, Marcos! Chocante!* A thousand *reais* for you, my friend," he yelled into the radio, lying. His captain had done a piss-poor job of finding the woman, and he would pay for his incompetence once the whole mess was over and they were back in Manaus. And if by some unlucky twist of fate, Marcos lost the *doutora* before Eddie could get his hands around her throat, the captain was a dead man. Eddie had run out of patience.

DEEP IN THE RAIN FOREST on the edge of a clearing, Marcos understood his position—perfectly. He'd worked for Fat Eddie too long to overestimate the fat man's generosity or his magnanimity, and although what he'd told the man wasn't exactly a lie, it was definitely a stretch of the truth. They'd found something, a camp, which was more than nothing, and that was good enough for Marcos. At this point he was willing to take chances. He'd been slogging through the river drainage for three days in search of the little *doutora,* fighting flies and mosquitoes and heat and mud, and his own gnawing fear, and he was sick and tired of having big Fat Eddie Mano ragging on his butt.

He cocked his pistol, scanning the abandoned campsite for stragglers. His man Rubio kneeled over the remains of a campfire and signaled that it was still warm. Jorge and Daniel searched through the palm-thatched lean-tos, in case anything useful had been forgotten— an unlikely turn of events. Marcos knew the Dakú, and they traveled too damn light to be able to forget anything. The big question in his mind was whether or not Guillermo Travers had caught up to them.

Over the radio, Marcos heard Fat Eddie yelling for everyone to follow him.

The best-case scenario would be if Travers was lying dead in the rain forest somewhere. He'd had a lot of *bolas* jumping off the boat with a giant caiman in the water, and his escape had made Marcos look bad, real bad—the *ruim* gringo.

"What's your location?" the fat man demanded through the receiver. "I want to pick her up, before she can escape me again."

"We're on a tributary of the Marauiá, heading toward the Cauaburi." Marcos gave him their position, wishing he was anyplace else. He'd heard about the *noite do diabo,* and he'd planned on being back in Manaus long before the damn thing was supposed to occur. But hell, no. There he was, smack-dab in the middle of the area the damned devil was supposed to come ripping through, with enough sins on his head to make him a target, and his *estúpido* boss didn't have enough sense but to keep him chasing after a skinny little white woman.

Hell, all he wanted was to go back to Manaus.

He was about ready to do it, whether he found Annie Parrish or not, whether Fat Eddie liked it or not.

"*Sim, senhor,*" Marcos replied to Fat Eddie's continued instructions.

His man Lopes came jogging back into the camp from where he'd followed some tracks up the trail, and Marcos mouthed the word "woman" to him. Lopes replied with a wide smile, and Marcos heaved a silent sigh of relief.

Then Lopes held up eight fingers.

Marcos wanted to hit something. He didn't give a damn about how many women total were with the Dakú. He only gave a damn about one woman.

"*Sim, senhor.*" He humored Fat Eddie again, then mouthed the words "white woman" to Lopes, who answered with a shrug and a negative shake of his head.

That was it for Marcos, the straw that broke the

camel's back. They'd caught up with the Indians they'd been tracking, and Annie Parrish wasn't with them.

Findado. He was done. He was heading back to Manaus, and letting the devil have Annie Parrish and Guillermo Travers and anybody else who wasn't smart enough to get out of the northwest before the *noite do diabo.*

As a matter of fact, Marcos thought, maybe it would be best all around if the devil got Fat Eddie, too.

"Sim, senhor," he said again. "Yes, yes. We have her and are heading for the Rio Cauaburi on a course for Reino Novo." The place where the devil was supposed to begin his course of destruction. "Yes, *senhor.* We should be there by tomorrow night. Yes, *senhor.* I'll have her in chains. She will not escape. Do not worry ... wait ..." He made a strangled noise into the receiver, then made a few more. His mind was made up. "The static, *senhor.* I'm losing you, no?"

No, he answered his own question and flipped off the radio. He was done listening to Fat Eddie. By tomorrow night he'd be in Manaus, safe, while the fat man would be in Reino Novo, fighting it out with Vargas and whatever devil beast appeared. All Marcos had to do was get around the group of Vargas regulars behind him in the forest and make a break for the river.

Fat Eddie could go to hell, he thought, then grinned at his own cleverness, because, of course, hell was exactly where Fat Eddie was going.

BLUE ORCHIDS TUMBLED DOWN over three of the tree branches above where Annie was sitting. Two trees over, another group of orchids bloomed in luscious profusion. To her right, a *munguba* was literally drenched in blooming *Aganisia cyanea*.

Unbelievable, she thought. She knew botanists who would give a year of their career to see such a sight. And there she sat, no newspapers, no specimen jars, no camera—nothing to record or collect the second most amazing find of her life.

Or rather the third, she admitted, lowering her gaze from the trees to Will. He was so beautiful, sitting next to her in the half-light of the forest floor, his muscles moving in smooth precision as he repacked the arrows in his quiver, his hair falling across the back of his neck, the blond streaks gleaming a dull gold to match the bracelets hanging low on his wrist. He'd melted her down to a sated, wanton lethargy with his lovemaking, making more of a woman out of her than she'd ever been before— and being a woman was still the one thing she couldn't afford.

Hell.

She wanted him, and wanting him wasn't smart, wanting him threw all kinds of monkey wrenches into her plans for the future, if the two of them even had a future, considering the direction they were headed and what he was determined to do and notwithstanding her own commitment to doing whatever it took to get back what was hers—which she was finally ready to admit was a damn sight more than the orchid Vargas had stolen.

Will had been right. She wanted what Corisco had taken from her in Yavareté—a piece of her pride and some indefinable aspect of her sense of security. She'd always taken care of herself and come out in one piece, until the Woolly Monkey Incident, and that friggin' jail cell, and the creepy freaking things that had gone on in there, and the awful Fernando with his damned Instamatic.

Her face paled, and she looked aside—another memory she'd spent the last year avoiding every time it had come to mind.

"Annie?" Will touched her arm, and she let out a beleaguered sigh. She'd lied to him, and a part of her had known it even as she'd been doing it. She'd been lying a lot since she'd come back. She'd lied to Mad Jack before she'd left, telling him she was on her way to Costa Rica to do cloud forest research—and surprisingly enough, she could live with most of those lies.

But she didn't want to have a lie between her and Will. Not him. God, they'd been closer than their skin, and she wanted all of that free of lies.

"You were right in Barcelos. I came back to do some damage."

"To Vargas?" he asked, sounding like he already knew the answer to the question.

She nodded. "I tried to buy a shoulder-fired, antiaircraft missile and launcher in Manaus, but Johnny Chang absolutely wouldn't sell me one, saying Fat Eddie would have his head if one of his rocket launchers came up missing— but hell, we saw how much good that did him."

"A *rocket launcher*?"

She glanced up and caught his gaze, and had to work damned hard not to go all mushy. She had problems, real problems, and she still wanted to kiss him. She wanted to suck on his mouth and crawl on top of him, and she

could see where that was going to be a full-time problem
from here on out.

Damn.

"Yeah. I bought those guns from Chang thinking I
was just going to use them for self-defense, but it was a
hell of a lot of guns."

"A hell of a lot," he agreed, his eyebrows still arched
in surprise.

"Enough to go upriver and blow Corisco's operation
sky high," she confessed, "and I knew it. I could have
started in Reino Novo and finished in Yavareté and made
the world safe for ..." Her voice trailed off, and her
hand came up to her brow, rubbing at the sudden ache in
her temple. Damn, she thought again, forcing herself to
take a breath.

"Safe for what, Annie?"

"Well," she said, stalling for a second, trying to put a
good face on the destruction that somehow had always
been at the back of her mind. "I guess I was going to
make the world safe for me and figured a whole lot of
other people would benefit from it, especially if I blew up
the jail in Yavareté."

"What happened there?" His voice was soft but insistent, telling her he hadn't missed the implications of what
she'd said, or of what she hadn't said, and sitting in the
orchid-drenched glade, after making incredible love, he
wanted to know the terrible things that had happened in
Yavareté.

She took another breath to steady herself before she
spoke. "Technically speaking, it wasn't rape." And maybe
that's why she'd spent the last year dismissing what had
happened, shrugging it off. She hadn't been raped, and

she'd healed from the beatings with only one small scar to show for her time in chains, one small scar she could have gotten anywhere.

He smoothed his hand down her arm, his fingers coming to rest in a firm but gentle grip on her wrist. "Technically speaking, then, what was it?"

She looked up. His eyes were very dark, his face set in tight lines.

"Have you been to Yavareté?"

"Yes."

"Seen the jail?"

"It's cinderblock," he told her. "Looks unstable and wet and twenty bucks says it's crawling with cockroaches the size of rats, and rats the size of small dogs. It's close to the river, has no windows, and during the rainy season, another twenty says it floods."

"Yeah, that's the place."

"So what happened?" He moved his hand up to cup her chin and leaned in closer. "You never told Gabriela, but you *are* going to tell me."

Yes. She figured she was.

"It was very strange." She glanced away again.

"How strange?"

"A *ménage à trois* of sorts, I guess"—she shrugged—"where my part was to be manacled naked to the wall, which I really hated, with Vargas tripping out on some strange brew he'd cooked up in a pot, and his oversized guard dog, Fernando, clicking away with his friggin' camera. There was incense and blood, and for three days I pretty much felt like a living sacrifice just waiting to happen. But the worst part"—she paused for a moment, her brows knitting together—"the worst part is I know I got off easy. I wasn't the first woman to hang naked in that jail cell. There were clothes, some of them bloody, and I was just so damned scared that I was going to end up the same way."

"Was there anybody else? Any witnesses?"

"No." She shook her head. "People on the river leave Vargas alone. They don't mess with him, and I think because of that he's been getting away with murder. I don't know about the rumors of the virgins on the altar of gold, but I think he's murdered women in that jail cell." She lifted her gaze to his. "The place reeks of death."

She felt his hand tighten on her chin, saw the spark of fury light in his eyes.

"Gabriela said he beat you."

"Yeah, but he never really touched me, not inside, not where it would have counted. I was his prisoner, but not his victim. I never let him have that."

She never let him have that. Will lowered his head on a deep exhalation, releasing her chin and running his hand back through his hair. He'd wanted to know, and now she'd told him. My God. He'd underestimated her from the very beginning. The stories hadn't been wrong. She was no cat snack. She was Amazon Annie, and not because she'd managed to drag a load of illegal guns up the Rio Negro, or because she'd walked the Rio Vaupes, or because seeing Johnny Chang's head hadn't scared the holy shit out of her—but because even three days in the hellhole of Yavareté wasn't enough to make her forget who she was. He didn't know many people with that kind of strength.

"Somebody must have loved you very much when you were growing up," he said, looking up at her from over the top of his hand. "If it wasn't your mother, who was it? Your dad?" Amazing Annie, he wanted to call her, with her wild hair, sweet mouth, and those gold-green eyes.

"Partly," she said, a small smile curving the corner of her lips. "But I also had Mad Jack, and he told me I was the greatest thing since sliced bread every day of my life after my mom left. For a kid only a couple of years older than me, that was pretty cool."

"Pretty cool," Will agreed softly, falling even more in love. He offered her his hand, and when she took it, he rose to his feet, pulling her with him. "We better get going. We have to catch up with Tutanji and the others."

"Yeah. We wouldn't want to dawdle." Her smile broadened into a grin. She was so pretty.

"Yes, we would." He leaned down and kissed her, then kissed her again. "I'd like to stay here with you, in this place, forever, just let time and Vargas and the river pass us by, but today we've got to make tracks."

"To Reino Novo?"

"For me," he said. "I want to send you north with the rest of the women."

"North?" Her eyebrows rose. "Where north?"

He hesitated for a minute, then pulled a roll of paper out of his quiver. "Fat Eddie's men aren't too far behind us, and behind them is another bunch of guys who I think were sent by Vargas."

"By Vargas? For what?"

In answer, he handed her the paper, and when she unrolled it, she swore.

"Son of a bitch." It was the wanted poster, and now he knew the picture had been taken in Yavareté. "Where did you get this?"

"From Tutanji. He was going to turn you in for the money."

"Why?" she asked, legitimately confused. The Dakú were the least acculturated Indians in the Amazon. They didn't even have metal tools, not so much as an axe.

"Last night, by the fire, Tutanji told me Vargas is holding a hundred Indians and *caboclos* in cages at Reino Novo, many of them Dakú. He thought he could buy them back with the reward money."

"What do you think?" she asked.

"I think Vargas is going to kill them for his Night of the Devil."

Annie blanched. "A sacrifice. Yes. I can imagine him doing something that horrifying. He likes to kill things. In Yavareté, he used to kill pacas with this special poison he kept in a gold box. Then he'd cook up their blood and drink it with a bunch of other stuff in it. He spilled a lot. Believe me, it was not a pretty sight."

"What kind of poison?"

She shook her head. "I'm not sure. It's a powder, an iridescent powder, some kind of hemorrhagic toxin. After he gives it to the animals, all their blood comes gushing out."

"Kingmaker beetle," he said. "The ground-up carapace is an iridescent, hemorrhagic poison, but the beetle itself is extremely rare, worth a hundred times its weight in gold. That's kind of an expensive way to get paca blood."

"Yeah, well, I think he likes the way the blood gushes out way too much to care how much it costs." Her hand came up in an absent, fluttering gesture, as if she were trying to push the subject away, and he imagined that she was. "I don't suppose we have time to go back to where the *Sucuri* sank to try to salvage some of the guns I bought?"

"No," he said, reaching up and giving her cheek a brief caress, his gaze skimming over the scar above her temple. "Not today."

Whether she'd been victimized by Vargas or not didn't matter, not anymore. Will was going to kill him, because he wasn't nearly civilized enough to let the bastard live—not even close.

CHAPTER 24

THE SKY GREW OVERCAST AS THEY followed a game trail north through the forest. Annie had traveled with Indians and with other scientists, and Indians were quieter and faster on the trail. Will covered ground like an Indian.

About a mile or so from the glade of the blue orchids, the first rain washed down through the trees, a gentle shower dampening the hot earth and rising again as steam. In minutes, they were walking through a dreamscape of dripping leaves and white vapor. Will kept a steady pace, and Annie stayed with him. She hadn't argued with him about going north, but just like the night the *Sucuri* had sunk, she felt in her gut they should stay together.

She was about to say as much, when he came to a sudden stop.

She'd heard it, too—a gunshot. Their eyes met, and when the next shot sounded, they both took off at a run.

More shots came after the first two, and the sounds of

distant screams and shouting. By the time they reached
the place where the attack had taken place, the battle
was over and the Indians were gone, but plenty of
evidence to what had happened remained. Calabashes
of *chicha,* a fermented drink, had been smashed. Manioc
gratings were strewn everywhere. The trees and plants
surrounding the bare place in the trail where Tutanji's
tribe had been caught were riddled with bullets, their
leaves and fronds in shreds, but there were no dead
bodies.

"Gather what food you can," Will said after a quick
look around. "I'll be back."

He started to disappear into the forest, then stopped
and took off his machete.

"Here," he said, handing the big knife over. "Don't be
afraid to use it."

"I won't be," she assured him, slipping the knife
through the belt on her shorts.

"Good." He kissed her cheek, and then was gone,
melting into the trees.

Annie looked around the trail. The Indians had been
disarmed. Bows and blowguns were tossed aside. Everything they had been carrying had been haphazardly thrown
into the bush. All the food containers had been smashed,
their contents poured onto the ground.

Even abandoning all standards of sanitation, she
barely came up with half a dozen pieces of cassava, the
bread made from manioc. Abandoning even more standards, she shoved them into her pockets. By the time Will
returned, she'd salvaged what she could.

"They're not too far ahead of us," he told her, breathing hard. "It's not Fat Eddie's men. I would have recognized them."

"So who is it?"

"*Pishtacos.*"

"The fat-eaters?" *Pishtacos* were the bogeymen of the Amazon.

"According to Tutanji, they've been raiding all along the river, *pishtacos* and *garimpeiros,* and taking Indians to work in the mines. It's the ones who can't work anymore who are put into the cages."

"Indians don't last very long in the mines."

"And their women fare even less well in the brothels," Will agreed. "The best I can tell, Vargas must have sent out two parties of men to track you, the group on Fat Eddie's men's tail, and one down from the mines, the ones who did this. We're close enough to the Cauaburi now for them to have gotten this far."

"And we're following the ones who did this, right?"

"Right. Help me find some darts, and be careful. They're all tipped with curare." Curare was the famous hunting poison of the Amazon.

With a blowgun Will picked up from the side of the trail and a few darts found here and there in the bush and slipped into his quiver, they took off, running along the forest path, following Vargas's *garimpeiros* and their captives.

Hours later, Annie sank down on the trail next to where Will had stopped for a moment, her muscles aching, her breath ragged. She'd been up north for a year, and a week on a riverboat hadn't done a damn thing to reacclimate her to the equatorial tropics.

God. She was drenched in sweat, the air temperature felt about a hundred and twenty, and the humidity had been hovering all day between "downpour" and "drizzle."

"Tired?" he asked, kneeling down beside her.

"A little," she lied, wiping the moisture from her brow.

"Here," he said, pulling the top off a gourd kept tied on the same string as his quiver. "Open your mouth."

She did as he asked, and he scooped out two fingerfuls of a green powder and put it on her tongue. It was like talc, very fine and smoky tasting.

"Make a paste out of it with your saliva, and just let it sit in your mouth for as long as you can," he said, dipping out a larger scoop for himself.

"What is it?" she asked.

"Something from Tutanji." He smiled. "It's good for you."

They sat silently for a few minutes, waiting for the plant powder to take effect, and eventually, Annie wasn't so hungry, the heat wasn't so terrible, and she had the strength to get to her feet.

When he asked if she was ready to go, she didn't hesitate. The next time they stopped, dusk was falling and they were nearing the river, and she could hear Vargas's men and the Indians up ahead. Women were crying. Men were shouting, and Annie wondered how in the hell they were going to save anybody from a bunch of armed men.

Will had a plan, though, and it started with him taking feathers out of his hair and working them into hers. He tied them on top, a dark green parrot and the black toucan, letting them stand straight up.

"There," he said with a quick grin, sitting back on his haunches and checking out his handiwork. "You look like a bird. Now I'm going to make you look like the forest."

Using a handful of mud like an artist's palette, he

painted triangles and stripes on her face, and she helped by putting stripes down her arms and legs. When he was finished, he handed her his bow and the gourds on his quiver, keeping only the blowgun.

"We'll follow them to their boats and make our move on the beach. You stay hidden where you can see what's going on, and when the time comes, head for the last boat. That's the one we're taking to Reino Novo."

She nodded, hoping to hell it was dark by then, because feathers or no feathers, she would stick out like a sore thumb in the company heading down to the riverbank.

Will slipped into the trees, and Annie followed, until the river came into view. Five boats were moored on the beach. She knew there had been exactly twenty-three Indians in Tutanji's group, and there looked to be half again as many *garimpeiros*. There were a ragged bunch in ragged clothes ordered about by a few men wearing the uniform of the Brazilian army. Vargas, for all his grand schemes, was still exercising his commission, which made the Brazilians culpable in the forthcoming massacre—unless she and Will could somehow stop it.

With a touch on her arm to stay, Will left her, disappearing into the forest.

Annie looked down at the machete and the bow. Even given his blowgun, they were woefully underequipped for the task ahead.

A fire was started on the white sand beach for the miners to cook their food, while the Indians were herded into a makeshift compound guarded by the soldiers with the automatic weapons.

Standing silent and still behind the buttressed roots of a strangler fig, she concentrated on her breathing, keeping it gentle and even, keeping herself calm. Whatever Will was going to do, she needed to be ready.

Down by the river, two of the *garimpeiros* walked up to the compound and tried to take a woman, her friend from the morning, Ajaju. The other Indians immediately became excited, objecting loudly and scrambling to keep Ajaju with them. Ajaju screamed, her face stark with fear, but the miners kept pulling at her, hitting the Indians who were holding on to her. Her children began to cry, and for a minute, Annie feared the *garimpeiros* would succeed, but finally, one of the soldiers interceded, threatening the miners with his rifle.

Angry grumbling ran through the other *garimpeiros*. Rape was their expected reward.

Annie grew even more still, her breath even softer as she witnessed the further rough treatment of the Indians, the *garimpeiros* throwing things, the soldiers ignoring them. Up until Yavareté, she'd lived a sheltered life. She'd seen hardship and poverty, had experienced a little poverty herself on the ranch, at least compared to the other kids at school who'd had new clothes instead of Mad Jack's way too big hand-me-downs to wear. In South America, she'd seen real poverty, the kind that crushed people, the kind perpetuated by ineffective governments run by people whose sense of privilege far outstripped their sense of justice.

But in Yavareté, she'd witnessed brutality, psychotic brutality. She'd experienced it for herself, and it had changed her more profoundly than she'd thought.

She had come back for vengeance, an inarticulated vengeance that nonetheless had compelled her to buy guns. Standing in the trees, her body no more than another living, growing part of the forest, her breath no different from the transpiration of the leaves, she quietly came to the realization that she could kill.

The knowledge shifted her awareness of the world around her. She was no longer carefully apart, separated from the people in front of her by virtue of her intelligence and her education, or by her culture and her passport. She was no different from any of them, soldier, miner, Indian. Her hand went to the quartzite crystal and the jaguar fangs hanging around her neck. She was no different from Will.

She knew where he was, to her left, about fifty yards away near the far end of the beach, and she knew what he was doing—waiting like a jaguar with his curare-tipped darts. He had eight, and she knew eight men would die.

She was a jaguar now, too. Like a cat, she kept herself still, waiting, and when her chance came, she would not hesitate.

Vargas's men had eaten and were breaking their quick camp, when a cloud passed over the sun, laying a shadow on the river.

That's when the first man died. No one else saw, but Annie had watched the *garimpeiro* wander into the edge of the forest at the far end of the beach and unzip his pants. Then his hand had come up to his throat, and he'd crumpled, falling into the forest vegetation and disappearing.

Another *garimpeiro* followed blindly in the first one's footsteps, heading to the edge of the forest to relieve himself, and meeting an instant, silent death.

Dusk had fallen with the shadows of the clouds. Night would come quickly. Annie felt her muscles tense in readiness. The Indians were already being put on the boats. The fires were doused. Someone hollered a name into the deepening darkness and shouted louder when he didn't get a response.

"*Jose! Agora mesmo!*"

"*Um momento!*" An answer finally came from the forest, and Annie recognized Will's voice.

She couldn't remember ever having stood so still for so long, so painlessly. She could have waited hours longer, if necessary, being a jaguar.

Another movement at the far end of the beach caught her eye, someone coming out of the tent. Food had been brought to him there, but now two soldiers were standing by, ready to strike the canvas. It was time to go.

At first Annie thought two people were coming out at once, and was quickly revising her and Will's odds in her head, but as the two came farther out on the beach, their bodies remaining in perfect synchronization, the truth dawned on her with growing distress.

It wasn't two people. It was one very large man, a six-foot-eight-inch giant with a huge barrel chest and trunk-like legs.

It was Fernando.

Her instinct was to flee, her breath instantly becoming ragged and fast, and she actually moved, before she stopped herself.

She was a jaguar. A cat. Even a giant was no match for her. She believed it, but she couldn't stop trembling, and she couldn't take her eyes off him. He was dressed as an officer, something she hadn't known about him before, and he was carrying an assault rifle.

He went to the lead boat out of the five moored on the beach. There was one armed soldier for each boat, and two *garimpeiros* to guard the Indians. Darkness fell with the sudden swiftness of the tropics, and one by one the boats took off up the river, leaving the last soldier to holler for dead men. As the fourth boat turned into the current, Will struck with uncanny accuracy, hitting the soldier, who slumped over the wheel. The man's rifle went clattering into the bottom of the boat. The bound Indians reacted instantly, jumping into the shallows and onto the beach, but no more instantly than she did. She broke into a run, bursting out of the trees the same time that Will hit the beach.

With her knife free, she cut the Indians loose. Neither Tutanji or Ajaju were among the five. Will spoke quickly, and in seconds the freed man nodded. Gesturing for the two women and the children to follow, he took off into the forest.

Annie was already on the boat, firing it up, when Will jumped on board. In the darkness up ahead, someone shouted back at them, and Will answered, saying something that made the other soldier laugh.

"Take the wheel," he told her. "I'll put the dead man overboard."

She guided the boat out into the river and heard the body hit the water with a splash.

Will came back to her side and leaned close to her ear to be heard above the sound of the outboard engines. "Try to get some sleep. We've got a few hours to the mines."

She nodded. "You saw the giant come out of the tent?"

"Yes." He took the wheel from her.

"Fernando," she said.

He nodded silently and touched his hand to the feathers in her hair. "You look like a bird, but you're really a jaguar. I saw you in the forest, waiting."

She held his gaze for a moment, the wind whipping at their hair, the stars shining above.

"Yes," she said. "That was me."

He grinned, a flash of white in the dark night. "Get some sleep."

She was too tired to object, and when her head rested on the wooden bench running the length of the starboard side, it was like settling into a down-filled pillow.

HOURS LATER, it was the silence that woke her, the silence and the chill of early morning, before dawn had broken the sky.

Will had cut the engines and the lights, and they were drifting down the shoreline. Branches and leaves slapped at the boat. He grabbed for them as they passed, holding on just long enough to keep the boat from slipping farther into the current.

Annie raised her head to a startling sight—Reino Novo, as she'd never imagined it. In the middle of thousands of miles of unremitting darkness, it was a city of lights, ballpark lights illuminating the gouged and gaping holes of the mines, the yellow and orange hoses of the pumps and generators snaking out of their black depths like miles of intestines.

All along the scarred faces of the mines, miners scurried like *formigas*, ants. Some manned the hoses, blasting away at the earth with high-powered jets of water. It was a twenty-four-hours-a-day operation awash in water and mud and misery, a cacophany of noise and violence within the great womb of the forest.

She'd seen gold mines before, but never anything on such a scale. There were open pits on both sides of the river, each as horrible as the other.

"Are we still on the Cauaburi?" she asked.

"No." Will stopped them by tying off on a sturdy branch. "We came off the main river a couple of hours ago. This is a tributary off to the west."

"Where are the other boats?"

He pointed toward the mines, and Annie saw a series of docks jutting out into the river from both sides. Four boats were pulling up to the docks on the south bank, their side, and a commotion was being made.

"Come on. We have to hurry, if we're going to keep up."

She was glad he hadn't asked her to stay with the boat. She could see the Indians being herded off onto the docks, and she could sense their fear and confusion. Reino Novo had changed to the point of being unrecognizable compared to what she'd seen a year ago. It was huge, completely contained. Fires from a smelter belched smoke and soot into the sky, laying an added pall of stench over the area.

On the north bank, a town had risen up, muddy streets of whorehouses and cantinas. Farther upriver, hundred-gallon tanks of the gas and oil needed to run the generators lined both shores, the iridescent smear of leaks making a glossy coat on the water. The smell of the place alone was enough to terrify the forest people. It was enough to terrify her.

"This place is unbelievable," she said.

"Yeah," he said. "Take this." He handed her the rifle and the extra rounds of ammunition he'd taken off the dead soldier. "It's about a thousand times bigger than I expected. We'll try to keep out of sight, until we can see where they're taking the Dakú. Hopefully, it'll be near the cages. Our first priority is to get as many people out as possible. Secondly, if we can"—he pulled a duffel bag out from under the wheel—"we'll try to use this stuff to blow the place." He unzipped the bag, revealing a cache of dynamite.

"Vargas's guys like to travel prepared for anything, don't they," she said, stuffing a stick in each pocket.

"Yes." He smiled. "Come on. Let's go."

CHAPTER 25

F$_{\text{AT EDDIE SLOWLY MOTORED UP THE}}$ river, nearing Reino Novo, his swivel spotlight swinging from side to side in smooth, battery-powered arcs. It had been a long night with little to eat, and he wasn't in the best mood. He'd been on the rivers of the northwest for a solid week. Unbelievable for a man who prided himself on never having to leave the Praça de Matriz in his beloved city of Manaus.

The woman, she was a demon to have done this to him. He'd been trapped for hours, days, in his speedboat, sneered at by the likes of Corisco Vargas, lost his plane, ten pounds if he'd lost an ounce, and the woman, by the blood of Christ, for about the hundredth time.

What was it with her? he wondered. What made the little cat so hard to hold on to? So hard to catch?

He'd like to know how Vargas had held her for three days in the Yavareté jail. Or maybe that's what it took, a jail, to keep her in her place. He'd completely changed his mind about her head, and was damn close to changing it about turning her in to Vargas. She was a smart woman, a damned smart woman, like Guillermo was a smart man. The two of them together, working on his side, maybe could make him the richest man in Brazil.

Vargas still had to be dealt with, possibly killed.

Eddie mused the idea over for a minute, his hand easy on the wheel.

Yes, he decided in the end. There was no doubt. Corisco Vargas had to be killed. The man was a menace.

He'd never gotten another radio transmission from Marcos and Eddie had a sneaking suspicion it wasn't because his captain had suddenly dropped dead in the forest.

No, he figured it had to do with the size of Marcos's balls, which must have shrunk up into his brain by now. The man had been taking the *diabo do noite* far too seriously.

"Night of the Devil. Night of the Devil," all the river people were whispering.

Night of the Devil, his ass, Eddie thought. Like everything else this last year that had been going to hell, the Night of the Devil was really the Night of Corisco Vargas.

Cristo, but he was really starting to hate that man.

Vargas had those Indians and those *caboclos*. Eddie would bet every ounce of fat on his body on the fact. What the hell Vargas was going to do with them, Eddie didn't have a clue, except to figure it would probably be pretty sick, and the Indians and *caboclos* would probably end up dead. Everything Vargas touched ended up dead, like this whole huge stretch of forest.

Eddie had seen plenty of mines in the north, and worked deals with the *donos*, the mine bosses, when he could. But he'd never seen anything like Reino Novo. It was no New Kingdom, but it was damn big.

His spotlight hit the top of its arc to the right and slowly swung back to the left, going from one riverbank to the next, and finally finding something of interest on the far shore. He grabbed the light, shining it full on the boat tied up to a branch.

Damned odd, he thought. There were five fully functional docks at Reino Novo not a hundred yards farther up the river. There was no reason on earth to tie a boat up to a tree.

He smelled a rat.

Or rather, he smelled a cat, a little cat. He smelled her like a feral dog.

"Jorge!" he called out, signaling the man piloting the next boat. When the man looked over, Fat Eddie lifted his arm and gestured toward the shore.

Possibly, just possibly, it wasn't too damn late to turn a profit on this whole damn mess.

WILL AND ANNIE scrambled over the slag heaps rising like small mountains around the belching smelter. Once they were off the river, its fires could be seen glowing like the fires of hell on the south side of the camp. Between the smelter and the mines was a stretch of no-man's-land, where hoses snaked, and water ran, and every makeshift walkway that had ever been tried was sinking into the mud. For all its riches, Reino Novo had not overcome the bane of rain-forest industry: once the thin layer of topsoil was gone, nothing would hold the rest of it together. The battle was always one of deterioration, with the rain always winning.

It was over the walkways that Fernando and his men were herding the Indians, past rows of shacks and burning piles of refuse.

Annie's heart was in her throat. There were men everywhere, but most of them were too haggard and tired to do more than jeer at the captives, or to look dumbly as they went by. The miners were captives themselves, captured by a false promise of riches and held by a debt servitude they could never repay. The company store would always be charging just a little bit more than the *garimpeiros* made, and too much of their hardearned share of the gold went right back into the *donos*'s pockets, spent on whores and *cachaça*, fleeting pleasures that few men could do without, but none could actually afford. To call their existence grim was almost naïve. The word "grim" didn't begin to sum up the misery of the mines.

Once past the smelter, the rain forest reasserted its dominance, sending viney tendrils burrowing under the slag heaps to reemerge as a spot of green in the middle of a gray wasteland. Trees grew closer to the trail, adding the cover Will needed to get closer to the Indians, but he was behind them, and he needed to move ahead.

"Keep following them, Annie," he said, dropping back to check on her. "Stay on this side, and you'll run right into me in about five minutes. If you don't, make your way back to the boat and get the hell out of here. Promise me."

"Promise," she said without hesitation, but he wasn't fooled. She was a terrible liar.

He kissed her hard, once, and slipped away, moving swiftly and silently through the perimeter of trees. He had five darts left.

Annie watched him disappear, an act that took him about two seconds flat. When the last soldier in line collapsed, she knew exactly where Will was—so did the Indians. The change in them was immediate. An alertness came over them, their faces turning to the forest. They knew they weren't alone.

Will's was a war of stealth, of hit and run with the darkness as cover. When the next soldier in line fell, his companions still oblivious to the carnage stalking them through the night, Annie thought they might have a chance at winning. The mines were behind them, the forest smelling greener, full of promise. If they could get the Indians released, they could melt into the trees as easily as Will.

Then she heard it, men's voices behind her, coming not from the walkways and the trails, but from the forest. She speeded up her steps, breaking into a loping run, wondering who in the hell besides her and Will was out in the jungle on a near moonless night—and so help her God, she could only come up with one name.

Fat Eddie Mano.

CORISCO SAT IN THE DARK in his office, the only light coming from the jungle-filled glass cage and the cylinder holding the orchid in his hand. He'd lost. Word had just come up from the docks. Fernando had arrived with the last *cordeiros,* and Annie Parrish was not among them. She would not be his to interrogate and torture one last time. Nor would she be his to sacrifice on *El Mestre.*

Perhaps he'd been wrong all these months. Perhaps she'd found the orchids elsewhere and was bypassing Reino Novo altogether.

Still recovering from his night of visions, brooding the loss was the limit of his energies at the moment. Later, he would take retribution.

He glanced over to a box lying open on the corner of his desk. A week ago, infinitely sure of success, he'd bought her a present, a little something his São Paulo tailor had sent up the river, a dress for her to die in.

He leaned over and lifted a handful of the silk. Gold and glittering, it would have been the perfect foil for her blond beauty.

His gaze came back to the cylinder in his hand. The orchids' location would remain a mystery now, and that was the true loss. He'd searched for the meaning of the flower's light in his *uyump* visions, and been denied an explanation. So be it. Many of the riches shown to him through the visions had come to him, and if at moments he remembered fleeting traces of a time before he'd partaken of the tiny frog devils, when his mind had been different, he didn't dwell on them for long. He'd chosen his path, and even a cursory look around would prove that he had chosen well.

And yet the orchid, he thought, watching it float inside its glass container. The orchid was more than it seemed, much more. He'd spent hours mesmerized by its vacillating light, many nights to the point where he'd been certain the plant had relayed something to him. But then he would come to himself, out of the trance, and realize he'd been drifting in dreams, not really paying attention, and the moment and the sensation would be gone.

For now, his chance to find more of the flowers was lost, as was his chance to have Annie Parrish, but he still had his *cordeiros,* his lambs, and he would not shirk his duty to them. Their sacrifice would make him infamous and bring him glory; the least he could do was go down and sort the new arrivals. The strong ones would go to the mines, the weak and the lame and the old would all go to *El Mestre*.

A loud bang against the glass cage drew his attention to the far wall of his office. The giant snake threw his body against the glass again, and something in the wall creaked, as if it might give way. With the anaconda's next attack, the wall actually bowed out.

Corisco smiled. Poor thing. He knew exactly what the beast's problem was—hunger, a hunger that would only be assuaged in the jungle glade on the Night of the Devil.

CHAPTER 26

WILL CAUGHT ANNIE AS SHE RACED BY, dragging her close with a hand over her mouth in case she screamed.

She didn't, recognizing him instantly. Her eyes were wide, though, wide with fear.

"There are men coming up behind us, out of the forest," she said, when he removed his hand. "Not Indians. They're making too much noise."

He met her eyes. "Fat Eddie." He couldn't believe it. Tenacious didn't begin to describe the fat man.

"The cages are just ahead, but let me warn you, Annie, the glint of gold you saw through the forest the last time you were here has gotten a lot bigger and taken shape."

"What kind of shape?"

"Snake." He was blunt. "Big snake."

Bigger than he would have dreamed possible. It was an unbelievable amount of gold to have all in one place, and Will could only wonder at the power Vargas wielded to keep his soldiers and the *garimpeiros* from stealing it by the handful. Fear would do it, an ungodly amount of fear, the kind of fear that made Will wonder what in the hell they were actually going to come up against, if they couldn't get out of Reino Novo as easily as they'd gotten in.

She swore, and swore again. He'd expected it. The woman did not like snakes.

"There's only two guards at the cages, both well armed, and one of them has a ring of keys. I don't want you to shoot, unless it's in self-defense. Bringing a bunch of soldiers and *garimpeiros* down on us is the last thing we want to do."

"Right."

They moved out, and Will couldn't begin to describe how awful he felt having her with him. Sometime, somewhere, over the last seven days, he should have been able to find a place to keep her safe. Her own damned insistence on coming had been part of the problem, but the rest of it was feeling like pure bad luck.

What in the hell, he wondered, had happened to his neat plan of gliding into Reino Novo on the *Sucuri*, an *invited* smuggler for God's sake, and taking a look around, seeing what had to be done, formulating a plan for doing it, doing it, and getting out.

Amazon Annie had happened, came his answer, and he knew in his heart that he wouldn't have missed her for the world, but he wished like hell that she was anyplace else but with him.

Annie wished she was someplace else, too, anyplace other than heading toward a giant gold snake in the middle of a hellhole, with a gun strapped over her shoulder, and her heart beating so fast she was afraid Corisco

Vargas could hear it above the sound of the pumps and the hoses and the hundreds of men he had working around the clock to mine more gold. Fernando for sure could hear it. He wasn't that far away, coming out ahead of them on the path into a circle of bright light.

As she and Will caught up to the group, she realized it wasn't a circle of bright light at all, but the reflection of a few torches on an unbelievable amount of gold. Vargas had literally paved a plaza with gold, and in the middle of the plaza he had erected the most stunningly unbelievable representation of *her* giant anaconda that she had ever seen.

"Will. Will," she whispered, pulling him to a stop. "Don't you recognize her?"

"Who?"

"The snake, the gold snake."

A trace of bafflement narrowed his gaze. "It's a snake."

"*My* snake, Will. The one that strangles me in my dreams, and it's your snake, too, the one on your boat."

That was the absolute last thing Will had wanted to hear.

"Don't tell me this, Annie. Please." He'd never seen her vision snake. Hell, he'd never even seen his vision snake. The only anaconda he'd ever seen up close and personal was the one that had sunk its teeth into his shoulder and bled all over him, and that snake had not been a vision.

"My God," she said, her voice full of awe as she looked up at the damned thing. "It's incredible."

Neither was that the reaction he was looking for.

"I've got three darts left, and four soldiers, including

Fernando. Let's do this, Annie, and get the hell out of here. Get the bow ready."

"Take Fernando first," she suggested, tearing her gaze away from the golden, snake-shaped tower. "He's got a Galil."

Excellent advice.

As they came up on the cages, a murmur of hope swept through the captives. Will said only one word, "freedom," and he said it in two languages, and three Indian dialects.

The stir put the soldiers on their guard, including Fernando and his last soldier, who had just reached the others and were quickly realizing that they'd lost a couple of men on the trail.

Fernando's realization was cut pretty damn short, though, when a curare-tipped blowgun dart caught him in the neck. Will downed the next man before he had a chance to shoot his gun. The third man was momentarily dumbstruck by his comrades all falling helpless to the ground for no apparent reason, and by the time he figured out that he was under attack, he had a dart sticking out of his chest.

He clawed at his shirt, trying to rip the dart out of his skin, but to no avail. As the curare took hold, his knees buckled and he fell to the plaza.

For Annie it was like watching a nightmare unfold in slow motion, the men crumbling, their cries of surprise as they were hit, and the grunts of terror when they realized what had hit them and that they were going to die. She felt her own breath slow in her throat, until a shot rang out, the last guard firing at them.

She reacted in an instant, swinging her rifle up and

pulling the trigger, her own shot echoing around the plaza followed by the guard's scream of pain.

"Will." She turned and found him holding his arm. Blood leaked through his fingers. He'd fallen to his knees.

"*Will,*" she gasped.

"Get the keys, Annie! Now!" He ground the words out between his teeth, forcing himself to his feet.

Annie ran across the plaza. The man she'd hit was writhing on the ground. The others weren't even twitching. Their muscles were paralyzed by the curare, their eyes locked open in terror as they slowly asphyxiated to death, their lungs no longer capable of moving air in and out.

Murmurs of excitement ran through the cages. The Indians and *caboclos* had been saved. All Annie needed was the key to release the locks bolting the iron doors, before more guards came running, alerted by the gunfire. All she needed was to wrestle the keys off the belt of the man she'd shot, while he twisted and jerked in agony at her feet, blood gushing from his stomach.

Oh, God. She was going to be sick, but she kneeled anyway and unclipped the ring of keys from his belt.

"Annie!" Will's warning cry rang out, but not before a meaty fist got a hold of her ankle and jerked her to the ground. She landed with a heavy thud, the wind knocked out of her as a half-paralyzed Fernando tried to roll her beneath him.

She kicked and swore, the arm she'd landed on throbbing in pain, the beast all over her, grappling her around.

The keys! She'd lost the keys.

Then Will was there with a knife, jerking Fernando's head back and slitting his throat.

Annie scrambled backward, revulsion turning into panic in her veins. Blood was everywhere, pumping out of Fernando's throat, running off Will's arm, pouring out of the gut-shot soldier. She dropped her rifle, trying to get away, her eyes riveted to the blood flowing onto the gold brick plaza. It slipped into the gold-mortared grooves, forming a tracery of blood, red veins running their course across the expanse of gold to the shallow indention in the middle of the plaza, a bowl, four feet across, with all the blood collecting in its golden pan.

Corisco drank blood. She remembered now. He cooked it into a hallucinogenic elixir with *uyump* frog skins. Devil frogs, the Indians called them, and a straighter road to hell had never been devised.

Will had drunk blood, too. Jaguar blood. She had blood smeared on her clothes and her skin, staining her shoes and getting all over everything. She'd lost the keys. Lost her rifle.

Merda. The keys. They were probably covered in blood from all the dying men.

"Will." She stopped her retreat, stopped sliding and pushing herself away from the dead guards. She lifted her gaze to where he was rising to his feet, one of the soldiers' knives still in his hand. "Help me, Will. We have to—"

Something behind her caught his eye, and the instant change in him warned her something was wrong.

"Will, we have to—"

"Stop, Annie," he said, keeping her from saying anything more. "It's too late."

"Too late, indeed," said another voice coming from behind her, a voice Annie knew down to the marrow of her bones.

She froze where she was on the ground, hardly breathing for the sudden fear gripping her heart. *Corisco.*

Soldiers crossed from behind her to go and stand on either side of Will. One took the knife from his hand. Two more grabbed his arms while three kept him in the sights of their rifles.

With a measured tread, Corisco slowly circled her, coming into her line of sight. Without meaning to, she drew herself back, her instincts more powerful than any source of pride or arrogance.

He was worse than she'd remembered—slicker, even more diabolical looking, with his black eyepatch and the bizarre white streak running back through his coal-black hair. His face was thin, nearly cadaverous, his uniform impeccably neat.

"Welcome to Reino Novo, Dr. Parrish," he said, his smile a sardonic curve. "Or should I say, welcome back?"

Corisco turned away, and Annie saw his gaze slide down Will's mostly naked body, one eyebrow quirked in disdain.

"I'd heard you'd spent some time with the Indians, Dr. Travers, but I seem to have underestimated the affinity I'd heard you felt for the native peoples. Are the other rumors true as well? The *sucuri*? A lost city of gold? People say you found one in the forest."

"This is the lost city of gold," Will said through gritted teeth, the soldiers holding his arms tightly behind his back.

To Annie's surprise, Vargas laughed.

"How very astute of you, Doctor. It is, indeed. Reino Novo, the new El Dorado. Lock him up." Vargas's smile faded as he turned his gaze back to her. "And bring the woman with me. We have much to ... discuss ... don't we, Dr. Parrish?"

Will lunged forward, but the soldiers held him back, and when he continued to struggle, one of them stepped forward and rapped him sharply on the head with the butt end of his rifle.

He collapsed like a stone, and Annie felt her life starting to flash before her eyes.

"Come, doctor," Vargas said to her. "We'll go up to the house. I believe you have a number of things you want to tell me."

Oh, God. She was going to die.

FROM WHERE HE SAT in his chair in the jungle, nearly catatonic with surging waves of greed, his men laboring mightily below him on his chair's poles to make even the slightest headway, Fat Eddie watched Vargas take the little cat away. The lost ten thousand *reais* meant nothing to him now, in light of the most magnificent mountain of gold he'd ever seen. A small measure of pride seeped through his greed. He had brought diamonds and emeralds for the eyes of the stupendous piece of work, and he would be careful not to lose a single one when he tore the whole thing down and had it shipped to Manaus. His men were already moving into place, securing the river and setting charges along the docks and in the fueling station.

Gold. More gold than he'd thought existed anywhere in the world, and it would soon be his, nearly as soon as Corisco Vargas would be dead. Given Guillermo's attachment to the woman, Fat Eddie figured Vargas would be damned lucky if he survived his little Night of the Devil whether Eddie got to him or not. Eddie figured that despite all his elaborate plans, the only devil Corisco Vargas was going to conjure was already in the forest glade, knocked out and lying facedown in the grass.

He chuckled quietly to himself, his belly rolling. Oh, yes. Corisco had gotten himself a devil indeed, a *brujo* who would take him straight to hell.

CHAPTER 27 ⨪

ANY DOUBTS CORISCO HAD HELD about his methods, designs, and goals were gone. She had come to him. Out of the dark of night and the deep forest of the northwest frontier, Annie Parrish had come to him.

He leaned back against his desk, sitting on the edge, his whole being awash with the pleasant glow of success and the early light of dawn. He had her, and now she would tell him what he wanted to know, or she would die. Behind her, the glass cage lay broken and empty, the occupant having become far too physically aggressive after its first bout of cage rattling early the previous evening. But Corisco even had that situation under control, the beast recontained in its alternate abode, awaiting its next meal.

And now its fated meal had arrived, in the shape and form of Annie Parrish.

He'd had her cleaned up, the mud washed from her face, the feathers removed from her hair. His servants

had done a commendable job of restoring her to beauty—
and the São Paulo dress was lovely on her, everything
he'd hoped it would be, what little there was of it.
"Death shroud" was perhaps a better description than
"dress" for the diaphanous wisp of golden silk twisted
artfully around her body. Plenty of skin had been left
naked to the touch, her breasts barely cupped in a golden
demitasse of a bodice, the rest of her torso left uncov-
ered, the remaining silk wrapped once low around her
hips and draping in a single fall to the floor down the
middle of her legs. It was too bad the two of them
wouldn't have more time to enjoy it, but the forest had
come alive with anarchy in the night and was going to re-
quire his attention. Fat Eddie had taken his invitation to
return a little too seriously, and Reino Novo was actually
under attack. No more than a few snipers, he'd been assured by his new captain, a man who had been with him
nearly as long as Fernando had been, snipers who were
systematically being taken out by his soldiers, but even
the best-trained troops needed the firm hand of authority
to guide them.

Cut down by a curare dart and a knife, Corisco
mused. He could not have devised a more fitting death
for his old captain—but he would have tried. He certainly would have tried. Failure was not an option in
Reino Novo, and Fernando had failed. It had been
Corisco's own efforts that had brought Annie Parrish
back to him. The truth had been in a small pack clipped
around her waist.

He held up her orchid next to his own, the pair of
them exquisite beyond belief. Having studied his for a
year, he was very sensitive to any changes in it, and when

held next to Annie's orchid, his did change, its light—so subtle in its vacillations—instantly began cycling on a different frequency.

Power was all he'd ever wanted, the power of the devil frog visions, the power of fear, and the power of gold, but perhaps in truth, the greatest power he'd brought to himself was in his hands.

"You see it, don't you?" he said, looking up at her.

And indeed she did. Her gaze was riveted to the pair of orchids. She'd had her year of studying her flower as well as he'd had his, and he didn't doubt that her observations were at least as astute as his own, probably even more so, given her profession.

"Do you know what it means? What they mean?" he asked, pushing off the desk and walking toward her.

Her eyes never left the orchids. Her expression, though, was hard to read. Awe was there, and rightly so. He felt the same emotion coursing through him. Whether he understood them or not, he was certain the orchids were responding to each other. But there was something else in her face, and oddly enough, it took him a moment to realize that it was fear. Not fear for herself, he would have recognized that instantly. She was afraid for the orchids, which left him slightly nonplussed. What did she think he was going to do? Smash the glass holding them?

A smile curved his mouth, condescending in its humor. "I won't destroy them, you know."

Finally, her gaze flicked up toward his.

"You won't understand them, either."

"And you will?" he asked, sounding deliberately doubtful.

"Given time and a lab. Yes."

It was an option he hadn't considered, having her work for him instead of dying for him. The idea was certainly intriguing.

"What about Travers?"

Her expression altered ever so subtly, and Corisco wanted to chide her for being so transparent. She'd been less easily read in Yavareté, more of a challenge, but love had a tendency to soften one's defenses as well as one's brain.

"He's brilliant. Far more so than me."

"So I should keep him and kill you?" he asked with feigned casualness, and was delighted by the frightened ambivalence he got for a response. It was his forte, really, torturing with chaos, churning people up and turning them inside out, usually metaphorically, though once he'd actually done it.

Ah, but he and Annie—they'd had such a time of it in Yavareté. Stripping her down for Fernando had been his only mistake. He should have kept her all to himself. Under the influence of the *uyump* blood potion, she'd nearly glowed, even in the dank gloom of the Yavareté jail.

Killing her would make his reputation. She was well known, high profile, and had once been highly respected. Killing her would prove to everyone how dangerous it was to come into the Amazon, into his Amazon.

But keeping her had its own obvious rewards.

"I could keep you both, if there were enough orchids to make it worth my while." It was a fair offer.

"It could take years to find more."

"Not if a person knew where to look, and you do know that, don't you, Dr. Parrish?" he said, his patience thinning. They'd danced the same dance in Yavareté, and he wasn't interested in a repeat performance. "This is your life we're bargaining with, Doctor, yours and William Sanchez Travers's. Don't doubt me on that score."

A shouting from down toward the mines pulled his attention to the window. Something was going on. Setting the orchids aside, he picked up a portable two-way radio off his desk and headed for the patio off his office, calling his captain. Before he could raise the man, an explosion rocked Reino Novo.

Corisco didn't miss a step, only walked steadily toward the doors, and when he reached them, stood tight-jawed, watching what was left of his number two dock flying in pieces up into the air. The number three dock exploded next, and Corisco felt a wash of cold anger pour down through his body.

He turned and gestured to his guards. "You'll be eating your balls for breakfast if she's not here when I return. Dr. Parrish"—he turned fully to face her—"I suggest you consider my offer very carefully. Without the promise of more orchids, you're worth far more to me dead than alive."

Annie believed him. Down to the core of her being, she believed him.

"What about Travers?" She had to know.

"Fat Eddie finds him more interesting than I do," he said dismissively. "Fighting has been going on around the plaza all night. Some of my *cordeiros* have been shot. Your Sanchez Travers was put in the main cage and wasn't in the best of health when he was thrown inside, having a bullet wound and a fractured skull. His chances of surviving the day were slim to begin with, and that he will die tonight with the rest of my sacrifical lambs is a foregone conclusion. It is your own life you are fighting for,

Dr. Parrish, only your own. Please us both by making the wise decision."

WILL WOKE UP in the night with a splitting headache, his skull feeling as if it had been cracked open. He was sweating and cold, and that wasn't good, not on the equator. Squinting, he gingerly investigated his scalp. From the matting of blood and hair and the size of the lump he felt above his left ear, his head just about had been split open. He tried rolling over to get on his feet, and stopped in mid-roll, a whole new world of pain coming to life in his arm.

He collapsed back down, a curse on his lips. What had he done to himself? he wondered.

The soft murmur of voices behind him brought his head around. A group of Indians, frightened women and old men, were huddled together not too far from where he lay on his back, backlit by flickering light.

Indians were good, he thought, better than soldiers, and he recognized Tutanji among them, which was even better. At least he wasn't alone. On the other hand, as his eyes adjusted to the night, he noticed they were separated from him by iron bars.

The disturbing bit of information slid into place, and suddenly he remembered a few things that made any sense of relief premature.

He'd been shot in the arm, and captured, and he was in a cage, one of Corisco's damned cages. The Indians were in another.

A burst of automatic gunfire stuttered through the night, coming from down by the river, and he jerked his head around—a big mistake. Lights flashed before his eyes, each one ripping through his head and leaving a path of pain.

Rolling back into a ball on the ground, he swore between his teeth. Either Corisco was starting his *noite do diabo* party, or Reino Novo was under attack.

He prayed for the latter. Destroying Reino Novo had been his goal for months, up until ... until ...

Something wasn't right. He was missing something important, something really important. He'd been heading for Reino Novo on his boat, the *Sucuri,* and he'd had diamonds and emeralds and ...

Annie.

Annie was gone.

It all came back to him in living color and an awful feeling of dread: the Night of the Devil, the race up the river, the dead soldiers, and Corisco showing up in the plaza and taking her away.

He swore, a savage curse. Vargas had gotten to her, before she could get to the keys. That's how they'd been caught, trying to save the Indians and *caboclos.*

The keys. He needed them. Pushing himself upright, he nearly passed out again. Shooting pains rocketed around the inside of his skull. A ragged groan left his lips. The keys. He had to get the keys and get out of the cage so he could save Annie, but he was a mess, a physical mess, wounded and beaten—like she had been in Yavareté.

"Here, little brother, drink this."

He looked up to see Tutanji opposite him, reaching between the bars to offer him a small gourd.

"You are back, little brother," the shaman said.

"Yes, I am back," he ground out in a whisper, careful not to cause himself any more pain. "The woman? Where is she?"

"The Jaguar Woman?" the old man asked, and Will was confused all over again. He didn't remember any Jaguar Woman, not ever. "She is there." The shaman pointed. "Inside the jaws of the golden anaconda, and truly, little brother, I fear her soul will be stolen tonight."

Will followed the old man's gesture past the cages to the tower of gold rising out of the plaza. The reflected flames of a circle of torches licked up the serpent's golden scales, higher and higher to the gaping jaws and the woman tied with her arms outstretched to the snake's gold fangs. Smoke curled around the curved, stalactite-like teeth, the flames making them glitter in chatoyant shades of red and yellow.

His heart stopped for one shuddering second. It was Annie, and she didn't look like a jaguar to him. She looked like a woman terrified of dying. He slowly rose to his feet and stumbled to the edge of his cage, his hands tightening around the iron bars. She looked like a living sacrifice, like she'd said she'd felt the last time Corisco Vargas had captured her.

Fear and guilt collided in his chest. He should have tried harder to get her out of Brazil, especially once he'd realized what was going to happen. There must have been a way.

A guard passed by on his rounds, walking between the cages, tossing insults to the Indians and using the butt end of his rifle to rap the knuckles of any hands clinging to the iron bars.

Will kept his hands inside his cage and waited until the guard passed, before returning his attention to Annie. The necklace he'd given her was still around her neck, though he doubted its ability to protect her now. The scrap of gold material wrapped around her body was

meant to make her look like a whore, and the sight of it
gave him a sick feeling in the pit of his stomach. Corisco
hadn't raped her before, and Fernando was dead. He
tried to take hope in the two facts.

"How long was I out?" he asked the shaman. It had
been dark when he'd been captured. Maybe he'd only
been unconscious for a few minutes, long enough for
Corisco to get her into that outfit, but not long enough
for him to have done much else.

Tutanji's reply destroyed that idea.

"You were gone the whole day, little brother. The sun
has come and gone and much fighting has started while
you were sleeping."

Then the Night of the Devil was upon them, the play-
ers put into place. He looked up through the bars to the
sky. There was no moon, only the sweep of the Milky
Way. The *noite do diabo* was a dark moon night.

His gaze came back to Annie. Anything could have
happened to her in the amount of time he'd been unconscious. His only consolation was that she didn't look
hurt. No blood marked her face or body, and even without the ropes tying her to the snake fangs, she looked as
if she could stand on her own two feet. She hadn't been
beaten.

He turned to Tutanji, his voice tight. "We need to get
out of these cages."

"Yes," the shaman agreed, lifting the gourd again.
"I'm waiting for the keys. Here. Drink this. It will make
you strong."

Will took a good-sized swallow from the container
and damn near choked on the bitter liquid as he handed
it back, the taste a warning that he should have asked
what the stuff was before he'd drunk it.

Hell. Tutanji had half killed him dozens of times. There was no reason to think their current situation would change anything. The old man ran on Otherworld time. Then again, elixirs for a man's strength were Tutanji's specialty.

And Will needed his strength. He needed it fast.

He shook the bars on his cage with his good arm, but none of them gave way, not so much as an inch.

A ring of keys, he remembered, had fallen to the ground in front of the cages. Now where had the soldier been when he'd killed them, and how far could the keys have fallen from that spot? He turned to check his position, but turned too quickly and had to slap a hand onto his forehead.

Sweet Jesus, his head *was* going to crack open.

"Do you know where the keys are?" he asked, his voice a pained whisper. Streaks of light ricocheted behind his closed eyelids.

"Yes. A monkey will bring them to us."

A monkey?

Will opened his eyes to a bare slit and slanted them toward the old man.

"What monkey?"

Tutanji pointed to a spot in the forest, and by the light of the torches, Will saw a small emperor tamarin monkey with a flowing white mustache sitting on a low branch in a tree no more than five feet away, the ring of keys clutched in its tiny hands. Its little face was turned toward the torches around the plaza, its expression one of pensive anticipation—as if it knew something terrible was going to happen.

Fucking doomed.

"Is that you?" he asked Tutanji.

"No. I am a caiman, an anaconda, a jaguar shaman, but never a monkey shaman. Call to him," the old man suggested. "Maybe he will come."

Maybe? That was the best Tutanji could come up with after three damn years? Will wanted to reach out and grab the little monkey by the throat, because he sure as hell didn't think the animal was going to walk over to the cage and hand him those keys.

Frustration made him shake the bars again, and this time they did make a small grating noise, enough to make the monkey turn and look him straight in the eye.

Will held himself very still, not daring to blink.

"Little brother," he said softly. Behind him, he heard Tutanji start to chant in a soft singsong cadence, the notes lifting on the slight breeze blowing through the trees.

The monkey just sat and stared, its jaws working on an invisible nut, its expression as worried as ever.

"Get your skinny little ass over here, little brother," Will crooned, working hard not to grit his teeth. "Get your skinny little ass over here, or I'll hunt you down with my bush knife and use your guts to string my bow."

Still staring right at him, the monkey stopped chewing, leaving its jaw hanging open. Then it screamed and took off up into the tree.

Will swore and hit the cage. So much for Tutanji's idea. He whirled around, searching for an alternative—and damn near passed out again, but with more of a hallucination problem than just the simple dizziness of before, a bright, neon-pink snake dancing before his eyes.

Slowly, he straightened back up, his gaze sliding toward Tutanji.

"What did I drink, older brother?" he asked. Now was not the time for visions and the Otherworld, not the time for *caapi*. If he was going to save Annie, he needed to be in this world.

"The snake will pass by," the old man assured him, "and then you will be strong. It is not *yagé*, not vine of the soul. A little tobacco maybe, to make you strong again, to make you forget where you were hit, where you were shot with the white man's bullet."

A nicotine rush then, Will realized. That's all it was, a slightly hallucinogenic nicotine rush. Ingesting the stimulant as brewed sludge was about a thousand times more potent than smoking it and just about guaranteed a man was going to see something that wasn't really there—like a pink snake phosphene.

"The mother of the mother of tobacco was a snake, little brother," the shaman continued. "You need the power of snakes."

Will bit back an irritated retort. According to Tutanji, he was always in need of something's power. In truth, what he needed was to get out of the friggin' cage.

A collective gasp in the glade brought his head around, and this time there was no dizziness, no hallucination. He was getting stronger, and in the nick of time. Corisco was coming. The sound of boots in a lockstep march could be heard approaching on the river path. Fear rippled through the plaza, a palpable fright jumping from cage to cage, making the Indians nervous as hell. The soldiers came into view, and Will swore. Corisco must have had a hundred men with him, each with a semiautomatic rifle and double bandoliers of ammunition crisscrossing their chests. There was enough firepower on the plaza to annihilate a thousand people, cut them down into shreds. Taking out a hundred unarmed Indian woman and frightened old *caboclos* was nothing less than slaughter—and there wasn't a damned thing Will could do to stop it.

Unless ...

The guard was coming back again on his next round, and when he got close, Will grabbed the bars of his cage in both hands and started shaking them.

CHAPTER 28 ⚑

CORISCO ENTERED THE PLAZA FLANKED
by a hundred men, each of them ready to die for him,
each of them ready to kill for him. Today he had required
both.

Fat Eddie's *jagunços* had descended on Reino Novo
like a swarm of mosquitoes, no match for trained soldiers except in their irritating numbers. His guerilla tactics had held Vargas's army at bay at the number two
mine for most of the day, his snipers picking off Corisco's
snipers in a game of attrition, but not for much longer.
Corisco had cut off the fat man's escape and was going to
blow the number two mine, Fat Eddie, and his mosquitoes to hell.

What a waste of a day, he thought with disgust. He
was unbeatable in a penny-ante war, and soon would be
unbeatable on a much larger scale.

Fools. Everyone who defied him was a fool, and
no one had defied him more than Annie Parrish. She'd
been such a disappointment when he'd returned for her

answer at midday, begging for the gringo's life instead of her own, telling him everything, promising him hundreds of orchids and her services in discovering their secrets, giving it all up with barely a threat between them.

Utter and abject surrender, he'd discovered, was the greatest defiance of all, depriving him of more sadistic delights, but he would take her offer. He would let her slave for him in exchange for William Sanchez Travers's life.

His mouth curled in distaste. He couldn't believe how cheaply she'd sold herself, and for nothing. The sodding gringo wouldn't last the night. She'd thought herself worth more in Yavareté. Much more.

He strode across the plaza and took the stairs up the tower two at a time, while his men lined up in formation in front of the cages. Despite Fat Eddie, the Night of the Devil was coming off as planned. Tonight, a legend would be born. He would not be made to look the fool, not by a fat man from Manaus, and not by a gringo whose preferred weapon was a primitive blowgun.

Good Lord. How far had the man thought to get with a blowgun? Corisco wondered.

Farther than most, he had to admit, remembering the ease with which Travers had dispatched his guards and the hapless Fernando. Fat Eddie had been wrong about the gringo's death on the Rio Marauiá, as he was being proved wrong about everything, especially his decision to bring war to Corisco's door.

But it was Dr. Parrish's capitulation that irked him even more than Fat Eddie's acts of aggression. If she wanted to enslave herself for the love of a drunken has-been who happened to be handy with a blowgun, fine. He would see to it that she paid the price in a thousand little ways every day. She'd stolen guns from Fat Eddie in Manaus, and the little *filha* been heading up the river to do him in with grenades and dynamite.

His man in Manaus had discovered the facts surrounding Fat Eddie's flight up the Rio Negro after the good doctor and his stolen guns. He'd even seen Johnny Chang's severed head, before it had been sent to Ecuador, an interesting item, but one that did nothing to address the real problem as Corisco saw it.

Scale. Simple scale.

The difference between him and all the other would-be river lords was scale. No one was thinking outside the box of their measly little existence, except him.

He made the landing where Annie Parrish was tied to the golden fangs twenty feet above the plaza, and knew he had his foolish moments, as well. He should kill her, let her fulfill her place in his planned ceremony. Her martyrdom would do far more to promote his cause than any amount of orchid research she might manage.

But her skin was soft, so very smooth, looking like gold satin in the light of the flames. The silk he'd wrapped her in was nearly transparent, it was so finely spun. Her hair was wild in its little-boy cut, but would grow in time, if he gave her time—and he was tempted, so tempted to keep her. He had a terrible sadistic streak when it came to women, and he'd hurt her before, but he actually thought that for her he could change. That he could control his more primitive instincts and perhaps relearn the art of tenderness.

She was so unusual, so unique, truly a prize worth keeping.

Or he could make an offering of her to the devil gods of the Amazon and send those images rocketing around the world via satellite and make himself a name unlike any other in history.

Decisions, he thought in irritation. He usually had no trouble making decisions, but just like in Yavareté, she made him hesitate, made him doubt.

He came up behind her on the golden platform and smoothed his hand over her bare shoulder, and felt her flinch. Sex had been so strange for him since he'd first taken the devil frog potion. The visions, which had made him powerful beyond his dreams, had also made him impotent, an odd contradiction he'd learned to live with in his own twisted fashion.

"What am I going to do with you, Dr. Parrish?" he asked, letting his hand continue to trail over her skin, all the way across her shoulders and then down the lovely curve of her back.

She trembled beneath his touch, and Corisco found her reaction appealingly erotic.

"Keep our deal," she said succinctly, and he smiled again. No one made him smile more than Annie Parrish.

"You should know better than to deal with the devil, Doctor." He continued along with his hand on her body, walking around the platform, breaking their contact only once when he rounded one of the fangs. Then his hand was back on her, trailing down the front of her arm and coming to rest on her breast.

With his other hand, he lifted her chin, forcing her to meet his gaze. Nothing but revulsion showed in her eyes, but he found that erotic as well, so much so, a spark of life actually stirred in his groin.

It happened now and then, but never with enough force to accomplish anything. So why keep her? he asked himself, and with his answer, her fate was sealed. He lowered his hand from her breast. She was unique, yes, but still no match for him.

As for the orchids? The Amazon's single most unendangered species was the *Cientista south americanus*. They could be found hanging from the trees, snorkling through the water, padding around after the Indians, cutting plants, stealing insects, tagging mammals, tracking birds, and generally sticking their noses in, under, and around every single living thing in the rain forest. If he needed one, he wouldn't have to look far to get one.

ANNIE HEARD CORISCO descend the stairs behind her, and she wanted to scream in frustration, which beat the hell out of giving in to her fear. She'd seen the look in his eyes, and he was going to kill her and Will. She knew it. Her strategy had backfired.

Biting off an oath, she jerked against the ropes tying her to the golden fangs.

She'd clung to stoic resistance in Yavareté, close-mouthed, unyielding resistance, and gotten herself beaten from head to toe and hung naked in chains. She'd thought she'd try a different tack this time, and though Vargas hadn't raised so much as a hand to her, and she was still clothed—in a manner of speaking—overall, she feared the consequences of capitulation, even feigned capitulation, were going to be far harsher.

And where was Will? She'd been brought to the plaza hours ago and had yet to see him. The light from the torches caught every ounce of gold on the paved courtyard and the snake tower, making the plaza shimmer with flickering brilliance, but it also made seeing into the cages on the perimeter impossible. Everything outside the circle of gold was cast in the deep darkness of the rain-forest night. Now and then, she glimpsed the movement of one of the guards patrolling the cages, or caught a brief shift of shadows inside the iron bars, but nothing she could identify, and certainly not Will.

Below her, row upon row of armed soldiers were standing at attention, their assault weapons in their hands. It was going to be a massacre, a bloody, bloody massacre, and she was going to have a bird's-eye view.

Corisco was crazed.

And she was trapped in the mouth of a giant snake hammered out of gold. Tied to its teeth, for God's sake.

She jerked her arms again and swore beneath her breath, her fury and her fear rising to the surface in equal measure. She had to get free. Will was down there, wounded, and if she couldn't get free, she was going to end up watching him die.

CHAPTER 29 ✄

WILL DRAGGED THE UNCONSCIOUS guard into the forest, his knuckles still smarting from the hit he'd taken, before he'd grabbed the man's rifle and jerked him hard into the iron bars, knocking him out cold. As soon as he'd unlocked his own cage, he'd tossed the keys to Tutanji. The captives were already swarming out of the cages, keeping to the shadows, and as soon as someone noticed—any second—all hell was going to break loose. Will was going to use that chaos to get to Annie.

He grabbed the guard's rifle and pumped a fresh round into the chamber. He'd seen Corisco bound up the stairs to see her. The bastard hadn't stayed long, just long enough to manhandle her a bit and cop a feel.

He jerked the guard's knife out of its sheath and took off running, his jaw tight with anger. He'd graduated from Harvard *summa cum laude*, but he hadn't played this hand smart at all.

He was halfway to the snake tower, skirting the outside

edge of the cages, when a huge explosion from down by the river stopped him dead in his tracks and almost stopped his heart. The earth shook with the force of it, the tremors racing beneath the ground and knocking half of Corisco's troops in the plaza off balance. Will rode the tremor out and knew there would be hell to pay, a thought he no sooner had than he heard a tree crash in the forest behind him, taking out everything in its path. Above the river, a huge fireball lit up the night sky, with smoke and flames spewing from its core, and Will wondered who in the hell was blowing up Reino Novo.

FAT EDDIE SAT in his big wooden chair with the detonater in his hand, chuckling, his big belly rippling in cadence with the sound. What a day, he thought. What a hell of a day.

He and his men had taken over the camp of the number two mine on Reino Novo's northernmost boundary early in the afternoon, and he'd had the *jagunços* hauling out gold all day—up until Vargas's troops had flanked them and cut off their route to the river.

Things had gotten sticky then for a while, but in the end, sheer numbers had prevailed. When they'd discovered Vargas's men rigging the camp and mine to explode, they'd taken over the job and done it right.

Maybe too right, Eddie thought, grinning through the soot and ash that now dusted everything in sight.

One of his men came running up to where he sat, mouthing words and gesturing, and Eddie realized he couldn't hear him through the ringing in his ears. But he understood exactly what the man was saying—"The second blast, she is ready, *senhor*!"

ANNIE HUNG PETRIFIED from her ropes, trying to stand
perfectly still, a near impossibility with the snake tower
swaying from side to side. As terrifying as her situation
was, she found herself suddenly fixated on who in the
hell had designed the tower, and if its infrastructure had
been engineered to withstand small earthquakes.

She didn't think so. She could feel the tremors running through it.

In the aftermath of the explosion and all the chaos
erupting on the plaza, with downed troops trying to
scramble to their feet, and her own immediate problem,
it took her a moment to realize the captives in the cages
were escaping.

Her thoughts immediately flew to Will. He had a
chance.

But in the next moment a second explosion rocked
the sky, sending another shock wave through the ground.
The tower shuddered beneath her again, a long, deep,
aching shudder centered in its core, sounding a lot like
collapsing panels of steel, or the opening up of a giant,
squeaky door hinge.

Not good, she told herself, wrapping her fingers more
tightly around the ropes, and when she heard a higher
pitched noise from above, her assessment dropped even
lower—until she looked up and saw a deep crack inching
its way across the top of the snake's right fang.

She jerked on her rope, using all her strength, trying
to help the crack along. If it gave way, she might be able
to get free.

A similar high-pitched noise sounded from behind
her, and she swung her head around to see what else was

giving way. It was another crack ripping down the snake's throat, following the pattern of the golden scales and leaving an ever-widening gash in its wake.

The tower was going to collapse, one way or another, and the only question in Annie's mind was whether or not she'd still be on it when it did.

CORSICO PICKED HIMSELF UP off the stairs for the second time, his jaw clenched to the point of pain.

What were those fools down at the number two mine thinking?

Looking around the plaza, he saw utter chaos, but not the chaos he had planned, and his *cordeiros* were escaping, sneaking off into the night, running for their miserable lives.

He jerked his head at the lieutenant on his right. "Round them up! *Imediatamente!*" Frightened women and old men shouldn't be too hard to corral, not by armed soldiers. "The ones you cannot catch, shoot."

The lieutenant snapped off a salute and quickly barked off a set of orders to the others.

Corsico watched his soldiers regroup, some to follow the lieutenant, others remaining to secure the plaza.

More trees crashed in the forest surrounding the plaza, convincing him to stay put until everything could be set back in order. He looked up the tower to see how his most important captive had taken the explosions, and felt the oddest sensation—a ripple of unease, a first niggling of doubt about the immediate future.

El Mestre, his beautiful snake tower with the diamond and emerald eyes and the seven-foot-long golden fangs, was cracking. He took a step down to get a better view and felt a second ripple of unease. The biggest gash was going straight down the throat, and if it didn't stop, the golden snake was going to break open like a cracked egg, and like a cracked egg, everything that was inside it was going to come pouring out.

Everything.

More than a ripple of unease washed through him at the thought.

Carefully, he took another step down, and suddenly the whole world came out from under him.

CHAPTER 30 ✠

Fat Eddie lay smashed into the ground where he'd landed after coming flying out of his chair. The only thing that had kept him from being broken into a hundred pieces by the last explosion was the resiliancy and the sheer quantity of his fat, and that the forest had sheltered him from the worst of the flying debris.

Saved by his fat, the words ran over and over in his mind as he lifted his head and looked around. He'd been saved by his fat. Two of his skinniest men had been broken against the trees. They hadn't been heavy enough to fall to the ground. Not so Eddie. It took more than the biggest fucking explosion he'd ever heard to throw Fat Eddie Mano into a tree. Just as it took at least three of his strongest men to get him to his feet.

"Getulio!" he shouted. "Joaquin! Alberto! Come help me!"

One by one, his men picked themselves up out of the forest and brushed themselves off. Most were cursing, but cursing happily. They were all rich men tonight, their boats loaded with gold and the night full of the promise for more.

The explosion, though, she'd been a mother, and Eddie doubted if Corisco Vargas still owned a fuel depot on the Cauaburi. No, no, no. There was no more gas, no more barrels of oil at Reino Novo. Nothing but the destruction of the fuel depot could have made such an explosion.

He hadn't done it. Neither had any of his men. Gold was their only desire. Corisco sure as hell hadn't done it to himself, which only left Guillermo, but Eddie would bet his portion of the gold that Guillermo hadn't done it, either. Guillermo, if he was still alive, would be where Annie Parrish was, and the little cat had been tied up on that great gold snake all night.

Which meant there was someone else, someone damned serious about taking Corisco Vargas down and Reino Novo apart.

Night of the Devil, Eddie thought, grunting as his men got him rolled over onto his back. He was beginning to like this Night of the Devil.

Getulio had the strength of an ox. So did Joaquin, and Alberto was built like a bull. Between the three of them, they got Eddie back into his chair, where he settled in with a contented chuckle.

Yes. The *noite do diabo* had already made him a very rich man. There was only one more thing he needed, *El Mestre*, the towering snake altar where virgins died and terror was born, though Eddie had his doubts about Annie Parrish's virginity after all those nights with Guillermo.

"To the plaza," he ordered, and four men came forward to help with the lifting of the chair.

NOTHING MOVED in the plaza. Everyone lay on the ground, stunned, knocked down by the sky-rocking explosion. Will had been sent flying—and he'd lost his gun.

"*Damn,*" he swore under his breath, feeling every ache and pain.

Bracing himself with his good arm, he slowly pushed himself to his knees. His head swam, but he rode it out. A soldier near the edge of the gold paving looked up and saw him, and for a moment, Will wondered if he was going to shoot, but the look in the younger man's eyes told Will he didn't give a damn about one more Indian escaping. The look in the soldier's eyes said he didn't give a damn about anything except finding a way out of Reino Novo and saving his own ass.

Too hurt to feel much relief, Will shifted his gaze to Annie and the tower. The altar was holding, but he didn't think it could last for long. Corisco was lying facedown halfway up the tower stairs, bleeding from a gash on his forehead.

He had to get Annie free.

Pushing himself the rest of the way to his feet, he didn't take his eyes off her. She looked very still, hanging from her ropes, her slight body limp, the wisp of gold cloth wrapped around her fluttering in a gentle breeze. The size of the explosion and the huge flames shooting into the sky down by the river told Will there probably wasn't a gallon of fuel left to be had in all of Reino Novo. The night was lit up by the fire, and the heat of it had created wind on an otherwise windless night.

He didn't think the tower could take much more. Its basic structure was cracked all the way down the middle now, and as he watched, a shadow moved out of the crack. It didn't look like much to him at first, maybe no more than an odd flicker of flame, but as he stumbled forward, forcing his senses to clear, he realized it wasn't a shadow at all, but a fer-de-lance sliding out of the tower in a long, sinuous movement. The snake, like any other wild creature, no matter how deadly, preferred the dark, safe forest to a glittering, firelit stage and quickly chose the shortest route to the ground, a speedy transverse of a curve of golden scales.

The snake that came after the viper probably didn't give a damn about dark, safe forests or anything else, Will realized. It just kept coming, yard after incredible yard of huge, gargantuan anaconda, its tongue flicking, its powerful muscles bunching and stretching as it slid onto the stairs and started climbing upward toward the golden snake's mouth.

He needed to move. He needed to save Annie.

But the snake ... he came to a slow, stumbling halt. My God, the huge snake was like the one before—Tutanji's anaconda, the snake of his nightmares, the snake from the *Sucuri.*

The scars on his chest and back began to burn, transfixing him with the memory of pain, agonizing pain, reminding him of the night Tutanji's anaconda had gone hunting in the lost world, of the night the giant serpent had found him asleep on the shores of a black-water river and devoured him deep in the heart of the rain forest.

He had to go, had to get to Annie, but the snake was enormous.

Monstrous, and the sight of it paralyzed him.

WITH THE LAST of her strength, Annie raised her head to look out on the plaza. Will was still there, looking shell-shocked, and her heart went out to him. She was so damned tired. She had no fear left. She was just going to hang from the ropes until Will could get up the stairs and set her free.

"Will?" she called out, and his eyes slowly lifted to meet hers. She knew the instant they cleared, the instant he came back to himself and truly saw her. It was the same instant he started running.

She slumped back down, and a smile almost touched her lips. He'd been wounded, and had to be at least as exhausted as she was, but the worst was over now. He was free, and—and what was that?

Her body stiffened.

What was that flickering over the edge of the platform?

Was it a darting lizard? The Amazon was full of lizards.

The thing slithered like a lightning bolt over the edge again, and the hairs rose all along the nape of her neck.

She'd been wrong. Dead wrong. She had plenty of fear left, and when a huge, blackish-green head of the biggest snake she had ever seen lifted into view and came swinging toward her, she let loose with a scream so bloodcurdling it echoed off the trees.

CHAPTER 31 ⚔

THE SNAKE, LOOKING LIKE A QUARTER of a ton and well over thirty feet long, actually backed off, swinging away from the shriek that emanated from one small woman's mouth.

Will didn't stop running. Even with the head backing off, the giant body was moving itself up into the golden mouth where Annie hung from the gleaming fangs, one great coil slapping down and sliding off another, yard after yard of snake slowly gaining the higher ground.

Will took the stairs three at a time, going right over the top of the unconscious Vargas and the dozens of kingmaker beetles scrabbling out of the broken tower. He had his knife in his hand, ready, but before he could reach the platform, the snake attacked him with a hissing strike, lowering its huge head from Annie's level down to his and lunging.

Will dodged the wet, gaping mouth and glistening teeth, his body running on pure, primordial adrenaline, his mind nearly completely shut down. He couldn't think about what he was doing, because any thought he might have would freeze him solid with fear.

The snake lunged twice more, hissing each time, while its tail glided in long, graceful arcs across the stairs, detached from the tension in high display along the rest of its body. After the third strike, the snake withdrew, keeping a slight distance from him and holding his gaze with its abysmally black eyes, while its body continued the slow steady climb to the platform.

Will had to make a move. Annie had stopped screaming, and the silence pushed him to full-out panic. He leapt up the final stretch of stairs, certain the snake was coiling around her body, making it impossible for her to draw another breath, but before he could make the platform, he was tackled from behind, his legs banded in an iron grip.

He fell to the stairs, twisting around, expecting to see the snake's tail tightening around him, but instead he came face to face with the end of a gun barrel, the pistol in Corisco's hand. The man weighed down on him, his other arm in a death grip around Will's legs.

"Let it have her," the man rasped, cocking the pistol. "That was the plan."

Will didn't think so.

"The plan's changed," he growled, whipping his hand back and slinging his knife with a lightning-quick action.

Corisco's one open eye widened in shock, his blood flowing from where the blade stuck deep in his chest.

Without wasting a second, Will reached down and jerked the knife free, before rolling over and scrambling the rest of the way to the platform.

At the top of the stairs, he stopped, his way blocked by thick moving coils of dark-skinned green anaconda.

The snake was the only thing moving. Annie was utterly motionless, nearly nose to nose with the monstrous reptile, transfixed by its unwavering gaze. From the back she looked like an angel, her arms outstretched and hanging from the ropes, her fingers curled in a supplicating pose, and the diaphanous swath of golden silk wafting about her.

Cold dread washed through him. He didn't know what to do, what move to make. He stood perfectly still, his heart racing, his hand clutching the knife, watching the snake and the woman hang in timeless limbo together.

Incomprehensibly, the snake wasn't attacking her, only staring, its body swaying in front of her, its black gaze taking her measure.

The shot, when it came, caught him unaware. He didn't hear it until after it had hit him, and when he fell, he fell forward ... *into the endless green coils of the giant anaconda.*

Annie jerked her head around, the spell broken, and saw Will collapse on top of the snake. Beneath him, the anaconda continued to bunch and move its powerful body. Corisco was oblivious to the danger, holding the smoking pistol with a look of triumph flashing across his face, but his victory was brief.

A second shot came quickly after the first, from out of the forest with all the force of a high-powered rifle. The bullet caught Corisco in the chest, and the man sank lifelessly against the stairs.

Its loops slowly uncoiling, the snake glided down the stairs to investigate, moving past Will to hover over Corisco's body. Long moments passed in which Annie feared any number of horrors might unfold, but the beastly serpent did nothing, only slid quietly off the tower and into the dark forest.

"CRAZIEST BLOODY THING I ever saw," Mad Jack said, ripping open another sterile bandage to press over Annie's cut and bleeding wrists, doing a quick job of bandaging the raw wounds left by the ropes that had bound her. "A snake big enough to eat my horse and you hanging there like friggin' Fay Ray out of *King Kong*. God, Annie, I ought to tie you up myself and send you home on a slow boat. What's his name? The one who was going up the stairs with just a knife, for Christ's sake, to save you."

"Will. William Sanchez Travers," she said, though she truly wasn't paying any attention to him. Her throat throbbed from screaming so much. Mad Jack had brought three men and a woman with him, all heavily armed, and the four of them were up in the golden mouth, working quickly and efficiently to put Will in a body sling and lower him over the side of the tower to the plaza.

"The scientist guy who disappeared? I've heard of him. Don't worry, honey. I've got a floatplane on the river. We'll have him in Manaus in a couple of hours. We just have to get the hell out of here, before the soldiers decide to come back. There's another group working around these mines, but they're too busy stealing gold to bother with us."

Fat Eddie, she thought, but what really got her attention was Mad Jack calling her "honey."

He never called her "honey." For years he'd called her

"Pip Parrish," as in "pipsqueak," and during his teenage years, he'd called her "Pain Parrish," as in pain-in-the-butt-Parrish-quit-following-me-around. She'd been twenty before he'd started calling her "Annie" on a regular basis, and for the last four years he'd taken great pride in calling her "Doc," as in Dr. Parrish.

But he never called her "honey."

She must look worse than she thought, and she knew she felt worse than she looked—all wobbly inside, really wobbly, from her brain to her toes.

"I'm in shock."

"You've got that right, Doc," he said, flashing her a quick glance. He looked worried. Worried as hell. He finished a cursory check of her body, then took off his shirt and put it around her shoulders. "You stay put." He pumped another round into his rifle and laid it across her lap, before rising to his feet. "I've got to help your friend, Will."

"Sure," she said, and her voice sounded weak, even to her.

Frowning in concern, Mad Jack kneeled back down. A swath of midnight-black hair fell forward across his brow, and he brushed it back with a quick, restless gesture. "Annie. I'm going to get you out of here. You can count on that, and you know it, don't you?"

"Yes." She nodded. Mad Jack never let a person down.

"And you know I love you."

She nodded again. He'd always loved her, always been there, from as far back as she could remember, and after her mother had hightailed it out of Wyoming, Mad Jack had still been there, all of eight years old and ready to fill in the void her father had been too angry and too proud to notice.

"Good," he said. "So I know you won't take this wrong."

She watched as his gaze strayed past her to a sight she knew she couldn't handle—Corisco, where he lay dead on the tower stairs. His mouth tightened into a grim line.

After a brief, intense moment, his gaze came back to her, his eyes a blue so dark they bordered on a no-man's-land between black and slate-gray. Like a glacier-fed lake in high summer, a smitten, fifth-grade girl had once written to him in a heavily decorated poem. Boy, they'd sure gotten a hoot out of the perfumed note—but that little fifth-grade girl had gotten it dead-on.

"Annie, I know holding on to people is not your specialty," he said, "but whoever this guy is, you might want to consider holding on to him. I love you, but there's no way in hell I would have gone after a thirty-six-foot anaconda with just a knife to save you."

She gave him another little nod.

"You need to remember that, Doc." He was frightfully serious, his voice low. "There are lines you can't cross without getting hurt, and I thought I taught you where those lines are."

He had.

"And I thought I told you that if you wanted me to come back and take care of Corisco Vargas to let me know, and that I would see to it."

He had.

"And I thought I told you to stay the hell out of Brazil."

He most definitely had.

He swore, one succinct word, and then his gaze soft-ened the slightest degree.

"And I taught you to stand on your own two feet. Cover me, Annie. I'll be back." He stood up and strode toward the tower, where two of the men were holding a belaying rope, while the other man and the woman were putting Will over the side in the body sling.

Annie started to tremble. She was in shock, and she was in love, and more than anything else, she wanted to hold Will.

They'd survived. Against all the odds, they'd saved the Indians and *caboclos,* destroyed Corisco Vargas, and survived Reino Novo.

She'd lost her orchid, though, her beautiful, luminous orchid. Vargas had left both of the specimens in his of-fice, and his whole house had gone up in flames when Mad Jack's team had blown the fuel depot.

She lifted her gaze to where Will was being belayed off the broken snake tower, and in her heart, she let the orchids go. They didn't matter now. Nothing mattered—except Will.

EPILOGUE ⚔

Mmmm, *GATO*," ANNIE PURRED AS will slowly pulled her into his arms.

He met her gaze in the deepening twilight, his eyes dark and slumberous, before he lowered his mouth to take hers in another wet, deep kiss. She tasted herself on his tongue. She smelled herself on his skin.

She'd marked him. Every time they made love, she marked him as hers, letting him absorb her until she was a part of him. And he was doing the same to her, in the most intensely physical way possible.

Still kissing her, he smoothed his hand over the curve of her stomach, letting his hand rest on the place above her womb.

A son, Tutanji had said, the only other person in the world who knew where they were. The old shaman had brought them in over the mountains, the promise he'd made to Will fulfilled. Some days, looking out over the ancient, rounded hills and the dark green canopy of the rain forest flowing to the horizon, even Annie forgot where they were. She forgot the place they called home was connected to the rest of the world. Some days she wondered if it really was, or if they had somehow disconnected and were floating free.

Not even Gabriela knew where they were. Their supply drop-off was miles and miles from where Tutanji had led them after Will had healed. There was only one way in to their lost world, and it was not a trail for the faint of heart.

He broke off their kiss, and she sighed in contentment, running her hands up along his scalp, holding him close. He'd loved her well. He was the jaguar, more so now than ever, and she was the cat's favorite snack, all of her.

Will knew when she drifted into sleep, and he pulled her close to hold her next to his body. Looking over her shoulder, he checked the sky. She wouldn't get much of a nap, but he would let her have what she could. She would never forgive him if he let her sleep into the dark hours of the night.

That time was for them, for the work they did, and it tied them together in a way as profound as their lovemaking. When the sun fell only a few minutes later, he kissed her ear and gave her a gentle shake.

"Annie."

"Mmmm," she murmured, lazily opening her eyes and stretching.

A smile curved his mouth. She was going to get loved again, if she wasn't careful. It had happened more than once, and they'd lost a night's work.

"It's time, *querida*."

In minutes, they'd thrown on some clothes and moved

to the highest platform in their five-tiered tree house. Tonight was for panorama pictures, not for collecting. When the cameras were set up and ready, they sat down together on the edge of the deck. Walkways and ladders connected the tiers of the tree house together. Each platform was strung with ropes and, where necessary, safety nets. Each held its cadre of supply cabinets and lab equipment, food caches and cisterns.

Below them, on the forest floor, a silver ribbon of water wound its way to the horizon, illuminated by starlight. At the edge where earth gave way to sky, the river made a subtle transition between this world and the other, seeming to lift into the dark forest of space and flow into the starry wonder of the Milk River.

With Corisco dead and Fat Eddie busy counting his gold in Manaus, their lives had drifted into the quieter rhythms of peaceful days.

Slowly, as the night deepened, the forest of trees began more and more to resemble the Milky Way, thousands of small lights appearing where before they'd been outshone by the sun. *Epidendrum luminosa,* Annie's orchid, the Messenger in Tutanji's language. All plants talked, Tutanji had told them, but truly, he'd said, not all of them have a lot to say. The Messenger was different; its language more complex; its knowledge going back to the beginning, when it first opened its petals in the first misty morn of an Amazonian Eden, a gift from above.

Listen to the light, he'd said, and a lifetime's work had been born. A hundred flowers had been catalogued, the photons of light emitted by their DNA measured and graphed in anticipation of the day when the Messenger's message would be heard.

Until then, he and Annie would stay in the place time and the world had forgotten.

She reached over and slipped her hand into his, and he bent down to press his lips to her cheek. It was a sweet kiss in the dark, while below them, the wonders of the ages blossomed in the night.

ABOUT THE AUTHOR ✍

GLENNA MCREYNOLDS has won numerous awards
for her writing, including a RITA from the Romance
Writers of America for *Avenging Angel* (1994), and a
Career Achievement Award in Romantic Adventure
from *Romantic Times*. She is also the author of the
"dazzlingly sensual"* medieval trilogy: *The Chalice
and the Blade, Dream Stone,* and *Prince of Time*.

Glenna and her family live in Colorado. She loves
hearing from readers and can be contacted through
her website at **glennamcreynolds.com**.

*Kirkus Reviews